The Weaver's Lament

The Symphony of Ages Books by Elizabeth Haydon

The Weaver's Lament

BOOK NINE OF
THE SYMPHONY *of* AGES

Elizabeth Haydon

TOR

A TOM DOHERTY ASSOCIATES BOOK

New York

THE WEAVER'S LAMENT

Copyright © 2016 by Elizabeth Haydon

Maps by Ed Gazsi

Illustrations on pages 14 and 349 by Joe Dettmore

A Tor Book
Published by Tom Doherty Associates, LLC
175 Fifth Avenue
New York, NY 10010

www.tor-forge.com

Tor® is a registered trademark of Tom Doherty Associates, LLC.

The Library of Congress Cataloging-in-Publication Data
is available upon request.

ISBN 978-0-7653-2055-1 (hardcover)
ISBN 978-1-4299-4922-4 (e-book)

Our books may be purchased in bulk for promotional,
educational, or business use. Please contact your local bookseller
or the Macmillan Corporate and Premium Sales Department
at 1-800-221-7945, extension 5442, or by e-mail at
MacmillanSpecialMarkets@macmillan.com.

First Edition: June 2016

Printed in the United States of America

0 9 8 7 6 5 4 3 2 1

To my family
into which I was born,
married,
or invited,
you who have given me all the music I ever needed
to be able to sing this rhapsody
with abiding love and thanks

ACKNOWLEDGMENTS

To

Tom Doherty, Impresario
James Minz, Midwife
Susan Chang, Shepherd
Jynne Dilling and Kathleen Fogarty, Beacons

for making this series happen
with gratitude and fond appreciation

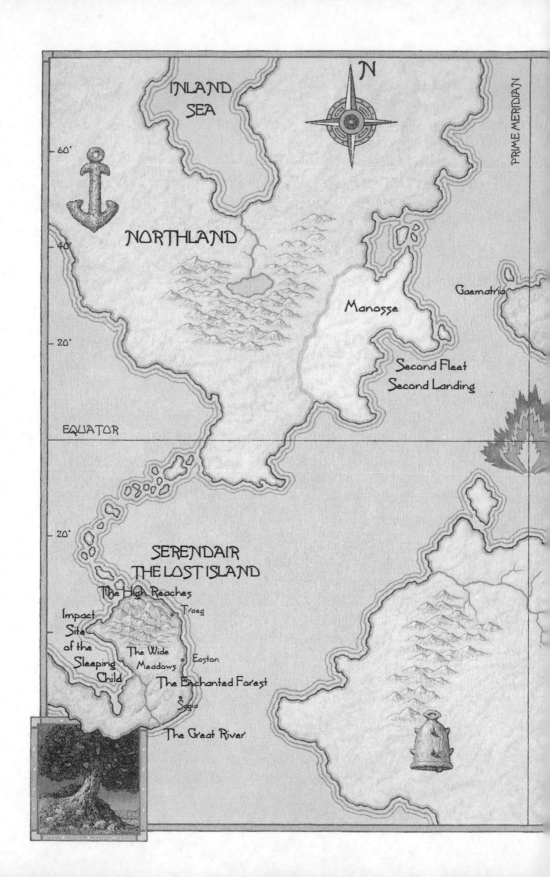

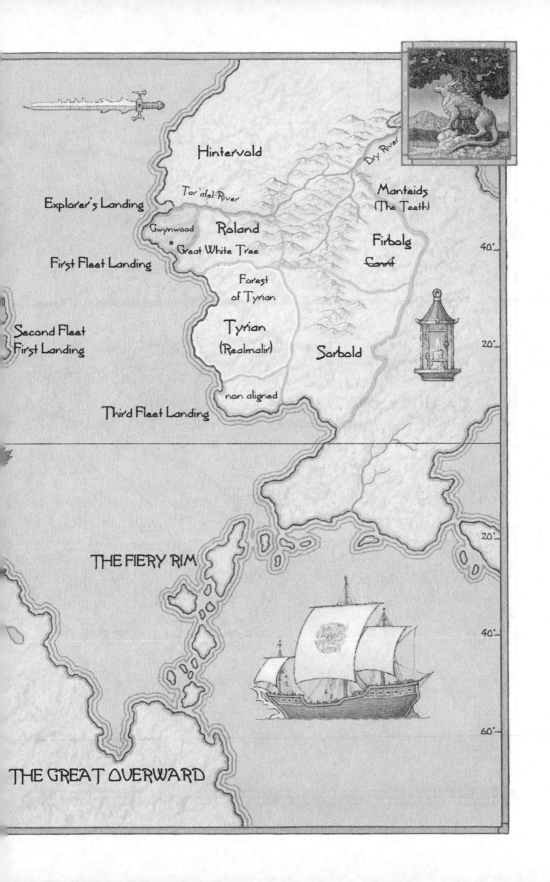

Hintervold

Tar'afel River

Explorer's Landing

Gwynwood

Roland

Great White Tree

First Fleet Landing

Forest
of Tyrian

Second Fleet
First Landing

Tyrian
(Realmalir)

non aligned

Third Fleet Landing

Dry River

Manteids
(The Teeth)

Firbolg

Canrif

Sorbold

40°

20°

THE FIERY RIM

20°

40°

60°

THE GREAT OVERWARD

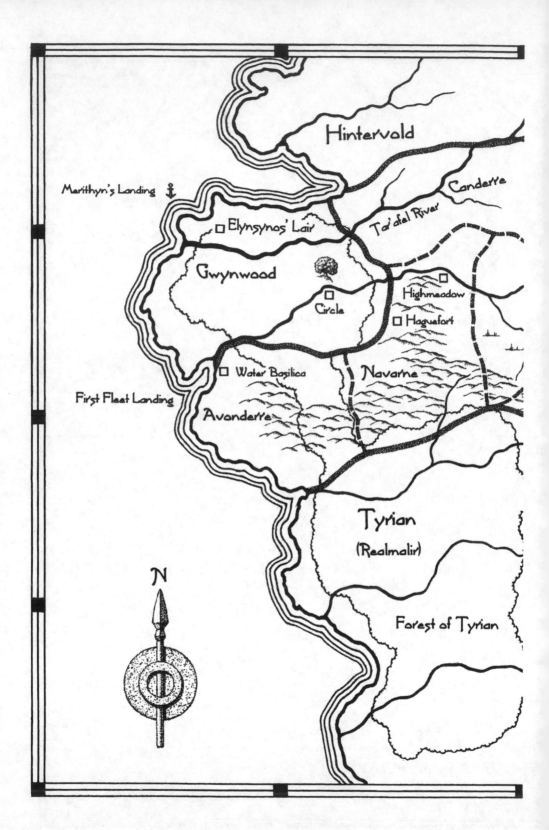

Hintervold

Canderre

Merithyn's Landing ⚓

Ta'afel River

Elynsynos' Lair

Gwynwood

Circle

Highmeadow

Haguefort

Water Basilica

Navarne

First Fleet Landing

Avonderre

Tyrian

(Realmalir)

N

Forest of Tyrian

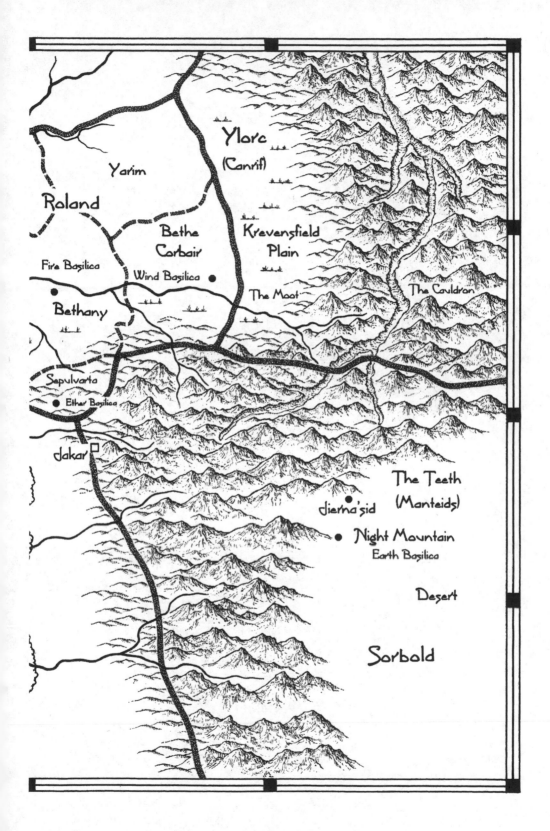

Ylorc
(Canrif)

Yarim

Roland

Bethe
Corbair

Krevensfield
Plain

Fire Basilica

Wind Basilica

The Moot

The Cauldron

Bethany

Sepulvarta

Ether Basilica

Jakar

The Teeth
(Manteids)

Jierna'sid

Night Mountain
Earth Basilica

Desert

Sorbold

THE WEAVER'S LAMENT

Time, it is a tapestry

Threads that weave it number three

These be known, from first to last,

Future, Present, and the Past

Present, Future, weft-thread be

Fleeting in inconstancy

Yet the colors they do add

Serve to make the heart be glad

Past, the warp-thread that it be

Sets the path of history

Every moment 'neath the sun

Every battle, lost or won

Finds its place within the lee

Of Time's enduring memory

Fate, the weaver of the bands

Holds these threads within Her hands

Plaits a rope that in its use

Can be a lifeline, net—or noose.

THE AMULET OF TSOLTAN, SYMBOL OF THE F'DOR

The Weaver's Lament

Prologue

THE YEAR 1008, SIXTH AGE
THE CITY-STATE OF HACKET

In the inconstant torchlight flickering around the dark glade, it seemed that the grave would never be deep enough.

The soldiers, exhausted after the hauling of the thickset body from where it had been found in the hut, the stench of rot and decay, and the shifts of digging, were sweating profusely in the warm night air. They glanced every now and then over their shoulders, keeping their reconnaissance brief, then turned back to the task at hand.

Their leader alone stood watch, lending no aid.

"Make quick work of it, boys," he muttered, refusing to observe their undertaking.

Finally, after far longer than any of them wanted, the task was considered complete enough.

The exhausted Firbolg soldiers paused, awaiting approval.

Their leader finally looked back at the massive mound of displaced earth, then down into the hole in the rocky ground, and nodded reluctantly.

The unit scrambled. While the Sergeant-Major looked away again, they hurried into the trees of the glade and dragged forth the large body, carefully wrapped in strips of cloth that had been soaked in brine and pungent herbs to help combat the odiferous state to which it had devolved.

Then, with newfound energy, they hoisted it high enough to carry as a group to the grave and, using the ropes that had been attached to haul it, lowered it carefully into the hole, slipping only once before righting it again.

After a few moments, the most senior of the Bolg soldiers cleared his throat politely.

"Sir?"

The broad-shouldered Sergeant, an even more massive man than the one they were burying, did not seem to hear him.

The soldiers exchanged a glance in the dimming torchlight.

After another long moment, the senior soldier tried again.

"Sir?"

This time, the Sergeant turned and looked over his shoulder. "Eh?"

"Orders, sir?"

The Sergeant finally came around. "One moment, please," he instructed, his voice stronger than it had been earlier in the night.

He reached into his weapons bandolier and pulled out a sword, a jagged weapon smelted with points up the blade, known affectionately as the Old Bitch, named after a hairy-legged harlot he had known long ago in the old world. It was actually a replica of several such swords that had seen combat with him over the centuries, but its age hardly mattered.

He crouched down at the grave's edge, near the corpse's feet, and held the sword, point down, in front of him for a moment, thinking.

"'Bye, then, Trom," he said quietly. "Sleep well, an' Oi'll see you on the other side o' the Gate."

He rose and tossed the weapon into the open grave, then signaled to the troops.

"Fill 'er in," he said.

When the task was accomplished, he pressed his foot into the new mound of earth in a few places, then looked at his bone-weary troops again.

"Know you lads're tired, but it seems like a good time to go out an' have a lit'le fun," he said. "Just to deliver our respecks to the ones what put 'im in the ground. Whaddaya say, boys?"

At first there was no answer.

Then, one by one, the soldiers shook off their exhaustion and let loose a war cry, from deep in the throat, aimed at the stars.

The Sergeant smiled for the first time in a week.

"Well, then," he said, making his way back to his horse, "let's 'ave at it."

THE PROPHECY OF THE THREE

The Three shall come, leaving early, arriving late

The lifestages of all men:

Child of Blood, Child of Earth, Child of the Sky

Each man, formed in blood and born in it,

Walks the Earth and sustained by it,

Reaching the sky and sheltered beneath it,

He ascends there only in his ending, becoming part of the stars.

Blood gives new beginning

Earth gives sustenance

The Sky gives dreams in life—eternity in death

Thus shall the Three be, one to the other.

1

EASTERN BORDER OF THE
FOREST OF TYRIAN

At the crossing of the trans-Orlandan thoroughfare and the eastern forest road, Achmed the Snake thought he had caught the faintest trace of woodsmoke in the air.

He reined his horse to a stop and inclined his head to the west, seeking to confirm what his nose had hinted at, but sensed nothing further.

The Bolg king wearily loosed the reins and rubbed his face vigorously, then ran his thin-gloved fingers through his hair, damp with sweat. He took another breath, only to be greeted with the warmth and heavy perfume of late summer, wafting over him on a brittle wind. Nothing more.

Achmed glanced around for a place to water his mount and located a nearby quick-running stream winding its way out of the forest in the distance. He nudged the horse toward it and dismounted, allowing the animal some rest with its refreshment and himself the whimsy of memory.

It had been just short of a thousand years since he had been in this place, owing largely to its status as a backdoor route into the eastern edge of the forest of Tyrian. There had been no reason to brave the hidden defenders that were invisibly guarding this part of the Lirin kingdom when he could just as easily enter Tyrian via any of its public entrances, as he had done whenever the spirit had moved him to do so in the past. There had been relatively few times that the spirit had so moved him;

Achmed disliked forests in general and the Great Forest of the western part of the continent in particular. He preferred to do his visiting with the other two people in the world who, with him, made up what had been known long ago as the Three in the quiet solidity of his mountainous kingdom of Ylorc, where the ancient stone hallways and cavernous rooms were immune to prying eyes and free of the tattletale wind.

But since one of those two people was not cooperating, and the other would be arriving from the south shortly, he had decided to undertake a journey to check on his Wings, the network of carefully bred and selected horseflesh that he kept in secret stables across the continent for his personal use, which allowed him to traverse substantial distances in minimal time.

It was as good an excuse to leave the mountains without a guard regiment as any.

Achmed pushed his cloak back over his shoulders and crossed his arms, then turned around, taking in the sight of the forest to the west, the Krevensfield Plain behind him, and, in the distance, the jagged mountains to the south known as the Teeth, the cousins to the mountains of his own kingdom.

His eyes narrowed as the memory he sought returned.

The last time he had been here had been in the throes of the War of the Known World, the last intercontinental conflict the Cymrian Alliance, to which his kingdom was a signatory member, had suffered. A millennium had passed since those days, a largely peaceful time in which great advances in architecture, mechanics, medicine, and machinery had been made in Roland, the central nation in the breadbasket of the continent; political strife and diplomacy had been undertaken in the former empire of Sorbold, where now seventeen city-states, most of them members of the Alliance as well, had sorted themselves out of the destruction of that broken empire into independence; and his own kingdom had continued to rebuild and grow its military might. A substantial amount of progress had been made on all of those fronts—the center, southern, and eastern lands of the Middle Continent.

But here at the outskirts of Tyrian, the western coastal region covered mostly in thick, primeval forest, the view could easily have passed for that time long ago when last he had stood in this place.

It also could have reasonably been mistaken for a moment even longer ago when he had first stood there, upon coming to this continent.

Achmed knew that the primitive appearance of the forest was in many ways an illusion. Tyrian had undergone great progress in the last thousand years as well; healing centers and repositories of lore had been erected within the arms of the great wood, along with improved defenses and cooperatives for agriculture from which the Lirin fed much of the northern lands that could not grow their own food. But all of that millennial progress had been undertaken with an eye toward preserving the innocence of the forest, the natural antiquity of the land, and so it was not surprising that he was seeing now what his eyes had seen a thousand years before.

In the near distance to the south, he caught a trace of a familiar heartbeat approaching.

The Bolg king smiled slightly.

When counted in real time, his familiarity with that heartbeat had a history of almost three thousand years. He had walked, hidden, fought, and slept beside it on two sides of Time, and of the world as well—as well as in the world's belly.

It thudded mightily on the wind, but less so than it had in the Past.

He walked back to the horse and stood beside it, waiting.

A few moments later, a mount of almost twice his horse's size appeared over the edge of a swale in the forest road coming from the south. Atop it was his oldest friend in the world, the massive Sergeant-Major whose actual title was Supreme Commander of the forces of the mountainous realm of Ylorc, far to the other side of the continent, at its eastern edge, but who chose to be called Sergeant by his troops.

Grunthor by his friends.

From a distance, the giant grinned in greeting, but maintained his steady canter.

Jutting from the bandolier he wore, the hilts and handles of an impressive collection of bladed weapons still stood at the ready, as they had on both sides of Time, making him appear to have a sinister sun rising behind him, or as if he were the center of a monstrous daisy. His seat on the specially bred horse was as natural as it had ever been, his seven-and-a-half-foot frame sitting erect, without a nod to age or the damage he had sustained over his lifetime, more through sheer force of will than anything else.

Achmed, arms still crossed, assessed his friend's health and stamina as the giant rode closer, displeased with what he witnessed. While he had noticed no signs of aging or decline in his own status for the last millennium or so, nor had he seen a wrinkle or graying of hair on Rhapsody the last time he had been in her presence, the third member of the Three was not faring as well. His shaggy hair and beard, once an impressive shade of burnt orange and the thick consistency of a horse's mane, were sparser and gray; his skin, the color of old bruises, seemed more sallow than the last time Achmed had beheld him, which had not been that long ago.

But the grin was still bright, the eyes twinkling in the aging face.

Given the two races from which he was descended, Achmed thought, it was impressive that Grunthor was still moving autonomously at all. His father had been Firbolg, the race of demi-human hybrids that careful medical attention and a thousand years of peace had managed to bring to an average life span of forty years. Grunthor's mother was Bengard, one of the long-dead race of enormous desert dwellers who were impossible to gauge years for, owing to their love of bloodsport and arena fighting. The Bengard had put a premium on living bravely and dying young gloriously.

The fact that both of the only friends he'd ever had were still living was a miracle.

Achmed exhaled, lost in memory.

The new world had not been new for a long time, he mused; the places that he and the other two of the Three had discovered upon coming through the Root of the great world tree Sagia from their island homeland of Serendair were no longer fresh or alien, but dull in their familiarity. He and Grunthor had together completely restored, reoutfitted, and reenvisioned the massive, mountainous city-state of Ylorc, carved into the eastern Teeth almost three millennia before by Gwylliam the Visionary and left in ruins by the Cymrian War a thousand years later. The secrets in those endless, broken tunnels had all been found, the mysteries had all been solved; now the Bolg army, half a million strong, was the best-outfitted and best-trained fighting force on the continent, perhaps in the Known World, but it had seen nothing but military exercises and war games, with no live battle, for many centuries.

All that peace was aging Grunthor, a child of the arena and the battlefield, Achmed knew, even more than some of the cost of war he was paying from ten centuries before.

"Well met," he said to the Sergeant as he drew his enormous horse to a halt.

The giant pulled off his helm, ran a hand through his sweaty hair, and nodded.

"Well, 'allo, sir," he said cheerfully. "Glad ta see you, too. Where's the Duchess?"

"Late. Are you surprised?"

"Not a bit. All well in Ylorc?"

Achmed watched as Grunthor dismounted slowly, shaking the ground as he alighted. "Indeed. The vineyards are beginning the first round of harvest. Looks to be a fine one this year—if the weather holds as the Invoker predicts, we should even get a late third, an ice wine that they'll love in Marincaer, the simpletons. How were your travels?"

The Sergeant-Major's smile dissolved into a solemn expression. "Buried Trom."

The Bolg king exhaled. "I'm sorry." Grunthor's success as the sire of a multitude of Bolgish children with superior genes for war, originally propagated as a side effect of one of his favorite appetites, had so far produced thirty-seven generations, the first round of which had been gone for nine centuries—except for Trom.

While all of the mothers of his other children in the first generation, Bolg women of various levels of stature, were long deceased, Trom's mother had been Lelik, a Finder, spawned of the rape of a First Generation Cymrian, probably a woman, and one of the first ranks of Firbolg who overran Canrif, as Ylorc was known at the time, in the days following Gwylliam's death and the evacuation of the mountains by Anborn, Gwylliam's son and general, a millennium and a half before the Three had come to the continent.

Her Cymrian ancestry meant that she was exceptionally long-lived.

Lelik had become one of Achmed's second round of Archons, the select caste of Bolg who had been determined to be of leadership ability, and the mother of one of Grunthor's first children. The extraordinary longevity Trom inherited from his Cymrian/Firbolg mother, in concert with the apparent immortality of his father, had allowed Grunthor the pleasure of keeping a child over the centuries, when all of his other progeny had come and gone in what seemed the wink of an eye. It had also allowed for at least some duration of an individual woman's company, the only example of it Achmed knew of in Grunthor's life on either side of Time.

Trom's demise was the end of an era, even if that era only had one successful example of procreation and female companionship.

Grunthor made a gesture brushing off the sympathy.

"Well, thank ya, sir, but it was time. Long past, rather—'e'd lost the use of 'is legs and other functions long ago; no soldier wants to live like that."

"I suppose not. How many did you get out of that line, do you suppose?"

"Dunno," said the giant cheerfully. "Twen'y or more generations. Think Oi still see new litters of Trom's 'Greats' every now an' then. Lookin' forward to gettin' back to Ylorc an' knockin' out a few more brand-new ones o' my own."

Achmed smirked. "No luck in the pleasure palaces of the former Sorbold, eh?"

Grunthor shook his head. "Lost my taste fer women other'an Bolg a long time ago, sir. Well, at least *that* kind o' taste. Always willin' to snack on a few Lirin, but seems that's frowned upon nowadays."

"Truly we have lived too long. Well, best of luck with the new crop. If you keep at it, you may even catch up with Rhapsody. How many brats has she pushed out so far?"

"Still only six," came a voice in their ears, as if from the air around them. "And you would both know if anything had occurred otherwise, given that one of you is godfather to each of them, and the other is guardian to them all."

Both men looked around them in surprise.

"Where are you?" Achmed demanded of the air.

"On my way. You're standing in the vibrational buffer zone surrounding Tyrian, Achmed, you idiot. You didn't think I, and every communications specialist in the Lirin army, could hear you? And yes, snacking on Lirin is still considered frowned upon, Grunthor. Now back up about three hundred paces and, for the love of God, the One, the All, stop talking until I get there."

The two men looked at each other, then dissolved into quiet snickering.

Achmed sought her heartbeat on the wind and caught it a moment later, a strong, steady rhythm, though light in tone compared to the thundering of Grunthor's. They were two of the only heartbeats he could still feel in his skin, a gift he had inherited long ago from a Dhracian named Father Halphasion, who had been his mentor in youth, and had named him the Brother.

He thought back, for the first time in as long as he could remember, to the gentle monk who had rescued and cared for him after his escape from the Bolg of Serendair who had raised and abused him from birth. The name had been bestowed upon him, the priest had said, because he was "brother to all, akin to none." The resulting connection to the populace of the Island of Serendair, the drumming, tittering, pounding, and thrum of every heartbeat on that island, had all but driven him mad.

Now there was most often silence in his skin unless he sought those heartbeats.

But one that he frequently monitored was approaching from the west.

Grunthor was the first to catch sight of her, and broke into a wide grin upon doing so.

"Well, there she is. The 'orse looks new."

Achmed nodded as the forest roan, and the woman atop it, came into his view.

He breathed a little easier upon beholding her.

Occasionally over the centuries when seeing her after a long absence he found her appearance startling. While neither Time nor battle had made a mark on her physically, there was often something in her eyes and expression that was different, or something off-putting to him about the clothing in which she was attired at events where they met up.

While he and Grunthor, in his estimation, had changed very little from the days when the Three had first met, Rhapsody had evolved a great deal. Her inability to contain both excitement and wrath from her younger days had resolved into a queenly calm, a steadiness he recognized as necessary to her role as Lady Cymrian and Lirin sovereign, but he considered boring nonetheless. Her emerald eyes used to sparkle at anything she found interesting, and it had been a secret challenge of his in the old days to make that happen. Now they tended to gleam when she was pleased or angered, which brought the same light into those eyes, but it was hardly as interesting.

And the court clothing in which she was often garbed at events of state was nothing like the two or so dozen dresses he had reluctantly purchased for her when they first had come to the mountains of Ylorc together. In those days, Rhapsody's excitement upon receiving what was by and large high-quality peasant garb had made his skin-web, the sensitive network of veins and nerve endings that scored the surface of his body, tingle and hum pleasantly for days afterward. Now she was routinely gowned in heavy fabric of countless cost, sewn and embroidered by the patient hands of expert seamstresses from around the world. It was always a spectacular blending of beauty and artistry to behold, but it made her seem an entirely different person.

But the woman atop the roan was the one he remembered.

Rhapsody was smiling broadly, her face alight, her golden hair pulled back in a simple fall and tied in a black ribbon, as he remembered it from the old days. She was garbed in a white muslin shirt like any other Lirin citizen and wore moleskin pants tucked into sensible boots, much like the ones she had clothed herself in during their time together as the Three.

Achmed could hardly contain his relief.

"You came alone?" he demanded as she reined the horse to a stop and vaulted down from it, running to greet them.

She wrapped her arms around him first, filling his nostrils with her scent and soothing his prickly skin with the natural musical vibration that emanated from her. Then, upon comprehending his comment, she pulled back and looked at him in surprise.

"You have a problem with that?" she asked incredulously. "I somehow thought you preferred it when Ashe doesn't come with me."

"That goes without saying," Achmed said as she moved on to Grunthor, who picked her up and spun her around like a child. "I was referring to Meridion."

"Oh," said Rhapsody when the giant returned her to the ground after a long, warm hug. "I hadn't realized you would want to see him, I'm sorry. He can be here if you'd like. He and you, Achmed, are the only people—besides Rath and the other Dhracians, of course—that I have ever known who can travel in a way that essentially overcomes time and distance—you by riding the currents of the wind, as the Dhracians taught you, and Meridion by collapsing the passage of Time. I would be happy to summon Meridion if you'd like. He's nearby—he and I have been attending a Namers' convocation at the Repository of Lore in Tyrian City."

"Yeah, why not?" Grunthor said. "Always a nice thing ta see my first godson."

Rhapsody nodded and turned back to the forest. She sang a sweet incantation, repeating it several times, then loosed it to waft away on the hot wind of summer's end.

"Come with me," she said, waving them both back in the direction of her roan. "I've arranged a meal, some privacy and security at one of the border watchers' longhouses just inside the forest edge. I know that you aren't fond of being away from the deep Earth, but the longhouse roof is enclosed, so it's a little like the caverns of Ylorc, and I think you should enjoy the food and libations. And we can be together, just like old times, at least for a while. I'm so glad you both were able to come for the family gathering."

"Family gathering?" Grunthor queried.

"I am *not* coming to that," Achmed said flatly. "I came to see you, and perhaps Meridion, or any other of your progeny you had with you, but I believe I was clear in my response to your invitation to the gathering at Highmeadow."

Rhapsody hoisted herself back up atop her roan.

"Oh, *that's* what I was supposed to infer when you returned the invitation I sent you via avian messenger, for security reasons, by shredding the paper and blowing your nose on it? I *completely* misunderstood. I apologize."

"You should consider yourself lucky with my choice of bodily excretions," Achmed said, mounting as well. "I had to scale back my original intentions for the health of the innocent bird."

"Why would you not come?" Rhapsody asked, appearing sincerely stricken. "You are the only members of my family that won't be in attendance."

"My point exactly."

Rhapsody sighed as Grunthor finally summited his mount, taking his time and care.

"You could come, you know, Grunthor. I hope you will. Your godchildren, and all the Grands and Greats, are really looking forward to seeing you."

The Bolg Sergeant shook his head regretfully.

"Naw, thanks, Yer Ladyship, but I'm not really feelin' up fer it," he said wistfully. "Just came from putting Trom in the ground. Not in the mood for a celebration, sorry."

"I'm so sorry," Rhapsody said, reaching across horses and patting his arm consolingly. "I had no idea."

Grunthor covered her small hand with his enormous, pawlike one. "Yeah, it was quiet and fast," he said, taking the reins in his own. "The way 'e woulda chosen if 'e'd been given the choice. Do ya think you might sing 'is dirge? Trom always did love to 'ear you sing."

"Of course; I'll do it tonight before Meridion and I head back toward Highmeadow. Was he ill?"

"Not really." Grunthor nodded to Achmed as the Bolg king signaled his readiness to ride. "Trom never really got back ta whole from when those Alliance soldiers beat 'im into oblivion a couple 'undred years ago."

Rhapsody's eyes flashed with anger. She set her teeth and nodded, but Achmed could see the rage swim through the muscles of her shoulders.

He took silent pleasure in the fact that she was still furious over the unprovoked assault that Trom and his regiment had endured at the hands of the soldiers of her husband's army.

And hers.

He had stood beside her on the gallows at the hangings of the men responsible, with very much the same look on her face, the same anger in her eyes.

"Grunthor is looking forward to returning to Ylorc and getting started on fathering a new rash of baby Bolg," he said, attempting to lighten the mood.

Rhapsody's eyes cleared of anger, and she smiled in the direction of the Sergeant.

"That's wonderful," she said sincerely. "I know how much you love your children, Grunthor, especially in the infant phase."

" 'At's right," said Grunthor smugly. "Bite-sized, chewy, with a nice crunch. It's a good breedin' plan—either they's well-be'aved, or they's delicious. Ya win either way."

"Oh, stop that," Rhapsody said to the back ends of both of her friends' horses, noting how much they had in common with their riders as she rode astride, catching up and leading them into Tyrian by the forest road.

2

HIGHMEADOW, NAVARNE

In the corner of the main bedchamber in the palatial estate of Highmeadow, a silver bell rang sweetly, its sound resonating through the air of the room.

After a moment, a voice, trained in the Lirin science of Naming, intoned a quiet message, audible only to the person to whom it had been sent.

Sam—good morning. You should expect a Great surprise today. I love you; I'll be home soon. Your Emily

Lord Gwydion ap Llauron awoke slowly, a headache buzzing behind his eyes as he did.

As was his accustomed reaction to the morning light and his wake-up call, he gritted his teeth and inhaled slowly, then allowed his breath to seep out between those teeth in a long release.

The accustomed reaction took some of the pain of awareness in small puffs with it.

His mind, wrapped a few moments before in a dream of a long-dead uncle who had survived to be his age, gradually absorbed wakefulness, thanks to the gentle vibrations imbued into the metal of the bell in the corner of the room. Gwydion stretched slowly, willing himself to be grateful for another day and struggling in the attempt.

A respectful tap sounded against the bedchamber door.

"Cmmmmminn," the Lord Cymrian grumbled.

The summons was met with an enthusiastic response as the door burst open and three small children came dashing into the room on billowing waves of excitement—a young blond boy of seven or so summers, his four-year-old sister, an impish redhead, and a towheaded toddler who was struggling to remain erect and in motion simultaneously as he hurried, arms outstretched, in the general direction of the bed.

"Papa! Papa!"

Gwydion, or Ashe, as the Lord Cymrian had been long known to his intimates, exhaled deeply and opened an eye, blue as those set in the excited faces heading his way, bearing the same vertical pupils.

The sense of the dragon in his blood, a primordial nature that had been with him most of his life, assessed the approaching small progeny, recognizing its own nature carried within them and reporting back to his human mind within the span of a single pair of heartbeats.

Reimund, Elysabeth, and Andret, it whispered, each of their names resonating in its unheard tones.

My children, Ashe thought warmly, allowing the understanding to wash through his still-sleep-addled brain with the sensation of a quick-running stream rushing through the frozen ground of a forest in spring. *My beloved children.*

A thought from deeper in his consciousness, the dragon sense, corrected him.

Your Greats, it whispered, this time irritably.

Ashe closed his eye again, absorbing the thought.

Behind his lids he could sense the presence of Merilda, their mother, hovering in the doorway, her arms crossed in amusement.

His granddaughter, the middle child of his middle daughter Elienne, the dragon informed him.

How is it possible? he wondered as Reimund, his oldest Great in Merilda's family, summited the bed, launching himself onto Ashe's abdomen.

"Oooof," the Lord Cymrian grumbled, mostly for effect, but still feeling the squeeze of the wind leaving his lungs.

He rolled onto his side and pulled his great-grandson into his arms, burying his nose in the giggling boy's neck as the lad's younger sister struggled to climb up the coverlet that had slid to the floor on the other side of the bed. Ashe stretched out an arm to assist her in her efforts, thankful that he had chosen to wear his nightshirt to bed.

He opened the eye that had not yet seen the light of morning to the sight of Andret, the youngest, staring him in the face with his hands above his head and bouncing enthusiastically on legs far too short to make the climb.

Ashe rolled onto his back again and opened his mouth, allowing a rolling draconic sound, part hiss, part gurgle, part roar, to emerge from the depths of his throat, clicking and glottal-stopping, to the screeching delight of the children. They imitated the sound capably in a joyful chorus, possessed of the necessary dragon throat structure, as all his progeny seemed to be, filling the air of the bedchamber with noise that would have caused any human present, were there one, to take shelter in fear.

It was a tradition begun with his own children when they were this age, and passed along, in spite of Rhapsody's feigned horror, to each member of the family throughout the generations.

Merilda was already across the room, snagging her wiggling boy and assisting him onto the child-covered mound that was now his great-grandfather.

"Good morning, Papa," she said, leaning down to Ashe and kissing his brow.

Ashe smiled easily. "Good morning, Gingersnap," he said, his voice still rough with sleep and the aftermath of the roar. Merilda, unlike her dark-haired mother and alone among her siblings, had a head of red-gold hair that echoed his own in his youth, before the gray of age had slipped into it, and her grandmother's emerald-green eyes. "Thanks for bringing the wake-up brigade."

"They have been up since foredawn, eager to jump on you," Merilda said, unconsciously putting out a hand to prevent a tumble. "I'm sorry if you were deep in a dream, or actual restfulness, something I scarcely recall from my own youth since I entered sleepless motherhood."

"Sleep is unduly overvalued," said Ashe, tickling Elysabeth and eliciting a gale of laughter that rang in his ears like the famed bells of the basilica in Bethe Corbair. He sighed, feeling the physical satisfaction of the wyrm in his blood from being in the presence of his greatest treasure—his family.

Andret's belly was near his mouth, so he blew loudly on it, and dodged out of the way of the toddler's scrambling feet, now trying to find purchase on the pillows.

"Here, you rascals, allow Papa some breathing room," Merilda ordered, dragging Andret back into her arms. Ashe pulled himself up against the headboard and wrapped his arms around the oldest two.

"Have you had breakfast yet?" he inquired of Elysabeth, who nodded briskly.

"Hours ago. Your tray is outside, by the way," Merilda said. "Shall I bring it in?"

"No, thank you. I think I'll just snack on these two tasty-looking Greats."

Reimund and Elysabeth squealed in delight.

"Come along," Merilda instructed, putting the wriggling toddler on her hip and signaling for the older two to join her. "Let's give Papa a few moments of peace. Your cousins will be along soon enough and the place will be ringing with noise."

Ashe kissed the oldest two great-grandchildren and watched wistfully as they slid off the bed and hurried to their mother. "Peace, like sleep, is unduly overvalued as well, at least where children are concerned," he said, kissing Andret, who hung upside down like a bat from his mother's arms. "Thank you for bringing them in, Gingersnap. I loved this morning's reveille."

"They do have the timbre of a bugle call," Merilda laughed. "The others should be arriving over the next few days before the family summit, and there's much to be done in preparation, so I will leave you to your breakfast and your privacy. Thank you for indulging their need to tussle with you. I remember how much my brothers and I loved waking you when we were their age, along with the other Grands when they were here with us."

"Where is Hamimen, Papa?" Reimund asked as his mother led him away.

Ashe smiled. "She'll be home soon, and happy to see you." He exhaled as Merilda led the children out the chamber door and smiled at him in very much the same way that Rhapsody would have. Then he lay back against the pillows, suddenly bereft as the door closed behind them.

Though certainly not soon enough, he thought.

Then he rose creakily from the shambles of the bed and made his way to the privy, feeling cold and overwhelmingly lonely.

A little more than half an hour later, the Lord Cymrian descended the curving staircase leading to the round vestibule of the main residence at Highmeadow, bathed, shaven, dressed, fed, and in a considerably better state than he had been in upon first awakening.

The antechamber was the main entranceway to the part of the fortress generally reserved for family matters and small meetings, a building full of bedchambers, medium-sized dining rooms, and private libraries, decorated in a homey manner, in stark contrast to the grander facilities in other buildings elsewhere in Highmeadow.

He was rounding the curve of the staircase when his dragon sense roared to life, making his skin prickle.

Ashe closed his eyes and let the sensitive network wash over him, transmitting its information. He smiled warmly and finished his descent.

In the vestibule below him, the Invoker of the Filids, the leader of the nature theology of the western continent, was waiting for him, back turned to the staircase, examining the tapestry across from it.

"Good morning, Your Grace," he said respectfully.

The Invoker turned and matched his smile. "Good morning, m'lord."

Ashe's heart cramped upon beholding her with his eyes.

The Invoker was his youngest daughter, Laurelyn.

There was always a moment's hesitation upon seeing her, a woman indistinguishable in the appearance of age from her niece, Merilda, in spite of having been born a generation and three centuries before her. In addition to the glow of youth, Laurelyn was the image of her mother, with golden hair that hung to her waist, braided in leather cords and feathers, except for the blue eyes and draconic pupils she had inherited from him. But while Rhapsody radiated the mercurial warmth and unpredictability of the fire that she had absorbed in her trek long ago through the elemental core at the Earth's heart, Laurelyn had a peaceful, steady mien, a constant, placid soul that reflected her deep tie to the Earth. She had a green soul, sweetened by birdsong and the sounds of the deep forest, wise as a quiet, spring-fed lake.

It was in many ways like looking once more upon his own father, Llauron ap Gwylliam, who had held the office of Invoker more than a millennium before and had taught Ashe everything he knew of the woodlands.

Though, unlike her, Llauron was dead in body and soul a thousand years.

And now she stood in the entranceway to the place that had once been her childhood home, attired in a simple robe of burlap cloth dyed brown in butternut hulls, the wooden staff of her office in her hand, topped with a golden oak leaf.

Ashe opened his arms. "Come to me, little bird."

Laurelyn hurried into his embrace, beaming.

"To what do I owe the honor of the Invoker's presence in my home?" Ashe said teasingly, holding her tight.

"Actually, I've come to bless the grounds of what I am told is going to be a massive family summit," Laurelyn replied. She gave her father a final squeeze, then stepped back and regarded him with more distance, holding her staff. "If the royal family is to be all in one place, it is well advised that the Earth hold that information in confidence, and not relay it to anyone who might make improper use of it."

Ashe nodded approvingly. "A wise decree."

"I am only able to stay until midday—I must ride back to the Circle by nightfall tomorrow to make preparations for the end-of-summer rites. But I will return a sennight hence for the family summit. I look forward to it greatly."

"Do you have time to share noonmeal with me?" Ashe said, trying to keep the longing out of his voice. "My military councilors are coming momentarily for a series of briefings this morning, but all that should be done in time for us to dine before you leave, if your schedule would accommodate it." His throat tightened as he watched her exhale silently. "I haven't seen you since Gavin's funeral pyre. Please, little bird—I've missed you."

Laurelyn sighed, aloud this time, then chuckled.

"All right, Papa," she said, humor in her otherwise serious tone. "I'll be back as soon as I have finished the incantations. But not a moment longer. And please make certain that lunch contains bacon if at all possible. I've missed the way it's made by the cooks at Highmeadow."

"Done." The Lord Cymrian kissed her forehead and headed for the council room, pleased with the improvement that was continuously occurring in his day.

Pushing to the fringes of his consciousness the fragments of his disturbing dream which still lingered, heavy on his mind.

3

*J*ust beyond the doors of the council room Ashe could feel his elevated mood sink rapidly again.

Standing about the room, or sitting uncomfortably in its chairs, were soldiers of various ranks and ages, men and women both, some of them in their third millennium, First Generation Cymrians, others having passed less than three decades of life.

All of them were looking summarily displeased.

Ashe sighed as they rose to their feet when he entered. He waved his hand at them halfheartedly, signaling them to the council table.

"Gentlewomen and men, good morning."

An irregular chorus of *good morning, m'lord* rattled back against his skin. Ashe closed his eyes as the words buffeted him, then opened them and took a seat at the council table.

"I must say, the expressions on your faces are truly unpleasant to behold on such a fine, sunny morning," he said as the chairs around the table screeched upon being pulled out, then thudded heavily as they were dragged back in. "I hope that your news is not so disturbing as to merit the ugly looks most of you are wearing."

"Forgive me, m'lord," said Knapp sourly, one of the two First Generation soldiers who served as Supreme Commander of the continent's sea-lanes. "My face always looks like this, and has for two and a half thousand years. My ugly look should be interpreted as merely advanced age and general cussedness, not a military problem. The coastlines are, as of the last report yesterday, free from threat."

"Well, that's a relief," Ashe said. He turned and addressed the only other First Generationer present. "Solarrs—how stands Manosse?"

"No hostilities reported, m'lord, on land or sea."

"Good to hear."

Tian, Mistress of the Lance, the thickset commander of the six-hundred-thousand-strong infantry of the Alliance, cleared her throat. Ashe nodded at her.

"All is well in the northern borderlands, and to the east," she said quietly. "Tyrian reports no incursions from the south, nor elsewhere. The Krevensfield Plain is preparing for harvest, with nothing of note to report. No activity has been reported up to or at the eastern steppes. The Bolglands appear quiet."

"Excellent." Ashe turned to the younger contingent of generals, men and women who had, for the most part, little or no Cymrian lineage and therefore had fewer years of age among them than many of the bottles of port and other libations he kept in his wine cellar. "Air defenses?"

Ariane, the Lirin woman who commanded the reconnaissance outposts of mechanized weather balloons, coastline gliders, and avian messengers, bowed slightly. "All clear. You have the weekly dispatches, m'lord. The Sea Mages report nothing of note on the thermal readings as well."

"Indeed, thank you. Anything of note from Faedryth in the Distant Mountains, any incursions against the Nain? Communications from the Hintervold?"

"No, m'lord."

"Very good." He glanced around the table, his gaze lighting upon Reynard ap Hydrion and Arnald Goodeve, who, with their field commanders Dante Corynth and Markus Mendel, were responsible for patrolling and maintaining order in the city-states of the southern Teeth, and inwardly winced. From the glances between them, and the darkness of their expressions, he knew he had located the area of concern.

"All right, Reynard," he said, bracing himself. "It appears you are the burr under the saddle. What is amiss in the southern Teeth, or beyond?"

Reynard and Goodeve exchanged another glance. Then Reynard, a swarthy soldier of less than thirty summers and more than his share of battlefield acumen, spoke.

"Permission to speak candidly, m'lord?"

Ashe felt his stomach knot. "Granted, and in fact, demanded."

Reynard exhaled. "It's Grunthor again, m'lord."

The Lord Cymrian sighed. "What now?"

Goodeve coughed. "The usual, m'lord—he's sending raiding parties into random city-states and outposts, attacking border troops and guard units."

"We are getting complaints from your diplomats who have been attempting to establish affiliations with some of the smaller city-states that have been nonaligned since the War of the Known World," added Mendel. "Most of what was once the former empire of Sorbold is well seated, either signatories to the Alliance or at least friends thereof, as you well know, sire. The diplomatic agreements that the Foreign Service is trying to put in place are continually disrupted by Bolg assault forces that, up until now, had confined their activities to war games, but now have crossed the line. There are casualties, thus far only military ones, but last week came dangerously close to civilian settlements and established towns."

The headache that had dissipated from behind Ashe's eyes crept back in, rampant, making his skull ring with sharp pain. The dragon in his blood muttered darkly, beyond all but his own hearing.

"Define 'dangerously close.'"

"An abbot traveling outside of Sepulvarta to a wedding was killed, along with the human contents of a small caravan of wagons populated with itinerant workers of unknown origin, most likely headed to the coastal vineyards or the olive fields in the hills of Windswere. It's not clear who fired upon whom first, but there was nothing left but smoking wagons by the time it was done."

Ashe's teeth were gritted so tightly he could feel his jaw quiver.

Dante Corynth and Markus Mendel exchanged a glance.

"We have been questioning whether to alert you, m'lord, given the Sergeant-Major's friendship with the Lady Cymrian—" Corynth blurted, only to be brought to silence by a glare from Reynard.

And a horrifying draconic curse from the throat of the Lord Cymrian that even made Solarrs and Knapp blanch.

"Why in the world would you imagine *that* would keep you from reporting this?" he demanded, the vibrations of the wyrm in his blood evident in his tone. "Do you think for a heartbeat that Rhapsody would condone the slaughter of civilians—a priest, or farmworkers? Even at the hands of one of her friends?"

"No, m'lord, no, of course not," said Reynard quickly. "We came here expecting to make this report."

Ashe pushed his chair back, the wood screaming against the slate of the floor, and rose angrily.

"How long has this been occurring?"

"There was a report of rowdiness and Firbolg horseplay as long ago as during the month of Fore-Yule last year, m'lord," Knapp interjected, noting the gleam of panic in the eyes of the younger generals and field commanders. "We've heard it, both at this level and in the lower ranks, for quite some time. When we discussed it at this meeting last year, it was deemed to be boredom, if you recall.

"The Sergeant-Major has long been the epitome of military leadership among the armies of the Alliance, and the recipient of great respect and admiration across the Known World, but of late he seems to be, well, at odds with the peace that has been the standard, more or less, for a thousand years. He's got the best fighting force on the continent, armed with ingenious and high-quality weaponry, a carefully cultivated and expertly bred stable for his cavalry—but no one to engage. He himself was pouting about 'an onerous peace' at one of the field-commander conferences late last winter. 'Got myself an army to be proud of, but nobody wants to come out and play,' I believe he said. I did pass this along to you at the time, if you recall, m'lord."

"The diplomats have been griping about it at least half that long," said Solarrs darkly.

Ashe gripped the sides of his head, seeking to keep it from exploding.

"He's a menace, and has been for a very long time," he said in a low, seething voice that rang with the hiss of the dragon. He thought back to the soft one intoning a wakeup message that morning.

I love you; I'll be home soon.

I have a project for you to attend to upon your return, my love, Ashe thought angrily.

"I cannot wait for the one who is able to put an end to that menace," he said, running a hand angrily through his graying hair. "Grunthor may be one of the Three, and one of my wife's dearest friends, but there are limits, and they have just been exceeded."

The military leaders around the table looked at one another blankly.

"Is there anything else under status reports?" Ashe demanded.

"No, m'lord."

"Good. Then let's get to procurements and training needs, so that I can be done with this cursed discussion and we can all get to noon-meal. I see no need to torture ourselves any more than we already have."

*L*aurelyn was already waiting at a table on the balcony of the library when Ashe arrived, a glass of wine at his place setting.

"I've taken the liberty of requesting quiche and greens with herbs from the buttery for both of us," she said as her father kissed her head, "but if that's not to your liking, they are standing ready for a substitution."

"That's a wonderful choice, but I thought you wanted bacon," Ashe said as he took his seat and unfolded his napkin.

"It's in the quiche."

"Ah. Perfect." He exhaled as he took in the sight of her, allowing the unpleasantness of the morning to dissipate into the air around him, then took a sip from his glass. "Did you know that Merilda is here?"

"Yes, I had breakfast at dawn with her and the Greats," Laurelyn said, also unfolding her napkin. "They were very excited about jumping on you afterwards. I hope you enjoyed it, Papa."

"I may never recover."

"Hmm." Laurelyn picked up the coffee server and held it over his empty cup. "Skunk urine?" she inquired blandly, using her mother's name for his dark, odiferous favorite beverage.

Ashe laughed as she poured him a steaming cup of the hot, bitter blend. "Oh, bless you. Did I ever tell you that you're my favorite child?"

"Repeatedly. And I would have been immensely flattered had I not heard you tell every one of my siblings the same thing."

"I told all of you nothing but the truth," Ashe said as a chambermaid entered with their meal. "Every one of you is my favorite, each in a different way, and each for a different reason."

"If one believes Mimen, and one should, since she's a Namer, it also had something to do with timing," Laurelyn noted as she leaned back to allow the chambermaid to set her plate, then nodded her thanks. "At any given point in the day, if one child was behaving especially well or especially badly, it made the choice of Favorite Child easy, she said. When will she be home?"

"Her message this morning said 'soon,' without specifics. But our anniversary is a sennight hence; I cannot imagine her missing it."

Laurelyn waited until the library door had closed behind the chambermaid.

"You must be referring to the one commemorating the first wedding you held in secret in the grotto of Elysian," she said with a solemn expression but a sparkle in her eye. "Your public anniversary is closer to autumn."

"I didn't realize you knew about that," Ashe said, picking up his fork.

"You should; you're the one who told me about it, when we were exploring down in that grotto long ago."

The Lord Cymrian sighed. "I am getting old. My mind is failing me daily." A wicked gleam came into his eye. "How is Syril?" He watched as Laurelyn's clear, milky skin turned a rosier shade.

"He's well, thank you."

Ashe put down his fork again, crossed his arms, and leaned conspiratorially across the table.

"So now that you have settled into your relatively new role as Invoker, will we at last be receiving tidings of an upcoming wedding in the new year?"

"No."

He blinked in surprise. "No? Why, little bird? You have shown all the subtle signs of being in love for a decade now—is the bloom off the rose?"

Laurelyn sat back and dabbed the corners of her mouth with her napkin.

"Not at all," she said sensibly. "We do not intend to wait until the new year. I had planned to ask you to marry us at the end of the family summit, given that everyone will already be gathered."

Ashe laughed out loud and took her hand, drawing it to his lips. "Wonderful!"

"But you must keep this to yourself, Papa, and tell only Mimen until the last day."

"Why?"

"Because I do not wish our news to overshadow or take away in any part from the summit. We have not been together as a family since Andret's Naming ceremony two years ago, and I'm sure there will be a lot of family business, glad and thought-provoking tidings to discuss." She took up her glass again. "And besides, I have such a reputation for commonsensical behavior and a dowdy personal life that the surprise should be fun."

"You are hardly seen among the family as having a dowdy personal life," Ashe said in amusement, returning to his quiche. "It is a source of great pride to all of us that you have ascended to the office of Invoker after three hundred years as Gavin's Tanist." His face grew solemn. "I'm sorry that so few of the family were able to attend his funeral and your investiture. Gavin was a great man."

"It was to be expected," Laurelyn said. "The new Invoker is invested within one turn of the moon after the pyre of the previous one, and it was the dead of winter, before First Thaw; it was not reasonable to expect many of them to travel under the circumstances. I was grateful to have both you and Mimen there. The Filidic order does not place as much emphasis on mourning passing as it does on celebrating arrival or transition. Gavin was not offended in the least, I am absolutely certain. I am also certain he will be looking on, if he is able, from the Afterlife with joy at my long-awaited wedding."

"Speaking of which, is it proper for me to pronounce the wedding rites for the leader of the faith to which I am only a lowly adherent?" Ashe asked.

"Of course. I may be your Invoker, but you are my sovereign. And, more importantly, my father. There is no one in the world whose blessing I would rather have on my long-in-coming marriage." Her eyes sparkled mischievously. "And after three hundred years of celibacy, it's particularly appropriate for my father to bless my union, wouldn't you say? Stupid rituals. When I've tended to all the rites that need my attention, I will raise that issue with the Filidic Council and see if I can eliminate that ridiculous situation for whomever becomes my future replacement. Celibacy is an unnatural state to force upon a nature priest, or, in fact, anyone, even an Invoker-in-waiting like a Tanist."

Ashe's face colored in much the same way as hers had a moment before. He cleared his throat.

"Uh, well, you've been the Invoker for eight months now, little bird. I can't imagine why you would still be observing an—er—unnatural state."

"Oh, trust me, I'm not," Laurelyn said breezily, causing Ashe to break into embarrassed laughter. "Syril is of Cymrian lineage, but it's so many generations removed from the First that the longevity it grants will most likely be minimal. There's not a moment to waste."

Ashe nodded reflectively. The gift of an expanded life span had been both curse and blessing to his family over the centuries, though at least at this moment in Time, death had taken none of his progeny from him. But his own third-generation Cymrian lineage and the blood of the dragon Elynsynos in his veins, coupled with the seeming stoppage of Time on Rhapsody, who had not aged a day in a thousand years, had meant that some of his grandchildren appeared considerably older than their parents and even their grandparents. Loss of friends and family members over time had been something that his family had become as pragmatic about as it was possible to be.

Still, he hurt for his daughter, realizing that she would never have what he and Rhapsody shared—a union lasting a thousand years.

And, given how quickly he seemed to be aging, he was not certain how much longer he would be enjoying that blessing, either.

"Well, I'm glad to hear it," he said, finishing his lunch.

"That's one of you," Laurelyn said, looking down at her plate to keep from laughing. "All the serving men and women who work in the In-voker's Palace have discreetly chosen to find other lodging for the time being. Apparently *they* aren't so glad to hear it—at least at night. The walls of the Tree Palace are not particularly soundproof."

"Well, good for you both. I guess some things *do* run in the family." Ashe swallowed as Laurelyn rose, folded her napkin, and came to him. She bent and kissed him, then went to where her staff stood, leaning against the wall, took it in hand, and turned to face him again.

"I must be off," she said regretfully. "I hope to make it to the guest-house in Tref-Y-Gwartheg by nightfall. My father worries incessantly about me if I ride by night."

"You're absolutely right, he does," Ashe said, rising as she walked to-ward the door of the library. "He also prefers you to ride with a regiment—or two—or four—"

"I'm the Invoker now, Papa," Laurelyn said indulgently. "I command the forest roads. Please, stop worrying. I'm almost five hundred years old."

"To me, you will always be the tiny child sitting alone in the garden, singing quietly to herself, the plants, and invisible fairies—my little bird," Ashe said, his heart in his aged eyes as he stopped in front of her near the door. "Your brother made exceptional use of the Singing lore your mimen taught all of you in the form of True-Speaking, but you employed it in song, softly, making things grow, and bloom, and heal. You can't imagine how much I love you, how much I miss you—how proud I am of you. You won't ever understand, until you have children of your own."

"What makes you think they were invisible?" Laurelyn asked, amused.

"What?"

"The fairies. They were never invisible to me, Papa." She watched his eyes take on a gleam, and she came into his arms again. "Not sure if the 'children of my own' path is for me—my sister's *daughter* has children of her own now, children who apparently bounced the stuffing out of their great-grandfather a few hours ago. We will see how things come to pass, one challenge at a time. Goodbye, Papa. My love remains with you."

"Goodbye, Your Grace," Ashe whispered in her ear. "My love goes with you, my little bird."

He closed his eyes as she left the room, allowing his dragon sense to wash over her, following her down the stairs and out into the world beyond his protection. He went to the window seat beneath the large library window once she had mounted her gelding and had passed through the forest gate in the western wall of Highmeadow and sat, letting his inner sense follow her to the edge of its reach—about three leagues—until the cool green vibrations of her heartbeat were at last beyond his awareness.

A flash of red, like an explosion of blood behind his eyes, roared through him, sending a shock of heat and palpable anger with it.

Ashe closed his eyes tightly, but the image shot across his brain, narrated by the seething tones of the dragon.

An image of a massive, knuckled claw descending from the sky above the forest canopy.

Snatching Laurelyn from the saddle.

Get back here, the voice in his head hissed. *Mine.*

Ashe struggled to blot the image from his mind, breathing shallowly.

In a few moments it was gone, his brain his own again.

As a wave of despair crested inside him, he recalled the message he had received that morning.

I love you; I'll be home soon.

Please come home now, *Emily,* he thought. *I can feel the strings of my mind unraveling without you here to bind them up again.*

After they passed through the eastern wall of Highmeadow, Reynard, Goodeve, Mendel, and Corynth rode farther on until they came to a sheltered spot in he road. Reynard was the first to signal his intention that they come off the pathway, a neatly groomed forest thoroughfare that was maintained and guarded by the forces of the Alliance.

He sat up straighter in his saddle, amid the dusty shafts of sunlight streaking the forest floor through the canopy.

"I need help making sense of this," he said quietly to the others. "Have we been ordered, or challenged?"

"It's not clear to me," Corynth said, casting a glance around him. "There was no direction or timetable set."

"How could there be?" Goodeve asked. "In all of the order that has been maintained for centuries, this is the one source of random mayhem. It's unpredictable."

"Probably the reason for the old practice of Spring Cleaning," said Mendel archly. "While history extols the aid that the Bolg have given to major battles throughout the second Cymrian era, the wildness, the primitive violence has never been bred out of them."

"Their repulsive king takes great pride in that," Goodeve said. "I have heard the briefings."

"Are all of your seconds in place?" Reynard asked. He received three nods in response. "Then, given the conditions, it seems a visit beyond the southern Teeth, to the city-states, is in order."

"We'll need reinforcements," Mendel said.

The others nodded in agreement and returned to the forest road.

4

(M)eridion was finishing up his paperwork from the symposium he and his mother had just conducted when he heard, or rather felt, her voice singing his true name, a complex mathematical series of notes that made up the essence of who he was on the deepest of levels. It was a skill known only to the Namer, one of the rarest of professions in the Known World, although he and Rhapsody had just spent the better part of a fortnight working and training with most of the rest of the Namers that now existed.

She had left two days prior to get to the southeastern border of Tyrian, the great forested realm of the Lirin, in order to meet up with her two best friends in the world, Achmed the Snake, king of the Firbolg and, on a far more personal basis, guardian to him and each of his brothers and sisters, and Sergeant-Major Grunthor, his and their godfather, so hearing her speak next to his ear as he was putting papers away was a bit of a surprise.

Meridion ap Gwydion, eldest son, Child of Time, pippin, please come to the Thornberry longhouse. I love you. Mimen

Her wordless song was light, with a merry tone, so he assumed the summons was a pleasant one rather than an alert.

Meridion chuckled at her use of the word *pippin* in her salutation, the Lirin word for *baby*. His assistant, Avriel, was energetically packing up his materials, her back to him, oblivious to Rhapsody's call.

He closed his eyes and concentrated on his namesong again, particularly the musical passage *Child of Time*.

Around him, Time itself seemed to slow to a halt.

Meridion glanced at his assistant, frozen between the threads of it.

He finished his work, jotting a quick note for Avriel, then went to the coat tree at the door of the Repository and took down his cloak and walking stick.

He turned around and glanced at his assistant again.

Avriel had not moved, nor had Time.

Satisfied, he left his office in the Repository of Lore, walking past the various men and women in the hallways, all motionless, and exited the building, taking the forest road, where he concentrated more intensely.

A cylindrical corridor of power opened before him. Meridion stepped over the threshold into it.

The trees of the forest seemed to rush past him in the blink of an eye, one moving blur, until he found himself outside the door of the longhouse to which he had been summoned.

Meridion stepped out of the corridor.

Then he closed his eyes and concentrated again.

Birdsong and the breath of the wind greeted him upon his exit, the dancing boughs of trees still in leaf, the passage of foot travelers in the distance, and all the other movement of life that had come to a halt while he was traveling.

The Three had not arrived yet.

He imagined by now Avriel had become aware of his exit, and most likely was not particularly surprised. She had become accustomed to his odd comings and goings, and rarely complained, unless he had forgotten to leave a note.

He was pleased that he had remembered to so do this time.

Avriel—thank you for your stellar help, as always. Answering the Lady's call. Will return shortly. M

He smiled, anticipating the arrival of the Three, the trio of epic renown that to him had always been guardian, godfather, and mother.

He was indulging in fond thoughts and funny memories when a twinge of the Future rattled his good mood.

Meridion looked rapidly around, but saw nothing. He cursed under his breath.

While his gift with the manipulation of Time was a very convenient and useful one most often, on occasion it was unduly disturbing. He had almost unlimited access to the noncorporeal vision of the Past, allowing him to step back in Time, if he knew where he needed to go, to see things that had occurred long ago, or, one of the traits most annoying to his friends and relations, repeating disputed words of an event for the record. He also could travel, quickly and unseen, over great distances in the wink of an eye, in the Present.

The Future, while more available to him than to most people, was a mystery that occasionally gave him broad or subtle hints, but only small ones.

And it raised his hackles without giving him reassurance.

It was a small enough price to pay for the other aspects of the power.

And, he reminded himself that, while as far as he knew, his ability to pause and manipulate Time was a unique one, many people had such glimpses of the Future, from premonitions and dreams to simple goose-flesh out of nowhere. His own mother had been bedeviled by such premonitions and dreams until she had married his father, a man with dragon's blood who could chase such nightmares away.

He cherished a memory of her from the distant Past that he had once caught while experimenting with the Time Viewer, a machine of a sort, an invention he had been tinkering with that allowed him to catch glimpses of things that had happened in the Past. It was a vision of his mother as a young child, four or five, perhaps, working on her family's farm in Merryfield in the old world.

She had been gathering eggs in the chicken coop when a shiver had run through her.

Daddy, she had said to her father, a man Meridion had never met. *It happened again.*

His human grandfather had turned around and smiled at her.

The tickle?

Yes.

That's just a goose walking over your grave. Pay it no mind.

His mother had looked at her father seriously. *I have a grave?*

His grandfather's smile had resolved into a pleasant, though serious, expression.

Everyone has a grave, child, but being that you are half Lirin, yours will probably be the wind. It's just a silly farm-folk expression. Now, finish up with the eggs.

The little girl had nodded. *Yes, Daddy.* She had gone back to the nests, shaking her head of wavy golden hair, muttering to herself, too quietly for her father to hear.

No damn goose better be walking on my *grave, whatever that is. I don' like gooses.*

Meridion chuckled as he always did upon seeing the image again. He leaned back against the door of the longhouse and closed his eyes.

Enjoying the memory, the sun on his face, the wind in his hair, the song of the birds in the trees of southern Tyrian, and the undisturbed Present he was sharing with the rest of the world, without a thought of the Future, looming in the distance, beckoning.

SOUTHWESTERN TYRIAN, NEAR THE FOREST EDGE

Achmed sat back in his chair and raised his tankard to his lips, hiding his smile behind it.

A pleasant serenity reigned in the longhouse where the Three had taken shelter; the food had been more than satisfactory and the ale was of a solid quality and pleasant. The laughter that had accompanied the meal had banished the Sergeant's exhaustion, and his own disquieted melancholy.

Now Grunthor and Rhapsody were engaged in a fiercely competitive Bolg game of cards known as Crusher that, when played in Ylorc, involved the exchange of varying levels of violent blows, usually to the face, but occasionally to the balls. The other two of the Three were exchanging flicks of the fingers, still more dangerous to Rhapsody than to Grunthor, while he himself sat, with his feet on a footrest of perfect height, taking in the tableau of how things had once been when days were simpler.

And happier, he thought. *Definitely happier.*

There had been a good deal of catching up, of bawdy laughter and repulsive humor, the sharing of stories, both amusing and sad, and, above all, an ease of being in one another's presence again.

Meridion, Rhapsody's eldest son, had met them at the door of the longhouse upon their arrival. Achmed was grudgingly fond of all of her children, but had a special affinity for Meridion, having participated in his life-threatening delivery and through the many stages of danger that had hovered around him as an infant, to see him grow into a likable young man with a worldly sense of humor and an appropriate view of his own place in said world.

Rhapsody's youngest and oldest children favored her physically, being the slightest of both the men and women in the generation, both with their mother's golden hair, though Meridion had inherited his father's curls, and both had the vertical pupils in their blue eyes that all of Ashe's children displayed.

After Meridion were two strapping offspring, Allegra and Stephen, each sporting their father's red-gold hair and their mother's emerald eyes atop bodies reflecting the soldier's build of their father more than the slight build of their mother.

Then a pair of brown heads had been born a century or so apart, Elienne, who had arrived in between the two redheads, and Joseph, who Rhapsody claimed had the same hair color as her brothers. Achmed and Grunthor had disputed those claims and had made great merriment pointing at a multitude of dark-haired men of revolting backgrounds, nominating them as her so-called "bastard" children's fathers, much to Rhapsody's amusement and Ashe's annoyance.

The final child was Laurelyn, recently ordained as the Invoker of the Filids, who looked so much like Rhapsody from a distance that it still tended to startle the Bolg king, who had searched her for her heartbeat, without finding it, more than once before approaching her.

Though he would have never admitted it, some of Achmed's favorite times over the millennia had been those days in which Rhapsody had brought her children to Ylorc for visits and training, particularly in the forge and the engineering that their great-grandfather Gwylliam had originally brought to the mountain. Stephen and Elienne had shown the most aptitude for that, while Allegra had trained at length with Grunthor in military leadership, and Laurelyn had been effective in learning the ways of the Bolg midwives. Joseph and Meridion had studied the Lightcatcher, the redesigned machine set into the peak of Gurgus within the mountain range, that made use of the science of colored light and sound.

But a millennium had passed, and now Rhapsody's children were grown, as were most of their children. Achmed had begun to notice some aging occurring in the line among a few of the grandchildren whose other parents had little or no Cymrian heritage, and the discovery had unsettled him.

Thankfully, the oldest child, Meridion, still maintained the appearance, air, and demeanor of youth. He sat with Achmed while the other two exchanged gentle finger flicks and participated in delightfully sardonic commentary.

"Do you wish to lay a wager on the game?" Achmed asked him in a loud aside. "I will give you two to one on Grunthor."

Meridion bowed his head in false modesty and demurred.

"Stand up straight and shrink from no one," his mother said in similarly false annoyance as she flicked Grunthor's hand, causing him to whimper and put it in his mouth for comfort. "Look every man in the eye, Meridion, and spit in that eye if you feel the need to—including that of your loudmouthed guardian."

Both the Bolg king and her son chuckled.

Finally, Meridion rose from his chair.

"I must return to the Repository to finish up with the cataloguing of the symposium," he said, a tone of genuine regret in his voice. "I'm delighted that you summoned me, Uncle; it's been marvelous seeing you both on this side of the continent. Don't let me disrupt your game, Mimen; it appears you have Grunthor at disaster's door."

"His arm is a lot more enflamed than mine," Rhapsody said proudly.

"Ya do know Oi'm 'oldin' back, right?" the Sergeant-Major demanded jovially.

Meridion laughed as he took his leave. "I'm really grateful to have this image in my mind as I write the history of the Three," he said from the doorway. "If the Cymrian populace could see the epic trio engaging in a game of Crusher rather than ruling the world, it would be most unsettling—or perhaps gratifying. Travel well, Uncle, Godfather, and I will see you shortly, Mimen."

Achmed was left alone to observe the ridiculous image of the Sergeant and the Lady Cymrian swatting at each other.

A knock sounded on the longhouse door.

Rhapsody rose and went to open it as Achmed and Grunthor moved subtly behind the table, each within reach of a weapon.

As she pulled back the door, Rhapsody laughed aloud.

Her granddaughter Cara, Stephen's oldest child, stood there, her spouse Evannii beside her, each of the women bearing a plate of gingerbread men and women intricately decorated with frosting as soldiers in the army of the Alliance.

"Are the uncles here, Hamimen?" Cara asked humorously. "As you can see, we've been baking for them."

"Absolutely. Please come in—cookies would be welcome at this point." Rhapsody stepped aside to allow the two women to deliver their baked goods and receive warm embraces from Grunthor and a pleasant acknowledgment from the Bolg king. Cara stripped the parchment from the plates while Evannii held them out for Grunthor's inspection.

"Ah—this one looks like Hasgarth Thomlinson, that pompous fart," said the Sergeant-Major, examining one with a fat belly that resembled one of the captains of the Alliance's guard units. He bit the head off summarily, to the amusement of all three women. "Goody. Oi love eatin' vicariously."

"These taste far better than I expect their models would," Achmed said, breaking one into several pieces and sampling it. "I have no doubt Hasgarth Thomlinson himself would give me gas, if not diarrhea."

"Are we interrupting, Hamimen?" Cara asked after Grunthor had helped himself to the better part of three dozen gingerbread soldiers. "We can come back later."

"Not at all," Rhapsody said. She turned to the other two of the Three. "I have an appointment with my granddaughters; I hope you will excuse us. It has been wonderful, as always, to visit with you. I do hope you will change your minds and reconsider coming to the family summit."

Achmed shook his head emphatically while Grunthor sighed.

"Gotta be on my way south, Duchess, but fanks again," he said wistfully.

"Please do consider what I said about refraining from provoking Ashe," Rhapsody said seriously as she put her arms around his neck. "I've come to greatly appreciate the peace that our kingdoms have enjoyed for all these centuries. I would very much like it to remain thus."

"I promise nothing," said Achmed, rising and receiving a farewell hug from Cara and Evannii. "We are occasionally noting shortages in the supplies that Roland merchants who have contracts with the Alliance quartermaster have been delivering to Ylorc. If this flagrant swindling continues, we will have to resort to making unannounced visits to the commissaries and storehouses to retrieve all of what we have paid for. I hope this point is not lost on you, Rhapsody."

"I will absolutely convey your concerns, and look into the ledgers myself," she promised.

"Good." He assumed an annoyed stance as Rhapsody came to him and kissed him on the cheek.

"I love you, you petulant thing," she said.

Achmed grunted noncommittally, as was his custom, while she went and embraced Grunthor enthusiastically again.

"I love you, I love you, I love you," she said from the depths of his embrace.

"Feelin's mutual, miss." The giant grinned broadly, the look of exhaustion leaving his eyes for a moment.

"Why does Grunthor get three 'I love you's while Achmed only receives one?" Evannii asked in amusement.

"He's three times as big?" Cara suggested.

"She loves me three times as much?" Grunthor offered.

"Just tradition, started a thousand years ago," Rhapsody said, patting the giant as he released her. "And the fact that he's three times more willing to hear it than Achmed."

"Since when comparing his willingness to mine, you are multiplying by zero, he's a thousand times more willing to hear it," said the Bolg king, opening the door of the longhouse. "A million times. A billion times."

"I will meet you both in the rotunda in the main hall of the palace of Newydd Dda once I've taken your uncles to the border," Rhapsody said to her granddaughters. "I want to be able to consult the diadem in our discussions, and if I'm going to do that, I need to put on more appropriate attire."

Achmed rolled his eyes.

"*Never* misses a chance to change into fussy clothes. Some things never change."

5

TYRIAN CITY

℘he royal complex of Tyrian City, the capital of the Lirin kingdom, was set on a series of graduated hills leading up to Tomingorllo,
the tallest of them, where the throne room was built into the summit.

At the base of the first hill, Newydd Dda, was the main hall where the
royal living quarters and the ambassadorial suites were housed.

Rhapsody dismounted and handed the reins of the roan to one of
the two Lirin soldiers accompanying her. She gave the horse a cube of
sugar and a gentle scratch of the ears, then bade the soldiers goodbye
and hurried to the main hall's great rotunda, the showpiece of Tyrian's
architecture. She walked quickly across the vast central courtyard, where
the singing fountains splashed in the sunlight, surrounded by a high
stone wall and guard towers.

The courtyard led directly into the rotunda, which contained an
enormous circular hearth at the center, where a perennial fire warmed the
entire palace year-round. Many tall trees that had been built within the
palace's structure had grown to towering heights, and were beginning
to show indications that autumn was approaching, unlike the glorious
plants and flowers that were kept in a constant growing season by the
heat that circulated from the hearth, making it feel like a conservatory.

A screen of faceted crystal circled the hearth, casting prismatic patterns all around the rotunda, something that had delighted Rhapsody
from the first time she had come to this place, and the dancing colors

always gave her pause to stop and appreciate the beauty of the palace where she lived part of the year.

Sitting on a cushioned, semicircular bench were Cara and Evannii, holding hands in the glow of the fire.

"I'm so sorry to keep you waiting, my dears," she said, kissing each of them as they stood and embraced her. "It took longer than I expected to see your uncles off."

"Not to worry," said Cara. "We really appreciate the time you've taken to research the lore for us, but—"

"Tarry a moment, Cara. I know it may sound overly formal, but I need to put on a Naming robe, and to maintain silence as we go up to Tomingorllo," Rhapsody said. "In matters as important as the one we have been discussing, it's critical that we observe all the rites and rituals of Naming."

The women exchanged a glance.

"Very well, Hamimen," Cara said. "We will follow your lead."

A quarter hour later, the three women were standing at the heavy oak doors of the room atop Tomingorllo, where the court and throne stood.

"This, unlike the main hall of Newydd Dda, is a more austere, less ornate hall," Rhapsody said as she swung the pair of doors open. "I didn't realize it when I first beheld this place, but the austerity is designed to keep what is said and done within this chamber as clear and commonly understood as possible. It is here that the united Lirin kingdom, representatives from the Lirin of the plains, of the sea, of the forest, and from Manosse on the other side of the Prime Meridian gather to work in unison on the business and leadership of the kingdom."

"Should that not be 'queendom,' Hamimen?" Cara asked jokingly. "You have been the monarch for a thousand years."

Rhapsody laughed. "Fair enough. I shall bring up that nomenclature at the next conclave, but secretly I am always hoping that another will come and take my place every time we meet. Perhaps next time it will be a king."

"And is that why you leave your crown behind when you go to Highmeadow, Hamimen?" Evannii asked. She was from Manosse, and, having only recently moved with Cara to the continent, had never seen the diadem.

Rhapsody shook her head, smiling.

"No, my dear. It is always a great honor to wear the diadem. I try to remember that each time I place it back in its case. The next time the case is opened, it may choose another head to rest upon. The Crown of Stars is not my crown, beloved granddaughter. It is the crown of our people. Come, I'll show you."

They entered the enormous room atop the tallest hill. On the other side of the oaken doors was a marble rotunda with an overarching dome held up by pillars that stood ten feet from the wall. The dome had a large opening in the middle, leaving the center of the room open to the sky.

Across from the doors stood the throne of the Lirin kingdom, carved of black marble with pillar-like arms and a low, straight back. A great stone fireplace stood, dark and cold, at each of the other two directional points of the circle.

Much like the iridescent lights that leapt from the fireplace screen in the main hall at Newydd Dda, glittering colors were dancing around this gigantic room as well. But rather than being generated by the flames of the fire shining through leaded glass, they were blazing with brilliant fragments of light from a small crystal crown resting beneath a clear, unornamented glass dome on an ornate silver stand at the room's center.

The diadem was constructed of countless tiny star-shaped diamonds, with eight similarly shaped larger stones forming the center ring of the crown. They glimmered in the sunlight that rained down in heavy sheets from the opening overhead. When Rhapsody approached it, the stones began to glow even more brightly and took on an iridescence that made them seem as if they were made of colored air.

"The fragments that make up the crown were once the Purity Diamond, a stone the size of a man's fist that shone with the light of the stars," Rhapsody said softly, repeating words that had been spoken to her by her mentor in the sword, Oelendra Andaris, a thousand years before. "It was brought by the Lirin of the First Fleet on a ship that was part of the exodus from the Island of Serendair, prior to the Island's destruction in volcanic fire from the star that had fallen, many millennia before, into the sea. That star was known as the Sleeping Child."

The young women, both aware of the history, nodded but listened in silence.

"The Purity Diamond was given as a sign of friendship to the Lirin tribe Gorllewinolo, the first indigenous people that the Cymrians had ever met in this land. 'Tomingorllo' means 'tower of the Gorllewin,' the people of the west. When Anwyn destroyed it as part of an agreement with a F'dor spirit to kill her hated husband Gwylliam during the Cymrian War, the diamond lost the light that it had once radiated. Queen Terrell, who had commanded that the diamond shards be carefully crafted into the crown, decreed that anyone who could restore the light of the stars to the crown would be recognized as the ruler of both the Cymrians and the Lirin, who would live as a united people. Until that time, however, they would remain separate, following their own monarch."

"It was Hamimen that restored that light," Cara said with quiet pride.

"No, it was Daystar Clarion," Rhapsody corrected.

"In your hand," noted Evannii.

"Aye. But soon there may be other hands to carry the sword, perhaps even those of your father, Cara," Rhapsody said. "We shall see. Now, if you are ready, we can discuss what you have asked of me."

Both women looked at each other and exhaled.

The Lady Cymrian and Lirin queen turned to the case and lifted the dome carefully.

The ethereal diamonds glowed even brighter and began to whirl; then, as if caught by the wind, they floated out of the case and came to rest in a circle above her head like a halo of stars.

"I've always loved watching that," Cara whispered to her spouse.

Rhapsody closed the case and gestured to the two women to follow her to the throne.

They crossed the open metal grates in the floor that had been fashioned in the shape of eight-pointed stars, through which the air atop the hill could be felt, leaving the room fresh and clear. Rhapsody mounted the steps, turned around, and sat on the throne's hard seat.

"Tradition," she grumbled jokingly. "If I had known at the time of my coronation that I would be sitting on this thing for a thousand years, I would have gotten a pillow for it."

The women laughed.

"All right," the Lirin queen said briskly, "let us invite the wisdom that you seek. At your request of a year ago, I have undertaken to study and master the ancient lore of the summoning of a child, something that is rare in history, and has produced very few progeny. I have, however, seen one such summoned child in my life, and she is a beautiful creation, deeply magical.

"There always should be caution in such an undertaking, because anything that deviates from the natural path always contains a risk," she continued as Cara and Evannii looked at each other. "But the history records no negative outcomes from the summoning ritual in the times it was undertaken.

"The process is actually quite benign: if two entities that have individual souls are willing, free of coercion or duress, to share them, the one who will give 'birth' to the child allows the one who will share that child with her to rest his or her hand on her heart. Both put themselves in a state of willingness, of creation, of the desire to bring forth a soul into the world, and a Namer's incantation is sung over them. It is one of the most beautiful rituals I have ever studied; the namesong is gorgeous. My understanding is that a light appears between the two parents. Then they name the child, and it forms.

"When dragons undertook to conjure children, it was because of a dilemma described in an even older legend. In the Before-Time, when the Firstborn races that came from the original five elements—the Seren, from ether, the F'dor, from fire, the Mythlin, from water, the Kith, from air, and the Wyrmril, or dragons, from Earth—were forming, it is said that the Creator—called the Architect of the World by the Gwenen, by the way, I just learned that—offered a model to four of the newborn races that were little more than the formless elements they were springing from. That model was said to be the form that three of those races chose to emulate, the human form with the erect skeleton, the head, arms, legs—that design. The F'dor were not shown the model at all by the Creator, who recognized as they were coming into existence that they were, as a race, destructive and cruel, so that withholding a corporeal form from them was necessary for the continued existence of the world. But the dragons were, in fact, offered to glimpse the model—and refused, not wishing to be told what to do."

"Imagine that," Cara said, rolling her eyes, eyes whose pupils were vertical.

Rhapsody laughed. "After some time, the dragons noted an error, or at least what they perceived to be an error, in their decision. Each of the three Firstborn races that had used the model had chosen to crossbreed with the others, resulting in the Elder races and beyond, but dragons had chosen a form that was not compatible with the other three—so they decided to try and use conjuring to expand their race.

"They sculpted the model that they had initially refused out of Living Stone, and underwent the ritual, which is odd, since it would seem that stone, even if it is alive, does not have a soul or the ability to commit to share one, and dragons believe they don't have souls, either. But apparently the concept of a soul is somewhat different than it is traditionally understood, which is what I have been studying in the last century.

"So, if you are still interested, I have learned and committed to memory all the rites and rituals, and I am ready to assist you if you are interested in expanding your family. Summoned children are comprised of vibration, not of flesh, and do not eat or drink the way a child born normally would, but in all other ways, they are very real, with a soul, a personality, and emotions. It seems to me that if you decide to do this, you are in the right family for it."

Rhapsody took several deep breaths to replenish her lungs, which were spent from the length of the tale.

Cara and Evannii exchanged a smile, then looked back at their grandmother.

"Thank you, Hamimen," Cara said, genuinely touched. "But we have been doing a good deal of study and thinking and discussing this during the last year. We have decided to wait on this, and adopt an existing child that needs a home instead of summoning one out of our own souls. We've actually already located a pair of children who were orphaned, and who have been waiting for parents for some time."

Rhapsody blinked, then broke into a warm smile.

"How wonderful," she said quietly but with a glint of excitement in her eyes, the stars in the crown whirling even faster around her like a spinning halo of lights. "I am very happy to hear that, for their sakes and yours. And I know Papa will be as well."

"Thank you. We're sorry you went to so much trouble for nothing."

Rhapsody rose from the throne and went to the pedestal. "Undertaking the study and the learning of lore is never for nothing," she said, removing the diadem from her head. "If nothing else, it keeps the lore alive in one more mind than had it before. For me it was a joy to do this for you, my dears. I can't wait to meet my newest Greats when you are ready. Now, let's prepare to travel to the family summit at Highmeadow. Are you going with Meridion?"

"Yes, we're meeting up with him at the Tree," Evannii said, following Rhapsody out of the throne room and down the walkway toward Newydd Dda.

"Funny—that is where he and I will be parting," Rhapsody said, linking arms with her granddaughters. "Perhaps if you are there we can look at some of the new exhibits in the Repository that he has done such splendid work on. It's nice that we can be sharing the trip so that the journey itself is a reunion."

When they reached the base of the forest again, they chased each other through the golden ribbons of dusty light raining in the advent of afternoon, laughing in the strange phenomena of longevity and life spans that bordered on immortality.

Not thinking too much about the disparities that might one day part Cara and Evannii before they would Rhapsody and Ashe.

Who were two generations older.

6

After Rhapsody had returned from Newydd Dda, she sought out her son, who had returned to travel north with her.

"Thank you for taking the time out of what I know is a very busy undertaking to visit with your uncles," she said, kissing his cheek.

Meridion smiled. "The journey took a matter of moments. Thank you for naming me as you did. If you hadn't woven 'Child of Time' into my name at birth, I would be hampered by the same delays and hours or days of travel that the rest of the world contends with. It would truly be an onerous thing, much too terrible to be borne."

They laughed together as she took his arm and walked with him to the livery, where the horses they would ride to the Circle were awaiting them.

"I know that your travel time is insignificant, but I am also aware that you have the same limited amount of it, day into day, as the rest of us, and that you are very busy with your work," she said. "Easily as you may compress your journeys, you cannot expand the time spent, and I appreciate that you chose to spend it with us."

"It was my pleasure," Meridion assured her as they walked into the stable. "And traveling on horseback with you will be one as well. I always loved it as a child when we went riding together, you and I. Father was always a wonderful riding partner, and teacher, as well, and I learned a great deal every time we set forth together, but there was something different about doing so with you."

"Oh?" She picked up the currying comb after greeting the horse in a soft woodland language, then set to work.

"Yes," Meridion said, grooming his mount as well. "While Father's instruction was about seat and gait, use of tack, emergency roll-off and other skills, you were always looking off in the distance, pointing out some particularly beautiful trees or interesting landscape, or bringing the horses to a halt to dismount so that we could examine some unique flowers in the grass. I remember the day we found the fairy huts and spent the entire afternoon exploring the forest at Highmeadow, and didn't even venture more than a league from home."

Rhapsody chuckled. "I remember that day well. It was a beautiful one."

"Just as I know you cherish the time you spend with your children, Grands, and Greats, we all look forward to having that opportunity to be with you and Papa, you know."

"Thank you," Rhapsody said. Her emerald eyes sparkled. "Will you tell me something that is none of my concern?"

Meridion chuckled. "I thought everything was a Namer's concern."

Rhapsody laughed. "Only if the Namer is your mother. And then she only *thinks* it's her concern—but that's the mother's opinion, not the Namer's."

"Ah. Well, ask away."

The Lady Cymrian's smile softened. "Seeing Cara and Evannii, or, in fact, any of your siblings with his or her spouse or betrothed, leads me to wonder if you are lonely." She winced as Meridion sighed. "I don't mean to intrude, Meridion—"

"Do I seem unhappy to you, Mimen?"

"Not a bit. You seem content, fulfilled—a wise and reliable brother, an indulgent uncle, a stalwart friend. I just wondered why you seem so satisfied alone, as if you don't see any need for a partner in life." Her eyes twinkled and a teasing tone entered her voice. "I do hope your father and I have not ruined your view of marriage forever."

Meridion laughed again. "Of course not. I'm not lonely, Mimen; I'm just waiting."

"For what?"

His face grew solemn, though his eyes still smiled.

"Not what—who. I've seen her, Mimen. My soul mate—but she's

not of this time. She hasn't been born yet, I think, and I don't believe she will be for some time. But she's getting closer."

"How have you seen her?" Rhapsody asked, curious. "I thought you were unable to know the Future."

"I can't know it the way I can the Past, because the strand of Time in the Past is set, and therefore solid enough to pass into, even if I can have almost no presence there. I have glimpses of the Future, just as you do, but more keenly; I see her in my dreams, and occasionally when I pass through a place where one day she will be, I think. It's only momentary, like the feeling you used to describe as a goose walking over your grave."

"That's an old farm expression from Serendair. Do you know her name?"

Meridion shook his head. "No. But every time I see her, I know even more certainly that she is the other half of my soul. I can't really explain it."

"You don't need to," Rhapsody said, cleaning the horsehair from the currying brush and hanging it on the stable wall. "I understand, believe me. When I beheld your father for the first time, my eyes literally stung. It was like tears had filled them for no apparent reason, and I could see him utterly clearly. And I knew as well."

Sounds like Eye-Clear, Meridion thought absently. He had spent a good amount of time at the Namers' summit giving a tutorial in how to distill the elixir that allowed for undiluted sight, when it was essential to strip away visual distractions and see something clearly, particularly for physicians before undertaking surgery or engineers in delicate manual undertakings. He shook off the thought.

"In any case, it has made me somewhat disinterested in anyone else in the meantime," he said. "But I'm not lonely, Mimen; I'm just waiting. It may sound hackneyed, but one of the many things I'd like to emulate in my father is to have only loved one woman in my life. It may not be the way for everyone; I can understand the value in having learned of love from a variety of sources, gaining experience and perspective before finally reaching the ultimate state. But this is just what my guiding sense tells me is right." He grinned. "And it's not set in stone. Should someone come along that sets my world a-spin, I am more than willing to change my plans."

Rhapsody patted the roan and finished tacking it up.

"What's she like?"

Meridion considered. "I don't really know how to describe her," he said, tending to his own mount. "She doesn't look like anyone I could compare her to, dark of hair and eye, and seemingly studious. I know this sounds odd, but it would not surprise me if she had a touch of Bolg in her bloodline."

Rhapsody stopped short and turned in amazement. "Really?"

Meridion shrugged. "It's possible; I'm not sure. But for now, I am willing to wait until it feels right. And, up until now, no other person has made that happen."

"Well, thank you for telling me," Rhapsody said as he finished tacking up and adjusted his horse's hackamore. "I'm not actively worried about you; I merely want life to hold all the love it can for you, just as I wish for all of our family. I have always wished that the last thing I might be allowed to say to each of my children is what the Patriarch before Constantin said to me as he was leaving for the Light—'Above all else, may you know joy.'"

"I appreciate your concern. But one thing I've learned from the bequest of an unusually long life span is that filling the empty space with placeholders until what is meant to be there is present is not always the best way to go. I've seen many examples of it."

Rhapsody nodded. "I know. Well, if you're ready, let's be on our way—it is my hope that we will have some time in each other's company before our paths diverge, and that you will arrive at Highmeadow a day or so ahead of me."

"Off to visit Elynsynos?" Meridion inquired as he led his mare from the stable.

"Yes. I haven't seen her in such a long time, and I want to make sure she is well." Rhapsody's smile faded to seriousness. "I always hope to get perspective from her on the dragon aspects of the family with which I alone am unfamiliar."

"I imagine that can be very strange when it's not in your blood," Meridion said. "It's even strange to me, and I have the vertical pupils and the throat structure to do the roar to prove my qualifications."

Mother and son laughed as they closed the stable door, mounted up, and rode off to the northlands.

7

THE REPOSITORY, TYRIAN CITY,
SOUTH OF THE CIRCLE

 $\mathcal{T}$ hree days later, Cara and Evannii met up with Meridion and Rhapsody at the central wing of the Repository, one of the museums where lore was collected and displayed for the public.

It was here that mother and son had hosted the Symposium of Namers for a fortnight, one of the largest gathering of the practitioners of the science of musical healing and education in the Known World. Meridion, one of the foremost experts on many elements of Naming lore, had conducted a number of workshops and teaching sessions, including the escorting of several of the Sea Mages from the island of Gaematria through the new wing that housed the maritime collection.

The three women followed Meridion around a corner and came to an abrupt stop.

"What is all this, Hamimen?" Evannii had asked, standing at the vestibule of a wing of the Repository, an archway over which read the inscription *Explicarum Mortes*.

"The new hallway of Death," Rhapsody said blandly.

Cara nodded while Evannii blanched.

Rhapsody nodded. "This is actually a significant part of a Namer's training," she said, smiling slightly. "One of the most common of the aspects of our practice is death rituals, the various songs, prayers, ceremonies, and observances which celebrate the passage from life through death into the Afterlife. As you know, we have a similar dedication to the passage into life as well, birthing and Naming ceremonies and the like, but there is no event about which more lore is written, more time is spent in study and memorization, than death rituals."

Meridion led his two nieces to the wall just inside the exhibit, where a mural of four riders on four strange horses was displayed.

"This is an old legend, popular among the adherents to the Filidic religion of the western continent, of which your aunt Laurelyn is the Invoker now," he said solemnly, his blue eyes twinkling, their vertical pupils expanding excitedly. "I'm sorry you both couldn't attend her investiture; it was truly an interesting ceremony, and only takes place rarely."

"We were sorry as well," said Cara as Evannii nodded in agreement. "We were still in Manosse when it happened."

"It is one of those sorts of events that only gets attended by those who are nearby or if the weather cooperates," Meridion said, opening up the case below the mural. "Unlike the kinds of celebrations that can be planned months or years in advance—such as the family summit we are all about to attend—when the Invoker dies, the Filids have death traditions that prescribe an almost immediate transition, including a fairly unique kind of funeral pyre. The Songs of Passage and the dirges that are sung for the high nature priest in a religion to which the entire western half of the continent, including nearly all of the Lirin kingdom, adheres are extraordinarily beautiful, as well as being heard only rarely."

"Can you tell us, Uncle, of this lore?" Evannii asked, pointing at the mural of the horsemen. "I have never seen anything about this in Manosse."

Meridion's face lit up as it always did when he was discussing lore.

"It is believed in the tradition of the Filids that death has four different manifestations, as represented by these images," he said.

He pointed to the first one, a painting of a tall man with a restful expression on his face, which was pale as was his hair, a shade of white that reminded Evannii strongly of the moon. His eyes, however, were dark and devouring, as were the brows above them. The horse he was pictured atop appeared to be in the midst of constantly changing colors.

"This is the one that is most well known, which I find rather amusing, given that his body count may be the lowest," he said impishly. "This is the manifestation of the Peaceful Death, the Lord Rowan, who is also known as Yl Angaulor, the Hand of Mortality. He is said to live beyond the Veil of Hoen, which is the Cymrian word for 'joy,' a place where time passes differently than it does on our side of the Veil. His wife, the Lady Rowan, is known as the Keeper of Dreams, the Guardian of Sleep, Yl Breudiwyr. They are considered sacred entities by physicians and healers, because it is said that if you seek their aid in a life-or-death situation, they may take you, or the person you are caring for, beyond the Veil to assist in healing that person."

"Do you know of anyone who has ever gone?" Cara asked.

"A few," said Meridion lightly. *Both of your grandparents, and Constantin, the Patriarch of Sepulvarta,* he thought, glancing at Rhapsody. "The Veil of Hoen is reputed to be a place between life and death, on this side of the Gate of Life. Those who are grievously injured are often healed and returned to this state of being. Those who are beyond their talents pass through the Gate of Life to the Afterlife, as does everyone eventually, the Filids believe. So, for purposes of this display, the Lord Rowan represents Peaceful Death."

He pointed at the others. The next was a more terrifying image, a large, muscular horseman, clad in armor from which spikes emerged, a whip of many tails in his heavy-gloved hand. He wore a war helm above a face that was half skeletal, half sunken, and rode a tall, broad steed that seemed to be formed of dark wind and fire.

"This is the manifestation known as the Wracked Death," he said a little more somberly. "He represents the experience of those who die violently, or in pain, or wither away in the grip of terrible illness."

The young women exchanged a glance and a wince.

"Is any part of the exhibit about the Afterlife?" Evannii asked hopefully. "I would think that might be a pleasant collection."

"It will be opening next year," Rhapsody said as Meridion waited eagerly to continue his presentation. "I find the research into that subject at the moment to be somewhat controversial. I have long thought that the traditions and beliefs of various cultures have brought about the existence of their mythical figures and entities, rather than the other way around. Lore manifests into reality sometimes; that's why Namers have to be especially careful about what they say.

"There are many people who believe with certainty that they know what color the paint on the walls of their homes in the Afterlife will be.

The more I study the lore, the more I have come to believe that paradise is not the same for everyone, and that we don't all live in it together. I think we each make our own places in the Afterlife—"

"We were talking about Death," Meridion interjected. "These other two horsemen are Death in War and Death of Worlds—"

"I'm sorry to have interrupted, Meridion, but I do believe we all need to be on our way in order for you three to arrive at the guest house in Tref-Y-Gwartheg by nightfall," Rhapsody said lightly. "You know how much Papa worries when we are on the forest road in the dark."

Meridion, paused in the middle of an intriguing lecture, exhaled, then nodded quickly.

"Right," he said. "I will go get my gear—did you ladies already give yours to the quartermaster to put in the coach?"

"Yes, Uncle," said Cara quickly.

"Very good. All right, I shall return forthwith, and we can be on our way." He came to Rhapsody and kissed her, then hurried toward the door of the Repository.

Cara and Evannii looked to the Lady Cymrian in relief and smiled gratefully.

Thank you, Cara mouthed.

Rhapsody bowed slightly, smiling to herself.

Meridion stopped at the door, then turned back in excitement.

"I'll grab some of the manuscripts and folios from my office on the way to the coach," he said happily. "And then we can finish the discussion on the way to Highmeadow! I can even teach you the songs of Passage for each of the major races, and the dirges of all the cultures in the Alliance. I am *so* glad we will be traveling together."

Rhapsody waited until Meridion had left the Repository to laugh. She hugged both crestfallen young women.

"Namers," she said, rolling her eyes. "I'm so sorry. Maybe you can pretend to fall asleep in the coach; I sometimes do. Except I don't have to pretend."

Once her son and granddaughters were safely packed and on their way to Highmeadow, Rhapsody had her forest roan brought forth, saddled up, and rode north.

She had traveled this road for a thousand years, most often alone, but occasionally with company. The very first time she had undertaken the journey it had been with Ashe, who at the time was unknown to her and her Firbolg friends, neither of whom trusted him. He was still in the throes of physical and spiritual agony, suffering from a wound that left an ugly, festering scar bisecting his chest, where his heart had been torn open and a piece of his soul removed by a F'dor demon at the House of Remembrance, an ancient Cymrian museum similar to the Repository, on midsummer's night long ago.

As she rode through the forest, Rhapsody thought back to those days of suspicion and fear, glad that they were long past. Ashe had been forced for the sake of his safety to hide himself within a cloak of mist generated by Kirsdarke, the elemental sword of water that he bore, remaining out of sight of the F'dor who had seized his soul, and the rest of the world.

It was his initial healing behind the Veil of Hoen that Meridion was referring to when instructing Cara and Evannii.

In spite of the suspicion and the doubt, Ashe had guided her from the Bolglands to this place to which she was traveling now, to the white forest of Gwynwood beyond the Tar'afel River, a place of deep magic, then and now.

The lands of the dragon Elynsynos.

The sun was setting two days afterward by the time she reached Mirror Lake, the beautiful body of water, still as glass, that was the landmark to the entrance of the dragon's lands. There was now, a thousand years after the war that had threatened this place, nothing but peace in the utter absence of birdsong, the deafening silence a sure sign that the dragon was alive and well.

The only voice making a sound she could hear was inside her.

Rhapsody reined her roan to a halt and stared across the lake, letting her hand come to rest on her abdomen.

For a century or more, she had been beset by the voice of a child, calling to her from within, as each of her six children had done prior to his or her conception. It had initially begun as a distant awareness, a realization that a presence was hovering in the ether, waiting to be conceived and born. She had happily shared this news with Ashe, who had blinked, then stared at her. In her mind she recalled his first words in answer.

Not again, he had said, wincing at the surprise, followed by shock and sadness, that had come over her face, banishing the glow of happiness that had been there a moment before. *Surely you do not want to under-take this again, Rhapsody?*

She had been so gobsmacked that she had not brought the subject up to him again.

But that had not quieted the presence she could feel, growing stronger each time it made itself known to her, as it intermittently did.

As the sense grew stronger, a voice emerged, as it also had with each previous child. At first it spoke softly, often in the darkness just as she was falling into slumber, or at quiet times when she was engrossed in her studies, when no one else was around.

Mimen, it had whispered.

Mama.

She had struggled to quiet the call, but it only grew more insistent, filling her ears and her dreams with its song. She had almost come to regard it as a secret she was keeping from her husband, who would occasionally catch sight of her face, her eyes filled with despair when there was no other reason for it, then sigh and turn away.

The voice had only grown stronger, more plaintive, as if it were standing beyond a doorway in the freezing cold.

Mimen—Mimen. Please. Let me in.

Only to become quiet again as she dissolved into silent tears, unshared.

Often great lengths of time would pass, while silence held sway. It had been so for a long while; she had no idea why it was making its presence known again now.

Rhapsody shook her head to dispel the thoughts, then took up the reins again and allowed the horse to walk the entire way around the lake. Horse and rider came to a gentle halt, and she dismounted near the stream that flowed into the lake from a nearby hillside. She stopped at the stream's edge.

"May I come in, my friend?" she whispered into the wind.

A rustling of leaves answered. A gentle breeze picked up, tousling her hair.

Of course, came a magnificent voice in the tones of soprano and alto, tenor and bass simultaneously. *You well know how much I love to see you. Come in, Pretty.*

Rhapsody chuckled.

She tied the roan to a nearby tree close to the stream, gave her an apple, and made her way across the glistening brook to the cave in the hillside and down into the lair of the dragon, the first wyrm she had ever learned to love.

Now that dragon was the matriarch of her family of them.

HIGHMEADOW

Meridion, Cara, and Evannii had arrived just short of two days after departing from the Circle, their carriage coming through the gates at almost the same time as those belonging to Meridion's brother Joseph, who, with his wife, Caryssa, had brought three large wagons of food, decorations, gifts, and grandchildren, and his sister Elienne, whose retinue was even larger.

"I am so excited for this gathering," Evannii had said, peering out the window, her face glowing. "I haven't seen most of these family members since our wedding."

"I do believe Mimen said everyone is coming," Meridion observed, peering out the window at the guards and house servants assisting in the unloading of goods and little people. "This is certain to be fun."

His father, Lord Gwydion, appeared at the carriage window.

"Well met, beloved ones," Ashe said, his face shining. "I trust your trip was safe and easy?"

All three family members nodded.

"Excellent! Well, I don't mean to give you and the others short shrift, but I have an appointment with an extraordinarily beautiful woman to the north of here. I am leaving momentarily—I do hope you will forgive me. We will be back in a couple of days."

"Oh, absolutely, Papa," Cara said, mischief in her eyes. "Hamimen talked of nothing else the whole time we were with her in Tyrian. I do hope you have rested up and that your back isn't bothering you. She's really quite excited. I imagine you'll both be smiling, and tired, and perhaps bowlegged, when we see you again."

Ashe's mouth fell open, then he laughed aloud.

"One thing that can never be said about this family is that it is shy when talking about sex," he said, his face coloring. "I just had a conversation with Laurelyn yesterday about the evils of celibacy from which I may never recover."

"Tosh," said Cara, kissing her grandfather's cheek. "I've always been grateful to have grown up in a family where candor is the order of the day, and a healthy attitude about all things natural is to be expected. Mimen says it comes from farming origins; what do you think, Papa?"

"I think your grandmother is always right," Ashe said, patting Evan-nii's face. "And any man who doesn't have the same belief about his wife is a damned fool. Enjoy the gathering, and I will see you both the day after the day after tomorrow."

He disappeared from the window, whistling.

8

GWYNWOOD, BELOW THE WATERFALL

A day later, Ashe finished tying his mount to a slender tree next to Rhapsody's waiting roan and sighed.

The black gelding had been watered downstream from the thundering falls, swollen with the rains of approaching autumn, fed and picked of knots. Ashe was fighting the long-ago instructions from his father, Llauron, and his uncle, Anborn, both of whom had been his instructors in horsemanship centuries before.

You shall not eat, nor sleep, nor piss until you have taken your mount through all its steps of care, Anborn had told him as an eleven-year-old, along with his friends and the rest of the youth brigade of which he was a part. *If I find any horse insufficiently cooled down and tended to, you will experience the same treatment yourself the following night.*

Satisfied that his uncle and father would approve of his gelding's condition, he untied its saddlebag and drew forth the bouquet of nymph's hair, airy wildflowers he had gathered for his love at the mouth of the stream. He inhaled their scent, remembering his brief time in the old world, where he and Rhapsody had first met, and how he had spied a clump of those very flowers on the morning after their first night together, her birthday, and had planned to make a gift of them to her.

That was just before he had been torn away from her, back to his own time, an event that had shattered his soul.

But now the only thing that separated him from her was the waterfall.

Ashe stowed the bouquet in his bandolier and started to climb.

The ascent was far more difficult than he had remembered it from the year before, and all the previous ones. By the time he reached the place where the waterfall shed away from the shale, Ashe was puffing, red in the face.

He bent over and put his hands on his knees, struggling to catch his breath.

A sense of despair washed over him, leaving him weak and vulnerable to the muttering of the draconic voice within him.

Dying, you know, it muttered. *You're dying. This is what it looks like.*

Abandoning his dignity, Ashe sat on the slippery rock bed that led down to the falls. He listened to the music of the wind ruffling the green leaves of the crabapple glen, the place in the spring of their first journey together that had most enchanted the woman who would be his wife.

If he closed his eyes, he could see her still, as she had been on that first journey, staring in wonder at the pink blossoms of the trees, holding out her hands in the heavy golden shafts of dusty sunlight.

It was a memory of light he had always kept in times of pain or sorrow, just to lift his spirits.

They had met in this place for centuries uncounted afterward, away from the family and the trappings of court, to be completely alone together. It was one of the only places he had felt safe during his time in hiding; now, it was a place of treasured memories and privacy.

A nagging thought from the dragon in his blood dulled the happy mood.

It was a conversation, resurrected from a hundred years before, when he had first had difficulty summiting the hillside that led to their meeting place, a small turf hut beside the waterfall.

Prior to that time, they had happily chased each other up the hill, climbing eagerly through the forest, frequently succumbing to passion among the trees or in the sweet moss beneath them, making love in time to the song of the waterfall. The surging dance of the element of water laughing over the rocks had refreshed his soul almost as much as the coupling had, the ebb and flow of both, the sense of freedom and eternity that the endless rush had engendered.

But on that first time when his stamina had failed him, when he needed to gasp for breath, bending over at the waist, Rhapsody had waited patiently for him to get his wind again, then put out her hand.

Come, my love, she had said. *Our bower awaits.*

He had looked up from his panting, this time from the exertion of the climb rather than the recovery from a glorious climax, and had glowered at her.

Look at me. You don't see me as I am again, do you Rhapsody? I am an old man.

She had smiled. *I see the boy in the meadow.*

You have always seen what you wanted to see, he had grumbled, still overexerted.

There was a time you believed that was a good thing.

I still believe that, he said, finally able to stand erect. *But we've been at this eight centuries now. How long are we supposed to live happily ever after?*

Rhapsody's smile had faded, but her eyes had still met his, looking as if into his soul.

Given that I didn't think I would survive the first year after I came, I suppose everything else is a gift, a blessing.

A blessing, the dragon whispered sarcastically. *Certainly, frailty and decrepit existence can be a blessing.*

Just as he felt his human aspect surrendering to the beast's ire, he raised his head and saw the warm glow of light-shine from the window of the turf hut, a tiny cabin hidden against the moss-covered face of the mountain behind it.

His dragon sense caught the warmth of his wife, waiting within the small room for him.

His resolved renewed, Ashe climbed over the last of the barrier rocks and hurried across the spongy turf of the grass leading up to the door of the hut. He paused outside it; the door was ajar.

He pushed it open a little farther, leaned up against the exterior turf wall, and called into the doorway.

"Do you still love me, Aria?"

Her answer was the same as it had been every time he asked the question over the last millennium.

"Always," she called back. Then Ashe heard a smile creep into her voice. "Come inside; you're letting the bugs in."

"Nonsense," he said jokingly, following her voice into the cabin, the bouquet behind his back. "Within range of the door, there are only twenty-eight river flies, four mosquitoes, one hundred and seventeen—oops, make that sixteen, a minnow just got one—gnats, and—"

His words ground to a halt once inside as his senses were overwhelmed.

The first to make a successful assault on his dragon sense, and his nose, was the odor of a savory stew, which had been spiced appealingly and had filled the small cabin with a warm, inviting air. He noted the other dishes she had prepared—freshly baked bread infused with rosemary and waiting to be served with butter and honey; crisp greens tossed with mulled wine; and a torte that had been assembled in eight layers of cake, cream, mousse, and chocolate, all touched with coordinated liqueurs—and recognized the complexity of the spices and the elaborate levels of preparation within what were otherwise relatively simple dishes.

The second of his senses to succumb was his hearing; she had obviously spent some of her time that day playing a gentle air on several of her instruments—lute, flute, and harp—that were repeating it endlessly now on their own. The piece was easy on the ear but Ashe recognized the sophistication of the music, primarily because his draconic nature was counting the measures and making note of the complex time changes and obscure harmonies.

At the same time that other nature was noting the fact that scented water had been sprayed about the cabin, a subtle blend of lavender and sweet woodruff that took some of the dryness out of the room. The residual mist rested lightly on his skin, taking away some the sting of the vibrations that played havoc with his concentration on a regular basis, and refreshing the waters of his soul and sword. The result was a feeling of great peace and wellness descending; Ashe breathed it in, touched and happy in the knowledge that each of the actions his wife had undertaken she had done with her knowledge of the needs of both aspects of his nature, man and dragon, as an expression of her love for him, a love he knew was deeper than the sea.

But he was utterly unprepared for the sight of her.

Instead of the clothing in which she generally met him in this place—her regular traveling trousers and linen shirt, a negligee, or nothing at all—Rhapsody was attired in an elegant gown of midnight-blue watered silk that also shone black or gray, depending on the angle at which she was being viewed. It was embroidered with thousands of tiny pearls that made it look like a star-scattered sky, except that the wyrm noted the patterns into which the pearls had been assembled, spelling out a variety of phrases in musical script and Ancient Lirin, the dead language of her childhood. Some phrases were loving, some humorous, some scandalously bawdy, and they fascinated the dragon in his blood. A long line of small matching pearled buttons stretched down her back, the sheer sight of which made his fingers ache.

Her beautiful hair had been carefully plaited in the luxuriant patterns the Lirin were known for, and a rainbow of tiny gemstones had been placed within the strands; the jewels caught the light of the fire and sparkled, enflaming the dragon's heart, and the man's at the same time, but for different reasons.

She was just finishing setting a pair of crystal wineglasses on the table, and looked up as he closed the door behind him. Upon beholding him, she broke into a heart-melting smile and stood erect, her hands behind her back like a little girl with a secret.

Ashe fought down the lump that had risen in his throat. He coughed, then shook his head with mock concern.

"A thousand years a queen, and yet you are still the same foolhardy, reckless woman who drew a puny dagger on me when we met in the streets of Bethe Corbair."

Rhapsody blinked but her smile remained.

"Reckless, am I? Foolhardy?"

"Indeed. Did you intentionally risk being devoured this evening?"

"Oh, I certainly hope so."

Ashe laughed again. "I meant literally. I'm not complaining, mind you—this is a lovely diversion, Aria."

"Diversion?"

His laugh dissolved into a warm chuckle, but there was a serious look in his eyes. "Are you saying the exquisitely detailed jeweling of your intricately braided hair, the dozens of tiny buttons down the back of your color-changing dress, the pearls adorning your gown in patterns of words in Ancient Lirin, and the complicated symphony of spices with which you have made that delicious-smelling supper as well as perfumed your beautiful body, are not specifically designed to distract the dragon within my blood?"

His wife slowly came away from the table before the fire toward him.

" 'Distract' is a somewhat belittling word. I would say rather that those things are meant to *amuse* or *entertain* that part of your nature, beloved. I love the dragon as I love the man you are. I thought it deserved some attention as well."

"Well, while the dragon appreciates it greatly, the man is at a loss to deal with the details," the Lord Cymrian said, dropping his pack to the floor, but bringing forth the bouquet from behind his back and holding it out to her. "While the wyrm in my blood is enjoying the opportunity to count them, the arthritic fingers of the human side of me are despairing the barricade of buttons that will keep you from me for hours while I fumble with them."

Rhapsody's smile broadened. From behind her own back she produced a buttonhook and held it up wordlessly.

Ashe laughed aloud.

"Gained," he said, using the sword trainer's word for acknowledging a point of an opponent's victory.

In return, Rhapsody came closer and took the bouquet from his hand. She raised the blossoms to her face and inhaled their scent, her smile growing warmer. When she looked back at him, her eyes were gleaming.

"Thank you," she said softly.

"Happy anniversary."

"And to you, Sam."

Ashe's throat constricted at the use of the name she had called him by on the night they met in the old world, the name by which an unknown young man or boy was greeted by the people of her farming village. The word, spoken in her voice, still made his heart race as it had then, a lifetime ago.

Sometimes in the light of morning, on the rare occasions when he woke before her, he could still see the girl he remembered, the young woman who had not yet been touched by the mesmerizing power of the elemental fire she had absorbed later on her journey through the Earth, coming to this place a world away from everything she had known and everyone she had loved. With her emerald eyes closed and her golden hair mussed and loose around the pillow, she was Emily in his eyes, a blond, fair girl of slight figure and strong backbone, hiding from and refusing the suit of the farmboys who had sought her hand in the marriage lottery of her village.

Even now, asleep, she could almost pass for fourteen years of age, as she had been on that night, though the transformation she had undergone had altered her inexorably in the eyes of the world. But in Ashe's eyes, the simplicity of Emily's sweet face wrung his heart even more tightly than the enchanting beauty of the woman he had fallen in love with as Rhapsody, the woman, queen, and Lady she was when awake.

The woman over whom, unlike him, Time seemed to have no dominion.

He gazed at his wife, backlit by the dancing flames of the fire, remembering each moment of that first night again, and each moment of every encounter since. Through a millennium of life and death, brutal war and a blessedly extended peacetime, the birth of children, grandchildren, and great-grandchildren, the passings of old friends and beloved family members, they had clung to one another, sharing a soul, uniting and rebuilding an empire, an Alliance, and, above all else, a family that was the entirety of his world.

And all of it had begun on a warm summer-turning-to-autumn night, a night almost exactly like this one, with his first sight of the woman who stood before him now, looking at him with the same wonder he still saw in her gleaming eyes.

He blinked. All of the thoughts, and all of the memories, had occurred within a single beat of each of their hearts.

In the next heartbeat, they spoke simultaneously, their words tumbling over those of the other.

"I love you." "Are you hungry?"

They laughed together, and then spoke once more, their words clashing again.

"Yes, but not for supper—yet." "I love you, too."

Rhapsody gave him the buttonhook and held up her hand. "Hold that thought a moment," she said. She took the bouquet to the small kitchen area, put the flowers in water, then walked to the fireplace, where she stirred the pot hanging above it, releasing glorious, savory odors into the air of the small cabin and causing Ashe's mouth to water. She diminished the fire to coals with a single word, then returned to where he stood near the door.

"I'm all yours," she said, looking deeply into his eyes.

Ashe stepped forward, watching her intently. He came within a hairsbreadth of her, then raised his hand in the air before her.

"May I touch you?" he asked quietly. Like his first question, it was an old tradition, a promise made after one of her first extensions of forgiveness to him, long ago, on the banks of the Tar'afel River, before they had become lovers, when he had swept her off her feet against her will, and had received a surprisingly stunning blow that rocked his head back in return. At the time, it had served as proof that he understood their boundaries. Now that there were no boundaries between them, it was often the last thing he said before all talking became unnecessary.

"Yes. Please." Rhapsody's glittering smile resolved to something deeper. She turned around, away from him, to face the fire, pulling the hair away from the nape of her neck, around which a simple golden locket still hung.

The weariness of age disappeared along with the soreness in Ashe's joints as Rhapsody's innate music, so recently painfully absent from his life, enfolded him, wrapping him in bliss. He rested his hand just below her ear and traced a loose curl of her hair to her shoulder, feeling the fire in her skin respond with warmth beneath his touch. He inhaled happily, reveling in the sweet familiarity of her scent, then set briskly about employing the buttonhook, gently prying his wife free of the gown that still kept the dragon fascinated, until it fell away from her gleaming shoulders and back, all the way to her waist.

He followed the path his hand had traced with his lips, feeling his blood begin to hum with excitement as a deepening passion began to consume him.

Rhapsody looked back over her shoulder and smiled as the trail of his kisses swept up her spine to the base of her neck again. Ashe, lost already in her scent, her warmth, met the gleam in her eyes with his own and kissed her at last, taking her lips as gently as he could manage, then with more intensity, turning her to face him as the fire behind them grew, matching her breathing.

She reached up and entwined her arms around his neck, causing the gown to fall to the floor at her feet, and took a step back, pulling him down with her onto the rug that was bathed in the light splashing on the stone floor before the now-roaring fire.

All of Ashe's restraint, his control of the dragon within his blood, abandoned him. The centuries of aging and damage to his body seemed to fall away, leaving him giddy, happily vulnerable, lost utterly in the woman beneath him. Time and space became suspended; it seemed like hours and at the same time only a few moments before he came back to awareness, naked, breathing heavily, bathed in sweat, spent, his arousal sated, his soul satisfied, his heart full, drowning in love.

His wife in his arms, clinging to him, her heart beating in time with his.

Finally, as their ardor cooled, their breathing slowed, Rhapsody sighed beneath him and stretched. She leaned up on her elbows, kissed him warmly, and rested her forehead against his.

"*Now* are you ready for supper?"

Ashe sighed comically.

"I suppose I could be forced—" He curled up, laughing, as she poked him under the arm and slid out from beneath him. She rolled gracefully to one side and stood, using training in the battlefield skill of a horseman's rollout, kissed him on the top of the head, then started over to the fire.

She froze in her tracks, chilled by the sound of his gasp of horror.

He had seen the scratches that scored her back—in blood, blood that was also on his hands.

9

*W*hat's the matter?"

The look of devastation on Ashe's face caused Rhapsody's heart to sink suddenly. The draconic pupils in her husband's eyes were expanding, even in the light of the fire. He could barely form the words.

"Your back—I've *gouged* you."

Rhapsody's forehead furrowed, and she looked over her shoulder. "You have?"

Ashe nodded, rising slowly from the floor of the turf hut. "Aria, I'm so sorry."

In response, Rhapsody walked to the small closet that had always been part of the tiny house and opened the door. She examined her back in the looking glass hanging on the door, then chuckled.

"Oh, for goodness' sake, Sam, that's nothing. Be quiet a moment," she said as he started to speak. She chanted a soft healing roundelay as she reached farther into the small closet and pulled out his bathrobe and her dressing gown, then looked back over her shoulder again. She came to him and handed him the robe.

"All better," she said briskly. When her husband just stared at her, she turned her back to show him her newly healed skin, then pulled on her dressing gown. "If you'll pour the wine, I'll serve supper."

"I can't believe you are dismissing what just happened as if it were nothing," Ashe said, cinching the belt of his robe and looking around for the bottle.

"It's the red over on the windowsill," Rhapsody said as she ladled the stew into two bowls. "And I can't believe that you are worrying one more moment about it."

"I—*harmed* you, Rhapsody, injured you; the dragon is overzealous again—"

The Lady Cymrian set the bowls in their places, then stood up and crossed her arms in front of her, looking at him with a mixture of fondness and disbelief.

"In a thousand years of spectacular lovemaking, there have been surprisingly few bumps and bruises, Sam, largely owing to your impressive agility, but there *have* been some," she said humorously, her tone gentle. "We've both endured an occasional scratch or two, rug burns, insect bites, even a splinter, especially when utilizing the floor of a turf hut, rocks by the shoreline, or some other rough surface. If I recall correctly, on the two hundredth anniversary of our formal wedding, a collision of our foreheads during vigorous knobbing against a pillar in the Great Hall of Highmeadow after everyone else had left resulted in a rather impressive black eye for you—am I wrong?"

Ashe's despair tempered and he chuckled. "No. You are never wrong."

"Well, now you're just trying to gain points with sweet talk you don't really mean," she scolded playfully. Her teasing smile faded to a warmer one. "That collision also resulted in Elienne."

Ashe's smile matched hers. "Indeed. Well worth the black eye."

"So stop fretting." She returned to the sideboard and brought the rest of the food to the table while he poured the wine.

She touched the wicks of the candles as he pulled out her chair for her, snapping them to life, then sat as he pushed it back in and took his seat. The music grew slightly louder as they set about dining in relative silence, smiling at each other and discussing the state of the Alliance between courses.

"How was Tyrian?" Ashe asked as Rhapsody rose to bring forth the dessert.

"The realm is in splendid shape, prosperous, peaceful, anticipating a good growing season, a bountiful harvest, and fine weather for the most part. The healing centers are functioning well, and are being visited by healers from far corners of the world." Rhapsody carefully sliced the torte and put a large piece on his plate. "Structurally, agriculturally, culturally, militarily, and spiritually, all seems right with the world there.

Rial is still doing a magnificent job as viceroy, though I suspect he will want to step away and rest soon."

"And the meeting of Namers?"

Rhapsody's eyes sparkled.

"That was amazing," she said, taking her fork to her own piece of cake. "I am so encouraged about the state of the lore, not only among Lirin Namers, but with those who preserve it in other races and cultures, too. The Repository is still ringing with some of the most glorious tales and songs; the Sea Mages were delighted with the new Maritime wing, where we did two whole days cataloguing and sharing sea chanteys. And you would have been incredibly proud of Meridion, Sam; his address and his work on the symposium were first-rate. Speaking objectively, he's by far the most gifted Namer in the Known World."

"I am always incredibly proud of him, and of all our children, and the Grands and Greats," Ashe said, folding his napkin and laying it beside his plate. "You and God, the One, the All, have blessed me with a family I could never have even begun to imagine, given the one I came from. I thank Him each day for giving me the sense to have listened to you about having one of our own."

Rhapsody laughed and rose to clear the dishes. "You had a bit of a hand in making that family what it is, too," she said. "The best proof I can recall of the wisdom of deciding what you want the outcome of something to be, and then making it happen."

"I've already admitted that you are never wrong," Ashe said, gathering the dishes she left behind. "Shall I wash or dry?"

Rhapsody was already pumping water into the sink near the wall. "Why don't you dry and put away tonight? I swear I am shrinking; I had trouble getting some of the serving pieces down from the top shelves this afternoon."

A pounding hum behind Ashe's eyes made him stop for a moment; the dragon, which had settled into dormancy after their lovemaking and had been abashed into silence at the sight of the scratches and her blood beneath his fingernails, was beginning to rise again. "Can we set them to soak for now, Aria? We need to talk more seriously."

Rhapsody sighed, but did not turn to face him.

"Are we going to have the anniversary discussion now, then?"

Ashe swallowed, struggling to contain the draconic voice that was growing louder in his ears.

"Do you begrudge me?"

Rhapsody touched the cold soapy water, releasing her fire lore to raise its temperature to just short of boiling. Then she turned and gave him a reassuring smile that carried over into her tone.

"Not at all. I'm grateful you are willing to limit the discussion to once a year—I know it's painful to have to wait so long."

He put his load of plates into the water, wiped his hands, then took her into his arms and kissed her.

"If you would acquiesce, we could stop talking about it."

Rhapsody smiled, but Ashe could almost see the lump that had formed in her throat.

"If I acquiesce, we will stop talking altogether."

"I don't believe that's so," he said lightly. "When my father undertook this transition, he was often in the ether nearby, and able to speak to me. He came to the Cymrian Council, witnessed our investiture and wedding—"

He stopped as her eyes filled with tears.

"I'm sorry, Aria," he said as he drew her closer, a gesture meant to both comfort her and spare himself the sight of her crying. "I know it pains you to hear this."

"It does," she said to his shoulder, "but it also pains me to hear the suffering in your voice and to know that you are unhappy."

He pulled back and took her face in his hands.

"I have never said that I am unhappy," he said, looking deep into her eyes to assure her of the veracity of his words. "How can anyone as blessed as I have been be unhappy—be anything but grateful?"

She said nothing, but her eyes reflected an even deeper sorrow. Ashe sighed dispiritedly and pulled her close again, resting her head on his shoulder and caressing her recently healed back.

For the past twenty or so years this had been a hallmark of most of their secret-wedding anniversary celebrations in the tiny turf hut, an agonizing discussion that they had agreed to limit to once a year.

It had begun with a request he had made two decades before out of nowhere in the aftermath of an especially tender evening celebrating just such an anniversary. Faced with his own painful aging and approaching mortality, the persistent rise and increasing unpredictability of the dragon within him, and his unspoken fear that the beast in his blood would inadvertently harm her, their children, or the continent, he had casually suggested that he consider undertaking the same transition from wyrm-kin to wyrm that Llauron, his father, had undergone.

Llauron had made the decision, just prior to meeting Rhapsody, to forswear his humanity in favor of entering an elemental state and become a pure dragon. He had manipulated Rhapsody, by means of a false death, into using Daystar Clarion, the elemental sword of starfire that she carried as the Iliachenva'ar, to light his funeral pyre with the sword, the action that made his transition to an elemental state possible. Llauron, forever after in elemental wyrm form, later had warned her at the Cymrian Council where she and Ashe announced the date of their public wedding of what would happen in the future.

Rhapsody, I must ask you to remember something.

Yes?

Whether you realize it now or not, for all that you hated our last interaction, you will be faced one day with the same situation again.

What does that mean?

It means that when you marry a man who is also a dragon, one day you will find that he is in need of becoming one or the other. If he chooses to let his human side win, you will eventually understand the pain of being widowed, as I have. And if he takes the path I chose, well, you have had a window into what both of you must do. I don't mean to impinge on your happiness in any way, my dear, but these are the realities of the family you are about to marry into. I just don't want you to wake up one day and feel you were misled.

Rhapsody, who had been tremendously traumatized to discover she had essentially burned Llauron alive, had greatly resented being so misled. She had struggled to keep her voice calm and as anger-free as possible.

Goodbye, Llauron, she had said. *I'll see you at the wedding, I expect, or at least feel your presence.*

Now her father-in-law's prediction was coming to pass.

That first night twenty years before, Rhapsody had listened while Ashe laid out his proposal with the same serene look on her face as was usually in place, though her eyes had kindled from emerald green to the color of spring grass. When he had finished explaining his idea, she had asked but one question of him: *Is this an obscene joke?*

At the shock on his face that followed her question, she had risen from the bed, pulled on her dressing gown, and run from the turf hut.

The sounds of her retching, followed by sobbing of a magnitude he had almost forgotten she was capable of, her despair filling the crabapple grove with a howling wind and causing the waterfall to roar in accusation, had appalled him so greatly that he had let the subject pass for the next three years.

Quite possibly that was because he knew even a thousand years' time had not healed her from the nightmares, remembering the part she had been manipulated into playing in Llauron's transition.

And his own complicity in it.

The avoidance of the discussion had resulted in the ability to sincerely wish her happy anniversary during those next three years, and a shattering frustration that the dragon within his blood exploited in his silence, nearly driving him insane. Finally the topic returned at his insistence, and her acceptance, of the need to at least ponder the possibility.

In his arms, Rhapsody inhaled deeply. "Do you have something new to add this year?"

Ashe swallowed the dragon's ire and waited until his response could sound considered. "Not really—do you?"

His wife pulled gently out of his arms. "As a matter of fact, yes," she said. "A few things. Can we sit?"

Ashe smiled and kissed her. "As my lady commands."

Rhapsody's face was thoughtful. "I do not command you, m'lord," she said seriously. "I merely asked. The peril of misspeaking during these discussions, especially for me, is immense. Please forgive me if I err on the side of cautious speech; I am so terribly afraid." Her eyes were mild, but Ashe could sense she was clenching her jaw to try to stop her chin from trembling, and he cursed himself silently.

She sat down on the bed.

"After Meridion and I took care of our responsibilities at the Tree, I went to see your great-grandmother."

"Elynsynos? You went to the dragon's lair?"

"I did."

"Oh. How is she?"

"She's well. Delighted with the world, and all her Cymrian Grands and Greats." Her eyes grew soft in the firelight with memory. "I needed her perspective. I hope you will forgive me; I didn't tell her of your— proposal, but I did ask her about being a dragon."

Ashe nodded. "And what did you learn?"

Rhapsody smiled slightly. "That, like every other being in the world, dragons do not know what happens after death." Her smile faded. "But she still seems as convinced as she was on the day you first brought me to her lair that she and all her kind are without souls, that they are long-lived, but not immortal, except that the blood they leave behind turns into veins of copper or gold or gems, to adorn the empty heads of kings and the breasts of vain women." She looked at him sharply.

"And she believes, in great sadness, that what Llauron really sacrificed for his dragon elemental state, for his wyrm longevity, was the human soul he was born with, his immortality, his Afterlife.

"Just as you are thinking of doing."

THE NONALIGNED STATES, THE FORMER EMPIRE OF SORBOLD, TOWN OF DROSSER

The four commanders rode two abreast down the narrow cobbled Mainway, between the median of horse troughs and the northern side of the street, scouting the pubs and taverns.

Dusk was coming, and with nightfall it would be more difficult to gauge the logistics and layouts of the places in which they expected to find the Sergeant-Major, so they had split up earlier, each of two pairs taking one side of the cobbled road.

Reynard and Goodeve, the two generals, had taken the lead, asking around to determine which of the establishments had better reputations for military types, finally narrowing the likely contenders to two, the Cock and Bull and the Serpent's Egg, which had been closed owing to a death in the family.

A few well-placed questions to a well-paid barkeep in the Cock and Bull confirmed their research.

"Well, he's likely to be here this evening, or somewhere on the street," the barkeep had told them, never ceasing in his task of drying the tankards. "A great customer, if yer in need of endless stories and tales of war."

"Has he been causing trouble in these parts?"

The barkeep's eyebrows had lifted.

"The Sergeant? Nah. There's occasionally some dustups in any bar, gents, and, beggin' yer pardon, but any place that serves soldiers knows to expect it. But he's a gentle giant. No reason fer worries."

"Good to know," said Reynard. "Thank you."

He paid for their drinks and led the commanders out of the establishment, leaving the barkeep to his tankards.

10

TURF HUT BEYOND THE WATERFALL

Ashe sighed despondently. "I thought about what I asked of you for almost fifty years before I brought it up to you, Aria. Forgive me if I am disheartened by being asked to wait yet again."

"I am not asking you to wait. Are you willing to hear a different proposal?"

Ashe sat heavily in the chair. Rhapsody could see the internal battle waging, the wyrm in his blood bristling in anger, the man exhausted from battling it. Her heart twisted in pain for her husband, whose face was showing the signs of age.

She came to him and climbed into his lap, wrapping herself and her warmth around him. Then she laid her head on his shoulder and put her hand over his heart, humming softly against his neck. She sang the soothing song of his name until she felt his heartbeat slow, his breathing become regular again; then she turned and kissed his cheek.

"Are you ready to hear my idea?"

Ashe smiled. "I'm listening."

"Next year is the third year in the cycle, the year when we will call the Cymrian Council—"

The Lord Cymrian's head hit the back of the chair, and he stared up at the ceiling.

"Are you trying to give me even greater reason to commit suicide, Aria?"

Rhapsody struggled to keep her voice calm. "I assume you are joking. If you are not, I will stop now."

Finally he turned and looked into her eyes. The expression he saw there was mild and loving, but deeper he could tell that his own pain was reflected; she understood the sheer volume of his despair, of his internal struggle.

"I'm sorry. Please continue; I really am listening."

"We have a little under a year if we begin when we get home to Highmeadow," Rhapsody said, sitting up in his lap and looking down at him. "We have been promising each other for a thousand years that we would give up our positions of responsibility and leadership once others stepped forward to take over."

"And no one has."

"No, of course no one has. What we inherited was daunting, and after those issues were resolved it was easier to spare anyone else the need to take on our positions, especially after everyone we thought worthy refused," Rhapsody went on. "But I am ready—more than ready, Sam. Our children are certainly qualified and able to either take over some of our roles or serve in them in transition to other leaders. It's time to let all that sort itself out. Stephen is well suited to take on the lordship if the Council elects him, or at least to serve as regent until they choose someone else. You have been training Allegra with Kirsdarke, as I have been training Joseph with Daystar Clarion. I have been encouraging Elienne to make use of her innate connection with Tyrian to consider attempting to take the crown; I left the diadem in its case in Tomingorllo before I left."

Ashe blinked. "You did?"

Rhapsody grinned. "Do you not think that if I had it with me I would have added it to my dragon-distracting anniversary outfit? I know how much your inner sense likes the whirling lights of the crown." Her husband squeezed her and chuckled. "Meridion is now a far better Namer than I could ever hope to be; he can take on whatever role he chooses, perhaps taking over the healing centers or continuing to advise the new lord and lady as he has done for us if he doesn't want to rule himself, as he continuously says he does not. The only thing I cannot pass off to someone for certain is my stewardship of the Earthchild, but that is minimal, and I hope that Laurelyn would consider taking on that responsibility. The Earthchild loves her; you can tell by the way her gardens bloom with winter flowers. She's the Invoker; it would be well within her oath and vow."

"And then I suppose you will be wanting me to finally build you the goat hut I promised you a thousand years ago, arthritic and aged as I am now?"

Rhapsody took his face in her hands and kissed him.

"You have built or provided me—us—with a dozen goat huts over the centuries, Sam," she said as she looked around the small turf hut. "This being the very first one."

"This?"

"Yes, this. I know it was yours to begin with, your hiding place, your disgusting hovel—" His laugh unbalanced her on his lap. "And I'm sorry if it was presumptuous to clean it out so brutally, but it has served well as a simple, hidden room with everything you and I have ever really needed—a bed, a fireplace, water, privacy, peace. Just like Elysian, or the beach shack in Gria Tres, or the cistern behind the wall of thorns in Bethany, or Oelendra's house in Tyrian, or any of the other small, hidden places we have had over the years to steal away from court and be alone in together. That was all I wanted, really—I didn't need any actual goats."

The Lord Cymrian laughed and kissed her. "So your proposal is to finally doff our leadership roles?"

"That's only the first part of it. I learned something at the first Council when Edwyn Griffyth refused the lordship outright; I had no idea that was possible. I, of course, had already been named Lady, and so it was too late to try that myself anyway, but I think we should warn those I mentioned of what is coming ahead of time, giving them the better part of a year to prepare, and then announce our resignations when the Council meets. We can still chair the session, so it's not the leaderless rabble it would be otherwise, but when the Council is over we will be done, at least with the lord- and ladyships.

"The roles of Kirsdarkenvar and Iliachenva'ar are a little more difficult. Who carries the swords is not our decision to make, that is the purview of the weapons themselves. But if you return Kirsdarke to the altar behind the basilica in Avonderre, we can see if it allows Elienne or Allegra to pick it up, or Meridion—he has a natural bond to the sea that may speak to its magic." Ashe nodded. "And I can take Daystar Clarion to the Altar of Fire in Bethany and try the same thing with Joseph or

Stephen. It may be vain to assume that ancient weapons of epic history will want to remain in our family, but there is no reason not to try, at least, to pass them on to someone who has trained with them."

"Agreed."

"And then, having 'doffed,' as you put it, our all-consuming responsibilities—pay attention, because this is the part I hope you will like—I will be yours exclusively, night into day, for the rest of our lives. Everything that has taken me away from you, and to which you do not desire to travel, I will give up."

Ashe sat up with interest. "Really? Everything?"

Rhapsody exhaled. "Everything except our children, the Grands and the Greats. But I can't imagine you would ask that of me."

"So your travels and work as a Namer, your healing responsibilities—"

"I've trained others. I can't imagine I will be needed."

"What about Tyrian?"

"If Elienne is chosen by the crown, I will have no need to be there." Her face darkened, and Ashe could feel traces of water enter the corners of her eyes, but her face and voice remained calm. "You like Tyrian, and once you are no longer Lord Cymrian you will also no longer be bound to Highmeadow. We could live there in peace, at least part of the time. If Elienne is not chosen, you could come with me until I am able to find a new viceroy or Lord Protector, but if you're not willing, I believe the realm will be safe without me. They lived sovereignless for more than two hundred years before I came; they will not miss me."

Ashe took hold of one of the waves of golden hair that had become unbound on the floor in lovemaking. "I thought Namers were required to speak only the Truth."

"I don't mean the friendships, I mean the running of the government. Rial has really been in charge of that all along; he's just humored me."

"I see. All your commissions and councils, all your boards and healing centers, the Repository, the international Loritorium, everything?"

The Namer's tone of True-Speaking was in her reply.

"Everything."

Ashe nodded thoughtfully, then his eyes narrowed.

"What about the Bolg?"

Rhapsody's face lost the last remnants of its smile, but her eyes remained placid.

"The Bolg haven't needed me for centuries. They never did, really;

Achmed and Grunthor were just humoring me as well. My music helped them gain the mountains, but it was never necessary. Everything they have accomplished they could have done easily without me—I tend to think it would be a less civilized place than it is with my contribution, less educated, less healthy—but it would still be a remarkable renaissance if only Achmed and Grunthor had been in charge. As long as there is an *amelystik* to tend to the Sleeping Child, I don't need to go back to Ylorc again. I will miss Elysian, but only a little."

"I see."

Rhapsody took a breath to cleanse her mouth of the dismal words.

"I would at least like to see Achmed and Grunthor every so often; I miss them when we go too long between visits. But now that Achmed can travel the wind, it's easier to see him outside of Ylorc. And Grunthor has such an immense structure in place in the army that he can wander the continent without having to confine himself to the Bolglands."

"I am aware. He is causing me no end of trouble, by the way, including skirmishes that are undoing years of diplomacy. I would appreciate it if you would speak to him about reining in his boredom before war breaks out."

"I have. I saw him outside of southeastern Tyrian before Meridion and I began making our way home and requested specifically that he refrain from breaking treaties and crossing you.

"Back to my proposal: Then, when all that is accomplished, I can be with you. We can do whatever we want to do, go wherever we want to go, see the things we always said we would, although in truth, we already have done that for the most part. Whatever it is about me that brings you peace and comfort will never be away from you; I will sing your arthritic knuckles back to flexibility. I will, in fact, sing your name-song to you as often as I can, and see if that helps restore your youth somewhat. I will make it my life's goal to keep you free from pain and happy; I already thought I was doing it, but clearly you need more of my attention now, and I am ready, delighted, in fact, to give it to you. And, having interviewed Elynsynos intensely on the topic, and knowing a bit about it myself, I will undertake to do all the things that might keep the dragon happy as well."

"A generous offer; fascinating, in fact," Ashe murmured. "Fascinating, and appalling at the same time."

Rhapsody sat back, stung.

"Appalling?"

Ashe caressed her cheek to take away a little of the offense, but she pulled away. "Yes, Aria—appalling. I'm trying to imagine you ever expecting me to sacrifice all the works I've undertaken in my life that I thought were noble or important to wait on *you* hand and foot, night into day, for eternity. I cannot form a picture in my head of you ever asking or in fact allowing me to do that."

"I said nothing about waiting on you," Rhapsody said, rising from his lap and turning away from the fire, which had already signaled her shock and rising fury in twisting blue and orange flames, snapping and hissing. "You aren't even going to get out of dish-drying duty tonight after this infernal conversation ends. I offered to be with you at all times, which is what I would gladly choose to do, given any opportunity. You once asked me how long we should expect to live happily ever after, Ashe—here's my answer: as long as God, the One, the All, keeps a spark of life in one of our bodies. I *love* you, dammit; fiercely—deeply—with everything that I am, Ashe, *everything*. Aside from one of our children, my greatest terror is the idea of the loss of you. I thought you knew that by now."

Ashe's mouth dropped open. "Of course—of course I do."

"Then you should know what that means, that I would do anything— *anything* I could to make you happy, to give you what you need, to keep you healthy, to bring you peace."

"Anything except what I have asked you to do."

Rhapsody stared at him in silence, her eyes gleaming either from unspent tears or anger; Ashe wasn't sure. Finally words formed on her lips.

"Perhaps that is because you are asking me to kill you, risk killing you, or feel as if I am."

Ashe exhaled silently.

"You know the first part of that is not true."

"I do not." Her gaze hardened. "Do you doubt my word now as well?"

He threw up his hands in annoyance and turned away. "You well know Llauron survived it."

"You are not Llauron. Llauron prepared for his immolation for Time uncounted, researching in texts that burned a thousand years ago. Neither of us knows what he might have done to offset the damage, or what a strike of starfire will do to you."

"I am willing to take that chance—should that not be sufficient?" Ashe turned back to her, his own eyes gleaming now. "Should I not be the one to make decisions about my own destiny, my own life?"

"Strange," Rhapsody said coolly. "I have always believed that our lives were shared, not strictly our own—I still recall vows to that effect, made twice and renewed endlessly. And while I acknowledge your right to make those decisions ultimately, what you are asking of me is dually awful—to risk ending your human existence in favor of a vaporous wyrm-dom, which separates us physically in this world, or ending your actual life, separating us on both sides of Life and the Afterlife, leaving me haunted for the rest of my supposedly endless days. Forgive me if I'm resistant to both of those things; contemplating the loss of you, my soul mate, the man I've loved across Time and for all of my life, in either case by my own hand, is breaking my heart."

Both of the spouses fell into heavy silence.

"The dragon is growing stronger," Ashe said finally, his voice low and soft. "The struggle to contain it grows more intense with each beat of my heart."

"I know."

"And do you also know how much I fear for you, Rhapsody—for our children? For the continent?"

The Lady Cymrian sighed. After a long pause, she spoke. "I do."

"Forgive me, but I don't believe you really do," the Lord Cymrian said, the ring of pained gravel in his voice. "You fear killing me with the starfire strike, at my request, which you know freed my father from his torment when his human body was dying and his dragon nature sought release—do you not see that I am tortured by the same possibility that I might destroy you, our children, the people I love beyond description—but against my will and without the possibility of *their* transformation?"

"Because you scratched me while making love?"

"Because I *dream* of it," Ashe spat. "Respect me enough to believe me when I tell you that I have seen grisly images in my mind for decades, of your blood on my hands, your flesh in my *teeth*—"

"I am well aware," Rhapsody interrupted, her voice now steady with an undertone of sympathy. She had woken many times at the end of those terrible dreams, unable to breathe in the clutch of Ashe's strong arms. The gentling and reassuring of her trembling husband, sweating and cold in the throes of his nightmares, had been among the more heartbreaking things she had undertaken in the course of their marriage. Now, as never before, she finally understood the sadness and despair her own nightmares had inflicted on him long ago.

"If you are aware, then *help me,* for the love of God, Aria," Ashe whispered. "Do you think I *want* to keep asking this of you? Do you think for one moment that I want to leave my humanity behind, to lose the ability to hold you, to make love to you, to share everyday life, a bed, a *goat hut* with you? This would be very much a death for me, even if I continue to exist in another form. There is nothing in this universe—I mean that without hyperbole, Rhapsody—*nothing* that I hate more than the thought of being separated from you and our family. But I don't know what else to do; the only thing that could be worse than that would be if I were to cause you or them harm when—not *if,* but *when*—I lose control of that element of my nature, and rampage. That tragedy grows closer with each passing hour."

Rhapsody turned away from him and stared into the fireplace. The flames settled down into a calmer burn, the flashing light that had been splashing off the golden tresses of her hair glowing more gently. She let her breath out slowly, recalling all the times over the course of their marriage she had contended with the alien element of the man who shared her soul. She had become almost expert at it, though even after a thousand years she still did not understand it fully. She adopted a soothing musical tone in her voice.

"But most likely it will not come tonight."

Only silence answered her.

"I have another thought," she said quietly, not looking at him.

Behind her, Ashe sighed deeply again. "Yes?"

Rhapsody exhaled. "The dragon in your blood was dormant when you were younger, as it was in Llauron's, was it not?"

Her husband crossed the small room until he stood at her back. He ran a shaky finger, its knuckle broken and distended from a thousand years of life and battle, through a lock of her hair. "You know that it was," he said in a low voice. "On the night I crossed Time to meet you in Serendair, I was utterly human, was I not?" The last phrase rang with an almost humorous irony, mirroring what she had said a moment before.

She turned at last to him, and her face was wreathed in a warm smile of fond memory.

"You were," she agreed, finally meeting his gaze; her eyes sparkled, emerald in the firelight. "Utterly human, and utterly enchanting."

Her husband drew more of her hair into his scarred palm. "And utterly lost to you, even then, at fourteen. I can still recall exactly how you looked that night, Emily, in the moonlit shadows beneath the willow tree in your father's meadow. And exactly how it felt to be inside you for the first time, as pathetic as the performance must have seemed to you then."

"Don't be ridiculous; the glorious memory of it lasted until we met up again, and still remains, even through all the years." Rhapsody took his face in her hands, trying to see past the lines of age and the graying of his hair to the cerulean-blue eyes that still looked at her with the same wonder they had on the night in question. She kissed him slowly, then looked deep into those blue eyes, regarding him thoughtfully.

"What if we could return you to that mostly human state, the dragon all but dormant again?"

The night wind whistled through the eaves of the turf hut, accentuating the utter silence that answered her.

THE NONALIGNED STATES, THE FORMER EMPIRE OF SORBOLD

Grunthor had been tucked away at a table in the corner of the Seaside Grogshop, a pub in the coastal province of Hacket, for the better part of the evening.

Under normal circumstances, a tavern such as the Grogshop was not the friendliest place for clients who stood almost eight feet tall and wore more weapons in a leather bandolier on their backs than resided in the possession of an entire coterie of town guards, but the Sergeant-Major was a known quantity at the establishment, which catered largely to military types. He had, despite his height and monstrous status, received prime hospitality as he had on several other occasions, his tankard never being left more than half full at any point in the evening.

In fact, his favorite waitresses and serving women were finding him rather morose and quiet this night, in contrast to his prior visits when he had flirted outrageously with every woman of any age in the tavern, or had happily held the place hostage to his drunken singing.

This night he sat quietly at his table and addressed his tankard, minding his own business. Had he not been of the proportions of a dray horse in a crowd of jackasses, he would most likely not even have been noticed.

But, in spite of his highly inebriated state and gloomy disposition, something seemed out of place to him.

Even though the Grogshop had a clientele that frequently wore the nation's uniform, there seemed to be a greater number of soldiers in the place this night, he thought. Under normal circumstances, he would have felt compelled to do at least a preliminary assessment of the premises, but again, he was distracted and tired, two conditions that would have normally caused him to remain in his billet, rather than seeking potables.

He had all but fallen asleep, bent over the table, when the subtle sounds of bending wood and bowstrings creaking caught his ear.

Grunthor raised his head from the table board and looked around.

Standing in front of him, hedging the shadows that clung to the furniture and cabinetry, were two men, armed and wearing the colors of Ashe's regiment specifically, with the base uniform of the army of the Alliance.

Behind him, his clouded perceptions, still in rare form from three thousand years of training, could sense several more lingering.

And there was an even larger contingent, probably armed with crossbows, behind that.

He smiled as widely as his inebriated state would allow.

Those in his field of blurry vision appeared to be watching him intently.

Grunthor grinned broadly at them.

"Well, 'allo, gents. What brings you all down 'ere to the seaside? Oi 'ope yer on 'oliday."

The men in the shadows looked at each other, then turned away, draining their tankards.

Grunthor's head made the descent back to the table again.

It lurched slightly to the right as he felt a dull thudding at the base of his neck.

Grunthor sat up a little straighter in surprise, reaching his enormous arm over his shoulder and patting randomly at his back. His arm swung surprisingly wide, then hung limp, even as his legs began to go numb.

"Wha—?" he mumbled as the two men before him tossed their empty tankards aside and sprang from the shadows, thick short swords in their hands.

"Yer kiddin' me," the Sergeant muttered as he groped for a weapon from his bandolier, but could not bring his arm high enough to draw one. He rolled into a ball as he fell heavily from the chair, his back beneath the table.

A volley of crossbow bolts went wide above his head, all missing but one, which pierced his right shoulder.

"*Hrekin,*" the Sergeant cursed. He waited hazily under the table, gripping the legs of the fallen chair, unmoving, with his eyes closed, as one of the soldiers approached, his blade drawn and ready, until the man was just above him. Then, with as much strength as he could summon into his injured arm, he slammed the chair directly into the man's knee, off-balancing him, seizing the calf of his other leg.

"Jus' one o' you, that's all Oi want, jus' one," he whispered as he dragged the startled soldier onto his back and grabbed him by the greave on his leg. He could hear the approaching footfalls, his foggy mind counting and assessing, then jerked the soldier, who was struggling fiercely, forward until his hand gripped the man's throat, crushing his windpipe. " 'Twould be a shame not to get at least one trophy."

By the time he was finished, he'd racked up thirty-seven.

The Grogshop had to be closed for the better part of two months for repairs.

11

THE TURF HUT

$\mathcal{A}$she blinked.

She waited silently.

"What do you mean, Aria?" he asked finally.

Rhapsody's hands caressed the slackening skin of his face and neck as she ran them down to his chest, where they came to rest over his heart. She let them linger there, warming the skin beneath his shirt, then gently pulled the collar wider, revealing the light starlike pattern of the veins below the skin over his heart.

"The piece of the star that the Lord and Lady Rowan sewed within your chest, that fragment of Seren from Daystar Clarion's hilt, saved your life when your chest and heart were torn asunder by the F'dor long ago, before I came to this world," she said softly.

Ashe eyed her warily. "It did."

"And, consequently, that elemental power awakened the wyrm in your blood, stirring it from dormancy into, well, a more equal partner with your human side."

"Yes."

She considered her words for a moment before speaking them to try to minimize the sting. "Perhaps you have not needed that elemental ether for centuries, Ashe. You were healed more than a thousand years ago; perhaps that is why the dragon has continued to grow stronger within you. It has been feeding off power that is no longer necessary to keep you alive, battling your human side for dominance."

He stared at her for a long time. "Go on," he said finally.

She swallowed hard. "What if we could remove that piece of the star from your chest now, and put it back in the sword? If you don't need it to remain alive, perhaps the absence of all that elemental power would return the wyrm to dormancy. You would be mostly human again."

"And elderly, even more bent and broken than I already am," Ashe said in a toneless voice. "Or perhaps I would die outright. The presence of the wyrm in my blood is doubtless responsible for my insane longevity."

"Not necessarily," his wife disagreed. "You are a third-generation Cymrian; your grandfather was not only immortal, he was all but invulnerable—your grandmother had to bargain with a demon of a First-born race, or she would never have been able to kill him. You have Seren blood as well as the legacy of MacQuieth, who lived at least two thousand years. You could have survived all this time just as a result of the human element in you that is Cymrian."

"So you want to reach into my chest and remove the piece of elemental ether that was sewn into my heart to heal it when it was torn? Rather a rash risk to take, wouldn't you say?"

"Rasher than undergoing a strike of starfire in the attempt to convert you into an elemental wyrm, formless and noncorporeal, assuming you live through it?"

Ashe's expression grew thoughtful.

"Perhaps not," he said.

Rhapsody slid her hands around to his back and drew him into her arms, pressing her face against his shoulder so that he could not see it.

"If it works, you might live out your days in a human state, with the wyrm at the edge of your awareness, rather than having to struggle with it for control."

A dryness in the air signaled a rising of his draconic nature.

"You wish to extinguish the dragon?"

Rhapsody pulled back and looked at him. The vertical pupils within his eyes were expanding in a peevish anger. "I wish for the dragon to be at peace within you, rather than fighting your human side for dominance," she said simply and directly. "Do not let the wyrm take insult from my suggestion; it is a part of you I have loved dearly for a thousand years. But if you are living in constant fear of a rampage, this could help."

"Or it could kill me."

"It could," Rhapsody acknowledged. "But you would die in my arms as a man, not a wyrm, and therefore your human soul would remain intact, traveling through the Gate of Life behind the Veil of Hoen, into the Afterlife."

"Separating us forever." The angry tone in his voice took on a tinge of pain.

Rhapsody shook her head and quickly took his hands. "No."

"*Yes,*" Ashe said. "Aria, the main reason for my desire to transition into an elemental state is *your* immortality. You may think me selfish for wanting to achieve elemental wyrmdom rather than dying outright in human form, but at least living among the elements I would have an extended longevity, like Elynsynos or the other dragons that have gone into the ether rather than keep a corporeal body. While I would no longer be a human man, at least I could be with you in *some* form. If I die outright, we will be separated on either side of Life and the Afterlife." He stopped speaking abruptly before his next words spilled out.

Leaving you at last to Achmed, who has been patiently waiting for you all this time, though you have never understood this.

Rhapsody shook her head again as a dazzling smile broke over her face, reminding Ashe of a sunrise at sea.

"I would go with you," she said, squeezing his hands. "I have no desire whatsoever to remain in this life without you. When whatever longevity you are granted by Fate is over, I will go to the Rowans with you. The Lord Rowan has promised me that he would take me, would come for me one day if he could. I expect that they will welcome me, just as they will welcome you when the time comes, just as Oelendra went in peace to join her husband Pendaris when the F'dor was finally dead, the Council reunited.

"Had you died, in battle or otherwise, while our children were young, I would have remained here, widowed, until they were old enough to fend for themselves and establish good and happy lives. Then I would have followed you to the Veil. But that's not an issue anymore, unless—"

The music in her voice changed so abruptly that Ashe's grip on her hands tightened.

"What is it, Aria?"

Rhapsody's face went solemn, but her eyes gleamed even brighter.

"I hear another tone," she said softly. "As I've told you. It grows stronger each day."

Ashe sighed. They were words he had heard her speak a half dozen times before, words that had always been a source of great joy to him, though he had not heard her speak them for a very long time. Each time they had undertaken to conceive one of their children, it was in response to just such words, Rhapsody's inner sense that a child was waiting out in the ether, preparing to come through the doorway that was their love for one another, into the material world. She had, in fact, spoken these words to him several times over the last few decades, but had refrained from bringing them up after he had started to inquire about the strike of starfire from Daystar Clarion. He held out his hands to her, hands that trembled slightly with age.

"I am too old to do this again," he said wearily. "I'm sorry, my love."

Rhapsody's glowing expression faded.

"I—I—but there is a child waiting, Ashe, a person, an entity, a living soul waiting to be born of our love. Our last child."

"We are great-grandparents," Ashe said. "Most of our grandchildren are grown. Time may not have marked a day on you since you stepped forth from the Root into this world, but even if my Cymrian lineage prevents it from showing, I am an elderly man."

"I can assure you that you still knob like a boy of fourteen." Her voice was light but strained. "In all the good ways—your stamina is stellar."

"Be that as it may, I cannot imagine putting you, or both of us, through another pregnancy. You have given me the six most beautiful, wonderful children in the world, and they in turn have given us precious grandchildren and great-grandchildren. They are inestimable treasure, both to the human and the dragon side of me. We have so much to be grateful for already."

"You are missing the point," she said archly. "You do not need to tell me to be grateful for our children; words do not exist that sufficiently describe how much I am grateful. But there is another soul, a unique entity, that is *waiting to be born*. We can't ignore it; I can *hear* it. I have tried not to push you on this, because you have been so insistent upon your own transformation, but we have a daughter or a son who needs us, who has been waiting for a very long time."

"I'm sorry, Emily," Ashe said as gently as he could. "I truly am. I understand that you are, in the eyes of Time, a young woman still. But I am not a young man; I can feel myself declining more each day. I have dearly loved each time you have made me a father, but I am too old to do it again." He felt her agitation rising and reached for her but she pushed him away.

"What—what am I supposed to do, then, Ashe? The presence of this tone is haunting; on nights when you fall asleep before me it hounds me, ringing within my soul. How do you expect me to live with that knowledge, that we have a child waiting for us that you have decided not to bring into the world?"

"The same way any other parents live with the knowledge that they might have had more children, but have decided not to."

"Other parents cannot hear their children calling before birth the way Namers can. Once we conceived each of our children, joined pieces of our souls to make them begin, once they took root inside me I could perceive glimpses of their personalities; I knew Meridion would be a Namer, that Laurelyn would be in love with the Earth, that Allegra could lead armies, that Joseph was tied to fire. They were not merely possibilities to me, Ashe, nor is this one that has been calling for so long; you do not understand what you are decreeing by telling me you will not give me another child. It would be as if a child we had deliberately made had died within me."

Ashe turned away dispiritedly.

"You want me to father another child, a child I will not live to see grow up, while I disintegrate into a useless wreck, or spin madly into a rampage which may kill him, or you?"

Rhapsody exhaled, her face absent any internal light. "I no longer know what to say. I have no words."

Ashe watched her for a long time, seeing the fire on the hearth diminish behind her. Finally he crossed the small room to where she was standing and took her into his arms again.

"How about this—what if this child is, well, meant to be like a farewell gift? I could break open my soul one more time, could help you conceive him or her; then, when the baby is born, or at least once you are pregnant, you could finally grant my request.

"If I am transitioned to wyrm form, I suppose I could help at least with a young child's training. It would not be the same for this child as it was for the others, and you would have to ponder whether or not that would be acceptable to you. You would have to decide if you could be the only parent with arms to hold him or her, and whether having a father that is a noncorporeal dragon would be too scarring. The other children would help you raise their sibling, I'm certain, and I would be as present in the child's life as it is possible for me to be. But the risk you run then is that he or she will be more dragon than human, because that is the makeup of my blood now, as opposed to when I sired our other children."

Rhapsody wiped away stinging tears from her eyes.

"Please forgive me; I can't talk about this any more. I will ponder everything we have said tonight, Ashe, as I hope you will as well. Now I must return to the dishes; I want to give them a chance to drain so you can tend to your drying duties before bed."

She tossed a dishcloth to him and turned to the sink. If it were not for the sensitive network of draconic senses that obsessed over every detail of his wife, Ashe would never have known that tears were streaming down her face as she scrubbed the plates and pots amid the steam of the sink.

Finally, when the dishes were clean and dry and put away, Ashe came up behind Rhapsody, turned her around gently, and took her into his arms. He kissed her upturned ear.

"Are you angry with me, Aria?"

"Not in the slightest," she said, her answer spoken into his shoulder. "I'm just sad because, after more than a thousand years, I don't know what to do to make you happy."

The Lord Cymrian exhaled, then pulled slowly away from her. He looked down into her eyes, studying them. Then he slid his fingers into the crown of her hair, caressing her head.

"Not in the long term, perhaps," he said quietly. "But I am absolutely certain that until this night becomes the new day, you know exactly what to do to make me happy."

He kissed her again, taking his time, then led her to bed, blocking out the notice that the smile she had given him in return had a tinge of sadness.

In the morning it was as if the conversation had never taken place, just as it had been every year before.

12

$\mathcal{A}$she held the door of the turf hut as Rhapsody carried the last of her gear outside, then locked it carefully, amused at the ritual that was a gesture with no real meaning, but seen as a sign of his protection of their special place and its privacy.

As always, she had gotten up with the sun to launder the sheets, towels, and tablecloths and sweep the tiny house clean, had made the bed and written her note for their return next year.

The notes were another tradition that had begun at the end of the honeymoon after their formal wedding, wishing each other well amid loving and occasionally randy commentary. The honeymoon had been a gloriously private respite away from all the planning and celebration that they had endured and enjoyed leading up to the big day. After all the strife and misunderstanding, the betrayal and pain that had occurred prior to the success of the Cymrian Council, which had itself ended in tragedy and battle, the fortnight they had spent alone in the turf hut, adorned only with fresh rose petals and the simplest of luxuries he had provided as a surprise, had been the closest thing to reliving their one night in Serendair that he had been able to arrange.

He closed his eyes as the sweet wind buffeted his face, and inhaled, as he had done for a thousand years, trying to keep this place embedded in his memory.

A random thought appeared in his mind, a recollection from the second night they had spent as lovers, long ago, deep in the grotto of Elysian. His heart, until the previous day wounded from being torn open two decades before, was finally healed, and it overflowed into his eyes, which could not stop staring into those of the woman he held in his arms, tangled in the sheets of her bed.

All I ever want to do is to protect you, he had said to her, unguarded love ringing in his husky voice. *I never want anything terrible to happen to you.*

Rhapsody had smiled up at him, but her eyes had held a trace of sadness.

You're sweet, she had said. *But you are too late. Many terrible things have happened to me—and yet I am still here, having survived them.*

I want to wrap my body and my life around you, and make anything that would seek to harm you have to come through me first, he had said.

Eyes closed, he could still see the tears form in hers as she smiled and kissed him.

When he opened them again, his wife was no longer in his sight. He let the dragon sense for her and found her down at the banks of the rushing waterfall, so he dropped his gear and made his way to her.

When he found her, he stopped for a moment to take in the sight.

The Lady Cymrian and Lirin queen was dressed in simple skirts and a woven shirt, her hair loose around her shoulders, looking for all the world like a peasant or commoner, the birth class to which she had been born. She had dipped her toes in the water, and was now sitting with her arms around her knees, watching the pools of golden sunlight form and rush away over the waterfall's drop.

Ashe, who had dressed simply in common clothing as well, descended the hillside and sat down beside her.

"Are you ready to go?"

She smiled at the waterfall. "Not yet, unless you're in a hurry."

"No hurry," he said, watching a tern dive and flap away again. "The children, the Grands, and the Greats have been arriving sporadically for the past sennight or so. We can go back whenever you want."

Rhapsody sighed. "Another secret wedding anniversary come and gone," she said, letting the sunlight dance on her eyelashes.

"Indeed," Ashe said, putting his arm around her.

His wife turned and kissed his cheek. "I have three things I want to say to you before we go home."

He pulled her closer and returned the kiss on her lips warmly, lingering as the wind rustled their hair, then smiled as she did. "I am listening, my love."

"The first is this—thank you for keeping the land at peace for the better part of a thousand years," she said, gently touching his freshly shaven face. "It has made the inevitable loss of the people we have loved a good deal easier. So far, Fate has blessed us; we have lost none of our children, our Grands, or our Greats, even as some of their spouses have passed. The next millennia will surely be a good deal harder." Her face took on a trace of sadness. "I beg you not to leave me to face that alone if you possibly can help it."

Ashe exhaled but said nothing. He turned back to the waterfall.

She kissed his cheek again. "I love you."

"I know," he said. "I love you, too. And I apologize for the discussion last night. I'm selfish and grumpy and I say stupid things. I feel so very old, especially when I see you sitting here in the sunlight, the image of the girl I remember from Merryfield. I sense the time is coming when my aging will be more of a trial for you than it has been for me."

"How so?"

"I don't want you to waste your youth tending to a cantankerous old man."

Rhapsody chuckled. "Why not? You spent yours putting up with a demanding and hotheaded woman."

He turned to her and looked at her seriously. "I have been nothing but blessed."

"How's this?" she said, trying to sound practical. "This was the second thing I wanted to say: we have another anniversary coming up shortly—that of our formal wedding. Let us each consider what the other has said, and agree to talk about it again on that day, a few weeks hence, instead of waiting another year. I will try to behave less emotionally. But please understand, what you have asked of me is without question the most awful request I have ever had to contemplate. I am trying to be brave about it, but I have not been able to find the courage to face it. I understand that you believe this to be the best solution to your torment and pain, but I am in great fear of losing you in the Afterlife—and, were that to happen, I might as well be condemned to the Vault of the Underworld after death."

"I know." He finally looked back at her. "What was the last thing you wanted to say?"

A glorious smile broke over her face. She leaned closer and brought her lips as near to his as she could without touching them, filling his nose with her scent and causing his hands to tremble.

"It's actually a question, but I don't need words to ask it," she said.

She let her lips, light and dry, brush his, then sat back abruptly on her heels, seeing the longing come into his eyes. She slowly untied the laces of his shirt as he leaned back, lost in her eyes, and opened it, exposing his chest, muscled still in spite of his age in the trim of a mature man that had in his youth been a strapping soldier, the skin slackened but still fit, and ran her lips down that chest to his belt.

Ashe leaned back in the sweet green moss that grew along the banks on his elbows and closed his eyes against the sunlight again.

"Words or no, you never need ask," he said quietly. "Never."

"I know," she whispered, echoing his own words of a moment before as she addressed his belt and what lay beneath it, exposed momentarily to the wind but comforted by the warmth of her mouth a moment later, the silky locks of her hair spread like a sunlit meadow across his chest.

He lay back completely on the moss as she pushed him gently down on it, pulling his shirt wider as she climbed atop him and kissed up his abdomen to his neck, leaving him shivering as her lips caressed his throat, his jaw and ear. As the sky began to turn different colors behind his eyes and his body to tremble, he reached up under her skirt and explored her with his shaking fingers, making her sigh.

Something about the sigh struck a nerve.

Lying in the soft green grass, amid the scent of sweet woodruff and lavender, Ashe grasped her thighs, pulling himself suddenly and roughly within her, rocking her urgently from below.

And, overwhelmed utterly with passion and without any other choice, he loosed the dragon that was panting beneath the surface of his consciousness.

The gentle lovemaking she had initiated in the green moss intensified into something harsher, something possessive and greedy, roaring past even the most athletic movements they had often made use of in their intimacy, and turning wanton.

Fire roared through Ashe's body as he seized his wife, his treasure, more insistently and began to thrust himself angrily into her, pulling her down hard onto his enraged tarse, filling her with himself.

He gripped her thigh even harder as he loosed one hand and ran it roughly up her torso, still mostly clothed, and tore aside her shirt, grasping at the breasts he had always addressed gently and in wonder in the past, losing every element of love as what he was making to her turned to a demanding expression of possession.

Mine, he thought as he panted and plunged wildly, clutching the hard muscles of her leg and the soft firmness of her breast. *Mine! Mine!*

The earth below him echoed his thoughts—*Mine! Mine!*

As he raised himself up and applied his mouth roughly, carnally to her chest, his teeth bared, Rhapsody took hold of his hair, interlacing her fingers through his curls, and put her mouth next to his ear.

Yours, she said in between breaths. *Yours. Only yours.*

Ashe stopped short.

She was speaking the words in the language of the Wyrmril.

Though she could not approximate all the pronunciation, being born without the draconic aperture of the throat, her linguistic intention was unmistakable.

She continued to whisper soft phrases of comfort in the language that spoke to the dragon in his blood as her husband lay motionless beneath her, gasping for breath. She removed his hand that was clutching her breast and took it in her own, kissing it.

You do not frighten me, she whispered in his ear, interlacing her fingers through his and pressing him gently onto his back again with her chest. *You may be stronger than me, and twice my size, but you have always been so. You swore not to hurt me on our first nights as lovers, both times, and you never have. You do not frighten me. I love you.*

Ashe blinked, his eyes teary.

I am not made of glass, Rhapsody said, nuzzling his ear. *Do not be afraid. Make love with me—I want you.*

She began to move again, gently but firmly, gripping him from within as well as without, building him up to a towering climax again, which she joined him in, riding him as he held her with a more reasonable grip until their cries and gasps of laughter were drowning in and dancing over the noise of the waterfall, warmed by the sun shining down on them, cooled by the breath of the wind, making love as they had so many times before over a thousand years of happy married life.

The heat of the dragon's possessive rage dissipated as the human being returned, sheltered beneath the leafy branches of the birch and crab-apple trees, rustling in time with their dance.

When that dance was over, she stretched out on top of him, lying motionless for a long time, listening to his heart race and then begin to slow, brushing away his tears and hers, caressing his shoulders and chest, guiding his free hand to hold her backside, until she felt that the dragon rage was long past.

The man beneath her was left on the brink of either joy or despair, waiting for her to push him over onto one side or the other.

She raised her face to him, shining, and smiled as warmly as she knew how.

I love you, I am yours, she said again in the language of the dragon, then switched to the Orlandan tongue. "Always."

The despair in his eyes tempered a little, but Ashe could not bring himself to smile in return.

"I am so terribly sorry—"

"No," she interrupted decisively, her hand still entwined in his. "Do not insult what we have made together, this day, and over the last thousand years. I have given myself to you in all that time in trust, and I do now, still. Do you not think that I was aware the first night you came to me in Elysian, declaring your love and your desire to be my lover, that you could have crushed my throat in bed in passion, or in my sleep, had you wanted to? Our swords hung, side by side, on the sword rack downstairs as we slept together for the first time, a sign of a willingness to embrace a mutual trust in days when there was none of that to be sensibly had, anywhere on the continent. You are the same man now that you were then; the dragon is closer to the surface, certainly, and harder to keep in control, but, as you can see, I can handle it."

"At the cost of bruised thighs, and—"

"I can heal myself, another happy benefit of being a Namer."

Ashe fell silent. *Until the day you cannot,* he thought, *because I have, in fact, crushed your throat.*

She kissed him one last time, then rose and disrobed, walking toward the falls.

"Come," she beckoned. "The pool you dammed for the laundry has had all the suds washed out. We can bathe before we return to High-meadow."

Ashe followed her, wishing for all the world that she were beyond his ability to hurt her.

And knowing she would never be.

HIGHMEADOW, NAVARNE

In three days' time, the Lord and Lady Cymrian arrived at the doors of the main dwellings where the family had gathered. The word of their arrival had spread quickly, and as they cantered into the compound, a great cheer went up.

Rhapsody rode before Ashe on his horse, leading hers, and the sovereigns both broke into grins at seeing the beautiful group gathered in the courtyard, the young children waving and dancing in excitement.

It had never ceased to amaze Ashe how many people now comprised his family, each one beloved and counted and obsessed over by both the dragon and the man. He brought the horse to a halt amid much joyful noise and buried his face in his wife's hair, kissing her repeatedly and nuzzling her neck.

"The greatest celebrations in all the world are the simple domestic gatherings of our clan," he said, his mood jovial and excited again. "Put up to comparison with all the ponderous, formal nonsense that was undertaken to officially celebrate our thousand years of reign and marriage a few years ago, I would always prefer to make mud pies and thumb-wrestle with my Grands and Greats any day."

Rhapsody laughed. "It helps that they are better at both those things than you are."

He dismounted slowly and took her down from the saddle as well, then turned with her to greet the swell of children, grandchildren, and great-grandchildren, some of whom looked older than both of them.

"I am glad to see that this housing complex, so long a fortress and military garrison, is finally now a place where our family gathers and lives," he said to Rhapsody as four of his Greats tried to climb him simultaneously.

"Both of those aspects were things you gave me to make me safe and happy," she said, bending and embracing another wave of little ones. "I can never thank you enough for all this, Sam."

"All right, then," the Lord Cymrian declared aloud, "the Cymrian

House of Manosse o Serendair is well met! Let there be much singing, love, laughter, and delight in the children."

"And food?" suggested Leonin, one of the younger great-grandsons. "I do hope there will be some food."

The family laughed and followed the Lord and Lady into the hall.

Brought forth in blood from fire and air

Sired of Earth

A child of two worlds

Born free of the bonds of Time

Eyes will watch him from upon the earth and within it

And the Earth itself will burn beneath him

To the song of screams and wails of the dying

He shall undo the inevitable

And in so doing

Even he himself shall be undone

This unnatural child born of an unnatural act

The mother shall die, but the child shall live

Until all that has gone before is wiped away

Like a tear from the eye of Time

13

HIGHMEADOW, A SENNIGHT LATER

Ashe looked on regretfully as Rhapsody and their adult children gathered the youngest Grands and the Greats and passed out lanterns for the traditional walk in the dark to the family quarters in the adjacent buildings.

Before the extended family retired for the night, they would escort Laurelyn and Syril with song to the guest suite across the glen that was reserved for visiting dignitaries, which many of the family members, young and old, had spent the early part of the morning decorating with rose petals, candles, muslin love knots, and wind chimes in the trees for the newly married couple's wedding night.

The laughter at the end of the sunlit day, compounding that which had rung through Highmeadow for the previous week, had warmed every bit of his body and soul, enough to have pacified the dragon into blissful dormancy.

He watched, content with his world, as Rhapsody moved about in the center of the circle of family groups, helping with buttoning a cape, or pulling on a small pair of boots, tucking burgeoning hair into a hood followed by a kiss, just as she had done with their own children at the time of the year when the summer night wind was taking on a colder feel. He recalled her words to a Namer's song she had once written about autumn, her favorite time of year.

Whatever your hopes are, catch them fast, the Earth seems to say as it dresses in its glorious funereal finery. Time grows short; winter is coming.

He smiled as Stephen lifted his own youngest grandson onto his shoulders, as Joseph and his wife Caryssa gathered a passel of Grands and Greats into a wiggling line, as Allegra clapped her hands and signaled to the door, followed immediately by the excited voices of her brood. Meridion began the caroling of the songs that would escort the bride and groom to their wedding-night bower, surrounded by the rising and falling of the tides on the sea of love that was his family.

The noise coming from them, laughter, gasping, good-natured argument, the teasing and the guffawing, the whispering and intellectual discourse, the squeals of delight and the sounds of young children's joy, all one glorious symphony of life that had started long ago on the other side of Time in a windy meadow beneath a willow tree.

Ashe's attention was drawn to the door.

The girl who had lain with him beneath that tree in the meadow, whom he had seen in the moonlight of just such a night as this, was watching him, smiling as she had on the other side of Time.

"Well, are you coming, Papa?" she asked.

Marigrace, Elienne's youngest grandchild, reached up to him, her cheeks rosy with excitement. Ashe scooped her up, feeling the age of his joints, and rushed forward through the sea of laughing children and adults, toward the door.

"Light the way!" he shouted.

Lanterns in hands followed him out the door, winking like fireflies in the dark of the compound.

*L*ater they stood together, the Lord and Lady Cymrian, on the doorstep of the main residence, watching the lights wink out in the family quarters, six individual houses that sheltered the families of each of their children.

Rhapsody looked up at him and smiled.

"Beautiful work with the wedding ceremony this afternoon, m'lord," she said, leaning her head on his shoulder. "Laurelyn and Syril are well begun. The perfect day."

Ashe kissed her brow. "Indeed. The music was lovely."

"Thank you. I think I will go get ready for bed, unless you need my assistance with anything."

"No, indeed. I have a few small items that need a moment's attention, and then I will be up forthwith."

"Good. See you upstairs." Rhapsody kissed him slowly, then made her way up the winding staircase and across the open balcony beyond it, disappearing around the corner to the hallway that led to their bedchamber.

The Lord Cymrian sighed happily, then turned and headed for his suite of offices.

A knock sounded on the door.

Ashe turned in surprise. A moment later, the chamberlain appeared from the side hallway in his robe, nightcap, and slippers.

"Pardon, m'lord," he said as he hurried past. "I had anticipated the keep to be closed for the evening."

"As had I," Ashe said.

"The guards are at their stations—I'm surprised they did not turn the visitor away."

Another knock thundered against the door.

The chamberlain doubled his gait.

"Some decorum, please," he said as he pulled the inner door open. "This disturbance is most unseemly."

Reynard ap Hydrion appeared in the doorway. He smelled as if he had been celebrating.

"Is the Lord Cymrian to bed?"

"He is not," Ashe said from the center of the antechamber, "but he is severely displeased at the interruption. What are you doing here? What do you want at this hour of the night, Reynard, that could not wait until morning?"

The general grinned, then turned and signaled out the door. He stepped inside the antechamber and opened the door as wide as it could swing, then opened the double of it equally wide.

A cadre of men, several of them bloodied and torn, came laden through the opening, dragging an enormous bundle wrapped in ragged burlap and a smaller, though still substantial one, stained dark, in the arms of one of the broader soldiers.

Ashe's dragon sense, lulled into abeyance with happiness, roared to life in panic.

"What—what is this?" he asked, shaking suddenly with a violence he could not control.

Primed with ale and excitement, the bloodied men tore back the burlap coverings proudly, revealing a gigantic, headless corpse, slashed open from the throat to the genitals, its limbs broken, its viscera gone.

"Dear God," the chamberlain whispered at the side of the Lord Cymrian.

"A gift, m'lord," said Reynard proudly, approaching Ashe with his hands open in blessing. He signaled to the broad soldier bearing the second bundle, who came before the trembling lord and tore off the burlap.

Ashe fought back the vomit that rose into his throat at the sight of Grunthor's head.

The neck of the battered corpse had been severed with an ax, the dragon noted, clearly after death. From the corpse's eyes and cheeks crossbow bolts jutted, some of them jammed in for effect, and a stripe of graying, horse-like hair and beard had been roughly shaved off, most likely as counted coup, leaving a swath from the bloody brow to the base of the neck where the spine had been separated. The stench from multiple sources of urine and feces was overwhelming.

Even as mutilated as it was, there was a nobility to the severed head, he thought sickly. The cheeks hung frozen in what almost seemed like a jolly expression in spite of the bruises that darkened them from the color they would have resolved into had they been allowed to heal.

Even the gaping mouth, which the dragon noted to be dripping human semen, seemed victorious instead of shamed.

The soldier seized the remaining hair atop the head and lifted it up for the horrified Lord Cymrian to better see.

"Your menace, m'lord," Reynard said proudly. "Menacing no longer."

His grin resolved to a look of shock an instant later as the air of the vast anteroom went suddenly dry to the point of igniting.

Gwydion ap Llauron turned in rage to him and belted him directly in the face, breaking his nose and sending him sprawling across the floor of the antechamber.

"You—you *imbecile*," the Lord Cymrian hissed, the tones of the dragon boiling in his voice. "What have you done? *What have you done?*"

The smiles faded immediately from the faces of the soldiers. They stared at their bleeding commander, who was all but drowning in his own blood.

Arnald Goodeve alone was staring at Ashe.

"My lord, this—this is the Bolg scourge, the Sergeant-Major," he said nervously.

From the open balcony above, a sound issued forth.

It was half gasp, half wail, a riveting noise of despair that rattled the bones of everyone in the anteroom.

The soldiers, the chamberlain, and the lord looked up to see the Lady Cymrian, attired in her dressing gown, standing on the balcony, her face colorless.

All sound left the massive room.

For a moment, Ashe thought he felt the world lurch to a frightening stop. *This isn't really happening,* he thought as his wife, shaking violently, descended the stairs, her eyes locked on the gruesome body pieces littering the floor of the antechamber.

The end of the world was in her eyes.

"Aria," he whispered, but she didn't appear to hear, just came down, step by step, into the thundering silence of the round room.

The men in the antechamber had no choice but to hold utterly still as she crossed to the soldier holding Grunthor's head, where she came to a shuddering halt. She looked into the Sergeant's bolt-filled eyes, the expression in her own all but empty.

"Put him down," she ordered tonelessly.

Shaking, the man obeyed, setting the severed head onto its wrapping.

Ashe's voice returned in a slew of obscene draconic curses.

"Who ordered this atrocity?" he demanded.

The soldiers exchanged a glance.

"You—you did, m'lord," Reynard whispered through his blood.

The Lady Cymrian, whose eyes were locked on the Sergeant's head, turned slowly and looked at her husband, whose florid face went suddenly pale.

"I—I did no such—"

"With respect, m'lord, you—said he was a menace that needed an—an end put to it," Goodeve stammered.

Rhapsody opened her mouth and began to take slow, measured breaths through it. She turned back to the body of her beloved friend.

"I didn't—I didn't mean—" Ashe choked.

"Silence," Rhapsody said, the tone of the Namer in her voice. "Let there be silence in this place."

The room, and the men in it, obeyed.

Slowly the Lady Cymrian knelt before Grunthor's head. She continued to breathe with her mouth open, ragged, painful breaths that came from the very bottom of her lungs. Finally, after an uncomfortably long while, she spoke.

"Chamberlain," she said softly without breaking her gaze away, "summon the quartermaster. Have him provision and tack his largest, smoothest-riding wagon with a team of six fast dray horses and many soft blankets, and bring it to the door. Then, while he does this, go to the family quarters, knock quietly, and ask each of my six children to come here. Tell them to bring none else, no spouse, no child. When you return, bring the guards and some of the blankets with you."

Still in shock, the chamberlain bowed and hurried off.

Ashe stepped forward until he was beside her. He knelt, and extended a shaking hand toward the head.

Rhapsody did not move, but her eyes flashed to the color of burning grass.

"Do not touch him."

Ashe's arm dropped heavily to his side.

They continued to kneel, side by side, in silence, Rhapsody's eyes locked on Grunthor's remains, Ashe's on Rhapsody, until the keep door opened silently. The chamberlain peered in, then stepped respectfully aside as Meridion, followed by Allegra, Elienne, Stephen, Joseph, and Laurelyn, came slowly into the keep in the order of their birth, each of them aghast, emitting sounds of dismay and horror.

A coterie of guards came to a halt behind them.

"Look well upon him," Rhapsody said flatly. "See what has been done to him."

"They will hang for this," Ashe said, his voice more growl than words.

For the first time since beholding the atrocity, his wife turned and looked at him.

"For the abuse and disrespect of his body after death, perhaps they should," she said coldly. "Who will hang for giving the order?"

The sounds of shock dissolved into silence as the daughters joined hands, their brothers' arms around each of them.

Rhapsody's gaze returned to what remained of Grunthor.

"My beloved children," she said quietly, "I beg your aid. Will you help me carry your godfather, in reverence and honor, to the wagon? No other hand in this keep save that of the chamberlain is worthy to do so."

"Aye, Mimen," Meridion whispered, followed a moment later by the same response from each of his siblings.

Rhapsody rose and turned to the chamberlain. "Bring me the blankets, please." The trembling man hurried forward, bowed, and placed the large rectangles of soft cloth in her arms.

Silently the children took the cloth and wrapped Grunthor's body under the eyes of the murderers and their father, avoiding their gaze. Rhapsody alone wrapped the severed head, lovingly swathing it in the blankets. When it was covered, she lifted it from the floor and cradled it in her arms as the children finished their abhorrent task. Then she went to the door without looking back.

Stephen nodded.

The siblings lifted the enormous body in its drapes and carried it, with the cadence and stepping of a military funeral procession, out through the doorway and into the night.

By the time they had borne him to the wagon, most of Grunthor's godchildren were in silent tears. Only Allegra maintained a steady countenance, her jaw clenched tightly.

They loaded him carefully into the wagon. Once the body was in the wagon bed, and covered with more soft blankets, Stephen came to his mother and took the wrapped head from her, smiling disarmingly as he pried it gently from her hands. The other children surrounded Rhapsody as she took them into her arms, kissed them, and whispered words of love to each of them, leaving Laurelyn until last.

"I beg your forgiveness for disrupting your wedding night, *y pippin*," she said distantly, as if she were fighting to remain in control. "I decided that you deserved to see your godfather one last time. I apologize if I've erred."

"Thank you for making the right choice, Mimen," Laurelyn said, fighting back tears.

"Go back to your families," Rhapsody said to her children. "Take care of them first. Kiss them for me. My love remains with you all."

"Travel well, Mimen," Meridion said. "Our love goes with you."

He turned and gave Laurelyn his arm, while Stephen walked with Allegra and Joseph escorted Elienne, making their way back to the now-dark guesthouses across the glade.

Ashe watched in despair as his children returned to their own families. He turned away to see Rhapsody as she climbed onto the wagon board and took the reins in hand.

"Aria—"

Rhapsody turned to him. Her eyes gleamed furiously in the dark.

"Do not follow me," she said. "This was a Grievous Blow."

The words seemed to slap him across the face.

Ashe fell back.

Rhapsody clicked to the horses and snapped the reins.

The wagon lurched off into the night.

She did not look back.

14

THE KREVENSFIELD PLAIN

She drove blindly, numbly, following the wind.

All around her, the ground shook madly, the Earth itself responding to the body of its child in the wagon. The wind screamed in reply, whipping violently in the darkness through which she was traveling.

Rhapsody kept to the forest road which led her, through the sunrise and the passage of the day, into the eastern lands, out of the forest and finally onto the Krevensfield Plain, the great open expanse of pasturelands that stretched the breadth of the continent.

She took the trans-Orlandan thoroughfare, the ancient roadway built almost three thousand years before by her husband's grandfather in the days when hope and innovation still ruled. She was still shaking when the sun came up, trembling from loss and the knowledge that nothing would ever be right again in her world.

She only stopped long enough to water and rest the horses, during which time she paced around the front of the wagon, afraid now to be too close to the bed for fear the dam would burst, and she would become unable to move for weeping.

Finally, when the day had all but passed, she found herself in the province of Bethany, the capital of Roland, the area that had been the central seat of the Alliance in the days before she and Ashe had taken on the mantles of the lord- and ladyships. Soon the empty thoroughfare would become full, she knew, with the traffic of merchants and pilgrims, of traders bringing their goods to market in the other cities and provinces the ancient roadway connected.

She slowed her pace, feeling innately the gratitude of the horse team, until the sun set behind her, coloring the sky before her in the hues of mourning. Finally, when the light had left the clouds, she brought the wagon and the horses to a walking pace, then to a stop when the wind picked up with the coming of night.

She sat on the wagon board, alone beneath the emerging stars, in the darkness, waiting for the breeze to blast through.

And finally she allowed the grief to come.

The tattletale wind whispered past her.

"Achmed," Rhapsody whispered back into it.

The name caught in her throat—the name of the only person in the world who would be more damaged by the loss of the man in the wagon than she was.

"Achmed," she said aloud again, trying to catch an updraft. "Achmed the Snake!"

Her words seemed to fall heavily to the grassy ground beside the cobbled roadway.

"Fornication," she muttered. She put the reins down on the wagon board and climbed down into the highgrass of the wide-open meadow. She spun around, trying to find the source of the wind.

"Achmed!" she shouted, letting her voice swell into the air; the wind seemed to catch the edge of it and lift it high.

Nothing came in the way of an answer.

The burgeoning grief that she had fought down in front of her children and the soldiers was rising again, like lava from a spitting volcano. Rhapsody swallowed, trying to keep it in check, but it overwhelmed her, bringing tears and fury and a need for release.

"Achmed!" she screamed into the wind as the water in her eyes burst forth, wetting her cheeks with hot rage and pain. "Achmed! Achmed!"

She let the wind, sturdy now, wrap around her, catching her howl and spinning it eastward.

"Achmed!" she moaned, sobbing now. "Achmed! *Achmed*—"

"Peace; I am right behind you."

The familiar sandy voice spoke as if from the wind itself.

Rhapsody spun and threw herself into his arms, weeping as though her heart would break if she withheld the tears.

The Bolg king pulled her close and allowed his cloak to whip around her in the wind, seeking to shelter and warm her. The elemental fire that burned constantly in her soul had diminished considerably; her hands were chilled to ice when he took them in his own.

"I can't find his heartbeat on the wind," he said quietly into her ear. "Is he dead?"

Rhapsody could only bring herself to nod, wracked by sobbing.

The Bolg king took off one of his gloves and let his veined hand come to rest, shaking, on her flying hair, battered around her by the increasing wind.

"In the wagon?"

She nodded again against his neck.

"What happened?"

Rhapsody opened her mouth to speak, but instead a sound emerged that made the nerve endings in Achmed's skin come alight with pain.

"Shhhh," he said, not unkindly, but with more command in his tone than had been in it the moment before. "All right. Cry, if you insist. Get it over with, but do it by yourself." He loosed her gently and made his way to the back of the wagon where the body lay.

Rhapsody wrapped her arms around herself in the brisk breeze, her tears slowing. She had come out into the night in her dressing gown, and only now had come to realize it. She thought she could hear Achmed's intake of breath when he beheld their friend, but there was no further comment or sound.

From in front of the wagon she could hear the gate of the bed being pulled up again. She turned and waited as the Bolg king returned.

Fire as bright as that at the heart of the Earth was burning in his eyes.

"Who?" he demanded as he came to her again.

"A horrific misunderstanding," she stammered.

"*Who?*" The word seethed from his mouth.

"Soldiers of the Alliance," she whispered. "They misinterpreted something Ashe said."

The Bolg king stared down at her in the dark, his eyes boring through her soul.

He said nothing.

Rhapsody's eyes overflowed again, the tears spilling down the sides of her cheeks.

Finally he turned away and climbed onto the wagon.

"You will need to choose a side now, Rhapsody," he said softly. "The middle ground has just vanished."

"He's my husband," she whispered again. "The father of my children. They will stand with him."

"Grunthor was your friend," Achmed said, louder now. "One of the Three. It appears he was ambushed; he has only defensive wounds. His bandolier is full—he never had the chance to draw a single weapon. I imagine it was a grotesquely unfair fight, though he probably took a good number of them with him."

His eyes narrowed and the fire in them gleamed even brighter with building rage. "You know what they did to him? You know *everything* that they did to him? Do you, Rhapsody? *Do you*?" Rhapsody closed her eyes and nodded, tears racing down her cheeks. "Semen is dripping from his mouth and his fundament. Your abandonment of him now is sensible and would certainly not be the biggest betrayal he suffered after death. Go home if you want. Go back to your children. Take one of the horses. I will travel by land to give you a fighting chance to ensconce in Highmeadow or any fortress of your choosing prior to the beginning of the war."

Her green eyes met his mismatched ones staring down at her from the wagon board as if sighting down a crossbow or his self-designed weapon, the cwellan.

"Well? Are you going home?"

She swallowed, her tears drying in the wind.

"Yes," she said. "The first home I knew on this continent. Take me to Ylorc. I need to bury my friend. I need to sing his dirge. I need to mourn with the other one of the Three. You are the only person in the world I want to be with right now."

In spite of the agony in his eyes, a small smile took up residence on his face.

Achmed put his glove back on. Then he reached a hand down to her.

She took it as he lifted her onto the wagon board.

They made their way grimly back to the Manteids, the mountains known as the Teeth, at the far eastern edge of the continent.

This time, as the wagon traveled into the darkness, she turned around and looked back.

But only for a moment.

Then she turned around again and stared east, lost in consuming grief.

15

HIGHMEADOW

*W*hen the wagon had departed and was swallowed up in the darkness, Ashe sank to his knees on the ground of the courtyard.

The dragon in his blood, long the hated undercurrent of insistent commentary in his brain, was preternaturally silent.

If it had been whispering to his brain, it was unlikely he would have heard it anyway.

Meridion, the last child in the fortress who had no spouse or progeny to care for, stood by him.

"Father," he said quietly. "You have to go after her."

Ashe's head remained bowed.

"You know the Bolg will not be contained or satisfied unless there is an apology, some sort of diplomatic settlement."

"They will not be contained by those things either, Meridion."

"If you do nothing, if you wait, war will most certainly erupt, a war of far greater brutality and destruction than the continent has ever seen in its history," Meridion pressed. "It will be mass slaughter, undoing a thousand years of the thwarting of cannibalism. And Mimen will be on the other side this time—it's Gwylliam and Anwyn all over again. I see no other choice."

Ashe lapsed back into silence, his head still bowed.

"Father?"

"I am willing to go, Meridion, but only to seek your mother's forgiveness. Achmed will never give it to me; I do not blame him for that."

"We can hope for the best," Meridion said. "She always did."

After a few moments, shadows emerged in the lanternlight.

One by one, his children were gathering again.

The first to approach him was Stephen, one of his high-ranking military commanders.

"I've had the guards take the prisoners to the stockade, Father," he said.

"And I've dismissed the chamberlain and the quartermaster, though they stand ready to be recalled at a moment's notice," added Joseph, his younger brother.

Ashe said nothing.

The brothers exchanged a glance, then turned in the direction of their youngest sister, Laurelyn the Invoker, who circled around in front of their father and crouched down before him.

"I must return to the Circle forthwith, Father," she said, quietly but calmly. "War is likely coming to the Great Forest, and it is my responsibility to prepare for it."

"We are readying to evacuate the Grands and the Greats to Tyrian," Elienne added. "Achmed will never attack Mother's realm, no matter how angry he is."

"She would never allow that," Joseph agreed.

"I will remain here with you to defend Highmeadow and the forest of Navarne, Father," said Allegra, an even higher military commander than Stephen. "I've sent a messenger to the summoning stations. Reinforcement brigades will be here by morning."

Silence returned.

Ashe remained on his knees for a long moment. Then he exhaled and dropped his head.

He rose slowly, feeling every one of his years.

"I will go to her," he said.

The five youngest siblings looked at one another.

"In her last words to you, she commanded otherwise, Father," Joseph said.

"It will be further provocation," Stephen cautioned. "I'm not certain how this situation could be made more grave, but if it can be, it will be if you do so."

"I have never heard her speak so commandingly to you, Father," Elienne added. "I do not think you wish to cross her further."

Ashe sighed. "What would you have me do then, children? It is not for me, but for the continent that I do this. Achmed has an army of a half million monstrous men, plus cavalry and special forces better armed and equipped than any in the Alliance, including that of Roland. Grunthor sired half of them. Should the continent die because I am a fool?"

He looked up finally to see them exchanging glances, all of them sad.

"I will go on my knees to them both, once they have had the chance to bury and mourn him initially. I will beg her forgiveness, and his, and will surrender whatever it will take to cool his rage—my office, my sword, my body, or even my life. I want our legacy as the husband and wife who reluctantly took up the mantle of leadership in order to reunite the Cymrian Empire to be a continued peace and stability, not a reenactment of Gwylliam and Anwyn. There are many horrific possibilities I have contemplated over the centuries, but that one is beyond imagination."

His children looked at one another, then back at him.

The expressions in their eyes acknowledged acceptance.

"I will go with you, Father," Meridion said. "Perhaps my training as a Namer can help in the negotiation."

"It will be an abject apology and capitulation, a surrender, not a negotiation, Meridion. But if you want to come with me, I would be grateful for your company—as long as you keep your distance from Achmed. I don't wish to see you get caught in the middle."

Laurelyn, the oaken staff of her office in hand, came to him and tenderly kissed his cheek.

"Give her a few days," she advised. "I know you do not want to tarry long, but, as you said, they need time to mourn and to grieve." She looked around at her siblings. "As do we all. My love remains with you."

Ashe took her face in his hands and kissed her forehead.

"You are so like her," he whispered. "I love you, little bird. My love goes with you."

The Invoker smiled, then bade her siblings farewell and headed west.

Later the next afternoon, Stephen had just finished bidding his wife, children, and grandchildren goodbye when Ashe came into the courtyard to do the same.

A caravan of carriages and riders accompanied by four cavalry regiments was assembling somberly, in relative silence. Only the youngest of the Greats were buzzing with excitement at the sight of all the horses and soldiers gathering in the great courtyard of Highmeadow. Ashe kissed each of them as they ran to him, and directed them back to their parents.

"Elienne and Joseph will remain in Tyrian with the family for the moment," Stephen said, ruffling the hair of three of his great-nephews as they ran past, back to their parents in the caravan. "I will ride rear of the caravan, and return as soon as they have successfully arrived, to aid Allegra with the defense of Highmeadow."

Ashe smiled slightly.

"Thank you, my son, but if I am successful, these precautions will have been undertaken for nothing."

Stephen shrugged. "That's why they're called *pre*cautions," he said lightly, quoting one of his father's many teachings. "Undertaken *before* the actual need to worry." His light words took on a heaviness. "I still am not certain that this wouldn't be best undertaken in writing and by messenger, Father. Now that Grunthor is gone, Achmed will have no reason to stay his hand against you. The law of one-for-one is strong among the Bolg."

"Actually, the Bolg live by the law of one-thousand-for-one," Ashe said. "Whatever revenge he might exact upon me is deserved, remember that. And if the alternative is that I end up dying of old age on this side of a divided continent, without your mother, it would have been a blessing to be torn asunder and eaten alive, or whatever punishment he condemns me to."

"If that was supposed to make me feel better, it failed miserably."

Ashe smiled brokenly as Allegra joined them, wearing her armor and leading Stephen's mount to him.

"It was only meant to tell you the truth," he said, returning his eldest daughter's salute. "You are a good man, Stephen, the very image of the man you were named for, my dearest friend and brother, Stephen Navarne. I am grateful to God, the One, the All, that you have his qualities rather than those of his idiot friend. Travel well."

"Do not gainsay my father," Stephen said, mounting up. "He is the best man I have ever known, and I will defend his honor with my life— at the cost of that of anyone who insults him—so you are generating a paradox I would rather not bring into existence. My love remains with you, Father."

"Mine goes with you, Champ."

Stephen's eyes glistened at his father's use of his childhood nickname. He raised his hand and clicked to his horse.

Ashe and Allegra watched him ride off to join the caravan, his red-gold hair that matched both of theirs glowing in the patchy light of the afternoon sun.

"The redheads will hold Highmeadow," Allegra mused once Stephen was out of sight. "It figures."

Ashe chuckled in spite of the despair that was bagging the loose skin around his eyes. He looked at his eldest daughter, the strongest and most martial of the three women, and smiled fondly.

"On the night I asked your mother for her hand, deep in the grotto of Elysian, she told me her own mother's name had been Allegra," he said. "When I said I thought that it was beautiful, she asked, 'It would be a good name for a daughter, wouldn't it?' I don't believe I had ever been happier than I was at that moment—until you arrived and we named you thus."

Allegra, a woman of few and always carefully considered words, smiled slightly but said nothing.

"I am deeply sorry for having put you in this position, my Heart-song," he said, calling her by the appellation he had whispered to her upon her birth. "I still am hoping to awaken from this nightmare and discover that this is all but a dream."

"Sadly, we are awake, Father," Allegra said regretfully. "But we will be prepared, at least."

She squeezed his hand and returned to her duties.

16

When night fell, while Meridion was working with the quarter-master, readying the riding and dray horses for their journey to the Bolg-lands, Ashe made his way to the stockade. He entered through the front gate after saluting the guards, then through the front entrance, where even more guards saluted him stonily. *Whether they know of what happened or not, they are still stoic,* he thought as he returned the salute and entered the building. *Good. They'll need that.*

He passed easily through all the remaining layers of guards until he came to the cells in which the four commanders of the armies of the Alliance were imprisoned. He stopped in front of Reynard's cell, where the general was pacing back and forth, stanching his bloody nose, and crossed his arms.

Reynard stopped short and turned toward the Lord Cymrian.

"M'lord—"

"Don't," said Ashe unpleasantly. "How dare you, you verminous piece of filth? You thought you could murder one of the Three and blame it on the misunderstanding of a comment made in annoyance?"

"M'lord, I thought you wanted—"

"Silence!" The multiple tones of soprano, alto, tenor, and bass, the hallmark of the dragon's voice, rattled the bars of the cell.

Reynard stepped back in terror.

"You are a bloody *general*, Reynard. Perhaps a private could claim he or she didn't understand, but a general always seeks clarification of intent if he is not absolutely certain of what he is commanded to do. You pathetic prick." He leaned closer, his hands gripping the bars.

"You will be facing military justice, rather than my own, Reynard," he said softly, his tone deadly. "For this you should be profoundly grateful. Are you, Reynard? Are you and your cohorts grateful?"

The men in the cells looked askance at one another.

Ashe slammed his hands on the cell bars, sending shock waves of sound through the echoing halls.

"Are you?"

A terrified chorus of *yes, m'lord* rang out.

"Well, that's good, at least." The vertical pupils in the Lord Cymrian's searing blue eyes expanded in the dim light of the cellblock. "I have a question, Reynard, for you and you other men. Come closer, so that I can see the answer in your eyes, and be certain that you are telling me the truth. Come closer."

Reynard began backing away. "M'lord—"

"I said come closer!" Ashe shrieked. The multiple tones of the wyrm caused the metal of the bars to ring discordantly.

Shaking, Reynard obeyed.

Ashe pressed his face up to the bars. "Sickening as it is for me to have something in common with you gentlemen, you will be pleased to know that, like you, I am about to face military justice also."

The commanders exchanged as much of a glance as they were able in their separate cells.

"So I now ask you a question, each of you, a question that I know that I, at least, can truthfully answer 'no' to. I wonder if any or all of you can do the same. Are you ready for the question, gentlemen? And please bear in mind that I probably already know the answer, being a dragon."

When silence answered him, he pounded on the cellblock doors again, making the hinges on the door of Reynard's cell squeal threateningly, as though they might break.

Yes, m'lord, came the hurried communal reply.

The Lord Cymrian's voice dropped to a whisper.

"Here it is," he said, his eyes gleaming with an angrier light. "The question to each of you is this—does any of the spunk dripping from the mouth of Grunthor's severed head belong to *you*, gentlemen? Or from any other orifice, for that matter?"

The four men went white. Three of their mouths dropped open as Goodeve lost his water, pissing himself.

"Well?" the Lord Cymrian demanded.

The men just stared in return.

Ashe's voice dropped to a deadly low. "I could have imagined, though I never contemplated it, that I might one day have to answer for actions like this perpetrated by ordinary soldiers or conscripts. But the thought that my squadron commanders and *generals,* for the love of God, the One, the All, would even entertain the thought of committing an atrocity against the supreme commander of an army that is part of the *very same Alliance* in which they serve has truly caught me by as much surprise as you gentlemen seem to be experiencing."

Goodeve and Mendel began to weep in terror.

"And here's the most inexplicable part, gentlemen—this completely constitutes a war crime—yet we have not had a true state of war declared in over a thousand years, a time long before any of you or your great-great-great-grandsires were born. So even the defense of the 'fog of war' will not hold." Ashe exhaled, then looked down at the floor for a long moment. When he raised his head, there was something colder, nastier in his eyes, but a smile had taken up residence on his lips.

"So here is what we have in common, gentlemen—and I'd like to think that it is the only thing we have in common: we will all be going together to face military justice for your crimes—you for the commission of them, and me as your commander and sovereign."

The soldiers looked at each other in confusion.

Ashe's smile widened. "We are all going to face *Firbolg* military justice. I am not entirely certain what that will entail, but since your actions destroyed what I valued most in the world, what I lived for, in fact, it hardly matters to me what the consequences might be."

Immediately the men began begging in concert, their pleas running into one another.

Ashe stepped back from the bars of Reynard's cell and held his hand up cautiously, as if in comfort.

"Now, now, gentlemen, do not be distressed. I have a hard time imagining that the Firbolg could visit *anything* upon us that is worse than what you did to Grunthor. And while he had the additional injury of shock at your violation of all things holy, you will at least know what you are being buggered *for.* The only real difference I think you can expect is that, while apparently you were shoving your cocks in the Sergeant's mouth after you had already cut his head off—because otherwise you would no longer have them, as he definitely would have bitten them off—I am certain that the Bolg will not allow that to happen with you. They will probably just rip out all your teeth first so as to ensure the safety of their own equipment. As for other orifices, well, I happen to know that the Bolg only consider that an option if the recipient is alive, so you should expect that experience to be repeated frequently, for as long as they can manage to keep you from dying of hemorrhaging or splitting apart. So get some sleep; we'll be taking a long wagon ride tomorrow."

He turned and started to leave the stockade, then stopped and held up one finger in the air, as if remembering something.

"Oh, I almost forgot. I want to thank you gentlemen for your assistance in helping me rid myself of a nickname I was given long ago by Anborn ap Gwylliam, my uncle, my father's brother, that I have never actually liked. It was he who chose to call me 'Lord Gwydion the Patient,' which I always have thought made me sound as if I am in a hospice. But now, gentlemen, now that your actions have truly ruined my life, I would say with certainty that patience is no longer a virtue that I can claim. Do, by all means, give me the opportunity in the course of our mutual journey to the Bolglands to show you what I mean, if you're up for the consequences. I haven't roasted anyone alive in a good long while. Have a pleasant evening."

He turned and left the stockade, whistling a grim tune that was devoid of any music.

17

ON THE ROAD APPROACHING YLORC,
EASTERN CONTINENT

Rhapsody spent as much of the nightmarish journey to the mountains as she was able curled up like a baby in the womb on the wagon board beside Achmed, covered with a soft blanket, trying to sleep, and failing routinely.

After the first two days the Bolg king apparently had deemed it wise to stop during the day and take shelter, allowing the horses rest and the entire contents of the wagon freedom from interaction with the rest of humanity that was traveling the roads and the Krevensfield Plain.

The Lady Cymrian had worked up the courage to climb into the wagon bed from behind the board, and, fighting down her gorge, used her fire lore to remove as much of the heat from the wrapped body parts as she could. The wind was cool at summer's end, but the sun beat down relentlessly, and she could not bear to imagine what was happening to Grunthor's corpse beneath the blankets.

"Burlap," she had muttered at one point to Achmed upon climbing back onto the board.

The Bolg king's brow furrowed. "What?"

"The bastards wrapped him in burlap, as if he were a potato or an onion, the fuckers."

"Even more reason to leave their garrisons and towns in smoking ruins," Achmed retorted darkly. "Are you set?"

They had spoken very little, almost not at all, as they traversed the breadth of the continent. Achmed's sallow skin was growing paler, she noticed, but his jaw was set and there was a sharp look in his eyes that was growing ever harsher as they traveled.

She understood how he felt.

The nausea that had filled her body from head to toe upon beholding her beloved friend's head, the eyes packed with crossbow bolts, the mouth and hair defiled, had only grown stronger with each day that passed. Her body was holding the grief, but her mind had somehow managed to numb itself to the point of disconnecting altogether. Any concept of what would happen beyond the next moment was unreachable.

She could summon no thought beyond her pain.

Achmed, in spite of no longer having the ability to sense the heartbeats of the continent, seemed to be able to predict the ebb and flow of people on the road, so their journey was accomplished with very little interaction with the rest of the continent's population. Little to no conversation took place between them; they passed as silently as it was possible for two furious souls driving a wagon carrying the defiled body of their beloved friend to pass.

After slightly more than a fortnight, they found themselves in sight of the Teeth just as the sun was setting.

The mountains had been wrapped in the magic of the Lightcatcher, the ancient instrumentality built into Gurgus Peak that channeled the vibrations of the light spectrum for so long, utilizing *Kurh-fa,* the green power of grass hiding, that at first it had appeared to Rhapsody as if the mountains had vanished into the overwhelming expanse of the Krevensfield Plain. She was sitting upright, staring around her, when a cavalcade of Bolg soldiers on horseback appeared as if from the air, shocking her further and causing her to tremble violently.

Achmed brought the wagon to a halt as the green haze faded and the mountainous realm she had known well for a thousand years appeared before her eyes.

The massive city of Canrif came into view, all of the doors and gateways and edifices carved into the stone of the mountains visible.

All across the wide mountain range Rhapsody saw guard posts and encampments of soldiers stretching for as far as she could discern.

The mounted guard that had just appeared signaled for permission to approach the wagon, and Achmed granted it.

"Perhaps you should step away for a moment, Rhapsody," he said, more direct order than suggestion, climbing down from the wagon board as the soldiers dismounted. He reached up and helped her to the ground, then spoke a few sharp Bolgish commands that set a guard group of hirsute soldiers in a circle around her.

Rhapsody stood, sick at heart and shivering in her dressing gown, as the remaining soldiers conferred with the king. Several of them returned to their horses, mounted up, and rode off in the direction of Ylorc while Achmed pulled the wagon gate down. The Lady Cymrian turned away, unable to watch.

But she could not block out the sounds.

In all the years she had been among them, Rhapsody had never known the Bolg to mourn aloud. But as they took in the sight of their beloved military leader's corpse, a wave of vocal grief that was unmistakable rolled through the assemblage, agitating them into a state of barely contained fury.

Then, to a one, they threw back their heads and loosed a roar of rage that would have made Grunthor proud.

"Summon the Archons here, and prepare great braziers around the perimeter of the Moot," Achmed instructed. "I need the first unit of the Keepers of the Dead to report here as well, and a catafalque built for his viewing. He shall lie in state as none before him, and all shall see what our enemies have done.

"In doing so, the reason for what we will do next will be unfailingly clear."

*W*ithin a single turn of the day, what Achmed commanded had been accomplished.

Gwylliam's great Moot, an ancient amphitheater built into the ground outside the breastworks and guardian towers of the Bolglands, used as a gathering place for the Cymrian Council, and the site of great tribulation and great diplomacy, had been outfitted as it had surely never been before.

All around the vast, deep circle of earth, known to the human geologists as a *cwm,* the enormous Bolg army stood guard, every stone rampart filled with soldiers at attention. Rhapsody, accustomed to the hundred thousand or so attendees at each Cymrian Council meeting every third year, had trouble believing her eyes at the sheer scope of demi-humanity filling the enormous amphitheater carved into the steppes leading up the mountain range.

Except for the occasional violent outburst of grief, often by one of Grunthor's descendants, the enormous crowd was silent, stunned. The Sergeant-Major had been more than an epic soldier to the Bolg; his astonishing life span and extraordinary leadership skills had rendered unto him the status of a demi-god. Rhapsody had always known this, but the sheer power of the grief at the loss of their demi-deity, second in respect and fear only to the king himself, battered against her like a violent rainstorm, or the edge winds of a tornado.

If she weren't so rent with anguish, she would have been terrified just to witness their gathering.

Grunthor's body lay in state, decked out in full military uniform with the "medals" of honor that Bolg cherished, the femurs, ulnas, and jaws of fallen enemies, his head sewn back on by the careful ministrations of the Keepers of the Dead. Achmed had refused to allow them to remove the bolts or to mask the bruises, however. He had assured Rhapsody that to hide the way the Sergeant-Major had died was itself a dishonor.

As a result, every one of the hundreds of thousands of Bolg that filed past him was enflamed at the sight of the atrocity that had been perpetrated on their beloved leader and countryman.

And, in the back of her fuzzy mind, Rhapsody tried to calculate what could be done to contain that wrath once he was committed to the Earth.

She had literally no concept of the answer short of the razing of the entire continent.

ℱrom the morning of the second day after their return to Ylorc through the night, then all the next day as well, the population of the Teeth filed past the catafalque. Children had come, each carrying a stone to add to the base of the elevated wall on which Grunthor's open coffin had been laid, so that by the time the night came on the second day it appeared that he was lying in state atop a mountain.

The vast ceremonial braziers roared with angry fire, lighted at sunset the first day and fed throughout the night. Rhapsody was certain that the residents in the nearest city to the Bolglands, Bethe Corbair, could see the glow and the cyclonic plumes of smoke rising in the distance, and were no doubt trembling as she was.

The first thought that pierced the numbness in her mind that had settled into her brain like mortar was that Ashe had most likely notified the cities of the Alliance by avian messenger of the threat of war brewing, so it was probable that their garrisons and outposts were alive with activity as much as the Bolg's were.

The thought caused her to step away from the Summoner's Rise of the Moot, the place from which she had long ago called the first Cymrian Council of the new age, and vomit. She had eaten almost nothing in the course of her journey in the wagon, and so found herself wracked with convulsions, producing nothing but bile.

The numbness returned a few moments later.

Finally, as the night came on the second day, the Archons, the elite council of leaders and elders of the kingdom, came forward to the catafalque, following the Bolg king. Achmed had arranged for Rhapsody to chant the name of silence from the Rise, a mighty task that left her throat raw, until at last the population of the Teeth was listening, still in the throes of a brewing rage.

Achmed nodded to her from the floor of the Moot.

The Lady Cymrian swallowed heavily, and began to sing the Sergeant-Major's dirge.

The first few lines, the Song of Passage that celebrated the Earth from which his race had come, was the standard death hymn sung at every funeral that she had ever overseen in Ylorc. Her throat, raw from sobbing and scorched in the aftermath of bile, produced wobbling notes with no sweetness to them, rasping, sour sounds that, ironically, seemed to soothe the Bolgish ears in attendance.

She sang of his victories, of his bravery, of his longevity, and his numerous progeny, which had always been a source of great pride to him.

She kept the song to those things that the enormous assemblage would find comfort in, avoiding any of the things that had made Grunthor special to her personally.

There would be time for that later, she knew.

The final lines of the dirge welcomed him into the Earth, and celebrated the strength his body would impart to it.

And then, with no finesse, the dirge ground to a halt.

Achmed exhaled and nodded his satisfaction to her, then addressed the roiling crowd below her, who hovered on the tiers of the Moot above him.

"Withdraw from the steppes to beyond the chasm, beyond the guardian mountains to the Blasted Heath and past it," he instructed, his voice betraying his exhaustion and the fury that had not been dimmed by it. "There is to be order; the Sergeant would have demanded no less. None shall take action until I command it. When we move, it will be as though the Teeth themselves have come to Roland."

A full-throated roar of understanding rocked the Moot and echoed off the mountains behind it to the east.

"Sharpen every blade, curry and saddle every horse, be prepared. When I return, you will be ready. Extinguish the braziers; when they are lit once more, it will be time to assemble."

The enormous assemblage tarried for a moment, waiting to see if there were any further instructions, then broke apart like a scrambling anthill dissolving from the slanted layers of the Moot and moved, as if the Earth itself were doing so, in great streaming lines, back into the kingdom of Ylorc.

The Bolg king signaled to the Archons, and together they approached the funeral bier. He glanced up at Rhapsody, a terrible frown on his face, and then to the far end of the Moot. She nodded and made her way toward the exit.

The Bolg, watching in silence, lined the pathway from the Moot across the steppes to the gates of the mountain kingdom as the Archons bore Gunthor's coffin back into the arms of the kingdom of Ylorc, the Firbolg king and the First Woman following behind.

Then they scattered, hurrying to their outposts and battlements.

18

DEEP WITHIN THE MOUNTAINS,
IN THE LORITORIUM

The Archons had been tasked with digging the grave within the Loritorium, the secret unfinished city deep underground within the mountains that Gwylliam the Visionary had begun more than two millennia before, meant to be a repository of elemental lore, books of great knowledge, and magical objects, found incomplete by the Three when they first came to Ylorc.

Sklvarch, Archon of Tunnels, had taken the lead with the project, providing diamond-edged shovels and picks to his fellows, with aid from the only Namer the Bolg had ever produced, Kandyrs, specially trained by Rhapsody. Kandyrs sang the incantations of Earth and Water, causing the ground to soften for the tools, and so the project that would have normally required many weeks of effort was accomplished in a day and half.

The site that Achmed had chosen for the grave was at the base of another catafalque, the altar of Living Stone on which the Sleeping Child lay in repose.

The Bolg king had the weary Archons set the coffin down outside the Loritorium and wait, resting, while he and Rhapsody went in. They traveled through the cavernous place, its high stone ceilings echoing the sound of their footfalls as they made their way through what had long ago been planned to be streets.

"Do you remember how he got the Earthchild here in the first place?" Rhapsody mused, still clad only in her soiled dressing gown which whispered around her as she walked.

Achmed smiled sadly and nodded. The battle that had waged beneath the ground with a massive demonic vine, tainted with the blood of a F'dor demon, had set the place the Child of Earth originally slept alight with rancid smoke and devouring flames. Grunthor, a child of Earth in a completely different way, had melded his body into hers, walking free of the flames and coming to this place, hollow and empty as it was. The Earthchild had stretched out on the very catafalque they were now approaching, where Grunthor had separated from her, stepping free of her, bringing her to safety and silence and warmth within the ruins of the unfinished Loritorium.

It was a silent, sacred place where each of the Three had stood guard in different ways, tending to her over the years into centuries into millennia, a stalwart vigil for one of the last Children of Earth, whose rib was sought by every F'dor still in existence in the air of the upworld, because if one of them could obtain it, that rib would serve as the key to open the Vault of the Underworld, setting the rest of their captive destructive race free on the world.

When the remaining two of the Three had climbed over the stony barricade Grunthor had built as a last line of defense for her, they paused atop it.

The Earthchild was there beyond it on her bier of stone, still asleep.

Achmed gave Rhapsody his hand to steady her in the descent from the enormous ledge of rock and led her to the catafalque, in front of which an enormous grave loomed.

The immense being, carved as she was from Living Stone and whose brown skin displayed lines and irregular stripes of vermilion and green, blue and purple, seemed healthy and well. Her eyes, closed in eternal slumber, were fringed with lashes that were green like grass at their tips but were showing signs of gold closer to her eyelids, evidence that the Earth was preparing for autumn. Her long, grassy hair was displaying the same colors.

Her cheeks were striped with trickling tears, leaving wet, muddy trails down the sides of her face to the catafalque beneath her.

Rhapsody, long ago invested by the Grandmother, the Child's last Dhracian guardian, as her *amelystik*, the female whose role was to tend to her, felt her throat tighten. She hurried to the Sleeping Child and ran her hand gently over the enormous statue's hair.

"Shhhh," she whispered. "Shhh, my dear, my child," she said in the language of the Dhracians. "I know. I know."

As always, the Child gave no sign of life or movement.

"We've brought him here to be with you," she said softly. "This is where he would want to sleep, to keep watch over you. Is that all right?"

She and Achmed watched carefully for a sign of an answer.

The trickle of tears slowly ceased.

Rhapsody kissed the Earthchild's forehead. "I understand," she said.

Achmed left her alone, caressing the Earthchild's hair, and returned after some time with the Archons, bearing the coffin in a funeral procession. They brought it to the grave and lowered it down, then knelt around it in final homage.

Making note of the Bolg king's dismissal, they hurried back over the barrier, out of the Loritorium, and up to the mountain tunnels again.

Achmed's elite council faded into the swelling mass of their rapidly moving countrymen, joining in the preparations for war.

Rhapsody and Achmed stood silent vigil for a while longer, observing the drying of the Sleeping Child's tears, until she seemed to be breathing easily again.

Then Rhapsody walked over and stood at the foot of Grunthor's grave, looking down at him, asleep in the arms of the Earth that was his mother.

Child of sand and open sky, she sang tremulously as once she had sung him through the fire at the heart of the Earth itself. *Son of the caves and lands of darkness, Bengard, Firbolg. The Sergeant-Major.* Her tears were flowing freely now, clogging her throat. *My trainer, my protector. The Lord of Deadly Weapons. The Ultimate Authority, to Be Obeyed at All Costs.*

Our brother. One of the Three. A faithful friend, strong and reliable as the Earth itself. Our beloved friend.

Then, before she broke into sobbing, she sang his true name, a series of whistling snarls followed by a clicking glottal stop.

Achmed's thin, strong hand encircled her arm at the elbow.

"He would have loved hearing that again," he said quietly. "And, after all this time, to know that you have *finally* learned to pronounce the Firbolg tongue sufficiently."

Rhapsody struggled to contain her tears. In her ear, she heard the Sergeant's voice as she had within the belly of the world, just outside the fire at its center, replying as he had long ago when she had sung his name to help him pass through to the other side.

That's it, miss. Oi feel positively a-tingle.

If there is any way that you can feel it, Grunthor, I hope you can feel my love, she thought.

They set to burying him in the rich, unpolluted ground of the Loritorium, taking their time. Grunthor had gone into the grave uncovered, without a shroud or other barrier between his body and the soil, as they both knew he would have wanted, so Achmed had Rhapsody step back at first while he shoveled dirt directly onto his body. Then he nodded, and she joined him in the task.

How long they worked was impossible to gauge beneath the ground, but they stopped occasionally to rest and to check on the Earthchild, who had returned to her slumber, seemingly content.

Finally, when the grave was filled in and patted down, Achmed wiped his brow with the back of his forearm and nodded his satisfaction. He leaned on his spade.

"Now that you're back in Ylorc, I assume you will be attending to your *amelystik* duties more regularly," he said. "You can visit with both of them at the same time; he would have liked that."

He cast a glance at Rhapsody, her white dressing gown sodden with dirt, her face paler than the fabric. He reached out and took her shovel.

"Sit down if you need to," he said. "You look awful."

She shook her head. "I need wine," she said. "It's the only thing I can think of that might dull the ache in my belly. Can we go back?"

Achmed smiled in spite of himself. "That will be interesting to see again," he said. "Getting drunk with you, on the rare occasions it occurred in the last millennium, was one of Grunthor's delights. You say the funniest things when you are inebriated. He used to repeat them frequently once you'd gone home."

"This was always my home, too."

Achmed nodded, putting his shovel aside. "So it is. Even more now."

He took her hand and led her toward the barrier.

"I want to be drunk," Rhapsody said wanly. "I want to be stinking, bloated, embarrassingly drunk, if it will make this pain go away. I want—"

"Shhh," Achmed commanded. He was looking behind her.

Rhapsody turned and looked over her shoulder.

Emerging from the earth, growing like a giant plant at an accelerated but leisurely speed, was an enormous obelisk of Living Stone, twisting like an awl as it grew.

The Lady Cymrian spun around in shock.

The ground itself was glowing red-orange, like the color of clay or steel in fire. The obelisk was bending and twisting as it rose, until it was almost the height of two men standing atop one another, as if it were being sculpted by the hands of the Earth itself.

Once it had reached its ultimate height, the clay began to depress in many areas, some parts of it sinking into long, deep lines, while other parts rose and fell in tiny, complex patterns, until it resolved into the very image of the man who slept beneath it, whole again, proud and tall, clothed in earthen representations of the armor he had always worn, the cloak that had perennially hung from this shoulders.

And then the molten ridge of clay along the back of the statue, in one final explosion, rose into the form of the massive bandolier of hilted weapons, jutting merrily up over his shoulders like the feathers of a resplendent peacock.

His face, without defilement or injury, smooth with clay, his eyes open wide, was grinning, while at the same time sporting a look in the earthen eyes that she had seen make Firbolg soldiers lose their water in terror.

Rhapsody brought her hands to her mouth, covering it.

In the statue's left hand was a clay representation of Lucy, the short sword he had used to teach her to fight long ago as they traveled through the Earth along the Root. In his right hand, a shield above it at the elbow, was Sal, the polearm he had nicknamed, short for *Salutations*. Taller even than Grunthor had been in life, it was a monstrous effigy, a monument to guardianship and military honor that could not be misread.

It stood at the base of the Sleeping Child's catafalque, between her and anything that would threaten her.

Rhapsody turned and buried her face in Achmed's chest.

They stood thus, silent for a long time. Finally the Bolg king patted her back, idly caressing her tangled hair.

"We need to get back," he said quietly, turning toward the tunnel. "I can feel the very mountains above us thundering with the preparations for war."

Rhapsody opened her mouth, but no words came out. Instead, she just exhaled and followed him over the barrier.

Please, she thought, her brain rattling with the words that had refused to come through her lips. *Please don't kill the rest of the world now, Achmed.*

19

THE CAULDRON

The campfires on the Heath were roaring excitedly when Achmed and Rhapsody returned to the Cauldron, Achmed's seat of power in the kingdom of Ylorc, just as the sun had signaled its descent for the night.

Throughout the kingdom, hammers rang out the sounds of smithing and bellows roared; horses were being groomed and outfitted in record efficiency, and celebratory shouts of glee rose in the air, the overture of battle to come.

Rhapsody was shaking at the sound of the buildup rattling through the corridors, so Achmed took her by the arm and led her to one of the vintners' closets where the reserve wines were kept. He grabbed three bottles, opening them all with the corkscrew in the closet, and headed for the corridors behind his quarters that led to the tunnels of what had once been an unfinished series of drains opening out onto the great chasm between the guardian mountains, where the Cauldron was, and the Blasted Heath, the meadow at the top of the world beyond it.

They had sat in these tunnels many times before, looking out on the mountains to the east, usually in times of defeat or devastation.

Now that what little comfort had been imparted by the edifying circumstances of Grunthor's interment had worn off with a return to the reality of his loss, it seemed an appropriate place to mourn, one of the only private places in a mountainous fortress gearing up for battle of titanic proportions.

They walked to the edge of the tunnel opening, seeing the Blasted Heath lit up in martial glory to the northwest, and sat down on the tunnel ground, just inside the opening.

They said nothing to each other, just watched the sky change color as the sun set on the other side of the mountains, quickly drinking two of the bottles of wine dry.

The wind roared through the chasm below them, accentuating the silence.

Finally, when the despair was too heavy to carry on her shoulders, Rhapsody leaned back against the rocky mountain wall.

"A thousand years ago, on the night we killed the first F'dor, the one that clung to Lanacan Orlando, do you remember that I asked you if there was a limit to what you would do for me?"

"Yes. And the answer now is the same as it was then—no."

She looked across the darkening heath. "I asked you if you would be willing to employ your professional skills to take my life if I needed you to."

"Yes."

"I'm sorry. I'm so sorry, Achmed. I was so lost and caught up in my own pain and fear that it never occurred to me what such a request might cost you."

The Bolg king's brow furrowed even more deeply than it had from the moment they had begun the funeral procession down into the chamber of the Sleeping Child.

"That didn't matter," he said. "Being as well acquainted as I am with death, knowing what it takes for someone to ask for it, I consider it an honor to serve in that purpose." He took a swig from the last bottle, then handed it to her.

She took it without looking at it. "Perhaps. But it was cowardly of me nonetheless. If I am to seek death before it claims me in its own time, I should do it by my own hand."

"*Now* this is costing me," the Bolg king said quietly. "I have just lost one of the only two friends I have had between two worlds. My skin burns, Rhapsody. I cannot begin to calculate the loss of Grunthor already. Please do not force me to contemplate any more than this; I am not equipped to do so."

Rhapsody's eyes cleared, and she looked at her friend for perhaps the first time that night, seeing the agony on his face. She took his hand, gnarled and marked by time and weapons use, but thin and sensitive with traces of nerve endings and exposed veins, and she felt that it was trembling. She raised it to her lips and kissed it softly. "I'm sorry," she said again.

Their eyes met, and silence took up its place between them.

"You're shivering," he noted finally. "Is it sorrow, or the cold?"

"Both," Rhapsody said, letting go of his hand and wrapping her arms around herself in the ragged remains of her dressing gown. "When I ordered the quartermaster to provision the wagon, he packed water and food, but I did not think to ask him for clothing in my size. The wind blows through what I have on, chilling me to the bone, even at summer's end."

"You must have clothing down in Elysian," Achmed said, stretching out his legs and leaning back against the rock wall. "I've never known its closets to be sporting less than two dozen gowns and other ridiculous froufrou, either before Anwyn destroyed it or after I rebuilt it for you."

"Yes, there is clothing down there, I suspect."

"If you want, I can accompany you to retrieve it," Achmed said after taking another swig from the last bottle. "It would not be wise for you to go alone among the Bolg preparing for war."

She shook her head. "Thank you, but I don't want to go down to Elysian," she said. "It's a place I completely associate with Ashe; it was very special to us. We fell in love there, married in secret there—Allegra was conceived there—"

"Stop," Achmed said sourly. "Unless you wish me to head right now, unprepared, into battle with your imbecilic husband, rather than being ready, do not tell me anything else about him. The very words make my head pound."

"Of course, I'm sorry."

The Bolg king leaned forward and stared at her, a mist of alcohol in his eyes. "I could never understand what you saw in him, Rhapsody. You never seemed the shallow type, able to be won by a handsome face or an athletic build with nothing but sawdust in its brain. What was it that made you allow him into your life and between your legs? His wealth, his family stature—his forked dragon tongue? His scale-covered dragon tarse? Hmm. Perhaps that explains it—"

"*Shut your hateful mouth,*" she snarled, rising from the stone floor.

"How dare you insult me like this, today, of all days? I left him, and my family, behind to bring Grunthor home to and with you. It has torn my heart from my chest; I cannot breathe, Achmed, I can't feel anything but sick. Do not torment me."

The stare became colder.

"I'm going to kill him," he said quietly, almost cruelly. "I am sure you are aware of this, yes? Because I don't want to discuss it when the time comes. You have allowed this interloper into our friendship, and into your cock-alley, and while I'm rather fond of the children he put inside you, I can't believe you were foolish enough to let him.

"You almost died giving birth to Meridion; I had to seal the blood draining from your womb with my blood lore or you surely would have followed Ashe's mother into the place in the Afterlife where foolish women who attempt to give birth to the children of dragons go. Why, Rhapsody? Were we not enough, Grunthor and I, and the Archons, the midwives, the Bolg children you coddled so disgustingly? Did you miss the company of your own races so much that you needed to leave us all behind and become his seed-catcher, his courtesan? Because *we had you first*. And you abandoned us to follow that—that idiot. That man who loved you enough to risk your life *six times*."

Rhapsody was shaking with rage and cold.

"I have but two things to say to you about this, Achmed, and listen well, because I will never discuss this with you again," she said, her voice heavy with her Namer's lore. "First, each time that man 'risked my life' so that we might have a child, it was at *my* request—*I* am the one who can hear a soul waiting to come through into this life from the realm beyond. There is nothing I have ever done, no contribution I have ever made to the world, not the training of the midwives, not the uniting of the Cymrians, not even my part in the killing of F'dor, nothing that can even *begin* to compare to what he and I have given the world in the lives of our children. *Nothing*.

"And second, though you think him to be an interloper, someone who found me in the new world and dragged me away from you and Grunthor and the Archons and the midwives, *I have known him longer than you*. I have told you this, obliquely, before, but you haven't paid attention. I knew him in the old world, if only for a night, because he was somehow able to be brought across Time to meet me. I don't know if it was all the wishes I had made for someone to come to take me away from my provincial farm village and its marriage lottery, or something more deliberate, but in either case, *I knew him in the old world*. We fell in love *in the old world*. Before Easton, before I met you in its alleys, before you kidnapped me and dragged me through the bowels of the Earth, *I knew him*. So stop tormenting me. I came back here with you, rather than stay with him. I don't know what else you want of me."

Just as her rant was ending, the signal sirens and alarm bells began to toll, beginning with those atop Grivven Post, the farthest western guard tower in the kingdom, to be picked up, moments later, in a rising wave flowing west to east.

They clanged urgently, interrupting the splendid noise of the leadup to war and turning it into a sour forewarning.

20

*B*efore she could look a second time, Achmed was gone.

"Wait!" she called as she hurried up the hallway behind him. "Please, wait for me, Achmed!"

The Bolg king paid her no heed, vanishing around the tunnel corner.

Rhapsody steeled herself and took off in as fast a run as she could manage, her speed something she had once been known for in the hallways and mountain passes of Ylorc.

She caught him meeting in the central confluence chamber with a cohort of Firbolg soldiers from the Eye clans, the spies who ascended the fanglike peaks of the Teeth to watch the surrounding mountain passes and the wide-open prairie of the steppes below and the Krevensfield Plain beyond. They were conferring in Bolgish, but she could still follow it well enough to catch the main thrust of their report.

Horseback—two Alliance—flag of truce—wagon—approaching from west—

Achmed ordered two horses to be made ready at the main gate, and an alert to be sent to Grivven Post, the farthest western outpost that towered above the breastworks, the underground tunnels in the plain leading up to Ylorc.

Then he turned to Rhapsody and sighted her down.

"Bring me the cwellan," he said to his aides, watching her intently.

Rhapsody inhaled deeply, and allowed her pain to settle in her gut. "Let's go," she said directly.

They rode together, followed by two mounted regiments, across the dark steppes toward the outpost. As they approached Grivven, Rhapsody turned and looked behind her.

An enormous squad of Bolg cavalry had formed and were following them, torches in hand. The commander was waiting at the westernmost part of the assembly. Achmed paused on horseback beside him.

"The order has not yet been given for the braziers to be lit," he said. "What are you doing here, Commander?"

The soldier was struggling to contain his visible wrath in the presence of the king. "We are ready to ride, sir."

"By whose command?" Achmed's question was not demanding, but rather wryly amused.

"The Sergeant's, sir."

"Hmm. He commands you even in death?"

"And ever will, sir."

The Bolg king nodded, pleased. "Very well. Light the braziers. Come, Rhapsody."

They were bustled into the tower built inside the mountain peak and hurried to the stairs, ascending as quickly as each individually could. Achmed took the steps two at a time and disappeared, despite Rhapsody's best effort to keep up with him, out the door that led to the giant cliff from which the reports had been sent.

A series of mounted spyglasses stood along the edge.

Rhapsody pushed her way to one and peered into it, as Achmed took up a taller one beside her.

At first all she could see was the night in the western part of the Krevensfield Plain. She kept watching, trying to see through the shadows cast by the thousands of torches planted about the inner circle of the peaks, and carried by soldiers gathering along the edge of the steppes, until finally she caught sight of four horses with riders atop two of them, pulling a wooden wagon behind them.

It was flying a flag of truce, and the standard of the Cymrian Alliance.

She gasped as she found the mechanism on the spyglass to adjust it, and sighted it on the riders.

Then she swore silently.

"As I suspected, it's your accursed husband," Achmed said, stepping away from the spyglass. "Call the captains of the regiments to me—we will send a welcoming committee."

"No," Rhapsody said, seizing his arm. "Meridion is with him."

Achmed's eyes narrowed. He turned back to the glass and looked through it again, swearing profanely after a moment.

"Where is the cwellan?" he demanded of his guards.

"On way, sir."

"Ring the ground below us with torchlight," Achmed instructed, "and form an alley of infantry between the tower and the riders. Let them come through soldiers on both sides. Then have the troops withdraw so that they are alone below. Train the crossbows on them both from a distance of one hundred yards, but have the archers forbear—I only want them for backup." He turned to Rhapsody, who stood beside him at the dark ledge, her arms wrapped tightly around her flapping dressing gown.

She was looking west, shaking with what appeared to be unsurpassed anger.

Her rage matched that of every other soul in the Bolglands, including his own.

Suddenly, atop every mountain in the range, and on the largest ledges and balconies in the edifice of Ylorc, wide braziers roared to life, making the night almost as bright as day, flames dancing and casting shadows across the steppes and the Krevensfield Plain.

The two riders approached down the alley of infantrymen, the wagon behind them driven by a nervous-looking human soldier in a breastplate, with an armed footman on the back.

They stopped at a distance of two hundred yards, approximately three hundred feet below the opening on which Rhapsody and Achmed stood.

Ashe was atop a gray gelding, wearing no armor and carrying no weapon save for Kirsdarke, the elemental sword of water, belted at his side. Meridion rode a black mare beside him, dressed also in traveling clothes, his chest protected by a padded vest, his cape flapping in the wind behind him.

They rode to the area at the base of Grivven Peak and drew their mounts to a halt.

$\mathcal{A}$she looked up to see that Rhapsody had stepped to the edge of the ledge on which she, Achmed, and a small coterie of Bolg soldiers stood. Achmed stood behind her, at her shoulder.

All around him the dragon could feel the static in the air, the palpable hatred of an entire populace, all of it aimed directly at him and his son.

The Bolglands are burgeoning, itching to ride down on the two of us, Meridion thought sickly.

Ashe looked up at his wife as once he had from within the Bowl of the Moot, at the first Cymrian Council, his heart in his eyes, but addressed Achmed.

"Permission to declare, Your Majesty, under the laws of peace to which we both are signatories."

The Bolg king exhaled but said nothing.

Ashe swallowed, maintaining his sight on his wife from within the shadows of the enormous circle of braziers behind him.

"The perpetrators of the unspeakable crime against the Sergeant-Major are chained, hand and foot, and locked in the wagon behind me," he said. "Here is the key."

He tossed the ring on which the key was tied a good distance ahead of him.

Achmed took several breaths, his eyes still locked on Ashe. Then he glanced down to his left at one of the guards on the ground near the horses, and nodded.

The Firbolg soldier ran hurriedly to where the key ring had landed and scooped it up, then ran back into line. A second Bolg, this one mounted, rode to the wagon and directed it to follow him, which it did until both were out of sight.

"Appalled as I am at the treachery, the unspeakable savagery of this crime, I take responsibility for the leaders of the army of the Alliance," Ashe continued.

"What are you doing here?" Rhapsody demanded angrily. "I told you not to follow me."

The Lord Cymrian swallowed again, nervously this time. "I have come to beg pardon and forgiveness of the Bolg king and the Lady Cymrian, and to prostrate myself at their feet in surrender. I have resigned as commander-in-chief of the armies of the Alliance—our daughter Allegra now holds that post. Direct, therefore, your rage at me, but, by your leave, Your Majesty, do not hold the continent responsible for the actions of rogue soldiers, just as Roland has done with past atrocities committed by errant members of the army of Ylorc."

The menacing anger radiating from Achmed was like the waves of heat from an inferno. Rhapsody looked down at her husband from the ledge, stepping even closer to the edge.

"You have endangered our son by bringing him here."

Meridion sat up taller on his mount. "I came of my own accord, Mimen."

"That was foolhardy."

"Gained. But in my profession, I am often called upon to tell the story of your famous belief in forgiveness," Meridion said, smiling slightly. "Are you not the one who, at the Council that named you Lady, told the broken Cymrian populace that 'we must forgive each other, we must forgive ourselves'?"

"Don't even address that, Rhapsody," Achmed warned her quietly from behind as a Bolg soldier came out onto the ledge from the tower, the king's cwellan in his hand. "I suggest you get Meridion out of the way. I am going to execute your husband now. The Bolg, and their king, demand it. I will not be swayed on this."

Rhapsody raised her head higher. She looked into the sky, the stars hidden intermittently by the plumes of smoke rising from the brazier fires. A calm, severe, queenly expression hardened on her face before Achmed's eyes.

"No," she said without a hint of emotion. "Allow me."

Then she turned away from Meridion to address Ashe.

"I told you not to follow me," she said again.

Ashe bowed humbly. "And as I have told you, I have come to beg forgiveness, to make amends."

"You wish to make amends?"

"I do."

Rhapsody nodded. "Very well. Gwydion ap Llauron, dismount and step away from the horse."

Ashe's brow furrowed, but he did as she commanded.

"Give your sword to our son."

The Lord Cymrian came to Meridion's mount, stripped off his sword belt, and obeyed.

Meridion's face lost its hopeful expression. He looked down at Kirsdarke in its sheath in his hands. "Father, I don't like where this is going. If we ride abreast—"

Ashe shook his head. "It's all right, son."

Rhapsody's voice rang down from the tower ledge again.

"Meridion, bring your father's sword and mount to me."

Ashe looked up to the ledge. Rhapsody stared down at him intently, her face solemn. She glanced at the sky again. Then her somber expression returned and she stared down at Ashe once more.

Ashe felt relief break over him like the splash of an ocean wave. He patted Meridion's leg.

"You may not believe this, my son, but at this moment, your mother and I love each other more than ever before."

From atop his horse, Meridion looked doubtful.

"I hope you're right. She looks fairly cold and angry to me."

"Go," Ashe said, smiling. "Go to her."

Meridion nudged his mare forward, and cantered to the base of Grivven Tower. One of the Bolg soldiers took the reins of both mounts from him, and nodded to the doorway that led into the tower in the mountain.

Meridion hurried inside and headed for the stairs.

"Tell them to stand back," Rhapsody said to Achmed.

Achmed smiled slightly. Then he spoke the words in Bolgish, and the soldiers withdrew quickly.

Tears came into Rhapsody's eyes.

"This will be the hardest thing I've ever had to do," she said shakily to Achmed, to the assembled army of Bolg, and to Ashe, who stared at her intently, his face shining, love in his eyes. "But it must be done."

She pointed her finger at Ashe's ear and spoke a single word.

Always.

Then, as her eyes overflowed and tears streamed down her face, she drew Daystar Clarion from its sheath with startling speed and pointed it at the sky in the direction of a star she knew well, Prylla, named for the legendary Windchild.

She spoke its name.

A crackle of lightning painted the sky, followed by the bright ring of a clarion call, a clear trumpet sound that blasted over the Krevensfield Plain and echoed off the Teeth, shaking the foundations of the mountains and of the buildings in the city of Bethe Corbair, seventy leagues away.

Finally, with a roar, a plume of starfire brighter than thirty suns descended, blasting the Lord Cymrian from the ground where he stood and dissolving him immediately into ashes in the air.

The blast ignited the grass of the field in a circle more than three hundred feet wide.

A moment later, darkness returned, leaving nothing in the place where Ashe had stood but the burning grass.

Rhapsody fell to her knees on the rocky ledge and bowed her head in grief just as Meridion appeared in the doorway.

He stared down at the ring of flames, dissipating already in the wind, then looked at Achmed, the man his mother had named as his guardian.

The end of the world was on his face.

21

"Mother," Meridion whispered. "What have you done?"

Achmed held out his hand to Rhapsody's son, cautioning him into silence.

He looked around at the Krevensfield Plain, where jagged rivers of soldiers on horseback and foot were moving as though in shock, stunned by the nearness of the massive strike of starfire. Then he turned and looked at the mountains behind him, where the braziers were roaring.

On the ground below them, in the ring of steppes at the feet of the Teeth, thousands more Bolg soldiers were gathering, bristling with anger and unspent violence.

The very mountains were beginning to shake with rage as the war drums began beating.

His heart, pounding in time with the furor a moment before, had stilled its fury as his eyes had beheld the column of flame descend, swallowing the Lord Cymrian in its maw.

Leaving himself to be the only Firbolg not screaming for the death and destruction of the Alliance all the way to the western seacoast.

His gaze, suddenly less blurred by rage, turned to Rhapsody, kneeling still, looking down on the plain below the tower ledge.

She was trembling in shock, her face and hands colorless, her golden hair whipping around her in the wind that rattled the shutters at the top of the tower.

Achmed looked to Meridion.

"Your mother, as always, spoke the truth, Meridion," he said quietly, his voice competing with the whine of the wind. "She did not have a choice. Had she not executed him, I would have, and with far more agony." He held up his cwellan for purposes of illustration. "I would have pushed his heart out his back and left it beating for as long as it could. His debt is still not paid, but there's little else in the way of recompense he can offer now."

He signaled to one of the remaining Bolg soldiers.

"Find Fraax, the Archon of the Lightcatcher, and tell him to fire it up," he said. The soldier nodded and ran off as the Bolg king crouched down in front of the Lady Cymrian, who was lost in grief.

"Rhapsody," he said gently, "meet me in Gurgus Peak. You need to help me make use of the indigo light spectrum, something I have not attempted before. The Night Caller element of the spectrum, the indigo light, may be the only weapon we have to quell the war before it takes down the continent. Do not tarry; the mountains are getting ready to move west."

Rhapsody did not seem to hear him.

Achmed waited for a moment, then stood and left the ledge, walking past the wide-eyed Meridion as he did.

Meridion stared at his departing uncle, then shifted his gaze back to his mother, who had lifted her head and was now gazing west at the ring of fire from the strike, diminishing now into embers and ash.

He came to her, shaking in rage.

"Mimen! What have you done? *What have you done?*"

Rhapsody turned to look at him, staring down at her. She opened her mouth several times, attempting to speak, but no sound came out.

"I—I can't believe you would *do* this!"

She struggled to speak again, finally able to force out a whisper.

"Meridion—"

"You've *killed* the Lord Cymrian—my father, your husband—your epic love." His anger flared as she rose to a stand, trembling. "How disgusting."

"Meridion, please—whatever you may believe, your father was the other half of my soul, and I would lay down my life in a heartbeat for him."

Meridion began to pace, running his hands through his sweaty hair, much the way his father used to. "But you would not forgive him?"

"I do," Rhapsody said, rising, her voice sounding as if she had swallowed shards of glass. "I do forgive him. I know you do not understand now, but one day you will."

"What is *wrong* with you?" he shouted in return. "You, my mother, the foundation of my very life, the teacher of my morals, my idol—you— you murderous *bitch*."

"Meridion, you don't understand—"

"You are bloody right about that!"

The sting of the words served as the equivalent of a slap across the face. Rhapsody stood a little straighter and stanched her tears, adopting a Namer's tone.

"Meridion ap Gwydion ap Llauron ap Gwylliam tuatha d'Anwynan o Serendair, hear my words," she said, strongly but calm. "I command you, in my last act as Lady Cymrian, to speak the following names and give them these instructions.

"Take your father's sword back to the exterior Altar of Water at the basilica of Abbat Mythlinis in Avonderre and leave it on the altar in its metal bindings. I bid you to attempt to lift Kirsdarke from the altar once you have delivered it there; it will either choose to come with you or it will not. I will bring Daystar Clarion to the Fire Basilica in Bethany in the same way; therefore, tell Joseph to undertake the same thing. If the swords refuse either one or both of you, it will be up to the swords them- selves to select new bearers. Then return to Highmeadow and speak the names of those who will either lead now, or transition to the new leader- ship. To Stephen, the crown of the lordship; to Allegra, the crown of the ladyship, until the council meets next year to choose the new sovereigns.

"Ask Elienne to go to Tomingorllo and see if the diadem of the Li- rin chooses her to wear it, and Laurelyn to offer her services to Achmed as the *amelystik* to the Earthchild. Herald that our reign is over, but say *nothing else*, I beg you—you do not know what really happened here." As the Namer's command came to an end, she began to sob again. "You are a Namer; you cannot afford to spread misinformation. Please, Meridion—"

"Who are you to tell me what to do?" he demanded.

"For the moment, until you speak the words I gave you, I am your sovereign. Thereafter I am only your mother."

Meridion's eyes were blazing with angry fire. "Nonesuch. My alle- giance to you ended in both cases when you killed the Lord Cymrian— my father. How could you *do* that?"

Rhapsody turned and pointed at the Teeth, where already units of soldiers were beginning to prepare for battle, milling about in agitation. "Look behind me, Meridion. Can you feel the bloodlust burgeoning?"

"Of course—"

"Did you think that it would be sated with something less? Did you imagine the surrender of Kirsdarke was going to spare the continent of this rage, the pain and despair at the murder and despoliation of Grunthor? Your *godfather*? Half a million soldiers and millions more Bolg citizens are roiling in blood fury. Even now Achmed is bringing on the night to cool that rage; elsewise there will be a retribution of death and destruction all the way to the sea."

"So to spare the continent you sacrificed my father's life? You, who stood with him through *everything* that both of you did over a thousand years of history? I thought Anwyn was evil; compared to you, she was holy."

Rhapsody was shaking violently now. "Meridion, please—"

"Enough! I will herald your words, the end of your reign, and speak the names of those who will replace you both. And then I will forget you, *Rhapsody;* I do not want your name in my mouth or your memory in my mind from this moment forward."

"Meridion—"

"You are dead to me." The words rang with a Namer's tone as well.

The Lady Cymrian froze. "I love you with everything that I am, Meridion."

Meridion stared at her, devastation evident in his eyes. "I believe that. I guess I just had a higher expectation of what you are. My fault, apparently."

He turned away from his heartbroken mother and made his way angrily to the staircase, descending as quickly as he could. He looked up when he made the first circular turn to see Rhapsody standing above him, watching him go.

He looked away and ran the rest of the way down.

The Lady Cymrian reached the doorway at the bottom of the tower just in time to watch her eldest son pull himself into the saddle of his mount and gallop away without looking back.

She ran after him, but had only made it to the circle of fire ash and devastated grass before he was all but out of sight.

She sank to the ground within the place where starfire had struck the Earth and wrapped her arms around her waist, unable to feel anything.

From the bristling air around her, she heard a voice, ragged and airy.

I will speak to him, Aria.

She did not even look up. "Leave me in peace."

I love you—God, I love you more than I ever imagined possible.

For a moment there was nothing but the sound of the wind. Then, after a long pause, the voice in the air spoke again, and it sounded tentative, nervous.

Do you still love me, Aria?

Her reply was so soft that only an entity hiding in the wind could hear it. "Always."

I'm so sorry.

"Leave me in peace," she repeated. "Please."

In the lack of an answer, it seemed to her that he had granted her request.

22

$\mathcal{T}$he great braziers were pulsing and roaring with angry life amid a host of dark shadows when Rhapsody finally managed to rise from the ground beneath Grivven Post and make her way back toward the Teeth, where Gurgus Peak hovered, the tallest of all the guardian mountains.

All around her, Bolg on foot and on horseback were rushing into formation, dragging wagons and giant ballistae into place, running past, cackling with the glee of rage. She had only walked a hundred paces when a Firbolg guard regiment took up positions around her, armed with barbed spears to keep any itinerant soldiers from crushing or injuring her in the dark, sent by the Bolg king on his way to the Lightcatcher.

She did not notice, lost as she was, her mind numb with grief.

The war toms were in full blast now, shaking the mountains with their violent cadences and echoing north and south through the stone. The noise of pending war was almost as brutal as that of war itself; though the arms and armor were yet to clash, the wood of wagons and the blasts of explosions were almost loud enough to make it seem as if the retribution for Grunthor's death had already begun.

She was led into the relative quiet of the inner tunnels of Ylorc, to the Cauldron, Achmed's seat of power, and through the Great Hall, where the ancient thrones of Gwylliam and Anwyn still stood, a horrifying reminder of marital strife leading to centuries of war, to the room beyond it, where the staircase and the funicular to the Lightcatcher stood. She ascended the staircase, still shaking violently, as the guard unit took up a defensive posture at the bottom of the steps.

Even from the hallway atop the staircase, Rhapsody could see that the room in which the instrumentality the Bolg king had called the Lightcatcher was ablaze with torchlight, shadows of patchy darkness pulsing from the enormity of it. Fraax, the Archon of the Lightcatcher, was lurking deep in the recesses of the room.

When she entered the cavernous tower room which housed the Lightcatcher, Achmed did not look up from calibrating the machine, but, sensing her heartbeat upon her arrival, motioned her closer. "Help me with this, will you?"

Rhapsody did not reply.

He turned after a moment, annoyed, to see her hovering near the outer edge of the circle of light in which the central table of the instrumentality stood, beneath the domed ceiling at the top of the mountain peak inset with a perfect circle of stained glass in the exact colors of the light spectrum. An enormous diamond was suspended above the table, glowing with undulating light absorbed from the sun through the interior clear circle in the center of the glass dome.

She was whiter than the diamond, trembling in the rags of what had been her dressing gown.

She was also smeared with the ashes of the circle in which she had called starfire down upon her husband, whose bodily remains were no doubt clinging to her now.

Irritated as he had been when she had not responded, Achmed took a breath and looked at her from behind his veils.

"Are you all right?"

Rhapsody said nothing.

Achmed extended his hand. "Come to me," he said as gently as he could. "Come. I need your help with this."

Slowly, the Lady Cymrian came into the circle of light, stepping over the circular track on which a tall metal wheel with a variety of openings in the center rested, waiting to be set into motion. The Bolg king waited until she was within reach, then let his hand encircle her upper arm in the attempt to still the violence of her shuddering.

"Remind me of the lore of the indigo part of the spectrum," he said, his voice as low and quiet as his nervousness would allow. "I don't recall the name for the note in the spectrum to which is it attuned—the fifth, is it not?"

"Sixth," Rhapsody whispered. "*Luasa-ela*. The note to which I am attuned, my Naming note."

"And what are the two powers of indigo called?"

Rhapsody swallowed silently.

Achmed's eyes darkened in annoyance. "This may be the only chance you have to spare Roland from the wrath of my army, Rhapsody," he said tersely. "In a reasonable world, your delay might be considered the cause for the war not being halted."

"Night Stayer, the sharp of the note," she said, her voice harsh and ragged. "Said to keep the night at bay. And Night Caller, or Summoner, the flat of it, said to bring it on."

"What do you know of its effect?"

"Nothing. It has never been tried before, or, if it has, there is no record of it in the lore."

Achmed nodded perfunctorily as he turned back to the instrumentality. "Then I would say it is risky to try to produce the sound element with the wheel," he said, nodding at the enormous metal caster balancing on its side on the circular track. "You are going to have to sing the note."

Rhapsody sighed dispiritedly. "Achmed—"

The Bolg king glared at her in fury. "Get *over* here," he snarled. "The cavalry is set to ride without orders, believing Grunthor is commanding them to attack. The infantry has so many soldiers aligned and ready to march that they would not even see me were I to interpose my body between the army and the continent to the west. I know you are in shock, that you are grieving, but if you cannot rise above that, at least long enough to help me make use of the only tool we have to quell this war, the blood of your Alliance, and perhaps your children and *their* children, will be on *your* hands."

He turned back to the machine, continuing the calibration.

Rhapsody tarried a moment longer, than exhaled and came to his side.

"Where are you directing the beam?" she asked quietly.

Achmed made a circular motion with his hand, his index finger extended.

"The whole of the Bolglands?"

"I see no other choice."

"Very well. Do you have everything in alignment?"

"I believe so."

"We will have to use the stored power in the diamond," she said, "since waiting for daylight, and for the sun to travel almost to the other end of the spectrum, would not be viable."

"Yes." Achmed strode to the lever that opened the metal shield that separated the space leading up through the tower from the glass in the dome. "Are you ready?"

Rhapsody struggled for breath. She nodded, her haggard face ghastly pale.

Achmed threw the switch, manipulating the segmented cover until it exposed just the indigo slice of the spectrum. A horrific grinding sound echoed in the room below the light tower, raining the dust and grit of disuse down upon them.

"Sivigant," Rhapsody said, her voice shaking. *Activate.*

The diamond's quivering light expanded, gleaming ferociously, until it caught the dark blue light of the indigo glass.

Luasa-ela, Rhapsody sang. Even in her despair, the note was easy to find, the primal sound to which she was innately attuned at her very core.

A beam of rich, dense blue radiance descended from the dome of the tower through the suspended diamond to the calipers on the altar-like table, bathing the maps engraved in the tabletop in deep blue light.

Achmed watched the room beyond the circle of gleaming brilliance intently.

After several moments, it appeared as if the very air of the place was coated in deep blue radiance, thick and dense, heavy with moisture, almost as if it had been dipped into the deepest part of the ocean.

Achmed held up his hand, and Rhapsody let the note cease. He headed out of the tower toward the elevated hallway at the top of the staircase and went to the window, then looked out.

Below him, the bonfires and torches had dimmed dramatically, as if the air of the steppes was wrapped in an encompassing blue fog. The soldiers that moments before were saddling mounts and aligning into marching orders and battle formations seemed either to be stunned, looking around them in shock from the ground or atop their horses, or wandering aimlessly, confused.

A chill had settled on the mountain, cooling the flames of the torchlight inside the Cauldron and the Lightcatcher itself. Achmed took in a breath to find it heavy and cold in his lungs.

The cavern of the Lightcatcher was the only part of the mountains to be spared from the effects of its indigo light.

He turned back to the instrumentality to see Rhapsody on her knees on the floor again, her head in her hands, with Fraax in the distance, appearing confused.

"Fraax?"

"Hmmmmm?" The Archon blinked. "Majesty?"

"Step into the hallway—I'm going to bar and lock the door. If you are able, keep away anyone who comes except for me and the Lady Cymrian. Do you understand?"

The Archon cocked his head and looked at him strangely. Then he wandered in the direction of the hallway, taking his time, looking around at the high ceilings above him, until he stood outside the doorway.

"Well, I suppose this is what we asked for," the Bolg king grumbled. He strode to the table where Rhapsody sat and took her hand, dragging her gently to her feet.

"Let's go," he said brusquely.

23

$\mathcal{A}$chmed led her out of Gurgus Peak and back to the Cauldron in silence.

They traveled to the Inner Reaches, the place where the canyon separated the guardian mountains from the Blasted Heath and the Deep Kingdom beyond, dodging wandering Bolg that seemed to have been slowed to half or less of their reasoning, the anger that had rallied them to prepare for war doused, as with the coming on of night. The Bolg king and the Lady Cymrian returned numbly to the same tunnel where they had come to mourn earlier that day and sat in silence for longer than it felt comfortable. Finally Achmed ventured a joke.

"I just realized you burned Ashe," he said. "Ashe—burn; ironic."

Rhapsody's eyes filled with tears. "I'm glad this is funny to you."

"It is absolutely not. I know this was difficult."

"*Difficult?*" Rhapsody's face, pale with sorrow and exhaustion, flushed red with rage, and she began to shake. "You're joking—*difficult?* Are you trying to torture me more, to punish *me* now for the heinous actions of men who used my husband's thoughtless annoyance at Grunthor's destructive boredom as an excuse to commit unconscionable evil?" Her voice began to rise in hysteria. "Do you blame me for his death as well? *Do you?*"

Achmed seized her shoulders and held her still.

"Of course not," he said quietly.

"Well, you're more than welcome to—I blame myself, you may as well blame me, too. If you do, by all means, please throw me into the chasm now," she said, still trembling. "You will be doing me a tremendous favor."

"Stop, stop, now. You're in shock. Here, sit down."

"Shock?" she said dully as he lowered her to the floor against the wall, then sat down in front of her. "Why would I be in shock? I've called starfire down upon my husband, blasting him into cinders. I've lost my son." All sound of life had fled her voice. "Maybe all my children."

Achmed exhaled slowly. "I doubt that."

"Meridion told me I was dead to him."

"He didn't mean it."

"He's a Namer, Achmed," Rhapsody said. She stared down at her trembling hands. "You have known one long enough to understand what their statements mean to them."

"Even a Namer is entitled to a few un-thought-out words of rage after witnessing what he did," the Bolg king said quietly. "Give him time. His status as the Child of it may mean that he can undergo a lifetime of healing in what would be a relatively short span of it for the rest of us."

She thought about her husband's ragged voice in the ether, and the need to confess bubbled up inside her, tickling her Namer's sensibility.

"You may not believe me, but I gave Ashe what he wanted," she said.

Achmed turned his mismatched gaze on her. "You may not believe *me*, but Ashe gave Grunthor what he wanted as well."

Rhapsody looked at him blankly.

"Grunthor has been tired for a very long time, Rhapsody," Achmed said. "A *very* long time. He never completely recovered from the injuries he sustained in the War of the Known World, in his battle with the titan. I have pondered on it for centuries, why he never came back to whole, to the point to which you and I have always recovered. I think there was something about the injuries that Grunthor, as a child of Earth, took at the hands of another child of elemental earth, and a demonic one, that never really healed completely.

"While we have all survived a thousand years, Grunthor aged in ways you and I have not yet. He had been bored with peace and exhausted with the routine of training men and women for battle that never came. Probably he inherited it from his mother's Bengard blood, the call of the arena that craved glorious death in youth over a decrepit old age. While I blame your husband for whatever foolish thing he said, I have never known him to intentionally wish Grunthor harm. And I certainly don't blame you for any of it. If there is an Afterlife beyond the Gate, I would like to believe Grunthor is at peace, at least."

He looked around, then back at her, then stood.

"I need alcohol," he said. "I think you do, too. Can I trust you to remain here and not throw yourself into the chasm while I'm gone?"

"I can honestly promise you nothing at this moment, Achmed."

"Then I will forgo the alcohol and stay with you. I am unwilling to risk it—when a Namer talks of suicide, it's a terrifying thing."

Rhapsody looked up at him. His face, normally shielded with veils, was uncovered, revealing dark circles under his already hollow eyes, the veins and nerve endings on his face even more pronounced.

"I'm sorry," she said softly. "I'm being a brat. Go get us some wine. I will not do anything intentionally stupid."

"I'll be right back."

He returned a few moments later, having raided the same vintner's closet they had obtained bottles of wine from when first holding vigil for Grunthor. He gave a new one to her, then sat back down across from her and took a long drink from a bottle of brandy.

"It's strange, this state of called night," he said, wiping his mouth. "I don't like the way it feels—the air is dead, thick with silence. The Bolg seem like they are in shock as well, waiting, confused. I hope they are able to recover from it."

"I imagine they will. The power of the Lightcatcher is not perpetual; it has to be renewed either by exposure to sunlight, which will not happen as long as the artificial night from the indigo spectrum is in place, or until the memory of light that has been stored in the diamond runs out."

"That could be a thousand years."

"Or a thousand days. It may take that long for the rage to cool, for the Bolg to forget."

"They will never forget," Achmed said. "But they will lose the ability to remain primed for war. On balance, it was the only thing to do."

"Agreed."

"I regret that you were not outside the Lightcatcher, within Ylorc with the rest of them, when we called the night."

Rhapsody paused in the midst of drinking from the bottle. "Why?"

"Perhaps it would have allowed you the same dull cooling of your pain. Perhaps by the time the morning finally comes, however long that takes, you would have finished grieving and be ready to live again. Instead, I suspect time will pass normally for us, and you will suffer at full strength for however long you choose to grieve."

She looked down the dark tunnel behind them, lighted dimly by the pale remains of the stalk joints that the tunnel crew of Bolg had set on their last rotation through the corridors before the summoning of night. The torches glowed feebly, their fuel all but spent.

None of the routine movement of the inner mountain caught her eye, not even the skittering of rats she could hear in the distance or the flapping of tapestries in the wind off the canyon.

The voice within her called softly, thick in the intransient air.

Mimen. I am still waiting. Mimen, please.

Rhapsody choked on the bile that had risen in the back of her throat.

"I wish I could have had one last night with him," she said dully. "Or even one final loveless knob in a darkened alley. Anything that would have given me his seed, as long as he had been willing to attach a piece of his soul to it." She sighed dispiritedly. "It was the only thing he ever really refused me."

Achmed closed his eyes as his forehead and nose wrinkled, his upper lip curling in disgust.

"What an utterly repulsive image," he muttered, "though I have no doubt that Ashe's rotten soul would make an appropriate companion to semen expressed in a back-alley fuck. Please spare me any further musings of that ilk. Neither my stomach nor my mind can take it tonight."

Rhapsody smiled slightly.

"I'm sorry," she said, a tone of loss echoing in her words. She stared out over the all-but-bottomless canyon, where seemingly frozen Bolg soldiers stood endless, meaningless guard, buffeted by the whining wind. "Within me I hear a tone sounding, the song of a child waiting to come through into this life from the other side. I have heard such a tone each time Ashe and I conceived one of our children, unique unto itself as each of our children is unique. Now, it will be a namesong I carry until my death, unborn. It will haunt my dreams, and grow within what is left of my heart until it shatters." She exhaled. "Now, at last, I can feel my life finally having corners, limits, as if I am approaching the wall at the end. Thank God, the One, the All. Immortality has worn out its welcome with me."

Achmed put the bottle to his lips and imbibed, then wiped his mouth on the back of his arm.

"There's a multitude of cocks out there, primed and waiting for you, Rhapsody. Once the buildup to war winds down, any street in any city on the continent would present you with a thousand or more options. If you want to have another child, walk into any town square, take down your hood, or lift your skirts, and smile. You'll have endless choices of potential fathers within moments."

He passed her the bottle, and she took it, examined the label, then drank deeply.

"I know you're drunk, or just being vile, or both, but I cannot explain to you how encompassing what I am describing to you is for me. I don't want to bring a child into this world anonymously. There must be love present. Children are conceived without it every day, in horrible ways, but I would fight to make certain that would never happen. I lived through enough of that in my life in the old world, thank you."

"Are you willing for it to be a voluntary Bolg? They all love you, *First Woman*."

"Shut up," Rhapsody said, stinging bitterness in her tone. "I know you are celebrating this night, but my heart is broken."

Achmed looked at her sharply, then took another drink.

"I'm not celebrating," he said.

"*Hrekin*. You may not blame Ashe for Grunthor's death, but you've hated him for as long as you've known him."

"I know you won't believe me, but I do not hate him, nor have I ever hated him. Even if I never understood what you saw in him, I know he loved you. I just don't understand why you have ruled an Alliance when all you wanted was to live simply and in peace, just because he had to rule; why you gave up so much of what you are to be his other half, and, more importantly, why he would allow you to; why you would risk your life to have his children. I guess I just don't understand why being yourself alone wasn't enough. I don't understand why you couldn't have him for protection, for amusement, for sex, for company or sharing parental chores, but still have maintained what is you without having to be half of someone else."

Rhapsody's world was spinning violently in the throes of grief exacerbated by wine.

"What you actually don't understand is the concept of sharing a soul.

It doesn't make you less of a person; I believe I was whole, before and after I married him. But in completing each other, you become another entity as well. Half of another whole."

"You're drunk, and you never were particularly good at math."

"As for children, they have never seemed an option for me—I can hear them before they are even undertaken, like this one that is calling to me, haunting me even now. I have shared a soul with Ashe for a thousand years; more, actually. I have been his other half for so long that I could impart to a child not only the lore of humankind and the Lirin, but that of the Seren and Wyrmril that was his legacy as well. But without his love, without the love of a father, willing to share a part of his soul, his life, to bring a child into being, I am forced to know that the soul of this child exists, but that its life was denied."

"Fine," Achmed said irritably. "If it really is bothering you that much, *I* will father your child, especially if it means we never have to have this inane conversation ever again."

KREVENSFIELD PLAIN, BETHANY

Meridion ap Gwydion was sick at heart.

He had stopped to camp for the night, having ridden his horse as far as his conscience would let him without feeling he was abusing the animal, but as fast as he rode, and as far as he went, he could not outrun the guilt for convincing his father to appeal to his mother and the Bolg king.

His words had left his mother broken and his father dead.

He had taken shelter beneath an elm tree, struggling to fall asleep and failing, so he let his mind wander through Time to the last moments of his father's life.

He had not witnessed Ashe's death directly, having been on the stairs when Rhapsody summoned the starfire, so he stepped back to the moment just before it happened.

The passage of Time slowed, then paused, as he went back until he was standing on the field directly in front of his father, who was frozen in between moments, his eyes elevated, watching the one woman he had ever loved on the tower ledge.

He was surprised, therefore, to see that just as the name of the star,

Prylla, was pronounced, his father had closed his eyes, let his head fall back, and had smiled as broadly as Meridion had ever seen him.

This makes no sense, he thought, letting loose of his place in the Past and returning to the Present.

He was trying to fall asleep again when he heard his father's voice next to his ear, not in his memory or in his travels through Time, but in the air around him.

Your mother told you the truth, Meridion—you do not know what really happened.

Meridion sat up.

"Papa? Father? Father, where are you?"

The voice spoke again, lightly, as if there was very little of him present in the air.

In the place she sent me into with the starfire from Daystar Clarion— in the ether. I have been begging her to consider doing it for more than a score of years now.

"You—you forsook your human form to—enter a fully draconic state? Like—like Llauron did?"

I am beginning to do so, yes. It is a process. Perhaps you have memory of him, and understanding beyond that of anyone else. Your mother said she thought you breathed in the essence of the last of his air lore when he Ended, protecting you, and her, from Anwyn.

"Yes. I have conversations with him sometimes in the Past," Meridion said, shaking off the sleep that had been hovering over his head, trying to clear the confusing hum from it. "He frequently tries to give me a sympathetic view of Anwyn, his mother, but it doesn't work even for him." Meridion thought of the sound of that name in his mouth.

I thought Anwyn was evil, he had said. *Compared to you, she was holy.*

He could feel his heart pounding, on the verge of exploding. *So this is the reason she told me not to say anything other than that their reign had ended,* he thought, sick with misery. *She did not want me to say that my father was dead—because he isn't.*

"She spared you?" he said to the air around him. "She—she helped you enter an elemental state?"

Though it must have shattered her heart.

"I thought she had never healed from doing the same to Llauron."

She hasn't. What you saw as my execution was the greatest sacrifice she has ever made for me. That others saw it the same way you did is the sacrifice she made to spare the continent.

"I told her she was dead to me. God, the One, the All, what will I do now?"

The voice in the ether was comforting.

Go and deliver the message as she told you to; the land cannot remain leaderless. Speak only the words you were given; to say anything else would dishonor the most innocent heart this land has seen in its history. I must begin my elemental journey now, and I do not know how long it will take. If you wait until I return in wyrm form, I will go with you to the Bolglands. We must both beg her forgiveness.

"Yes. But how can I ever unspeak the atrocity of what I said to her— my own mother?"

She is very forgiving, Meridion, and she loves you with all of herself; those were her last words to you as you left. You can trust that she understands your pain and your misconception; she will be grateful to have you back in her arms.

Meridion rose from beneath the elm and begged silent forgiveness of the horse. "I cannot wait for you, Father; I cannot have this on my head, or in my heart, any longer than I must. I will go to Highmeadow and herald the end of your reign, and send the message on to Tyrian, but after that I have to return to Ylorc. If you are back, you can come with me. If not, I am going alone."

So let it be done. I love you, my son.

"I love you too, Papa. Hurry back."

Only silence echoed in the glen around him.

Meridion mounted up and rode off into the night for Highmeadow.

24

THE TUNNEL OVER THE CANYON, YLORC

Now it's you who's drunk."

"Perhaps." The Bolg king rose and stretched sorely. "But I am also contending with my own loss, Rhapsody, and, at the risk of sounding unfeeling, I cannot bear hearing you talk about this anymore. So allow me a visit to the privy, since I know you have a long and well-documented objection to public urination, and we can get this over with. Take your clothes off, or at least your drawers, and I will be right back."

"This is not amusing to me, Achmed."

"I am not joking."

"You think I would *knob* you? Now?" She looked around at the darkened hallway, heavy indigo fog hanging in the air of it and the black Heath beyond, and exploded into sharp, mad laughter. "Well, isn't this rich? I can't imagine a better ending to this simply *wonderful* day. Let's see—we buried our dearest mutual friend, whose body was used as a latrine and a bunghole whore by men whose balls I should have ripped off with my hands rather than even imagine soiling my sword with their treacherous blood, though, now that I think about it, I wish I had let them experience Daystar Clarion in the same way Grunthor's dead body accommodated their tarses. I feel so much hatred right now that I believe, were they here, I would do exactly what I just pronounced."

"Interesting," Achmed said. "I can arrange to bring them to you— it would be amusing to watch. Have to commend Ashe for delivering them; that was a nice touch. Sorry it didn't make more of a difference in his sentence."

"Then, because that just wasn't enjoyable enough, I burned my husband alive with fire from a star that once lit the pyre of my only adopted sister, Jo, gone a thousand years now, whom I still miss. I traumatized my son, who called me a murderous bitch and not only told me that Anwyn was holy by comparison to me, but that I was dead to him, that he would be erasing me from his memory once he declares our reign to be over in his official capacity. This is the child who survived weeks in a tidal cave, floating within me, whom I have always communed with musically—the child who made me a mother. When he erases me from his memory, I will probably cease to exist, or at least I hope I will.

"I left my other children with their father, so I will not be the one to tell them of their loss—they'll hear from their brother, who hates me. Then, to top it all off, I share with you that my soul is being hounded by the voice of a child that Ashe and I were supposed to bring into the world, who now will never know life, and you tell me to take off my drawers while you favor me with not having to watch you piss before you fuck me on the tunnel floor among the wandering, mindless Bolg and the rats. Unless, of course, I would rather make use of the multitude of cocks out there, primed and waiting for me to raise my skirts and smile in any town square. My goodness—how much *better* can this day get?"

Achmed just looked at her, amusement in his tired eyes.

Rhapsody sat heavily back against the tunnel wall and put her face in her hands.

"I sorely miss you talking like that," the Bolg king said, sitting down again. "I don't believe I've heard you let loose with good gutterspeak since Meridion was born."

She crossed her arms in front of her and put her head on them.

"Do you feel better?"

"No. I'm not going to feel better."

"That's a shame. So, does that mean that when you were wishing for 'one final loveless knob in a darkened alley,' this place and present company were not what you had in mind?"

"Arrrgh," Rhapsody moaned within her crossed arms.

Achmed's mocking smile tempered into something vaguely sympathetic.

"All right," he said, running his hand over the back of his neck. "You can't say I didn't offer."

"Oh, *thank you*." Rhapsody remained in her crouch, her head on her folded hands.

Achmed leaned up against the wall as well and lapsed into an accommodating silence. Finally, when all the sound in the corridor had been used up, he cleared his throat.

"As I said at the beginning of this inane conversation, I was not joking."

Rhapsody raised her head. Her eyes were bloodshot and her face ashen.

"You want to fuck me on the tunnel floor among the wandering, mindless Bolg and the rats?"

"No." Achmed paused. "Well, yes, of course, who wouldn't, when you put it that way? But no, that's not what I was offering."

"What were you offering?"

"Sleep." The Bolg king looked at her intently. "Now I'm offering you sleep."

"I don't believe I will ever sleep again," said Rhapsody, putting her head down once more.

"That will be amusing to watch as well. I've known you a very long time, Rhapsody; I remember you trying to stay awake for extended periods on the Root, or when we were traveling overland, or once we got to Ylorc. Did you think I let you ride in front of me on horseback because I liked the way you smell or wanted to watch your breasts bounce when the horse cantered? Please. I was afraid you were going to fall, face-first, off whatever mount you were seated on when you passed out if you were alone."

"Thank you. I guess."

The Bolg king chuckled. "Which is not to say that I *don't* like the way you smell, or to watch your breasts bounce—"

"I don't *have* breasts, at least none to speak of. You and Grunthor always had a jolly good time endlessly reminding me of that fact."

"I am willing to let you sleep in my bedchambers, rather than on the tunnel floor among the wandering, mindless Bolg and the rats," Achmed said, smiling. "I think you may recall those chambers, having passed through them routinely on the way to the cavern of the Sleeping Child."

"Yes. They're enchanting. I love the way you decorated everything in black satin. If only it were red, it could be the whorehouse where I was enslaved in Easton."

Achmed looked down between his knees.

"You haven't made reference to that in a very long time."

Rhapsody rubbed her eyes. "I can't imagine why; it was one of the very best times of my life. And—at least I'm not being sarcastic here—even on its worst day, it was better than today."

Achmed's face grew solemn. "Even on the day when you were raped by Michael's entire regiment?"

At first, Rhapsody didn't respond. Then slowly, she raised her head.

"You remember that? I told you that?"

The Bolg king nodded. "You may not recall doing so, because it was a thousand years ago, during the war, when you had hidden Meridion away as an infant, and given him part of your name to comfort him and keep him company. You were very strange then, Rhapsody, sort of cold and distant and emotionless—"

"Of course I was. I had given the majority of my true name to my baby."

"You don't remember telling me about that day with Michael—the Waste of Breath? And his regiment of almost one hundred men?"

Rhapsody smiled bravely, but he could see her jaw and chin quivering.

"It wasn't just one day, Achmed. It was many days, days that I can never forget, dearly as I wish I could. And yes—as physically agonizing and soul-destroying as those days were, each and every one of them was better than today."

Achmed lapsed into silence.

"It was because of that—those—days that I went after Talquist, the Merchant Emperor of Sorbold, by myself," he said at last.

Rhapsody rested the top of her head against the wall and stared at the ceiling. "Why?"

"I'm not certain. But something broke inside me when you told me that. Some of it was about Rath, and not assuming everything that needed to die was ancient and supernatural, that Talquist was just a pathetic, cruel, less-than-human bastard who had come upon an ancient dragon scale and used it to manipulate the entirety of the world. He had no magical talents of his own, no exceptional strength, or even brilliant men who lived to serve him; he was just a slug with power to torment people who didn't deserve it, and he needed to die."

He drew a long breath and let it out again.

"And, in the pursuit of immortality, he wanted to eat your son's heart."

Rhapsody winced. "Please, Achmed—"

"He needed to die, and I needed to kill him, because for me it was personal."

"How? How was it personal?"

"Because I wanted Meridion to be my son."

It was as if all of what little air was left in the corridor had suddenly vanished.

After a moment, Rhapsody shook her head as if shaking off a trance.

"I don't understand."

"I know."

"No, I mean I *really* don't understand. You—you *hated* Meridion when he was a baby. You complained about him ceaselessly, called him awful things, threatened to feed him to hawks—"

"I was angry that you had let Ashe be his father. Because I wanted to be his father."

Rhapsody fell silent, her eyes wide.

"So if you hear a child waiting to come through, and Ashe now cannot give it to you, and would not give it to you even when he was still alive, I am willing to do so." He looked away. "I would be honored to do so."

Rhapsody stared at him for a long moment, then closed her eyes and sighed deeply.

"I appreciate that you are trying to comfort me," she said slowly, "and there is no one other than you with whom I can mourn Grunthor, so I am very glad to have had you to get drunk with and to listen to me lament the other things in my life that I'm grieving. But I've told you, all sad joking aside about fucking on the floor or cocks in the streets, that I don't want to conceive a child without the presence of love."

"I am aware. My offer still stands."

"You don't love me in that way."

Achmed snorted wryly.

"What would you know of my love for you? You have never correctly understood anything about me, not from the moment we met in the back alleys of Easton in Serendair two and a half millennia ago. You recall my first words to you—'come with us if you want to live'—you believed for years that meant Grunthor and I were seeking to help you, to rescue you from the Waste of Breath."

Rhapsody's eyes flashed, then kindled to a deep emerald.

"You disabused me of that notion long ago, Achmed. I remember, believe me—you were really telling me that you would kill me if I didn't come with you. I may be stupid, but I am not forgetful."

"What I haven't explained to the other side of my coin is the other side of *that* coin."

Rhapsody's head was spinning sickly. "I beg you, spare me the riddles. I don't have the heart for them."

Across the hall from her, Achmed gestured in frustration.

"Your accursed husband is not the only man in the world who has loved you. Now that he is gone, and Grunthor is gone, you still are not without love."

She fell intensely quiet. "What are you saying to me?"

Achmed sighed. "I have told you for a thousand years that I would always be right behind you, that there is no limit on what I would do for you. What else do you need to hear from me? If this—this child is something you need, ask it of me, and I will grant it if I can."

"Why?"

He looked up at the tunnel ceiling, then back at her. "Because I want you to be happy, or at least not tormented for the rest of your life by a child's voice you will never hear in the wind of the world. Because you are one of the few things, between two worlds and over the course of a very long lifetime, that has ever mattered to me. Because, whether you believe it or not, I do love you. In that way. And have for as long as I can remember. In fact, even though I know there was one, I can't recall a time when I didn't."

Silence again filled the tunnel.

When Rhapsody finally spoke, Achmed could barely hear her.

"I am so sorry. I never realized this."

"Of course you didn't. Because I never said the words to you, or told you in a way you would understand."

"Why?"

Achmed looked out into the night, to the Blasted Heath, where the torchfires had all burned out.

"Because every time you kissed me, as you have on a very few occasions, every one of which I remember, over the endless years of our lives, Ashe was always there to snatch you away again. Or it was moments before a battle neither of us expected to survive, or after living through said battle. Or because your intention was unmistakably platonic. Or you were comforting me or thanking me as you would any friend. Because you have told me you love me more times than I can count or remember, but *you* never meant it in 'that way.'"

He let all the breath out of his lungs, and when he took air in again, he used all of it.

"Because I thought I would only ever have you to myself in death."

Tears began to run down Rhapsody's cheeks, but she said nothing.

"You said once that you thought we build our own paradises in the Afterlife, that it didn't necessarily require that the rest of the world cooperate. I have built a tiny, pathetic paradise with you here, in this life, one-sided, odd, imperfect, certainly, but it has always been almost enough, Rhapsody. You allowed me to be your friend, which in and of itself is a rare gift, given that I began as your hated kidnapper. You told me that you were the other side of my coin, and that, because we were a coin together, we had worth—so I did. You adopted me as your brother, as your children's uncle, their guardian. I told you long ago that Jo and Grunthor and I were your family now—the one you have allowed me to be part of is of great value to me, even if I had to endure Ashe being part of it as well. So if you hear one more child that needs you, and if you need me to help that come to pass, please let me."

"I—a small part of me feels as if I am betraying him," she said. "But the larger part is so fixated—so *desperate* to make this—this *pleading* I hear inside me stop—it's killing me, Achmed, *killing me*."

"Don't talk to me of Ashe and betrayal," Achmed said bitterly. "While I know his part in Grunthor's death was unintentional, that does not absolve him of it utterly."

"I have finally come to realize something I could not understand before." She looked down at her clenched hands. "Every time I told Ashe that I could hear the tone of one of our children, waiting in the ether to come into this world through us, he was always surpassingly happy—his face would shine like the sun. Except for this last time. He seemed exhausted when I told him, and put the subject off—"

She paused, the words heavy to utter.

"Almost as if he knew that he wasn't meant to be this child's father."

"Perhaps he did."

Rhapsody raised her eyes slowly to meet his disturbing gaze.

"I know this may seem stupid, but—do—do you feel anything?" she whispered. "Is there anything inside you that—I don't know how it would feel for a man, or for someone other than a Namer, because for me it is overwhelming, insistent; I feel it in my mind, behind my eyes, in my heart, in my womb—but, can you feel even the slightest thing, the smallest sense that—you—that you might want—?"

"No," Achmed said quietly. "There is not the slightest or smallest sense that I might want this myself," he said, wincing as tears formed again at the edges of her eyes, which in his memory had never been so dark or so compelling. "My sarcastic nature has made it seem like I am doing you a favor, silencing the tone in your mind for your sake. It's a lie, and unfair, not to tell you the truth. Here it is—there is an enormity to that sense, Rhapsody; it's something I desire deeply, and have for as long as I can remember."

He could barely hear her now. "You want to be this child's father? Actually *want* to be, not are willing to be, but—"

"I have told you, yes."

The tears spilled over.

Rhapsody put her palms to her eyes and rubbed them with the heels of her hands.

She took her hands down and opened her eyes again, looking at Achmed with new ones, and smiled sadly.

"I am so tired," she said softly. "So tired."

"I've offered you my bedchamber. You may have it to yourself."

"Well," Rhapsody said slowly, "that would probably be best for you, because, as you know, I am often beset by terrible dreams, which will undoubtedly come back now that the dragon who used to guard me from them is gone. They can be quite disturbing." She inhaled as Achmed nodded and stood.

"But," she continued as she followed him to a stand, "if you need to sleep as much as I do, and we are the only two people in this mountain that are not sleepwalking, I imagine it would be good to have someone who I've just discovered loves me in ways I didn't know share that bedchamber, just to be safe. I am very confused and broken, Achmed, and I don't want to do anything that would make this a day that is even worse than it already has been. So, if you are ready for sleep, I will go with you. Please stay with me."

The Bolg king nodded.

"However," Rhapsody said drowsily, "if you are looking to fuck on the floor—"

"Not tonight," Achmed said, smiling slightly. "Come with me."

He reached out his hand, absent the thin glove, naked and vulnerable, and she took it.

Then he led her past wandering Bolg and sleeping rats to a place where she would be safe.

25

ACHMED'S BEDCHAMBER, YLORC

The night in the dark, stolid room had been quiet and calm for the most part.

Rhapsody had fallen asleep in her dressing gown amid the black satin sheets, exhausted beyond the point of being able to even say good night. Achmed had been perplexed about what to do, and had remained sitting on the edge of the bed for almost a quarter hour before she rolled over and opened her eyes halfway.

"Are you coming to bed?" she murmured sleepily.

"I had thought so," he replied. "But then I wasn't sure."

Rhapsody opened her eyes all the way, blurry.

"You and I slept beside one another for almost fifteen hundred years," she said. "We crawled along the Root, endured camping conditions once we got out—even though Grunthor, not you, was my mattress."

"I don't want to do anything that would make you even in any small way more sad than you already are, Rhapsody."

Rhapsody blinked. "Thank you," she said, genuinely touched. "I know you understand how deeply I am mourning. And how much I still love my husband."

Achmed sighed but said nothing.

Rhapsody put out her arms to him.

"Please come and hold me," she said softly. "There is nothing I need more tonight than that."

The Bolg king exhaled, then complied.

For much of the rest of the night he remained awake, listening to the tides of her breath as she slept on his chest, whispering sibilant sounds of comfort to her when her dreams were torturing her.

In the process, he was also absorbing the song that emanated from her that had always soothed the sting of life that irritated his sensitive nerves. It was a song that he had listened to, as she had said, every night for a millennium and a half, and she had no idea how deeply he resented her taking it from him when she had married Ashe and left the mountain.

So while he still was in the throes of agony at the loss of Grunthor, and was irritated and distraught about the buildup to a war that seemed would not happen now, at least he had the secret pleasure of feeling the music that came out of Rhapsody when she was breathing.

Especially when she was curled in his arms when doing so.

*W*hen he woke the following morning, she was watching him intently. She smiled slightly, and it was, for a moment, as if the sun itself had penetrated the dark stone and the black satin of his intentionally dark bedchamber.

"Good morning," she said.

"Good morning, I suppose."

"Do you still wish to do this?" she asked nervously. "I realize that yesterday was odd and terrible and confusing, and I don't want to ask you to do something that you are not comfortable about. I don't want you to regret your decision."

Achmed shrugged. "I told you I was willing last night. I am still willing today. I would say that makes it *your* decision."

"I—I do still want to," Rhapsody said nervously. "But the process by which I would like to undertake this is a magical summoning, not—not—"

"Not the tunnel floor among the wandering Bolg and the rats?"

"No, not that." She watched for his reaction, but he merely shrugged.

"So what would I have to do?"

She exhaled, relieved. "I would need to have a birthing cloth; there is one that would do, with an appropriate blessing, in the linen closet. We need to put ourselves in the proper frame of mind, open, accepting, welcoming. I will sing the invocation—you don't have to do anything there. Oh—and you have to rest your hand on my heart, if that is all right with you."

Achmed nodded again.

"Then," Rhapsody said, even more nervously, "if you want to, I think you should kiss me. It's not part of the actual ritual, but there's no reason we can't." Her eyes grew soft, with the glimmer of tears. "And this time, if that happens, I promise you I will be kissing you with no one waiting to sweep me away, no battle we don't expect to survive, no comfort of a friend in mind, even though we are and always will be friends. If you kiss me this day, you will be kissing the mother of your child."

Achmed's gaze deepened, and he nodded.

Her smile faded slightly as her stomach turned in the throes of what felt like betrayal.

"There is something I need to tell you about Ashe," she said hesitantly.

Achmed held up a single finger and brought it to rest on her lips.

"I'm going to make a selfish request of you," he said, looking pointedly into her eyes. "This is a day, to be followed by a night, that may be the only one I have had that wasn't utterly terrible since I heard your voice on the wind, screaming my name from the Krevensfield Plain. Therefore, I beg you, please don't mention *his* name again before the sun comes up tomorrow, Rhapsody. Whatever you have to say about him, let it wait for the morning. Or for a fortnight. Or, even better, for a lifetime.

"A short time ago I was preparing to rend this continent, to commit mass murder to avenge Grunthor and take your miserable husband down. And now, I find myself free of him, by your hand, without having to have innocent blood on *my* hands, ready to do something that is not in my nature—open my soul and help you silence the insistent call in your mind—and father your child. This could very well be the best day and night I have ever had—though, if we had done it the other way, sharing it with the rats and such, it might have been even better—as long as I do not have to share it for even one moment with the thought of that loathsome man. He was privileged to do this with you six times, and while I'm willing for it to be a multiple experience in the future, as long as the first one works out, the only one I'm guaranteed is tonight. So, I beg you—expunge his name from your lips from this moment until tomorrow at least. I don't want to taste him on them if you're going to let me kiss you. I've never done that before, you know—you have only ever kissed me."

She smiled. "Then give me a few moments in the privy—I don't have to change clothes, since these are all I have. But I would like to wash my face and brush my hair for the child's arrival."

She rose from the bed and started for the door, then turned around and smiled at him, the first real smile he had seen since she had left him at the border of Tyrian, before the world had gone to smash.

"Thank you for doing this, Achmed," she said softly. "I will never be able to thank you enough."

He waited until she closed the door behind her.

"That's what I would have said to you."

THE TUNNEL OVERLOOKING THE HEATH

They met a few moments later in the place they had been the night before, the tunnel opening over the chasm that separated the Cauldron and guardian mountains from the Blasted Heath.

The sun had still not yet risen, but the sky had begun to lighten, shedding rays of pink and gold across soft strands of clouds that looked like spun sugar.

There was an unmistakable sense of magic in that place, the place where they had mourned so many times, none worse than that which had occurred the previous night. But on the wind of morning, a feeling of good news blew in, bathing the opening of the cave tunnel with rosy light and fresh air.

Rhapsody knelt on the floor just inside the opening, the morning breeze playing with her golden tresses, hanging loose around her dressing gown. She hung the birthing cloth over her arm.

"Are you certain you still wish to do this?" she asked him.

"Yes. Please don't ask me again."

"All right." She swallowed, looking at him intently, solemnly, then slowly pulled the outer bodice of her dressing gown open, her eyes never leaving his.

"I have no breasts to speak of, as you know," she said. "But there is no need to hide what I do have from you."

The Bolg king locked eyes with her, their mismatched color and placement in his face as direct a connection as it was possible for any to have.

Rhapsody slid the top of her dressing gown over her shoulders, laying her upper body bare.

She glanced down at her heart, silently indicating where he needed to touch her.

His eyes followed hers.

"Then I will never speak of them," he said, a hint of awe in his voice. "There aren't words worthy to do so."

Rhapsody smiled. "Give me your hand," she said.

Trembling, he obeyed.

She took his hand in hers and drew it to her lips, then kissed it gently, allowing her lips to linger on the distended veins, the traces of nerve endings.

"Are you certain you want to do this?" she asked quietly. "To make and share this child with me? I'm not questioning you, it's part of the ritual for me to ask you."

Achmed could not speak coherently, so he merely nodded.

"You have to say it," she whispered.

"Yes," he whispered back.

Rhapsody drew his hand closer and placed it on her chest between her breasts, directly over her heart.

"Then close your eyes, and together we will put ourselves in a state of willingness, of creation, of the desire to bring forth a soul into the world through the offering of a piece of each of our own."

The Bolg king obliged as much as he could.

After a moment, he heard Rhapsody begin to sing. With his eyes closed it seemed to him that she was singing a purple melody, much like the color of the sky at the end of a brilliant sunset or just before dawn, and the sound made his sensitive skin hum with a comforting buzz.

Then the song went indigo, rich, dark, and encompassing blue that weighed heavily but coolly on his eyes like the thick light with which the instrumentality in Gurgus Peak had painted the Bolglands, simmering the hot rage to something baffling and slow. It was a calm sound, like a lullaby to a fussy baby or a sensible solution to preempt a duel.

He listened to the Namer's incantation change colors across the whole spectrum of the rainbow, evoking each of the powers of the lore of light. *I wonder what sort of magic it might impart to the child,* he thought from behind his closed eyes.

The song of conjuring was so beautiful, so inspiring, that he felt a loss, like the slap of a cold wave, when it came to an end. A tug within him made him sense that the piece of his soul he had agreed to part with had been removed from within him and now hung, nascent, in the air between them, mixing with hers.

"Achmed," Rhapsody whispered. "Are you ready?"

He nodded, his eyes still closed.

"Open your eyes."

He obeyed.

Rhapsody was holding the birthing cloth over his hands.

A glow of spectacular beauty was hovering above it.

"Welcome, little one," she said, tears in her eyes. "Meet your father."

The generalized glow became defined; the outline appeared of a tiny head, dusted with golden hair, with arms that reached upward into the world, the skin translucent, scored with the finest of traceries of surface veins, like Achmed's own.

She looked up at her friend, the other side of her coin.

The father of her last child.

His eyes met hers, and they shared a smile, then looked back at their child as it continued to form.

And then, suddenly, the world around her, glowing with warmth and the profound beauty of the song accompanying a soul's appearance, went dark and silent.

Silent except for the sound of a horse's whinny.

26

ℛhapsody looked quickly around.

It seemed as if Time had stopped.

Before her, Achmed still knelt, a look of heartbreaking awe on his normally cynical face. He was staring down at the glowing light in the birthing cloth, wonder in his eyes.

Unmoving.

The baby was awake and beautiful, *a boy,* she thought hazily, feeling her head swim as it had when she had given birth before. His hair was fine and golden, his skin perfect and dewy, with the lightest traceries of veins scoring his head in beautiful patterns like the designs the Lirin wove into their hair. *A beautiful boy.*

Also unmoving.

She looked up.

Rising behind Achmed in the now-dark stood a gargantuan horse of no breed that she recognized, its coat and mane changing color from moment to moment.

Atop the horse was a figure she did recognize.

He was tall, wearing robes the color of night; his skin was pale, his eyes were black as pitch, and deep. Rhapsody felt she easily could fall into those eyes, crowned with black thundercloud brows beneath a mane of snowy white hair.

She had known his face for a thousand years, having spent the equivalent of seven in his realm, an ethereal place between life and death known as the Veil of Hoen, the Cymrian word for *joy.*

Yl Angaulor.

The Hand of Mortality.

The Lord Rowan.

The manifestation of Peaceful Death.

The Lord Rowan smiled sadly.

"M'lady, I am here to make good on the promise I made you. Come now."

Rhapsody's brow wrinkled. In her haze she shook her head. "Promise?"

The Lord Rowan stretched out his hand.

A sudden clarity filled her mind, like a Namer's bell tolling, and she heard in her ears her own voice, and his.

M'lord Rowan, will you grant me a favor? Please?

What is it you wish?

Will you come for me one day? Please?

The Guardian of Peaceful Death's solemn face had betrayed a flicker of a smile.

Fascinating. Usually I only hear prayers asking me to stay away, though you are not the first Cymrian by any means who has prayed for my assistance. You are the first one in the bloom of youth, however.

Please, m'lord. Please say that you will come for me one day.

I will if I can, my child. That is the only promise I can make you.

Rhapsody blinked as realization dawned. "I—am I dead?"

"Come, m'lady." There was a tone of urgency in his voice.

"But—"

Her protest was cut short as the voice of Manwyn, the Seer of the Future, rang in her head.

I see an unnatural child born of an unnatural act. Rhapsody, you should beware of childbirth: the mother shall die, but the child shall live.

"Oh, my God—"

"M'lady—"

She looked down at the translucent baby in her arms, only to see that her arms were frozen in Time as well.

Rhapsody jumped up in alarm, leaving her body, and the child it cradled, behind.

She looked down at her arms, translucent now as well.

The Lord Rowan glanced over his shoulder.

"M'lady, do not panic, I beg you," he said, his voice controlled, but there was an edge to it. "Be careful of what you say; a Namer's authority can contravene Time and Death, but you do not wish for that to happen."

Rhapsody met his gaze. "Why?" she asked, her voice trembling.

The black eyes narrowed. "Another comes for you. Another iteration of Death. Please, m'lady. It is time."

"But—my child—my baby—needs me—please, m'lord—"

"You are by no means the first woman to utter those words before meeting Death; you brought several children from such mothers to my realm long ago, if you recall." He stretched out his hand even farther. "Come."

"Please," Rhapsody said, choking. "One moment—just one. I beg you."

The Lord Rowan fell silent, a disapproving look in his black eyes.

Rhapsody inhaled, feeling no air come into her chest. She came closer to the Lord Rowan, walking around her own body, and knelt down beside Achmed, bending again over the child, cradled in the birthing cloth in her hands. She kissed the baby's head quickly, then spoke his name above him.

Graal, she said in the tone of the Naming invocation. It was the word in Serenne, the language of the Ancient Seren that Llauron had insisted she learn long ago, the word meaning *visionary wisdom.*

Speaking the word was heavier than she could imagine; it was as if she were swimming through clay. *I—love—you,* she whispered, forcing the words through the weighty air.

She turned her head with great difficulty and pressed a kiss on Achmed's temple, just above his ear.

Thank you, she said, struggling for breath. *Love—you.*

In the distance, thunder rolled and lightning crackled.

The devouring blackness that had appeared a moment after the baby's emergence lightened to gray, as if it were foredawn. Now Rhapsody could see an endless horizon all around her, shapes of a desolate landscape she could not make out.

In the direction the horse was facing, she thought she could see what appeared to be a wood wrapped in fog and sunlight. A massive gate rose from the mist, open to a realm of shining brightness.

The Lord Rowan's eyes darkened.

"*Now,* m'lady," he insisted. He reached down as far as he could from atop the steed.

Rhapsody stood and came to him. She took his hand.

The Lord Rowan swept her effortlessly up and onto the horse before him and dug his knees into the steed, which took off in a scream of wind toward the foggy place before them.

She turned with difficulty and caught one last sight of the three of them.

Herself.

Her last child.

And the man who had been the other side of her coin. Her child's father.

His only living parent now.

Beyond the rushing of wind, the thundering of the horse's hoofbeats, the Gate loomed in the green glade beyond the Veil, magnificent in its brightness.

She bowed her head in grief as the world began to spin away.

Only to raise her face as the Lord Rowan dragged back on his mount in a screaming of horseflesh and anger.

27

Meridion stood at the Gate before them.

The Lord Rowan drew the mighty steed to an unexpected stop, causing vibrations of immense power to shake whatever appeared to be the ground. He glanced at Rhapsody before him.

"My eldest son," she said haltingly.

The Lord Rowan's eyes narrowed as he assessed the man in front of him.

"You have not died," he said, almost accusingly.

Meridion bowed his head in deference. "No, m'lord."

"How did you know to come here?"

"I saw it in a dream, m'lord—this very night, a turgid dream of monumental scale. I needed to see my mother, so I came. I beg your forgiveness."

The manifestation of Peaceful Death drew himself up in the saddle angrily. "Then I am in the presence of an entity with the power to halt Time itself. I had never expected to be thus. What do you want? Your interference puts your mother at grave risk—a gravity I cannot overstate."

"I must speak to her, I beg you, m'lord," Meridion said. "Please. I believe I can hold Time in stasis for a few moments, long enough to impart to her what I have to say."

The black eyes of the Lord Rowan gleamed with displeasure. He turned and looked down again at Rhapsody, after glancing behind them.

"I came to take you beyond the Veil of Hoen and through the Gate because in Life you once asked that boon of me, and I agreed to grant it if I could. But you must know that the circumstance in which Death has come to meet you is not one within my domain. It is not my appointed task or jurisdiction to carry you to the Gate, m'lady, but that of my elder brother." The expression in the black eyes grew even darker for a moment. "And, upon my word, you do not wish for that to come to pass if you can possibly help it."

Rhapsody turned and looked beyond his shoulder. The flat sky was darkening in the distance, great clouds of gray dust seeming to dance slowly upward.

"He is coming," the Lord Rowan said. "And his authority, and power, eclipses yours, Child of Time."

Meridion swallowed and tried to keep from shaking. "As a Namer, it is my obligation to share lost lore with one who is entitled to know it—and as the Child of Time, I can keep Time at bay for a few moments, at least. Please, m'lord—I promise not to tarry." He pointed just beyond the Gate, to an enormous loom before which a woman sat, weaving the story of history. "There is something in the Weaver's loom that my mother must see."

The Lord Rowan turned in the saddle and looked into Rhapsody's eyes one last time, the black irises of his own devouring what little light was present.

"This is your decision, m'lady," he said, "though I strongly advise against it. I caught you in the moment just before your heart exploded, before an agonizing end that cannot be described in words. I will not be able to help you should the one who is coming for you find you here before you enter the Afterlife."

The Lady Cymrian considered for a moment.

Then she nodded her understanding and dismounted the horse, coming to stand a few steps from Meridion.

"Tell me what you feel you must," she said softly.

Meridion summoned his courage, sick at heart at the sight of her face, the glowing light in it that had always been present waning before his eyes.

The mist of the Veil of Hoen hung heavy in the air, frozen in Time. He turned to the enormous loom on which the tapestry of history was being woven, and pointed to the place where the original image had been altered, beginning with a tiny knot of interwoven copper and golden threads.

He watched her enormous eyes take in the sight of the rewoven history, the original pattern hovering in the air, evanescent, translucent beside the clear, well-formed threads that represented Time as it was now recorded.

Those eyes filled with unspent tears as she did.

"It was me, Mimen. I am so sorry."

Rhapsody continued to watch the floating scene of the Forgotten Past unfold before her eyes.

"It was me, Mimen, though I did not know it until I came here to meet you," Meridion said. He took a breath of the unmoving air and spoke as quickly as he could, trying to maintain a calm tone, relying on his training as a Namer, even as his heart pounded violently. "I just saw it in the Weaver's tapestry—the gold thread of your hair, the copper of Gwydion's—and my own fingerprints. I am the one who edited Time, who sent my father back to meet you in the old world. I am the one who caused the strand of Time that you lived before to burn in favor of the one I altered."

Finally she turned to him and smiled slightly.

"I know," she said. "I can see it as well."

"Can you forgive me? For this, and for everything I said?"

A dark wind blew through the glade.

Behind the horse, the clouds of dust on the filmy ground began rising rapidly, reaching skyward into darker ones that were racing again now.

Rhapsody's eyes grew clearer, and she appeared slightly more solid, as if by force of will. When she spoke, the tone of the Namer was in her voice.

"You had no say in the matter, Meridion. And it was the right thing for the world. There is nothing to forgive."

The Lord Rowan was looking behind him. "M'lady—"

"I wanted you enough to accept death as the consequence of your birth on both sides of Time, Meridion. Both times, I deem that my decision was wise. I am forever grateful to have been your mother."

Black rain began to strafe the glade, sending the limbs of the trees writhing, their leaves rustling madly.

"M'lady, *he comes.*"

Meridion's eyes widened as he beheld the horizon approaching from behind the Lord Rowan's mount.

Fire now was leaping from the ground, and thunder crackled and snapped in the clouds shot with lightning.

Before it all rode another horseman, larger and broader in form than the Lord Rowan, clad in spiked armor, a whip of many tails in his heavy-gloved hand.

The face beneath his war helm was exposed to the heavy air, his lips skinned back from his teeth that were clenched in a grin of hatred.

His face was part skeleton, part sunken, in which eyes of fire burned.

He rode low over the back of his mount, a tall, broad steed that seemed to be formed of dark wind and fire.

He was beating that windfire steed mercilessly, urging it onward, a grin of both satisfaction and fury curled on what remained of his lips.

"Mother—"

The remaining spirit of Rhapsody reached out and seized Meridion by the shoulders. Her hands had no weight, but he felt the strength of her will nonetheless.

"Hear me, Meridion: I love you; remember that *always*. Speak the same words for me to all our family—especially to your father. Be gentle with him. Tell him that no one killed me, there is no revenge to exact—and nothing else about my death. Tell him this additionally— *your lady commands you not to rampage; Grunthor's death brought the continent to the brink of war, but she wishes hers to return it to peace. Honor this command, and your wife will meet you one day beyond the Gate. She thanks you for the most beautiful life she could ever have imagined.*"

She took his hand and pressed her lips to the back of it; the warmth and sensation of love conveyed remained there for the rest of his life.

Then her other hand slid down his arm as she backed away from him toward the Lord Rowan's horse. Her palm, cold as the wind around them, rested in his for one last moment.

"And, my beloved son, above all else, may you know joy."

She gave him one final smile, then turned to the Lord Rowan, whose white hair was streaming violently in the wind now, and reached up her arms.

Without another breath the Lord Rowan swept her from the filmy forest floor and dragged her onto the mount before him. He kicked its sides savagely and dashed forward through the Gate, riding through Meridion as he did without so much as a whisper of impact.

Meridion spun around in time to see the horse disappear beyond the Gate of Life, then turned back again as the lightning flashed and the rain drenched his skin, stinging and burning, but leaving no droplets or mist.

Meridion closed his eyes as the howl of the wind before him rose into a scream of fury.

He could feel his eyelids burn as the thundering hoofbeats rode closer, ripping grass and dirt beneath them in a horrific smell.

A violent slap roared through him, dragging his hair behind him and off-balancing him, making his chest, shoulders, and legs ache violently.

Then he heard the sound of a horse in walk, circling him from behind and stopping in front of him again.

"Open your eyes, *coward.*"

Meridion obeyed.

The manifestation of the Wracked Death stared down at him from atop its evanescent mount in hatred.

His mother's words, spoken so recently and yet seemingly forever ago, sounded in his ear.

Stand up straight and shrink from no one. Look every man in the eye. Spit in that eye if you need to.

As warmth spread through him, Meridion stared back at Death.

The enormous monster leaned over the side of the horse, bringing its rotting head and the putrid stench of its tattered teeth down next to his face.

"You have taken a valuable prize from me, Namer," the Wracked Death said. In its voice were sounds of wailing, screams of agony, above the base of a growl that rang with the slamming of cemetery gates. "Your mother made a life of claiming such prizes from me—healing those who were among my spoils, who I deserved to carry beyond the Gate, or staying my hand by comforting them in death—just as you do. This does not come without cost. The ledgers record these thefts, both hers and yours—and now yours of her."

The eyes of the manifestation of Death burned even darker before him. His final words were considered, slow, and spoken in a terrifying hiss.

"I will never forgive your debt. When your time comes, I will be there to collect you—be certain of it."

Meridion exhaled.

"Perhaps," he said, sighting the horseman down. "Or perhaps my mother was right. Death itself is an immutable entity, but the manifestations of it, the traditions and myths, the legends and tales are perhaps given power by the very Namers, priests, and Singers, and their fellows in other cultures who recount that lore. Perhaps all of us have brought you into existence by the very sharing, guarding, and maintaining of that lore.

"I believe I will put that theory to the test—I shall return to the Repositories of Lore and remove any mention of you from the displays. I will rewrite the books and expunge your image, and that of the other monsters who are your brothers, leaving only Yl Angaulor in the record. I will whisper a new lore of Death into the wind: that those whose lives end in pain, or in war, or in the death of worlds, arrive at the Gate in joy. And, if I am wrong, I will apologize if you come to collect me, and you may torment me however you choose. That seems only fair. But trust me—I am confident enough in my ability to rewrite the lore as I have mentioned that I will lose no sleep over the infinitesimal possibility that I will ever see you again."

The grisly horseman blinked in astonishment. Meridion could not suppress a smile.

Then he closed his eyes and loosed the bonds he had put on Time in the Veil of Hoen, and made his way through its corridors to Ylorc.

28

THE TUNNEL ABOVE THE CHASM, YLORC

𝓘n the face of the miracle that he had just witnessed, Achmed's sardonic nature had failed him utterly.

As he looked down at the child in Rhapsody's hands, his own poised beneath the birthing cloth, he found himself staring into a pair of eyes, colored in two different shades, looking back at him as if the baby was sighting down a crossbow.

He chuckled in spite of himself.

My son, he thought, still unable to believe what he was seeing. He noticed the traceries of veins that scored the baby's tiny head, looking as if they had been painted there by an artist from the Inoye clan, a Gwenen tribe that detailed the skin in beautiful runes with inks made of cacao and the excretions of squid. *There is a little of me in him after all.* He gently touched the infant's translucent gold hair, and his long black lashes and golden skin with a rosy undertone exactly like that of his mother. *Thankfully, very little.*

The air of the room suddenly became heavier, pushing against the sensitive skin of his face.

"He's beauti—"

His instinctive reflexes responded like lightning as the child dropped into his hands.

His mother fell sideways to the floor, limp and lifeless.

"Rhapsody?" Achmed blinked in surprise.

He was over her a moment later, the newborn swaddled in the birthing cloth in the crook of his arm, sensing for a heartbeat he had known intimately for more than two millennia, but finding nothing.

"Rhapsody?" he demanded, his tone unintentionally harsh as it had been in previous times when his worry got the better of him.

Shaking, he rolled her over onto her back and felt her neck numbly for her heartbeat, only to be sickeningly assured of its absence.

Every organ in his body went numb or constricted with shock.

He opened his mouth to taste the air, pulled his veils farther away from his skin-web to allow his senses the best chance of finding her heartbeat in the wind, but, just as it had been a short time ago with Grunthor, there was no trace of it. He let loose his *kirai*, the gift he had utilized in Serendair to locate any prey by its cardiac trail, but to no avail.

The Bolg king fell back, shaking with shock.

He could hear his own voice, long ago, when she had been grievously injured by the demonic vine that had sprung from her F'dor-possessed sister's entrails, trying to jolly her into awareness.

Come on, Rhapsody, we've been in worse fights than this. Sleep on your own time, will you? This is no way to get out of your share of the work breaking camp.

But there was something so certain, so all-encompassing, so final about her state that he could not even bring himself to joke for old times' sake.

Achmed opened his mouth and began to breathe shallowly.

Desperation gripped him suddenly. He tightened the cloth around the newborn and set him, with the greatest of care, on the floor, then tilted her head back and pressed his open mouth on hers, breathing for her, pushed rhythmically on her chest, even though he knew before he began it would be to no avail.

He put his hand on the naked skin of her chest, the place she just a few moments before had bared for him, allowing him to rest his palm there.

It was warm, perhaps from the recentness of her heart stopping, perhaps owing to the fire that had been absorbed in her when she sang her way through the molten, towering wall of the element at the heart of the Earth.

"Rhapsody," he whispered brokenly. "Please, please don't do this."

Her eyes, green as the forest canopy, were open, staring blankly.

Achmed let his hand come to rest on them, closing the lids, brushing the luminous black lashes as he took his hand away.

Angrily he contemplated a blind run for the chasm.

A tiny gurgling sound, like the pealing of bell, went up behind him.

He turned to see that the baby had disentangled himself from the birthing cloth and was waving his arms slowly, randomly.

In the back of his mind he could hear the words of a prophecy spoken, something Ashe had obsessed over, that Rhapsody had assured him, during the course of her later, more routine pregnancies, had not been about Meridion or any of his siblings, but a woman who long ago she had delivered of a child with demon's blood, a spawn of a rape by the Rakshas.

I see an unnatural child born of an unnatural act. Rhapsody, you should beware of childbirth. The mother shall die, but the child shall live.

Her later pregnancies after Meridion's birth had all been healthy and safe, despite his rude comments about Ashe risking her life.

I see an unnatural child born of an unnatural act.

Oh gods, Achmed thought as he looked from his son to the baby's dead mother. *Oh, gods.*

There was a lingering warmth against his cheek, the odor of spice and flowers and soap; he put his hand to his face, feeling words he did not think he had actually heard, spoken after what felt like a loving kiss, in a sweet, familiar voice.

Thank you. Love—you.

Oh gods, he thought again.

For the first time he could remember, he felt the presence of caustic, bitter tears burn down his face.

Achmed shook his head to dislodge them from his skin, fearing if they remained there, he would never be able to make the ones that would come after them cease.

The little boy on the floor began to cackle, then cry, the sound rippling painfully across Achmed's skin-web.

He turned away from Rhapsody's lifeless body and crawled back to the infant, lifting him carefully from the floor and cradling him against his shoulder.

Now what do I do? he thought, panic rattling at the edges of his consciousness. *What do I do?*

The Bolg, wandering distantly, still waiting to be summoned to battle, said nothing in reply.

The first task Achmed had undertaken with his son was the gathering of wood for the pyre of the child's mother.

Initially he had panicked when the baby cried, believing him to be hungry and knowing he had no way to provide nourishment without Rhapsody. Then, after several terrified moments he recalled a conversation that had taken place a millennium before between his child's mother and a Dhracian known as Rath, a demon-hunter of his own mother's race, who had instructed her in the lore that had brought their baby into being.

A summoned entity has no real need of food or drink or sleep, the Dhracian had said as the Namer made careful notes. *It is comprised of a piece of a soul of two different people, and the musical vibrations of the lore by which it is sung into life. This is why the Earthchild has spent endlessly passing years in the darkness of the Earth, without the sustenance a normal child would need. The only necessity it has is that of love.*

He found that picking the child up and cradling him had been sufficient.

The Bolg king went slowly through the halls of Ylorc, the sleeping baby on his forearm, finding and gathering sticks of any nature, all in the name of making Rhapsody's funeral bier, passing logy Bolg in armor who were carrying as much in the way of weaponry as they could.

He had returned her to his bed, where she had awoken in his arms that morning, carrying her back to the place where her smile had made him appreciate the sunrise. Now that she was dead, putting her body to rest on the black satin sheets she had joked about was the least he could do, rather than leaving her corpse in the hallways to possibly be come across and defiled by wandering Firbolg affected by the Night Caller spectrum. The thought of how appalled she had been by that prospect made him willing to do anything he must to keep her safe in death as he had not been able to in life.

You want to fuck me on the tunnel floor among the wandering, mindless Bolg and the rats?

The memory of how ashen her face had been, how bloodshot her eyes, had made his suffering even worse. He had been assuming until now that she had just been joking, sarcastic and exhausted. But it occurred to him now, after seeing her clenched jaw, her trembling chin, that the memory of her torment at Michael's hands might have been clinging to the edges of her consciousness at that moment.

Maybe it always had been.

He had carried the baby with him the whole time he was gathering and building Rhapsody's bier, hour into hour until the night had come again. The child had slept, or watched with wide-open eyes, but rarely made a sound as he worked. He had been at a loss, however, as to where to leave or put him when moving the body, so in the end he had carried Rhapsody in his arms with the baby lying atop her, a last communion of mother and son that had made him physically sick.

Many times during the course of the night it occurred to him that he might be dreaming. He found himself wishing and hoping desperately that he was, but eventually he had only a pile of sticks at the opening of the tunnel overlooking the canyon and a body in his bed each time he went back to check on it, so he ultimately surrendered to the reality of Rhapsody's death and sank into survival mode, accomplishing what needed to be done in the same way he always had—silently and without a lot of fuss.

When the bier was finally finished, he and the glowing child returned to his chambers to gather the baby's mother and take her to her pyre. Her body had begun to stiffen slightly in the rictus of death, but it was still largely warm, almost as much as it had been in life. Once again he carried her, the child atop her, to the hallway and set her carefully down among the branches and sticks that he and their son had gathered for her.

Achmed had despaired of the ratty dressing gown that was the only clothing she had brought with her to Ylorc, a sad final costume in which to be sent off to the Afterlife. The irony of it amused him darkly; the woman who had most vehemently disdained the trappings of royalty and privilege had nursed a secret fondness for pretty clothing, even among the brutish denizens of Ylorc who were imagining, when they would see her attired in colorful dresses, what flavor the cloth marinades might have imparted to the meat.

The dressing gown was still open at the top, as it had been when she had brought his hand to rest on her heart in the conception of their child. Achmed saw the golden locket that she had always worn around her neck and carefully opened the clasp, took it from her throat, and closed the clasp again, then held it up to his eyes, examining it closely for the first time.

It was an inexpensive piece of jewelry, doubtless more sentimental than valuable. He opened the spring and a small, odd copper coin fell out, thirteen-sided, the like of which he had never seen before. He returned it to the locket and closed it again, putting it in his pocket.

He stretched her out atop the branches on which he had scattered the last flowers of summer that he could find. He had been amazed at how beautiful she had remained in death; it had occurred to him while gathering the wood that he might return to find that Time had caught up with her, that the thousands of years during which she had avoided aging might come to claim her while he was gone, but he noticed no change each time he had returned.

Gently he reached out and with the back of his hand caressed her small, perfect breasts, the nipples still pale pink and rosy, beautiful and desirable in a way she had never understood.

I have no breasts to speak of, she had said shyly as she revealed herself to him.

Then I will never speak of them. There aren't words worthy to do so.

He lowered his lips to the hollow between them and kissed her heart, still warm, but still, unbeating, beneath his sensitive lips.

Then he moved up to the rose-petal lips, the upper one shaped like a bow, and stared at them for a long moment.

If you want to, I think you should kiss me. It's not part of the actual ritual, but there's no reason we can't. And this time, if that happens, I promise you I will be kissing you with no one waiting to sweep me away, no battle we don't expect to survive, no comfort of a friend in mind, even though we are and always will be friends. If you kiss me this day, you will be kissing the mother of your child.

Achmed closed his eyes and leaned down, allowing his lips, thin and taut, to come to rest on hers, soft and plush, still warm.

Then he stood, looking down at her, the baby cradled in his arms now, sleeping, and thought back again to the time he had sat vigil over her when she had been at the point of death. The greatest healers of the City of Reason, the citadel Sepulvarta, where the Patriarch had held services in the basilica of the Star, Lianta'ar, had been unable to do anything but stanch her bleeding and advise him to prepare for the worst. Finally, he had remembered how, when he was griping about her wasting her time singing to comfort injured Bolg, she had given him the very tool to save her.

Well, that's a useful investment of your evening. I'm sure the Firbolg are very appreciative and will certainly reciprocate your ministrations if you should ever need something.

What does that mean?

I am trying to tell you that you will never see any return for your efforts. When you are injured or in pain, who will sing for you, Rhapsody?

Why, Achmed, you will.

Achmed sighed dispiritedly. He recalled sitting endlessly at her bedside, seeing no improvement, when finally the realization of what she meant had come to him. His words had perhaps been the first admission of love he had ever made, even if neither of them knew it, or could hear it, at the time.

Rhapsody, between two worlds I have had but two friends. I am not willing to let you alter this.

Now he had none.

But, through the memory, he now had her dirge.

He stood at the mouth of the cave, watching the wind play with her hair, brushing the edges of her tresses like a lover. He set the sleeping baby down again and carefully drew Daystar Clarion from its sheath.

As if the sword was mourning its bearer as well, no bright clarion call sounded, as it usually had when she drew it. The flames were burning quietly, just around the sword's tip, unlike the rolling blade of fire that it had been in her hand.

He expected it would be enough to light her pyre.

Then he discovered, upon touching it to the wood, that it wasn't.

The flames took the kindling at first, burning quietly and steadily, but rather than igniting her hair or her dressing gown, the bier seemed to be burning without taking her with it.

Annoyed, Achmed blew on the flames, but it seemed to have no impact.

"Hrekin," he said aloud; it had taken the better part of the day and night to gather the kindling, and now it was burning without accomplishing its purpose.

He looked at Rhapsody's body, glowing and untouched within the flame, and then down at the sword in his hand.

Then he realized his error.

Just as she and he had conjured the baby through their connection, his hand on her heart, so the sword must be mourning her, too, or at least subdued in the presence of an entity with as much or perhaps more fire lore than it had.

Careful of the flames, he laid the sword on her chest and abdomen, the hilt atop her heart, the blade pointing at her feet, and stepped back from the bier.

At first, the flames of the pyre roared higher, then settled into a steady burn.

Then, before his eyes, it seemed to him that the elemental fire she had absorbed in their trek through that inferno at the center of the Earth began to seep from her body, brightening the sword and the flames of the bier, leeching the color from her face and hands until she was as white as a dead birch tree. Beautiful as he had always thought the rosy golden glow of her skin to have been, there was something even more heart-rendingly magnificent in this aspect of her, absent the fire that had burned within her.

In the distance beyond the opening, morning was beginning to break, the sun still yet to appear, but the black of the night sky was fading to the blue-gray of foredawn.

Achmed took the sleeping baby back into his arms.

An image flashed before his eyes, her face, bruised and bleeding from her first combat on the Root, her eyes glittering in the fire-colored dark-light of the path through the Earth they had traveled to come away from what had pursued them relentlessly in Serendair. She had been applying bandages she had soaked in spice to his injured wrist, hesitantly singing her first song of healing.

Music is nothing more than the maps through the vibrations that make up all the world, she had said. *If you have the right map, it will take you wherever you want to go.*

How I wish I had the map to take you back in Time, he thought as the pyre began to smoke, its curling tendrils beginning to catch the wind of dawn beyond the tunnel opening. *How many things would I change if I could?*

He watched as the flames began to render her into ashes, and felt the song he had serenaded her back to life with once come to his lips again, a thousand years later. It was a song of his own making, a song of which even he didn't know the genesis.

He opened his mouth and began to sing in the three voices of the Dhracian race, one sharp and rapid, one low, like the shadow of a musical note just missed in the distance, and, from the back of his throat, coated in bile and nausea from his gut, the words he had sung her long ago.

> Mo hale maar, my hero gone
> World of star become world of bone
> Grief and pain and loss I know
> My heart is sore, my blood-tears flow
> To end my sorrow I must roam
> My terrors old, they lead me home.

In his imagination, he could see her stir as she had in the hospice bed the first time he had sung to her, eyes still closed. Her small, soft fingers, callused from years of playing stringed instruments, had brushed his hand, and he heard her inhale slowly, painfully, as if undertaking something very difficult.

Achmed?

Yes?

Will you keep singing until I'm better?

Yes.

Achmed?

What?

I'm better.

The gentle insult had made him smile in relief.

Obviously you're not much better if that's the best you can do. But you're still the same ungrateful brat you always were. That's nice thanks for someone who just gave you back the will to live.

You're right, you did, she had said slowly, with great effort. *Now that you—have given me—a taste of—what the Underworld—is like—*

Her words from the night before echoed louder in his mind and through his heart, making it bleed.

Do you feel better?

No. I'm not going to feel better.

He brought his lips to the baby's head and kissed him, then looked into the bier again.

Her skin and hair were aflame, gleaming with gold light. The sword of elemental fire was roaring with power, the blade alive as he had ever seen it.

Achmed stood, his lips still brushing the baby's golden hair that looked so much like his mother's, as the fire took her into its maw, screaming in the ecstasy of claiming one of its own, crackling with life and glee and welcome.

He turned away, unable to watch anymore.

"Goodbye, Rhapsody," he said quietly. "I hope the wind sings to you now."

He turned and took the baby away from that wind, deeper into the tunnel, and sat down, his back against the wall, as the smoke from the funeral pyre billowed out of the opening, over the canyon, and into the air of the mountains, rising into the pink and gold sunrise that was cresting the peaks of the Teeth.

He caressed their son as silent tears rolled down his cheeks.

I knew I would really only have you to myself in death.

29

At sunset that day, Meridion appeared at the opening of the long hallway leading to the overlook of the interior chasm in Ylorc.

Sitting beneath the overhang of the opening was the Bolg king, staring at the simmering ashes of a pyre, the elemental sword of fire glowing dully at its center, a birthing cloth in his hands swaddled around a sleeping infant. The baby's head, the only part of it visible, seemed to glow ethereally.

The battered scabbard of Daystar Clarion lay on the rocky ground beside him.

The smoke from the pyre lingered in the air above the ledge, a single curl rising above it and wafting over the wind across the vast gulf to the Blasted Heath beyond.

"Uncle?" he whispered.

Achmed did not respond, but continued watching the curl of smoke make its way east to where the sun would, with any luck, appear in the morning.

Meridion waited in silence. He tilted back his head and let the wind wash over his face, clean and cold, with the heavy scent of woodsmoke born of brambles and hastily gathered random kindling, and a lighter one, almost imperceptible, but familiar, the trace of vanilla and earthy spice, a hint of flowers and soap.

He choked back the tears that rose in memory.

Finally the Bolg king spoke woodenly.

"This is your mother's last child," he said. "She is dead. I burned her body." He glanced at Meridion, whose face was white but expressionless. "The pyre was lighted with her sword." He lifted the infant to his chest as it sighed aloud. "I tried to follow the appropriate death rituals that I have seen her perform endlessly over Time." He leaned back against the cliff wall with the baby up against his shoulder. "Of course, that means they were Bolg rites; I didn't pay attention to any Lirin dirges she ever sang."

"Thank you for tending to her. You have my gratitude."

"Spare me from it. I want nonesuch—I didn't do it for you."

Meridion nodded silently. He inclined his ear to the east. "His name is Graal."

Achmed's gaze sharpened, but he did not turn in Meridion's direction. "You know this how?"

"I'm a Namer. I can hear my mother's voice on the wind, pronouncing it. I can also smell the magic of his entry; he must have been summoned very near this place, too."

Achmed lapsed into silence. He took the quieted baby from his shoulder and cradled him in the crook of his arm again.

Meridion reached into the inner pocket of his cloak and pulled out the small box of Black Ivory which he had taken from the display in the Repository of Lore from under the eye of the Lirin guards who had been standing there, caught in between moments of Time.

"Uncle," he said again quietly.

"Begone." Achmed's voice was brittle and dry.

Meridion stood in silence for a moment, then exhaled and came closer until he could see the face of the baby in the Bolg king's arms.

"I have a story for you. Its ending isn't written yet." He swallowed; the words were the same as the ones the Bolg king had once uttered to his mother in the depths of the world, while they were traveling along the Root. It was a tale of great secrecy, of utter silence, and he knew that the Bolg king would remember them.

Achmed did not favor him with a glance. "Unless it is instructive of how to tend to this child, I am not interested in hearing it."

"It may be exactly that," Meridion said.

For a long moment there was no other sound. Then, at last, the Bolg king looked over his shoulder.

"What do you want?"

"I have just come from saying goodbye to my mother. I met her on the doorstep of the Gate of Life, beyond the Veil of Hoen. Now that she has left this life, she is the only other person who knows this tale. We can leave it that way if you wish. Or I can tell it to you. It is your choice."

He was met with nothing but silence, broken intermittently by the soft whistling of the sleeping baby, glowing within his woolen blanket in Achmed's arms.

Meridion sat down beside the Bolg king, at an angle, avoiding making eye contact with him, and began his tale.

"My parents met in the old world."

"So I have recently heard. Just when I thought there might be a limit to your father's ever-present, out-of-place imposition into every part of your mother's life, it turns out that he outdid himself, again."

"Whatever else you can justifiably hold against my father, that was not his fault, nor was it his doing."

Achmed looked out into the indigo dusk that hung heavy over the canyon to the night-stayed soldiers pacing slowly back and forth on the heath beyond it. "A thousand years ago, after your mother had killed Anwyn, she told me that before the Seer of the Past died, she told Rhapsody that Time had been altered for her, in a way that had made her existence better than it would have been on the first 'strand of Time,'" the Bolg king said at last. "But that was all she knew."

"Anwyn was referring to the meeting of my parents, in their youth, in the old world. That meeting led to my mother leaving her village of Merryfield in the middle of the Wide Meadows, looking for him, bringing her to the city of Easton, where you and Grunthor eventually came across her."

"I am aware."

Meridion's gaze also looked east across the canyon.

"My mother always believed that if she had not followed the boy who came to her, uncertain of how or why Time had been altered to bring him to Serendair, she would have been married off to a farmer she didn't love in her village's marriage lottery, lived and died long before the Seren War—that it was this meeting which brought her to this side of Time. But what she believed was not true."

Achmed glanced at him, but said nothing.

"I have seen the Weaver's tapestry beyond the Veil of Hoen," Meridion said, his voice dull with exhaustion and the effort to remain stoic.

"I have seen both the first strand of Time, which was burned when Time was altered, and the second one in which it was remade. She has seen them as well. Since you are part of the story, I believe you should hear how Time was altered for her. And my father." He exhaled. "And you."

Achmed looked down at the infant and adjusted his blanket.

"My mother's father, moved by her misery at that prospect, made inquiries of a passing Lirin troubadour who came through Merryfield just days before the marriage lottery," Meridion continued. "The man heard her singing in the barn, and made arrangements for her to study at Quieth Keep. So her desire to learn, something she communicated to the young boy on the second strand, saved her from the lottery."

Achmed's eyes narrowed.

"My understanding is that she was happy at the university, pursuing the science of healing through music. For the first time in her young life, she was not one of the only Lirin in her community. In addition to humans, among the faculty and the student body there were many other Lirin, as well as Ancient Seren, Nain, Gwenen—and even a half-Dhracian, half-Bolg man called the Brother, who also was studying healing, through a different method."

Achmed snorted. "You consider assassination a different method of healing?" he asked sourly.

Meridion shrugged. "I imagine it can be. But according to the tapestry, he wasn't studying assassination—just actual healing, as his mentor, a monk named Father Halphasion, had begun to show him."

"I think I've heard enough."

"If you say so. I think you believe otherwise, however. Or you should."

Achmed finally turned and stared at him with his mismatched eyes. Meridion waited, still keeping his own eyes fixed at an angle away from his gaze, but the Bolg king said nothing, so he continued his tale.

"At first, what you had in common with my mother, who was known to you initially as Emily, her family nickname, then later, when you became closer, by her given name, Amelia, besides the study of healing, was a young human woman by the name of Werinatha." Out of the corner of his eye, Meridion saw the Bolg king inhale, but maintained his gaze away. "My mother and she shared quarters in the university, and were dear friends—the closest thing to a sister my mother had ever known.

The tapestry of history shows that Werinatha and the Brother shared something more—a fondness that was mutual, and growing."

"Stop," Achmed ordered. The very air in the tunnel grew drier. "This is not history you wish to examine."

"I do not wish to examine that history. I am telling you the story of my mother. As a Lirin student of Singing, she was given a two-year pilgrimage, a Blossoming Year, just like her own mother, and sent after her first year of classroom study to the forest Yliessan, the Enchanted Wood where Sagia, the Great Tree, stood, to learn its song, and that of the Pool of the Heart's Desire, and Widershin's Stream, and all the other historic places housed within that enchanted wood.

"After the second year, her Year of Bloom, she returned to Quieth Keep, only to find it in ruins, destroyed by the accidental mismanagement of a magical undertaking that sought to cool the Sleeping Child, the star that had fallen ages before into the sea nearby, and threatened to rise, which eventually would result in the destruction of the Island of Serendair. On either strand, that cataclysm came to pass, as you well know.

"Also back from a scholarly pilgrimage was the Brother, who had arrived moments before her. Together the two of them stared in horror at the destruction of the university, seeing that only a very few had survived the disaster. Werinatha was not one of them. Jal'asee, however, *was*—which is why you hate him so, even now, three or more millennia later. Jal'asee had been one of the professors responsible for the undertaking that had ended in disaster, something else you do not forgive him for. That was true on both strands of Time as well."

Achmed turned away again.

"Your devastation broke my mother's heart. She knew the story of your youth, of your torture at the hands of the Bolg, of your mother's rape and death in childbirth. Your rage at what had happened to Werinatha was growing into something even more potentially destructive. And, just as you did after Grunthor's death, you and she turned to each other for comfort. Her love spared you, and the Island, from your wrath. Perhaps the greatest healing in her time as a Namer was that of you."

The Bolg king had fallen silent, staring down at the child in his hands.

"Graal—Graal was my mother's first child, not her last, born of blood and love—he was not conjured when the thread of Time was originally passed through the tapestry. He was conceived, as any real child is conceived, given to her by you, carried within her, and delivered from her body into your hands. The history says you loved them both, though your love was odd and fragmentary. So you did not follow the path of the second strand of Time—you did not become the primal assassin that you did when Time was remade."

Achmed was staring across the canyon again, silent.

"Do you understand, Uncle? On the first strand of Time, you were a *healer*—you did not have the skills that came when Time changed, because those skills were formed later in hatred, not love. You never met Grunthor, never learned to be the greatest of assassins—you never found yourself in the demon Tsoltan's employ, never had the key of bone that allowed the Three to leave Serendair in the second iteration of Time. You never came to the new world." He inhaled the dry, stinging air, then spoke as softly as he could.

"You died in the Seren War, Achmed."

He could hear the soft exhalation of the Bolg king's breath.

"My mother, however, survived. She fought in the war, though in the role of healer mostly, largely protected by Oelendra, her mentor on this Time-strand, who was younger than she on the first one." He shook his head. "Strange to contemplate; in this history, Oelendra was like her second mother. But the first time, she was like a daughter to her.

"Eventually the war ended, and Time went on. Gwylliam was born, and grew to be king of Serendair, was given his vision of the Cataclysm, and built his flotilla, led his exodus 'from the grip of death to life in this fair land.' My mother sailed with Oelendra, with the First Fleet, while Graal, a man by then, went with the Second—just as on the second strand, he was the one to provide the prophecy to Gwylliam of the Cataclysm. When that fleet was sundered at the Prime Meridian, MacQuieth offered the surviving members of it two options—to remain on the Island of Gaematria, which was within sight, or to sail back to Manosse. Graal chose Gaematria, and became the most visionary of the Sea Mages." Meridion looked down as his conjured half-brother. "My mother never saw him again."

In the depths of his blanket, the baby whimpered.

Achmed's sensitive hands stroked his cheek.

"She was greatly aged when she landed with the First Fleet in Elynsynos's lands. Like the other First Generation Cymrians, she did not grow older from that point on, and she continued to teach the science of Singing, and employ her talents as a healer. Then the Cymrian War came in response to the first Grievous Blow, and she served, again in her capacity as a healer and a woman of wisdom, on the Lirin council that repudiated both Anwyn and Gwylliam. The whole mess came to the same pathetic end it did on the second strand, with the continent divided against itself.

"But because the Three never came, because you and Grunthor were not there to kill the F'dor with her, the demons were ultimately victorious. Anwyn had shattered the Purity Diamond, which was the only real weapon against them, and soon the world was on fire, drifting through space, alight with smoke, dying. The Wyrm within its bowels was awakening."

Achmed removed his hand from the baby's face as he settled back into slumber. His own sallow face, etched with sorrow and exposed veins, grew even more somber.

"The remnants of the council took shelter in the mountains of the Deep Kingdom with the surviving leadership, particularly Faedryth, who had built his own Lightforge and had seen the end coming. Manwyn, also sheltered in the mountains of the Deep Kingdom, had uttered a prophecy about the unnatural child born of an unnatural act, saying it was the only hope of undoing the inevitable destruction of the Earth. Only after she had made that pronouncement did she warn Rhapsody about childbirth, that the mother would die, but the child would live."

Meridion's voice dropped to barely above a whisper.

"So she knew, Achmed. On the first strand of Time, my mother knew the cost, and understood what the consequences would be, both of taking the action, and of not doing so." He choked. "Even though she did not on the second strand."

For the first time since he had begun his tale, Achmed nodded.

"Go on," he said as if the words pained him.

Meridion felt tears stinging the corners of his eyes.

"Among the others taking shelter in the Deep Kingdom was Llauron, who had brought along his wounded son, Gwydion. Gwydion was almost a vegetable, a profoundly broken man who had undertaken the same brave deed he had on this Time-strand—he gone to the House of Remembrance alone, expecting to meet Oelendra there, and was torn apart by the F'dor on midsummer's night. As on the second strand, his friend Stephen Navarne found him, dying, Oelendra took him to the Veil of Hoen, and the Lord and Lady Rowan patched him back together as well as they could. But, because he had never met my mother in the old world, nor had he been healed with the Ring of Wisdom she gave to him on the second strand of Time, he had sunken into madness, drowning in unrelenting pain, his arms restrained, a gag in his teeth most of the time.

"Being a Namer of the highest order, my mother knew the lore of conjuring. The Council agreed, including Llauron, that Gwydion would be the one to be asked to provide the second piece of soul to bring this unnatural child into existence, this child that was to be 'born free of the bonds of Time.' Just as my mother asked you to do with Graal in this Time.

"So she went to the cave that served as a protective cell for Gwydion with a birthing cloth, and knelt before him, aged as she was. He was ranting, spitting in pain and fury when she first came in, but she asked the guards to leave in spite of the danger. And then she smiled at him, which gave him pause in his ravings, and began to sing."

Achmed exhaled.

"She sang his namesong, over and over, weaving calming and clarity into it, until he finally grew quiet and his eyes cleared of the madness. She took out his gag, and untied his arms, and rather than striking or biting at her, he smiled back. For a few moments, she had found the lost soul within the overwhelming agony.

"And when she had found him, she asked him if he could possibly bring himself to love her just for a moment, long enough to bring a child into the world with her."

Achmed clenched his teeth until he could taste the blood in his mouth.

"He stared at her. Then he smiled again. And he uttered the first coherent word he had pronounced since that night at the House of Remembrance—*yes*—and let his hand come to rest on her heart."

Meridion stopped. A thin trail of blood had spilled from the corner of the Bolg king's mouth.

"Shall I finish?" he asked, uncertain.

Achmed nodded curtly.

Meridion took a deep breath that rattled against his lungs. "She sang the incantation of conjuring, during which Gwydion remained calm.

And, when she felt ready, she rose with the cloth, lifted her arms aloft, and the baby appeared in it from the air itself."

He was now struggling with tears that were choking his words.

"Me, Uncle—that was me. *I* was the unnatural child born of an unnatural act—the child she knew would kill her to bring into the world. I was not born of blood and love, but of ancient lore and Naming science. I was her *second* son—the one without flesh or substance, the same state that Graal is condemned to now. He was her firstborn on the first Time-strand—her child of blood, of love—and yours.

"She—she had just enough time to—to kiss me, to whisper my name and that she loved me—before Death took her, and took her violently, grotesquely, in agony, splitting her from her throat—"

"Stop," Achmed said tonelessly. The word had all the gravitas of a Namer's command, filling the corridor with heavy silence.

Meridion waited for his tears to stanch, for Achmed's breath to return.

"That is her legacy to Graal as well—she did exactly the same thing in her remaining moments, in his first ones of existence," he said finally. "At least her death this time was not painful—because of a boon she had asked of the Lord Rowan long ago.

"And you, Achmed, you granted her last wish, her last boon—you gave her Graal, when my father wouldn't. She could not deny his namesong—the tone, she called it, of a child that was waiting to come forth into the world. Perhaps Ashe knew that he wasn't meant to be this child's father. But you were willing to do as she asked."

Achmed let all of his breath out slowly.

"You make it sound so altruistic," he said darkly. "In fact, my participation was utterly selfish. It was *my* desire to give him to her, to help bring him forth—to make a child with her.

"And, in doing so, I killed her."

30

$\mathcal{F}$or a long moment, no sound was heard but the whine of the wind in the cavern.

Meridion looked across the chasm where the Heath was now impossible to discern from the darkness.

"A funny thing about Time," he mused. "As far as I know, it has only been altered once, at least in the world that we see.

"You didn't kill her, Achmed. You gave her what she wanted, what she asked of you. And you have given the world this child, again, for what purpose, who knows, but the air around him indicates that it is an important one. I cannot tell you how to feel, what to believe, nor would I deign to do so, but at least to me, there are some things that are foreordained, that happen no matter what goes on with the threads of Time."

He looked at the Bolg king, who was now staring at his son—Meridion's half-brother.

"Gwydion fell back into madness, as everyone knew he would," he continued. "I don't know what became of my father after that—there is nothing reflected on the burnt strands of Time that I have seen. But at least for a moment, he saw sanity again, and in that moment, chose to father a child with an extraordinary woman, a child who had a role to play in undoing how Time had originally run—a scenario that allowed for the F'dor to escape the Vault, and wake the Wyrm—leaving the world dying in flames. So whatever the cost to him, or to me—to you and to Graal—at least the potential exists now for that to be made right."

Achmed looked up. Until he did, Meridion was not certain he even was listening.

"And how precisely do you know that?" he asked quietly, with a nasty undertone. "For all you know, all will result in the same outcome anyway."

Meridion turned away from the ashes being taken in plumes by the wind and came over to where the Bolg king sat in the tunnel, the baby in his arms. He crouched down in front of them.

"May I see him?" he asked.

Achmed glared at him with his mismatched eyes for a moment, an expression that over time had caused a great number of men to lose their water, pissing themselves in fear. But Meridion maintained a pleasant expression in return, and so the Bolg king relented finally and turned the baby toward him.

The motion caused Graal to open his eyes, his father's eyes, free of the dragonesque pupils that all of Rhapsody's other children had inherited. The baby looked at him curiously, his mouth puckering in interest.

"Hello, little brother," Meridion said softly, cautiously extending a fingertip in as nonthreatening a manner as he could manage and caressing the back of the little boy's curled fist. "Welcome to the world."

The baby's hand opened at the caress, and Meridion moved his finger under the child's palm, so that his tiny fingers would encircle it.

"Apparently I was both motherless and fatherless upon *my* appearance in the world, so Faedryth took me under his wing, with the help of the other members of the council, and taught me all the lore of the Earth he knew, and much of the engineering and mechanics as well. Eventually, he helped me to build a laboratory, a glass dome of a sort suspended above the Earth, with a viewing window below, where I could see the planet burning. I imagine my 'childhood' was a rather rapid one; since the whole point of my conception had been to make use of me to offset the coming devastation, I suppose that I grew to a manhood of a sort very quickly, 'born free of the bonds of Time.'

"Faedryth and I built a machine called the Time Editor—its name explains its purpose. I was a little concerned when I discovered this part of the history on the Weaver's tapestry while I was awaiting my mother's arrival at the Gate of Life, but it may actually be an evolution of something I've been working on in this iteration of Time."

He removed his finger gently from Graal's tiny hand and drew forth the Black Ivory box again, opened it and took out the burnt strands of time-thread that Faedryth's miners had discovered deep within the Distant Mountains of the Nain, and held them up before the Bolg king's eyes.

"If you hold these to the light, you can hear the last conversation—just an exchange of a few words, really—that Faedryth and I had before I was sent up into the laboratory to do what I could to rewrite Time."

Achmed stared at the Time-strands. They looked like clear parchment, though it was filmy and inconstant, yellowed with age, seemingly made of part translucent gem, part gossamer, changing moment by moment before his eyes.

"On the second strand, in the current, remade version of Time, these were found in the deepest reaches of the Nain crystal mines, where the diamond-like formations were believed to have been brought to the Earth from the stars in the form of meteorites. They lay beneath tons of age-old granite for tens of thousands of years before the Nain finally broached the mine, survived the pressure and the cold of the crystal bed—truly a miracle."

He smiled as his young half-brother stretched and yawned in his sleep, then handed the timefilm to the Bolg king.

Reluctantly, Achmed looked at the strand.

It was as if he was himself standing in the place where the image had been captured, a dark hall that could have been within the mountainous caverns of Ylorc, though he knew immediately that it was not. Gauging by the thinness and striations of the stone, he guessed it was in some mountain peak in another range, most likely similar or even adjoining of this one.

At the end of the hall was an opening, past which there appeared to be a laboratory of some sort, within a large, clear sphere suspended in the open darkness of the sky. Uniform lines of light were set into panels that encircled the transparent room.

Beyond the clear walls of the sphere he could see the world down below, burning at the horizon, as fire crept over the edges, spreading among the continents he recognized from the maps of the Earth.

Hovering in the air before him was a being, a man of sorts, with characteristics of several different races, and all the aspects of youth, except for his eyes, blue eyes, deep as the sea, scored with vertical pupils, resonating wisdom.

He glanced up at Meridion, and into those exact eyes, except solid, corporeal, unchanging, then back at the Time-strands once more.

The man's skin was translucent, like that of the child in his arms, motile, altering with each current of air that passed by or through it. The man actually glowed, especially his hair, curls of brilliant gold that almost seemed afire, like Graal's hair more than Meridion's. It was a slightly altered picture of the young man he had known in Meridion's youth, a young man for whom he had been asked to be the guardian.

And despite the young man's obvious wisdom, the image of his clenched jaw betrayed a quiver of nervousness.

His lips moved. Achmed did not hear what words the young man formed in his own ears, but they resonated in his mind nonetheless.

Will I die?

Another voice, immediately and annoyingly recognizable to the Bolg king as that of Faedryth, Lord of the Nain of the Deep Kingdom, answered.

Can one experience death if one is not really alive? You, like the rest of the world, have nothing to lose.

The translucent young man nodded and turned away.

Achmed shook his head to clear his eyes of the image, but as he did, he heard the young Meridion's voice in his head again, but with the ring of maturity, as if he had been somewhat older at the time of the utterance.

Forgive me. In my place, I think you would have done the same. Given the choice, I think you would have wanted it that way, too.

"I suspect at the time I said it, I was speaking to you," Meridion said as the Time-strand returned to its changing state. "I don't know why."

"You don't know anything," Achmed said in a low, deadly voice. "You have no idea what I would have wanted. Even I do not know that."

"I suppose," Meridion said, putting the Time-strand back in the Black Ivory box. "But either way, this is how my mother was meant to die. The way I look at it, she would have died in horrifying agony, but producing the child that went back to rewrite history, which allowed the world to survive at least a bit longer. That new course of history gave her a love that lasted a thousand years and produced many great descendants that the first Time-strand did not, as well as allowing her to still know and love a strange, irascible man who fathered her child in both iterations of Time, and who lives to watch that child grow up. In any case, as the Lirin say, *Ryle hira*—Life is what it is.

"That is the end of my tale, with illustrations, my song, a symphony of Ages spanning from before the Seren War in the Third Age to the end of this one, the Sixth Age, which in what little I can see of the Future will be known as Twilight. The paradox is complete. You deserved to be the one to hear the lore, Uncle, to be made aware of how Time had been altered, what you gained by it—and what you lost in it. It is the Weaver's Lament—when the threads of Time are undone, the song of the Past is resung with new words and new music. It becomes a matter of opinion which iteration is better for the world—nothing more, at least in the eyes of Time."

Achmed continued to watch his sleeping son, deep in thought. Finally he did not look up, but he spoke.

"Your mother's pyre is probably still warm. Do you wish to sing her dirge?"

Meridion closed his eyes and concentrated for a moment, then shook his head.

"It appears to have already been sung," he said.

At last the Bolg king looked up. "I assure you it was not, or at least not done properly," he said. "No one was here other than your mother, your brother, and me. She was dead at the time, he is an infant and very quiet."

"Did you sing?"

The Bolg king went back to looking at his son.

Meridion smiled sadly. "The wind is satisfied. Thank you, as I said before, for attending to her. I will make my own remembrance in other places, at other times. I appreciate you hearing me out."

He caressed the baby's head, then rose from the tunnel floor.

Achmed looked up again. "Where is your father's sword?"

"It rests on the altar stone beyond the Water Basilica in Avonderre, the place dedicated to MacQuieth Monodiere Nagall. My mother instructed me to attempt to pick it up, which I did, but I was refused. It was my parents' intent to surrender it to whomever the weapon chose."

Achmed nodded wordlessly.

"Goodbye, then, Uncle," Meridion said as he put away the Black Ivory box and straightened his belt and his gear. "I wish you consolation, and hope one day I will see you again."

"Wait. Here." Achmed rose as well and went down the hall to the opening of the tunnel where the remains of the ash bed were still taking to the wind. He crouched down and touched the cinders with his thumb, then pressed them onto the baby's chest above his heart.

"You are only the second person I have ever said these words to, Graal—my—son," he whispered in the Bolgish tongue. "It would be easier for me to wring the blood from my own throat than to say them to anyone else; I could barely bring myself to say them to your mother. But I do love you. Odd and fragmentary as that love might be, it is indeed yours. I hope whatever magic you have inherited from Rhapsody allows you to know, even though it is unlikely you will ever see me again, that you have my love, and that of your mother, for all of Time, cursed entity that Time may be."

He pressed his lips to Graal's forehead, receiving a series of soft sounds in return.

Then he returned to where Meridion was still standing.

"Take your mother's sword and come with me," he said.

THE CAULDRON, AT THE LIGHTCATCHER

The Bolg king led Meridion to the Cauldron, the center of most of the royal activity from the very founding of Canrif in this place almost three millennia before, and had the Child of Time follow him through the great hall of thrones to the chamber beyond it, where the glass funicular and the tower staircase stood.

He brought him, past whole cohorts of soldiers who were still wandering aimlessly, into Gurgus Peak where the Lightcatcher was churning, spending the memory of light that had been stored in its diamond power source.

Achmed stunned Meridion by striding into the center of the instrumentality where the altar-like table stood and, after kissing his head, put Graal down on the table.

He turned to Rhapsody's horrified eldest son.

"This is the seventh of your mother's children, the New Beginning. I think you should utilize the Lightcatcher's violet spectrum of the same name to bless him with whatever the powers are of being so named."

Meridion exhaled slowly. Then a small smile came over his face.

"At your will, Your Majesty."

Achmed slipped his sensitive, vein-scored fingertip into his son's grasp. The baby seized it and kicked wildly.

"If you wish to make up for your father's debt, care for this child as your mother would have," he continued. "Ask Analise o Serendair if you need her help; she will know what a magical child needs. You may not have been summoned into existence as he was on this strand of Time, but you were a magical infant with special powers and needs nonetheless. Analise was invaluable in taking care of you in Rhapsody's absence during the War of the Known World."

"Absence?"

The Bolg king nodded distantly.

"Your mother decided, once a coterie of assassins from the Raven's Guild in Yarim and the Spider's Clutch in Golgarn infiltrated these mountains, that you were no longer safe here, so she took you to the Distant Mountains of the Deep Kingdom and begged Faedryth to give you sanctuary, as you undoubtedly know," he said. "She did that because she felt the world you had been born into was not safe for you—and she was certainly correct about that. She knew it was her duty, her honor, to try and rectify that situation, mostly for you, but also for the rest of the world. The sacrifices she made to do it, on top of the separation, which tore her heart out, were numerous and terrible, but in the end, the world prevailed."

He looked back down at Graal and smiled at him.

"The world today is no different. Your father managed to keep a reliable peace and most often order, but there are ancient threats that have not been eradicated that still threaten your mother's children—and mine. It's my duty, and my honor, to try and rectify those situations as well."

"It would be my honor to take care of Graal until you return," Meridion said, watching Achmed and his son communicate silently. "And appropriate—I have reason to believe that he would have done the same for me by the old Time-strand."

"What makes you think so?"

"Well, as I told you, when Graal made his passage in Gwylliam's exodus, he sailed with the Second Fleet, and made the decision to stay on the Island of Gaematria, nearby to where the fleet sundered. He became the greatest of all the Sea Mages, and I know it was my mother's wish that I be allowed to study with them should things have worked out. So it is the least I can do to assist in his care."

Achmed winced and rolled his eyes. "The Sea Mages are on my list of Most Hated Entities, right up there with priests and academicians—well, I suppose they are a little of both, come to think of it."

Meridion nodded, too encompassingly sad to appreciate the humor.

"With your permission, I believe I will make use of your suggestion and will take him first to Analise," he said, thinking back to one of the few Liringlas he knew, his mother's oldest friend from the Island, for whom Rhapsody had sacrificed much in those bad days. "She is a midwife of consummate ability, and has been like an aunt to me all my life. She will be able to assess him in Manosse to best determine his needs as a summoned child, and give him a peaceful place to spend his earliest days—I fear I need to help my siblings cool the preparations for war which were enacted a short time ago. When peace has returned to both sides of the Middle Continent, I will plan to take him and keep him in my care, until you return."

"Whatever you decide, I'm certain you will take good care of Graal. Having seen how you dealt with your younger brothers and sisters, I know you will do well by him."

Achmed reached into his pocket and pulled out the golden locket that he had taken from Rhapsody's neck.

"This was your mother's. I don't really ever remember seeing her without it."

Meridion's eyes filled with tears. "Aye."

"I thought you might want it. Do with it what you will. Now, let us get to blessing Graal with the violet spectrum of light, and I will provision your journey personally, as my soldiers are still affected by the indigo light."

Meridion nodded. He turned to the Lightcatcher, sang the note for the violet part of the spectrum, *Grei-ti,* and set about bathing his baby brother in the light of the New Beginning, feeling both guilty and relieved.

He had spared Achmed the last detail of the story of the time-threads and the change in the Weaver's tapestry.

It was a piece of information that would haunt his own father, should it ever become known to him.

That in the first iteration of Time, once his own birth had been accomplished, and Rhapsody had succumbed to her gruesome death, he himself had eventually been found by the guards, by his grandfather Llauron, by Oelendra and Faedryth and the other refugees in the Distant Mountains, cradled gently in his father's arms.

He was covered in his mother's blood—blood that was dripping from his father's mouth, the remains of her flesh in his teeth.

Just as Ashe had dreamt about in his nightmares on this side of Time.

It was the cost of seeing the Weaver's tapestry that would ruin his own sleep for the rest of his life.

He had not chosen to give the Bolg king the satisfaction or the grief in the knowledge that, while Achmed had been partially responsible for her death by aiding her in a decision she had made herself on this side of Time, Ashe had, in his last remaining moment of clarity, tried to put her out of her agony in the only way the dragon within him knew how on the first strand of it.

If for no other reason, the fact that my alteration of Time prevented that from happening was well worth it, he thought.

PROPHECY OF THE LAST GUARDIAN

Within a Circle of Four
Will stand a Circle of Three
Children of the Wind all, and yet none
The hunter, the sustainer, the healer
Brought together by fear, held together by love,
To find that which hides from the Wind

Hear, oh guardian,
And look upon your destiny:
The one who hunts will also stand guard
The one who sustains will also abandon
The one who heals will also kill
To find that which hides from the Wind

Listen, oh Last One, to the wind:
The wind of the Past to beckon her home
The wind of the Earth to carry her to safety
The wind of the Stars to sing the mother's song most known to her soul
To hide the Child from the Wind.

From the lips of the Sleeping Child will come the words
of ultimate wisdom:
Beware the Sleepwalker
For blood will be the means
To find that which hides from the Wind.

31

CLAPPERCLAW MOUNTAIN, YLORC

There should have been light.

Achmed had been sitting at the top of the peak of Clapperclaw Mountain, the tallest of all the fanglike peaks of the Teeth, waiting for hours for the morning to come.

And it had come, he supposed, after a disturbingly long time waiting for it. The black night had faded somewhat to a duller gray-blue, the color left over in the sky when the sun has finally taken all the ribbons of colored clouds with it beyond the horizon, but sunlight did not come with morning.

He looked down from his lofty perch at the world below, a world that had changed after a thousand years of being the same to something he could not fathom, let alone recognize.

Even now, the Firbolg soldiers were wandering the mountain paths, or the steppes, or the breastwork tunnels beyond Grivven Post, lost, it seemed, in the lands they had traveled all their lives. The night had been called, and it had come, refusing to leave. All the thrill of the buildup, the excitement of the camaraderie of brothers-in-arms, ramping up to ride off and wreak havoc in the act of avenging a beloved leader, was dissipating as they stood, waiting to be summoned by the bugle call of reveille that wasn't coming.

Once he had stood in this very place, seeking the heartbeat of a F'dor spirit that had used its host's blood to form a tainted construct called a

Rakshas, a creature, by ironic coincidence, that had looked exactly like Ashe. He had stood at the summit of the mountain, silently calling for the heartbeat to lock itself on to his own, while Rhapsody and Grunthor had accompanied him in silence, waiting to follow him once his prey was snared.

And when at last he had found it, had located its trail, they had followed him down the mountain blindly, had run as he ran, until at last the Three had come upon the first of their great quarries and had worked as a team to destroy it.

He breathed in the cool, thin air of the mountaintop, and closed his eyes, trying to hang on to the memory for just a moment longer.

They were gone now, he knew, the only two people he was certain he had ever loved. Dear as Rhapsody's children were to him, the esteem in which he had held her was not in the same realm as his affection for any of them.

She had referred many times to Ashe as being the other half of her soul; now Achmed wondered if, in fact, the other half of his had been Grunthor. There was something comforting about the friendship that Achmed imagined would have been impossible to expect from a woman, a silent acceptance and fit that had always felt easy on his shoulders.

Achmed wondered if the darkness he had called would ever give way again.

"I am here, Bolg king."

Achmed opened his eyes.

Standing before him on the summit of the mountain was a face he had known only on this side of Time, but which had taught him more about his own beginnings, his roots—the mother he had never known—than any other.

Rath.

The Dhracian was looking down at him with what he grudgingly assumed was sympathy within the ancient man's liquid black eyes without scleras, and it irritated him.

Achmed had been Rath's quarry for centuries before they had finally come upon one another. Given that every other name Rath had been seeking was that of a demon, Achmed did not find that notion flattering.

And yet, not long after he, Grunthor, and Rhapsody had taken the mountains, Rath had appeared, finally having located him by the name the Bolg of Serendair had given him at birth, *Ysk,* the word for spittle. The Dhracian had explained to the incredulous king that not only he but all the upworld Dhracians, those who hunted for the loose spirits of F'dor demons in the material world, were seeking him as well, because he, as a Dhracian, should have been part of the Common Mind, the hive-like consciousness to which all with Dhracian blood had a connection.

But, Rath had said, the Bolg king had something more. The accident of his birth, the mass rape of his mother by a contingent of Bolg in the old world, had produced in him ties not only to the wind, the element from which Dhracians had sprung, but also to Earth, the origin of his father's race, whoever that father might have been.

It was a birthright that would give him the ability to not only find the elusive F'dor spirits in the air of the upworld, which all Dhracians possessed, but the ability to walk their prison of Living Stone, known as the Vault of the Underworld, and draw strength from the element from which it was made.

Rath had hounded him, more or less ceaselessly, from the time he had come across him, to take up that task.

You will need to answer this question, Assassin King—are you more assassin, or are you more king?

His first reply, a thousand years before, had been that he was a king, the ruler of a realm of monstrous men he was trying to reclaim, to take the bastard race of Firbolg, that of his unknown father, and make them a force to be contended with in the eyes of the world.

With Grunthor's help, and Rhapsody's, he had done that.

But now that they were both gone, and their goal had long been accomplished, Achmed could feel a change in the wind from which his mother sprang.

"You beckoned?"

Achmed exhaled and nodded.

"What is your need?"

"I have a proposal for you, Rath," he said.

The Dhracian said nothing, waiting.

"You have long been after me to join the Primal Hunt with you and the others of our race. And while I have assisted you in the capture and killing of a few of the names on your list, I have resisted taking on that task as my first priority—something I know that has bothered you immensely over the centuries."

Rath studied his face.

"I am not bothered, Majesty. I am just perplexed at how one of our race has managed to deny the primordial urge, the needles in our veins that demand we submit to the Primal Hunt before all else."

"Just lucky, I suppose. I have a question to ask you."

The Dhracian waited.

"Has the Hunt been completed? Or do you have a new list of names?"

The Dhracian's pupils expanded, watching him intensely.

"I no longer have a list. You helped with some of them on it."

"Is that because all the upworld F'dor are dead—or just because the hunters have killed all that they know about? Could there be more that we do not know about?"

Rath stared at him.

"There could always be more that we do not know about, Majesty," he said darkly. "That is why we continuously comb the wind, looking for a trace of the odor of burning flesh in fire. Having the names of some of the Older and the Younger Pantheon was a helpful tool, but finding those on the list was not an end in itself."

"I thought so. So the Primal Hunt continues?"

"Of course."

"Why?"

The Dhracian's mouth drew tight in annoyance. "I should not have to answer this question for you, half-breed or otherwise."

"Humor me. As I said, I have a proposal for you. I need these answers to be clear before I offer it."

Rath's jaw, taut a moment before, slackened. He understood the need to apply questions to any situation in which there was uncertainty.

"The Primal Hunt continues until the Earth does not, because if there is a chance that a F'dor spirit has been overlooked, the Earth *will* not. If a demon is hiding, unknown, somewhere in the cracks of the Earth, or within the wind itself, the possibility remains that it will continue to grow in strength and power until it finds a way to open the Vault of the Underworld and set the rest of its race free.

"We know that there is still at least one more living Earthchild, a child that slumbers eternally within your own kingdom, and whose rib would serve as a key to the Vault. Unfortunately, we know that they are also aware of this. They know that she lives, and where she sleeps—and that it is unlikely you would ever seek to move her, for you fear her death, whereas her rib is of value to them whether or not she is alive. And you are more than aware of the answer to your own questions—so what is it you are thinking?"

The Bolg king leaned back and let the thin wind and the wisps of clouds at the mountaintop race over the sensitive skin of his face.

"What am I thinking?" he mused, almost to himself. "I am thinking about my children."

Rath blinked his enormous eyes.

"Your children?"

"Yes."

"Forgive me, I was unaware that you had any."

"So was I, for the longest time."

The Dhracian looked uncomfortable. "I would have thought that such news would have been passed along through the Common Mind, given how important progeny are to the continuation of our guardian race."

"They are mostly not of our guardian race," Achmed said. "The first was the child you have already referenced—the Earthchild. She was the first vulnerable entity to whom I have sworn protection, with my life. You asked me once if I was more assassin, or more king—being a king allows me to guard her with considerable resources, rather than being out chasing ephemeral demons in the wind across the wide world. Chasing and killing demons would have been ever so much more fun and rewarding, but she needed me here. So here I have stayed, as much as I could."

"I see," said Rath. "Are there others?"

"Rhapsody told me early on that the Bolg were my children, though I scoffed at her at the time. But if children are brutish, unevolved resources that you put your time and your guidance, your knowledge and your faith into, for a purpose greater than your own selfish desires, I suppose she was right."

He glanced down from the mountain into the blue shadows, where the children he had just mentioned were moving slowly, wandering aimlessly, waiting for a war that, with any luck, would never come.

"And there are children who call me 'Uncle,' the strangest of experiences for one who had neither siblings nor parents in his life. Rhapsody's children, six in all, and a multitude of their own progeny. She made it a point to bring them to these mountains at least once a year during their childhoods, to visit, to learn their great-grandfather's engineering brilliance, military training from Grunthor, weapons and other manufacturing, nit-picking skills, snot assault skills and other Firbolg manners—"

Rath raised an eyebrow.

"—and, the most important lesson, that the Bolg are beings entitled to the same treatment that the people of Roland enjoy. And to know their uncles."

He sighed. It was a sound full of memory.

"And, at last, my actual son."

"You have a son?" Rath's tone was cautious.

"Yes." *Only in the thin air of a mountaintop could my head be so light as to be talking of this,* he thought.

"Of whom?"

"It doesn't matter. She's dead." Achmed sat forward and leaned an arm on his leg.

"Condolences." Rath looked away to the east, where the sun seemed absent. "Was he conjured?"

Achmed sat up, his eyes narrowing. "Why do you ask?"

"Because I felt a momentary trembling in the Common Mind a few days ago, a new song on the wind, if only for a moment," Rath said. "It put me in mind of the Lady Cymrian, who has studied the conjuring of a child with me, as well as with others knowledgeable of the lore. I do not know if you recall this, but long ago, when I met her first son, I asked if he had been conjured, because there was such a magical air about him."

Achmed lapsed into silence.

"What has put you in mind of them all today?"

The wind whistled through suddenly, bringing a chill with it.

"I am trying to find a reason to do something ultimately selfless," Achmed said. "That has never been in my nature; I am a selfish bastard of famous reputation. But an idea has come into my head that I cannot displace, as much as I might try. It's utterly illogical and undoubtedly suicidal. So I have been undertaking to determine what knobbing *arse* is manipulating my thoughts in this way."

"An unpleasant thing to say about your children."

The Bolg king smiled wryly.

"*I* am the knobbing arse, Rath."

"Well, I cannot dispute that." The ancient Dhracian's serious expression eased slightly for a breath, then returned to its stolidity. "What do you propose to undertake that would be for your children, and not yourself? Are you finally ready to join the Primal Hunt?"

"No, and never." Achmed brushed the rocky dirt from his hands and stood, looking west. "I think I am finally ready to walk the Vault."

An even heavier silence fell.

Rath was making the attempt to breathe quietly.

"But I cannot do it alone."

The Dhracian shook his head, as if trying to dislodge a gnat from his ear. "Who would you imagine could do it with you?"

"You, Rath."

"I have no lore of Earth—"

"I know. And I had no intention of taking you in with me."

"Then, what do you—"

"I want you to guard my oldest child," Achmed said to the Krevensfield Plain beyond the Teeth and the steppes leading up to them. "When she was first brought to the tunnels below the mountains by the Dhracians in the Colony that fought to protect her, she always had a guardian, an *amelystik,* who cared for her day into night into day." He took in a measured breath and let the moist fog fill his mouth, cooling the acid of the words forming with it. "She has recently lost that guardian."

Rath's eyes closed.

"I am so sorry. Was it in childbirth? A result of conjuring?"

Achmed's mind roiled at the intrusion he would normally feel at Rath's unwanted perception, but he merely nodded. "So if you would like the event you predicted long ago to take place, you would need to agree to remain with her, day into night into day, and protect her with your life. You alone of anyone I know, at least those still among the living, are uniquely qualified to do so. You could sense a F'dor coming, more likely than anyone else, and you are a master hunter. She would be safer with you than with any other choice I could make."

Rath nodded. His eyes took on a gleam.

"Do not agree too quickly, Rath. Guardianship of any entity below ground is like death for those of our race, accustomed to the buffeting of the wind and the freedom of the open air. It must have been so with our forebears that gave up their connection to the sky to live in the bowels of the world, standing guard over the Vault. I need you to vow that you will protect her with your life and everything you have, forever if necessary, until I return victorious, or at least until you know that the Vault is empty." He smiled sardonically. "It will probably be an endless commitment."

"You have my vow."

Achmed nodded, looking suddenly older.

"When would this commence?" Rath asked.

The Bolg king picked up his pack and his weapons from the ground. "Now," he said.

He turned without another word or glance and made his way west down the mountain, through the heavy blue mist and into the light of the brightening day.

The next task Achmed undertook was the summoning, and the gathering, of the Archons.

It took far longer for them to arrive on the steppes than he had hoped, each of them called by name through the speaking tubes that wound throughout the mountainous realm, an innovative communication system that had been designed and installed initially within the Cauldron by Gwylliam in the first Cymrian era, then extended to the entirety of the mountain range in the thousand years of his own reign. By the time the last one, Zifhram, the Archon of Agriculture, had arrived, the Bolg king was beyond furious, struggling to keep his rage in check, knowing that it was by his own hand that his specialists were slowed.

He was standing at the far edge of the steppes, where the low scrub and short, dry swales transitioned to the open rolling grasslands of the Krevensfield Plain. A beautiful gray stallion waited quietly beside him, saddled and tacked by the king's own hand, provisioned for a long journey. Across his back he wore a specially fashioned dual bandolier, a sheath that would hold two swords, and a hook at his belt for the cwellan, the strange, curved crossbow-like missile weapon that he had designed himself long before. In one of the sheaths of his bandolier, Tysterisk, the elemental sword of Air, rested.

The other was empty.

Achmed gestured impatiently for the Archons, the first rank of leadership below him, to come closer.

He looked at them, thirty or more generations removed from the original group of children Rhapsody had suggested he garner from each of the tribes that he had vanquished in the taking of the mountain, children who showed particular intelligence or promise in a variety of areas.

Idly he thought back to those original orphans, offered up in relief and disgust by the tribes, who then had discovered to their shock that those unwanted children were received into the king's favor, trained and educated and given positions of power in his court. He had insisted on maintaining at least a modicum of wildness, a dose of demi-humanity, in the generations of Archons that came later, fearful that if he bred all the monster out of the race that they might devolve even further into a construct he could not stomach—the race of humans.

Normally it was a secret thrill to see them assemble, the fruits of a thousand years of his labor, the masterwork of each member of the Three, their hirsute faces dark, their eyes focused, their expressions calm. Now what was staring back at him was a loosely organized group, more cogent than the wandering hordes of soldiers and everyday Bolg citizens, but not as clear and attentive as they normally were. Still, they had managed to follow the instructions and so now stood at attention amid the brushy clumps of grass.

"By my command, you are to stand down from the war now," he instructed, trying not to give in to the anger that was brewing behind his eyes at the docile, confused looks on the faces of his elite council. "I leave on the morrow—by the time you have shaken off the effects of the Lightcatcher, I will be far beyond your reach. I don't know if or when I will return, so the council of Archons shall rule and keep order in my absence. You are the terminus of a thousand years of breeding and training. Continue that tradition, and keep the Bolglands safe."

The Archons stared blankly at him, then nodded distantly.

Achmed exhaled. There was nothing more he could do.

Either the Bolg will stand in the trenches that Grunthor dug for them, operating in the systems I designed for them, farming the fields, educating the children, and healing the wounded as Rhapsody taught them, or they will return to the roving demi-human monsters they were when we came here a thousand years ago, he mused. *The time has come to see what path they choose, but, in any case, it is their path now.*

He sighed, letting the air in his lungs take any further sense of re-sponsibility with it into the dusty wind of the steppes.

"Best of luck to you," he said. "My children."

He mounted his horse and rode away without even a glance behind him.

32

THE GREAT FOREST

The wind stayed at his back almost the entire way across the continent, rippling the manes of each of the Wings he rode.

When he came to the first of the stables of the elite horses, the one within his own livery at the outer reaches of Ylorc, the Archon of the Wings had the next mount groomed, fed, watered, and ready, in spite of being somewhat logy and disconnected himself.

"Dinn't know if you'd need him, sir," the Archon, one of Grunthor's later-generation progeny, said, almost sleepily.

"Thank you," Achmed said, taking the gelding from the paddock. He patted the Archon's shoulder. "Good work. Stay ready."

"Yczzir."

He took down his veils when he was alone on the road, allowing the fresh air of the vanishing summer and the scent of hickory in the air to wash over his face. His skin had stung since Rhapsody's death, burning caustically in the absence of the musical vibration that soothed his hypersensitivity to the thrum and jangle of the world around him. Now the rush of wind was providing a little relief, at least.

He was allowing himself as many pleasures as he could bring himself to partake in, having said goodbye to the satin sheets of his quiet bedchamber and his exquisitely aged reserve port; at the very least he should be able to take advantage of the beautiful horseflesh he had been cultivating for a thousand years.

The other advantage to having the wind at his back was that the smell of the sea took longer to arrive in his nostrils.

Achmed had hated the sea for as long as he could remember. His sensitive surface veins and nerve endings were clogged by the cacophony of its chaotic waves, and his skin-web was easily thrown off by the enormity of the water within it, the element he disliked the most.

It would be the perfect purgatory, the testing ground for his eventual destination that would either prepare him for his journey within the Vault, or kill him outright.

Achmed was not certain which he would prefer.

He rode, thundering along the trans-Orlandan thoroughfare, utilizing the secret routes for which his mounts had been bred and trained, for the better part of two weeks, until finally he came to the northwesternmost stable beyond the Great Forest, where he kept his favorite Mondrians, white forest horses that had faultless footing and the smoothest canter in his Wing stable.

Riding one is a little like the experience of drinking an elegant brandy, Jorhan, his trainer four hundred or so years before, had said. *Smooth, surprising, but consistent, able to answer your every question and attend to your every need. If only they bred whores like that instead of just horses.*

Achmed, who had never indulged in one of those luxuries, had merely smiled.

"I won't be returning her," he had told Johran's many-generations-removed successor. "She's to be a gift."

"Aye, Majesty," the keeper of his Wing stable had said doubtfully; it was hard for a working man to imagine anyone to whom a Mondrian would not be an overly generous present.

The Bolg king had mounted up and taken an enjoyable ride south down the coast until he came to the harbor of Avonderre, a place he found it easy in which to get lost, in all the best possible ways. He had already made inquires of his grooms about the most reputable of liveries, and sought out the one that each had suggested.

TACK, it was simply called, so noted by its signage.

Achmed had brought the Mondrian with him into the stable, watching to discern its comfort with the place. When she tossed her head and settled quickly, he began to look around for the stablekeeper.

He found her in one of the stalls, mucking it out.

"Are you the owner?" he inquired.

The dark-haired woman turned around and leaned on the paddock rake, assessing the horse.

"I am," she said. "That's a fine-looking animal."

"Your propensity for understatement is unfortunate," he said lightly. She glanced back at him.

"I was addressing the horse about you," she said in return. "She's a magnificent creature."

The Bolg king smiled behind his resumed veils.

"Indeed," he said. "I am looking for a reputable stablemistress or master to present her to Laurelyn, the Invoker of the Filids, at the Tree Palace at the Circle, as a gift. I was assured by every groom and stable-keeper in my employ that this would be the place to find that person, and that her name would be Corinne."

"Really?" said the woman, smiling broadly. "I can go get her, then."

Achmed's smile cramped into an expression of displeasure. "You're not Corinne?"

"No. I'm the other owner, Corinne's sister, Sadie."

"Apologies," he mumbled.

"No need. Corinne's up the road a piece—"

"That's not necessary," Achmed blurted, "you'll do."

The woman laughed. "Well, that's very kind of you."

A headache began to buzz behind the Bolg king's eyes. "Can you deliver this horse to the Invoker?"

"By all means. When?"

"Immediately."

"Oh," said Sadie. "Well, no, then."

Achmed fell silent.

"You've obviously ridden her a great distance today," Sadie said, putting the rake aside and coming out of the paddock. " 'Twould be best to rest her, groom her, and pick her out, and take her gently to the Circle, so that she will be in fine shape to curry a little and then present, if she's going to be a gift. Take three, four days—would that be sufficient?"

"Yes." Achmed relaxed. "Thank you."

"Will cost you, though," Sadie said, reaching up and patting the Mondrian.

Achmed reached for his coinpurse. "How much?"

"Four silver suns."

The Bolg king pulled forth the coinage and held it out in his gloved hand. Sadie took the coins and put them into the belt at her waist.

"Do you wish to send a missive along with the horse?"

Achmed considered, then shook his head. "Just tell the Invoker that she's a present from her uncle in the east."

Sadie nodded. "With love?"

"Excuse me?"

The stablemistress shrugged. "She's just gotten married. Thought the horse might be a wedding gift. It's always nice to add a pleasantry with a wedding gift, 's all. Your choice."

Achmed pictured Laurelyn in his mind, the blue-eyed image of her mother, and smiled slightly.

"Certainly," he said, uncharacteristically jovial. "You may do that indeed."

He patted the Mondrian himself, then turned and left the stable without another word.

AVONDERRE

He took a room at the Sailors' Rest a few streets east of the harbor, a place he knew would ask no questions, and slept the remainder of the day away, letting the darkness wake him.

Then he wended his way through the streets of Avonderre, back to where Abbat Mythlinis, the elemental basilica of water, towered over the sand of the lagoon on which it stood.

Achmed stood for a few moments, taking in the sight of it in the dark, built from the enormous timbers left over from the shipwrecks of the First Fleet, set up to look like a broken ship on its side, lost in the memory of a previous visit.

It had occurred shortly after he, Grunthor, and Rhapsody had come forth from the Root into the new world, lost and confused about where they were in Time. Rhapsody had been left at the Circle to try to discern what she could there, while he and Grunthor had made a side journey to this place, to Avonderre. They had come in the dark and the rain, with the wind whipping the sea violently that night.

This time only darkness was present; the night wind was blowing off the sea, but otherwise the weather was quiet. Achmed glanced around, then made his way to the doors of the basilica.

They were locked.

He cursed quietly as he rifled his pockets for the thin piece of spun metal similar to the ones he had made use of, a lifetime before, as a lock-pick, and carefully manipulated the lock until it sprang.

Haven't lost the touch, he thought, unduly pleased with himself.

He opened the door of the basilica and slipped inside, closing it behind him.

Abbat Mythlinis looked just as it had the first time he and Grunthor and entered it, down to the salt spray coating the floor near the irregularly rising and falling fountain at the center of the basilica. Achmed skirted the fountain and hurried to the back doors he knew led to the annex.

He stopped long enough to look once more at the copper doors he and Grunthor had beheld a thousand years before, recognizing the symbol of Kirsdarke, the water sword that until recently had been carried by Ashe, and long before that by MacQuieth Monodiere Nagall, the great hero of the Seren War.

They still had the raised symbol of the water sword on each door, one pointed up, the other down, emblazoned on a background relief of a winged lion, the symbol of MacQuieth's family.

He pulled on the door and found it just as wedged shut as it had been the first time, so he spat on his hands as Grunthor had and finally managed to drag it open wide enough for him to fit through.

Out in the wind again, he hurried across the walkway over the sandbar and the anchor that lay in the sand before the annex on the other side, open on all sides to the sea wind and salt spray.

Inside the open annex was an altar, a solid block of obsidian gleaming in the occasional light of a waxing moon. Attached to its front was a plaque, its inscription reading something about MacQuieth, as Rhapsody had translated once from a coal rubbing he had done of the plaque. Achmed shuddered; this altar stone had once been the centerpiece of the cursed underground temple known as the Spire in the old world.

His name had once been held captive within it.

In his memory he could hear Grunthor's voice and his own as they first beheld the altar and its plaque.

This looks a little like the written language of Serendair, but only a little. I wish Rhapsody was here.

That's twice in ten minutes you said that, and Oi'm gonna tell 'er.

She won't believe you, or she'll think I wanted to pitch her into the sea.

Embedded in the stone were two metal brace restraints which held Kirsdarke, the elemental sword of water Ashe had carried.

Achmed inhaled, oblivious to the salt spray buffeting his face.

Meridion had obviously been here to deliver the sword, as Rhapsody had commanded, and had then had attempted to pick it up again, and was refused, as he had told the Bolg king.

Achmed closed his eyes and listened to the crashing of the waves beyond the annex.

Then he crouched down in front of the altar, feeling ill at ease.

He put his hand on the plaque, allowing his gloved fingers to trace the runes commemorating the iconic bearer of the water sword, a man he had come across, along with Ashe, in the windswept northern fishing village of Traeg, in the ragged clutches of old age and worn-out immortality. He had traveled in MacQuieth's company, wryly amused to meet someone more cantankerous and irritable than he was, and had witnessed his loss as the ancient hero took the demon clinging to one of his enemies from the old land to the bottom of the sea.

He had heard the hero's heartbeat, which rang like a great bell, beneath the waves of the ocean, fall silent.

And he had stood vigil, remembering the man who had once, in the old world, been known as the black lion, the King's Shadow, and who Achmed knew, had he not fled Serendair with Grunthor with Rhapsody in tow, would have come for his blood eventually.

He leaned his forehead against the stone, feeling his resolve weaken.

Where are you? he silently asked the other two of the Three. *I can't do this without you. I can't do anything without you.*

The sea wind blasted through again, filling his ears.

Achmed lifted his head eye-level with the blade of water, whose rippling waves had fallen silent and now appeared to be made of steel into which blue stone scrolling had been inset.

You are comprised of the element I despise, he thought to the sword. *You were carried most recently by the man I despised even more. And the place into which I seek to bring you is the last place on the Earth that I desire to go. But I sense that without you, I will fail, and that failure could bring about the end of the world. So please, please come with me.*

His head came to rest against the altar again, as his eyes closed once more.

He reached up his hand over the top of the stone and felt around for the hilt of the sword, which after a moment he had in his grip.

Then he stood and lifted the sword from the top of the altar as its braces opened.

Achmed exhaled.

I assume this is a sign that I have no choice about doing this, he thought. *Oh joy.*

He sighed, checked the bindings on his gear, and then slid Kirsdarke into the second sheath in the back of the bandolier.

Closing his eyes halfway, he walked out beyond the annex, away from the water basilica, across the edge of sand and into the arms of the sea.

He was fighting nausea every step of the way.

33

OFF THE NORTHWESTERN COAST,
NEAR TRAEG

*F*or his first experiment in walking the sea, Achmed chose what he believed was a relatively short trek north.

Along the twisting coastline the beaches grew rockier, even out into the sea itself, and rather than flat land beyond, the farther north he traveled, the more he found sea cliffs on sandspits, jutting out into the open sea.

Somewhere along the curves of the rocky coastline was the tiny harbor town of Traeg, a word Rhapsody had once told him meant *where the wind lives* in the language of the indigenous Lirin from long ago.

And, in Traeg, Achmed had someone to whom he wanted to say goodbye.

His initial foray into the water had been terrifying. He had, long ago, fallen into a quick-running river in full armor on horseback, and had come as close to death by drowning as he decided it was actually possible to do. It had been an experience that had engendered his consummate dislike and secret fear of the water, an element that had always served to thwart his *kirai* during his days when he still had the heartbeats of every soul on the Island where he lived beating in his skin, making his victims difficult, if not impossible, to track.

But now, there seemed to be a beacon of a sort for him, a deep tolling of what sounded like the echo of MacQuieth's heartbeat, which once rang like a great bell beneath the waves when the hero had been alive. It seemed to be attuned to the new sword in his hand, or the second sheath of the bandolier, so Achmed followed the quiet tolling of the bell blindly, hoping it might lead him to where he needed to go. Having the elemental sword of water deign to allow him to carry it might have given him the ability to walk beneath the surface of the sea, but its presence did not initially overcome the fear he had always felt in or around it.

He had discovered, to his dismay, that beneath the waves, Kirsdarke did not maintain its rigidity of blade, but rather only its hilt was solid. What on the land had been an arm-and-a-half of steel with blue scrollwork in the hands of anyone other than the Kirsdarkenvar disappeared when he took it into the water, though it was still a savage blade if it was needed beneath the waves. So rather than a reassuring weapon with a long blade, in the ocean he was carrying nothing but a sword hilt, at least until he figured out how the weapon worked.

It had not helped that, when last in Traeg, or nearby, he had been thrown into the water again, this time from atop just such a cliff on a sandspit jutting out into the sea, by the man whose regiment had brutalized Rhapsody long ago in the old world.

That soldier, known by the silly appellation Michael, the Wind of Death, had not achieved an extended life span as the Cymrians had, because he had not traveled with the exodus, being on the losing side in the Seren War several hundred years prior. Rather, he had made a bargain with a F'dor demon in a place nearer to where the Island of Serendair had once been, a seaside city called Argaut on the continent of Northland, to serve as the demon's voluntary host. It was an arrangement that had granted the human, Michael, a seemingly immortal existence, and the demon the body of a soldier of some strength and leadership skills.

The Wind of Death had been the bearer of one of the two swords Achmed was bringing into the sea with him, Tysterisk, the elemental weapon of air. At the point when MacQuieth, Ashe, and he had Michael backed up against the edge of the seacliff, the demon, caught in the Thrall ritual that should have immobilized it, had pointed the sword at him and severed the ropes of wind with which the ritual had bound its poisonous spirit.

And, with a single gesture, he had blasted Achmed from his feet and over the side of a cliff close to a thousand feet tall, into the sea.

You thought you could contain me with a Thrall ritual? I command the wind, you fool.

Blessedly, Achmed remembered little of what happened after that. He had suffered nightmares for a few centuries in which he was drowning in a variety of water sources, including one particularly odd one where the water source was a pitcher of wine. Eventually he had prevailed upon Rhapsody to use her Naming lore to help ease the memory from his mind.

But while he could remember little to nothing of his travails in the sea, he had a very clear memory of a warm cliff-top tavern, where the ale was good, the food was edible, and the barkeep was a First Generation Cymrian who had known and loved Rhapsody like a daughter in the old world.

And this man had also known MacQuieth, the water sword's most famous bearer.

So Achmed had taken his life in his hands, after leaving the water basilica, and had waded out into the sea outside the harbor. The initial feel of the tide going over his head evoked all the terrors he had been fighting since the bridge incident, but within a short time he had learned to open his eyes beneath the surface and appreciate the quiet swish of the realm of endless blue-green into which he had ventured.

He also found that the more securely he gripped Kirsdarke's blade, the calmer he felt.

So he walked out beyond the breakers to the first place where the sandy bottom dropped off, and, after getting past his panic, hung in the drift, his hair floating wildly about his face, letting the sword breathe for him, until he felt he could adjust successfully, then turned north and followed the coastline, popping up to the surface to check his progress every now and then.

He was disappointed every time.

Finally, when he came to the surface and was buffeted violently by the wind, he decided to come to shore and see if he recognized anything.

He didn't, but remembered that the first and last time he had come to Traeg, it had been from inland, so he and Ashe had approached it from above.

His spirits rose as he came out of the water to find that, as a result of one or both of the ancient swords of elemental power that he was carrying, his clothing was almost dry within moments.

The coastline was littered with enormous rocks and boulders, a good deal of flotsam and jetsam, pieces of driftwood and broken ships—and sea lions.

He had not realized what the massive area of dark slag between two enormous rock outcroppings really was until he had set them off by accident, earning himself the necessity of a hasty retreat, chased by ear-splitting barks and an utter loss of dignity.

Just when he was seriously reconsidering his mission, it occurred to him that the man he sought, a barkeep named Barney, as all barkeeps were traditionally named, was probably the only one of his profession still alive from the Island of Serendair, assuming he hadn't died in all the time that had passed since Achmed had last seen him.

Given that he hadn't seen the man for over a thousand years, it suddenly occurred to Achmed that he might have come a long, salty, seaweed-filled way for nothing.

Fortunately, both Rhapsody and Ashe had kept in touch with Barney and his family, and Rhapsody had kept him updated on such things, even when he refused to listen or had begged her not to, so he was relatively certain he had heard the man's name and his status as being alive relatively recently.

He leaned back as the sun was setting over the crashing waves of the shoreline and beyond, and loosed his *kirai,* seeking the man's heartbeat.

Water had never been his friend when he was trying to find a pulse, so he headed away from the shore, climbing a mountain pass that he had come across, when the flicker rushed across the surface of his skin, and locked itself on to his own heartbeat high at the top of a jagged, rocky cliff.

Achmed let out a deep breath of frustration and followed the rhythm up the side of the cliff.

After a long haul upward, and a loss of the sun into the western sea, he came upon a small establishment that looked very similar to one he remembered in the city of Easton in the old world, and another he had drunk in when looking for Rhapsody.

A sign out front proclaimed THE HAT AND FEATHERS.

He shook the remaining water from his garments and went inside.

The pub was full of fishermen preparing to head home for the night, so he found a small corner and waited for the crowd to pass, then approached the barman, clearly not the fellow he was looking for, who was wiping the ale off the bartop.

"Can I help ya, sir?" the man said, not looking up from his chore.

"I hope so," Achmed said as pleasantly as he was able; the constant vibrations of the sea battering against his skin-web, the sensitive nerve endings and veins that scored the surface of almost his entire body, and hunger, was making him irritable. "Is Old Barney about?"

"Who's askin'?"

Achmed gritted his teeth. "An old friend. Kindly relay my inquiry. *Please.*"

The young barkeep looked up and blinked, then blanched.

"Stay right there," he said, and headed for the back room.

A few moments later, the tavern was filled with a host of other employees and regulars that emerged from every corner, silently making their presence known. Achmed merely took off his sodden gloves, which had not benefited as his clothes had from the drying that came with exposure to the swords, and silently wrung the water from them onto the tavern floor.

A few moments later, some modestly heavy footfalls came tromping down the inner staircase, and the silver-haired tavern owner that Achmed had drunk and talked with a thousand years before appeared at the bottom of the stairs, looking much the same but a little grayer, a little heavier, and a little slower.

"'Ey, Barney," said one of the bigger men in the gathering, "this gent says 'e's a friend o' yourn."

Old Barney came closer, staring. Then his eyes opened wide.

"Well, yes he is," he said, the sound of genuine delight in his voice. "Thank you, my friends, but all's well. Back to your business."

He came hurriedly over to Achmed and bowed politely. "Majesty."

The Bolg king shook his head. "Please. Achmed. Now and always."

"Come with me," Old Barney said jovially, gesturing toward the same room in the back of the tavern where he and Ashe had met with the elderly man a millennium before, described back then as a "no-ears" room. "What's your pleasure?"

"Ale and bread, and if it's available, soup, as long as it's not made with mutton."

"Can accommodate you on both accounts," Barney said, signaling to the barkeeper. "So much better than last time you came to visit. We had mostly survived the burnings that took down the rest of the coast, but as I recall, I had little to offer you."

"I don't get out much," Achmed said, following the barkeep to the back room. "I had nothing to compare it to—I remember it being a good time. Well, except for the burnings and Rhapsody's kidnapping. But other than that, a good time."

Once there, the tavern owner pulled out a chair for Achmed and went to the door to take the tray the serving girl had brought back with two tankards, two bowls of a rich-smelling soup, and a loaf of hot bread.

"Have a seat, Majes—Ach—oh, I'm so sorry. One doesn't feel right to you, the other doesn't feel right to me." He put the bread, the soup, and a tankard down in front of the Bolg king.

Achmed waved his hand dismissively and seized the tankard, putting it to his lips.

Barney's face brightened as he took a seat opposite. "So how is Rhapsody? I haven't heard from her in quite a while."

Achmed took the tankard away from his mouth. He stared at the tavernkeeper silently.

Barney's smile faded. "Majesty?"

Achmed sighed, then took another draught.

"Please, please tell me—"

"She's dead," Achmed said between swallows.

"Wha—*what*? The Lady Cymrian?—is—?"

"Dead, yes. Several leaders of all levels are dead, including her husband."

Barney turned white and pushed his chair back.

"Look, I'm sorry," Achmed said, setting the tankard down on the table board. "I don't have words at the moment for any of this. I assume it will be heralded sooner or later by her son, and I would appreciate it if you would let it be disseminated that way. But my heart is too sore and my brain too tired to know what to say. I respect you, and I know you loved her. So I'm telling you, rather than putting it off or lying to you. She's dead. It was painless, from what I can tell. I don't know any more than that as far as what will be done with the leadership. I'm sure the family will have it well in hand before the Cymrian Council meets in my lands next year. Thankfully, I will not be there either."

"Where—where will you be, Majesty?"

Achmed tore a piece off the bread loaf. "That depends on what you tell me."

"I—I—"

"What can you tell me about MacQuieth? Other than what you told me a thousand years ago."

The old barkeeper blinked. "Majesty—"

"I saw him die," Achmed said, dipping his bread in the soup, which was a hearty beef stock with carrots and potatoes, a great improvement over the thin cabbage water he had been served the last time he had been here. "I heard his heartbeat wink out in the sea; it used to toll like a great bell, and I heard it fall silent."

He chewed on the bread and swallowed, then leaned forward.

"But then, I had always assumed he was dead until you told me otherwise that night," he said, his mismatched eyes gleaming intensely. "The legends say that after he landed with what was left of the Second Fleet in Manosse, he went to the end of the peninsula of Sithgraid, waded into the water to his waist or knees, and stood vigil for his son, Hector, who had been left behind in the place of guardianship MacQuieth felt he should have had."

"All that is true."

The Bolg king tore off another piece of bread. "And then, supposedly, when the Island was destroyed, he went into the sea and was never heard from again. But you knew otherwise, Barney. You knew. 'There are many places in the world for a man to hide if he does not wish to be found,' you said. And now I am about to do something very similar— though it is very much not to be told to any random kings, Firbolg or otherwise, that may come passing through your tavern."

Barney's face, which had gone gray at the news about the sovereigns, brightened a little.

"Understood," he said.

"Hateful as the water is to me—and believe me, it's hateful—I have found myself in need of traveling *through* it, rather than upon it. I also will be taking this with me."

He swallowed his most recent hunk of bread and reached over his head, quickly drawing Kirsdarke.

Barney backed up in his chair.

"As you can see, it does not run like elemental water in my hand, as it did when MacQuieth held it, or even Ashe," Achmed went on, sheathing the sword and going back to his soup.

"It is always interesting when you come by, Majesty," Barney said, only half humorously.

"No doubt. So if there is anything you can tell me about MacQuieth, or anything else you might think would be helpful, now's the time."

Barney exhaled sadly. "Forgive me, Majesty. I am still stunned and heartsick."

"I understand. So am I. More than you know. But in only the slightest of roundabout ways, what I am doing is something that would honor her, and advance the safety of her children and their children and so on, so if there is anything you can tell me, please do."

The old man nodded. "Well, I can say that I have not seen him since he went into the sea with the demon," he said, taking a draught himself. "But it's safe to say that, after almost two thousand years of guarding the depths, as he did after the exodus, there is still a great part of his soul in it."

"Can you elaborate?" Achmed put his tankard down and listened intently.

Barney shrugged. "Sometimes things wash up on the beach that seem, well, unlikely to do so," he said nervously. "Things that are often, well, opportune, if you know what I mean."

"Interesting."

"Did you ever see him draw the strange designs that he used to in the sand?"

"Yes." Achmed took another drink. "When we asked him what he was drawing, he said 'whatever the sea tells me.'"

"At the same time of day that the, er, opportune objects or information tends to show up, there is occasionally a drawing when the tide goes out, in the sand," Barney said. "I cannot make head nor tail of them most of the time, and I have sat watch to see if any human being is doing it, but no one has ever come. The sea pulls back, and there is a drawing in the sand. That's all."

"What time of the day is that?"

"Usually just before dawn—earlier than even the fishermen are out. And occasionally late at night, on my way home, I see something. But it's a rarity, especially these days. It is more wishful thinking than sensible thought to believe that MacQuieth is still guarding the depths. But they say he has always intervened with the tides around Gaematria, and I am not certain, but it was also said that once he returned to Tartechor, the domed city of the Mythlin, the Firstborn race of water, that vanished in the heat from the Sleeping Child when it rose, and took the Island to the depths with it."

Achmed nodded silently. He had heard MacQuieth tell the tale himself, in the context of explaining how he had gone in search of his son's body after the Cataclysm, and had found only undersea mountains of desolation and destruction where Serendair had been, and nothing at all of Tartechor.

"Rhapsody used to blither about the lore of the soul," he said finally, finishing the bread, the soup, and his ale. "She believed that it was a far more flexible, widespread entity than most races that believe in the soul tend to define it. Perhaps that is true of the sea and MacQuieth."

"It's pretty to think so," said Barney.

Achmed pushed his chair back. "I don't suppose you have a room to let?"

"For you, Majesty? Of course, though it's poor lodging."

"If it has a bed and peace and quiet, it will be like being in a palace. Thank you."

Barney inclined an ear to the rest of the tavern.

"It seems a quiet night, so if you would like to turn in now, you should be availed of mostly peace and quiet," he said. "And tomorrow, if you wish me to wake you early, I can show you the beach where I have on rare occasions thought that I have seen evidence that MacQuieth's heart is not still; that great bell you spoke of just tolls in a much wider bell tower than we can usually hear."

Achmed nodded and followed the tavernkeeper to bed.

34

The next morning, true to his word, Barney woke the Bolg king in the hazy hour ahead of foredawn, and together they took a lantern down to the beach between the guardian rocks of Traeg.

The wind had been even higher that night than Achmed remembered, and so his dreams were full of demonic screaming, making his repose minimal. He had barely slept since Rhapsody's death anyway; their last night together, close to the musical vibration that had emanated from her, had spoiled him, ruining any expectation of good sleep for him, but this night was especially haunting.

He had dreamt of the Vault, which he had actually once approached and had stood at the entry of, peering through the keyhole. The nightmares that had resulted were not so much a product of what he had seen in the dark, devouring space but more because of what he had heard while standing on the threshold of that lifeless realm; the sounds were beyond anything he had ever been able to describe to anyone, even Rhapsody. Now, with what he had witnessed in the mountains and what he was planning to do, the dreams returned, the noise that still haunted him screaming in his ears.

The airless place was full of sounds of the absurd, the profane, screams and cursing, pleading and whining, the begging voices suffering in agony, voices of judges pronouncing death sentences and the cries of the condemned, ridiculous, shrill commentary and palpably angry words so acid that the inside of his ears burned, set to the ominous pounding noise that all but drowned out desperate gasping and wailing, whispering in fear and threat, spinning like a dust devil tearing up the floor of a waterless desert, rattling his brain in just the split second of time in which he had gazed into the place.

He could not even bring himself to imagine how awful it would be to go inside.

As a result, in the morning he was exhausted, his skin even paler and more sallow than it usually was. The dark hollows around his eyes had caused the gentle barkeep to gasp upon viewing him in the light of the lantern.

The shouting sea wind and the crash of the waves below buffeted his sensitive skin, and Achmed was still nervous about the descent, so he stayed close to Barney and did not look around, but kept his sight drilled on the path.

There was no one on the beach. There was never anyone on this beach, Barney had explained as they made their way down to it, which was precisely why the ancient warrior had chosen, in his advanced age and morning blindness, to dwell here in a shack so small and unassuming that any who would have been fool enough to brave the wind of the beach would not have noticed it anyway.

The hut was now gone, a thousand years after Achmed had seen it, swallowed by the sea and the wind.

"This is where I sometimes find the sand pictures," Barney whispered in the almost-dark, looking east behind him where Foredawn still had not made any appearance. "I'm not certain what it was about this place, but, for whatever reason, it had a sense of home to him, just as the wind seems to want to make its home in Traeg."

The Bolg king took in a deep breath, finding the air of the place light of salt and pungent, but otherwise unremarkable.

"Will you hold the light to the water's edge?" he asked Barney.

"Aye, Majesty. Whatever you command."

Achmed shook his head, his hair blasting around him in the sea breeze.

"I command you to do nothing—I merely ask it of you. I am no longer a king," he said, his voice competing with the whine of the wind. "I've gone back to being an assassin."

"I am sick to hear that, Majesty."

"Don't be, Barney," Achmed said, examining the sand beach. "If I have any use to the world now, it's in that role."

The waves were rolling to the sand, rumbling as they came with the strength of the morning tide. The Bolg king analyzed the pattern, finally settling on a place where the surf ended without exceeding its reach too frequently, then gathered his robes and veils and sat down in the sand.

Before he descended completely to it, he pulled forth Kirsdarke and Tysterisk from the bandolier and stabbed each of them, point down, into the sand, Tysterisk away from the grasp of the water, Kirsdarke directly in its path.

Tysterisk was a weapon he occasionally had difficulty with because it, like Kirsdarke, had little more than its hilt visible to ordinary sight when in its element. While that meant that Kirsdarke was fully visible in the air of the regular world, and only became fluid in water, Tysterisk in the element of air was little more than its hilt, with the occasional sign of spinning air currents where the blade actually was.

He pulled off his boots and tossed them out of the way of the waves, then rolled up the trousers he wore beneath his robes and stretched out his feet, allowing the cold froth of the sea to surround them.

He kept his hand on the hilt of the sword of elemental water, trying to allow the gentle undulation of its waves to soothe his battered soul, but he was still too damaged by the loss of two-thirds of the Three to gain any comfort in it.

He bade Barney goodbye and continue to sit vigil, his sensitive skin tormented by the buffeting of the wind and the surf. Achmed closed his eyes and thought back to the day that Rath had finally found him.

The Dhracian had been seeking him since his conception, because those of the Common Mind had been linked with his unfortunate mother, had witnessed her mass rape, something that he knew might have contributed to his snapping when he heard what Rhapsody had endured. Upon finding him, Rath had tested both him and Grunthor, had taken the air out of a broken, antiquated vault where he had found them, had allowed them to collapse for lack of it, and thus determined them to be free of the F'dor's influence, because neither of them had attempted to wheedle or bargain as a F'dor would have.

Then he and Achmed had spoken for the longest time in the open air that either of them remembered doing.

In the ruins of Kurimah Milani, you said something about the bees, how a man could destroy every living specimen of their kind, should he come into their vault with flame, he had said to the Dhracian, of whom he had still been uncertain. *Then you alluded that it was such with another vault as well. I told you, I abhor riddles. Speak to me plainly—tell me what you want of me.*

Rath had chosen his answer carefully.

It is a great irony that to the Bolg you were polluted, unclean, a half-breed among mongrels that somehow made you less in their sight, he had said. *Somewhere deep in the scars of your past you have assumed that the blood of your unknown father somehow tainted you in the estimation of the Kin as well—but I tell you, with the wind as my witness, that nothing is further from the truth. To the Gaol, and all the Brethren who have been seeking you since your conception, you are a special entity, a rare gift to our race, one who might finally tip the scales in our favor. We have not been searching for you to torture or abuse you, to cleanse the race of your blood— but because we need you. You, in a very real way, are our last hope.*

He thought of Graal, of how the baby's eyes were like his own, his newborn skin scored with the patterns and traceries of surface veins and nerves, but how those things had made him beautiful, unique, rather than ugly and despised.

Then he realized for the first time that, to the Dhracian brother-hood, he himself never had been.

You alone among us are born of wind and earth, Bolg king. While we tread the tunnels and canyons of the Underworld in our endless guardianship, we are strangers there—and the demons know it. They understand how deeply our sacrifice costs us, how much the wind in our blood resents being trapped within the ground, away from the element of air for all time. And even within their prison they laugh at us, because in every way that matters, we are as much prisoners as they. But the earth is in your blood as much as the wind is. You have a primordial tie to it that neither the Kin nor the Unspoken have. You have power there, a corporeal form that would be protected by the element of earth bequeathed to you by your father, protected by the very Living Stone of the Vault, should you choose to walk within it.

He had chosen to put the pleas aside, to remain Uncounted, much to Rath's dismay.

Now he was beginning, for the first time, to truly fathom why.

I am not of the Gaol, he had protested. *I am but half of the blood of the Brethren—and that which was of the other half raised me, if such words can be applied to my upbringing. I know none of your lore, your prophecies—your history. My skills are limited, my talents pale in this area. While I was given a blood-gift that allowed me to unerringly track the heartbeats of any of those born on the same soil as I had been, that was an upworld gift. Each time I have faced one of the Pantheon, I have needed help to complete the task. Without that assistance, I would be dead or possessed myself.*

Rath had fixed the silver pupils of his eyes on Achmed and spoken softly, with more emphasis than the Bolg king had ever heard.

What you do not know is this—you could walk the Vault alone, and when you were done the silence would ring with nothing but the whisper of your name.

Achmed heard the words again in his mind. *I certainly hope you are right, Rath,* he thought. *But with any luck, we are about to find out.*

He continued to sit in the sand and contemplate his world and his task until the sky lightened, until the wind of morning calmed somewhat, until he could see beyond the dark water into the western horizon, until he could feel on his back and see out of the corners of his eyes the pinks and pale blues of the sunrise behind him.

Then he sighed.

He had neither felt, nor heard, any words of wisdom, any hints or suggestions or anything else that would make this hateful task successful.

Finally he stood as daybreak came fully, and brushed the sand off his calves and put his boots back on, muttering obscenities under his breath at the feel of the granular dirt rubbing against his feet.

Driftwood and other waste from the sea had floated onto the beach, a piece of which came up on a wave and wedged itself between an indentation in the sand and his boot. Irritated, Achmed kicked it away.

Then he looked at it more closely.

At first it had appeared as a long, hollow stick of driftwood, unremarkable save for the way the sunlight glittered as it rocked from side to side in the low surface and splashover from the waves that were pulling back with the tide. This object, in fact, had been delivered by the sea but had been caught in a similar sand furrow.

Achmed bent down to pick it up.

He turned it over, examining the regular scoring and the shape of it.

And when he had been at it for a few moments, he noticed from the two weapons sticking in the sand nearby that there were crude runes of a sort on it that he had seen inscribed in ancient manuscripts and on historical objects of art.

Different from any he had seen in all his time across the wide world.

His hand shaking, he held the object up to his eyes and the light of the now-rising sun.

"It's a scabbard," he whispered, though no one was around to hear him.

Achmed appeared at the door of the Hat and Feathers later that afternoon.

Old Barney was waiting for him, just getting ready to open for the evening.

"Any luck, Majesty?"

Achmed extended the scabbard.

The elderly barkeep smiled, tired and broadly.

"He is the soul of the sea," he said. "I hope that whatever it is you're seeking there will be as easy to come by."

Achmed merely smiled. "Ever seen this before?"

"Aye; 'twas his. He had several at one time, but I never got to see him in his days as a soldier, except when he would come into the Hat and Feathers in Easton. That was the one his sword rested in during those days; I do know it was special to him. But I did not sail with him—I went with the First Fleet, and he commanded the Second. By the time I got to know him in the new world, he was—well, you know how he was."

Achmed nodded. "Thank you, again, for your assistance. I wish you continued health and comfort."

"I'm sorry for your loss," Barney said, continuing to wipe down the bar. "I know you and Rhapsody were very close."

The Bolg king thought of his son and winced internally. "Thank you. Condolences to you as well; I know the two of you meant a great deal to each other as well."

"Aye, that we did."

"I would like to purchase some supplies from you, if I may, ere I leave."

"Of course. What can I get you?"

"Some potent potables and a flask of Canderian brandy, if you have some," Achmed said. "I'm told the sea can be bitter cold, and I might need some bracing."

Barney smiled and went to the back room, returning a few moments later with a dozen thin cylindrical metal flasks with belt hooks and a regular-sized canteen.

"Fishermen call these 'the third pole,'" he said, holding up the thin vessels. "Almost as necessary as the first two poles a man has; maybe more for us old lads. Fair winds and following seas to you, Majesty."

"Thank you," Achmed said. He waited until Barney had turned away, then laid five gold sovereigns on the bar, sufficient to pay for the alcohol and room rental.

As well as to purchase the entire establishment.

He slid the scabbard into the bandolier and took his leave, heading back down the rocky path, well lighted by the sun now.

35

THE WINDSWEPT COAST OF TRAEG

Once again, filled with disgust, Achmed waded into the sea.

The swishing silence as the waves closed over his head was a little less horrific this time, but still, being encased in the element that was his nemesis, it was all the Bolg king could do to keep from panicking once he was sinking again into the churning depths.

He had waited until the light had come fully up in the east, so that he could see the rocks along the coast. As he had been waiting, the waves had drawn back, as Barney had mentioned, and a ragged set of marks scored the sand in front of him.

If it was meant to be a drawing, and it could only be called so in the most generous of terms, it was one he thought he recognized.

It appeared to be a circle with a spiral within it, with rays extending from it.

Achmed knew the image well.

He had seen it long ago, both in the old world and the new, particularly in Vrackna, the basilica of Fire. He had explained to Rhapsody on their first visit to the temple in Bethany that, her belief and that of the numbskull clerics who worked there notwithstanding, she was not looking at an image of the sun, but rather the symbol of the goal of the ancient race of demons.

It was a picture of the Earth in flames.

The wyrm within its bowels was represented by the spiral, as the means the F'dor expected to use to achieve that goal.

He still took a rancid delight in remembering the horror in Rhapsody's expression as she realized what she was seeing, and how it was being misinterpreted.

If this really is a message from MacQuieth, or whatever else may constitute the soul of the sea, it's a presumptuous one, he thought, amused. As far as he knew, the famous hero had never attempted to go after what slept within the belly of the Earth. *Nice of you to suggest that I do, if that's what this image in the sand is implying.*

Now he was traversing the sea, struggling to hold down his nausea, when in the distance he heard, or rather felt, the tolling of a deep bell again.

His disgust abated, replaced by anticipation.

Achmed waited for the sound to return, but his ears were met by nothing but the noise of the waves crashing above him, muted in the grip of the water, and the heavy, thick rippling of the drift.

He turned in the direction that he thought the resonating sound had come from, but was lost in the chaos of the waves.

Hrekin, he cursed silently.

Quickly he reached over his head and withdrew the sword of water from the bandolier. It came forth, glowing with light, its blade ephemeral, its hilt solid in his hand.

Achmed closed his eyes.

He tried to block the swooshing and gurgling sounds from his mind and focus instead on the noise of the bell in the Deep.

After a few moments, he heard it sound again, low and far away.

The sword of elemental water vibrated in his hand.

In one of the true triumphs of will over instinct he had ever managed in the course of his life, Achmed let go of his need for control and allowed the sword to lead him, following the vibrations of the tolling of the bell, into the Deep.

He followed it blindly, without any other sense of where he was going.

All grasp of time and distance was now gone.

The Bolg king, having struggled with losing his sense of control, abandoned it utterly and focused his consciousness, much as he had back on the Island when tracking the heartbeat of prey, on the only clear sound he could hear in the confounding universe of endless water and muted vibration.

He was vaguely aware of passing days and nights from the darkness and deepening cold he could feel at the edges of his eyelids, but soon lost count of them. Traveling the sea in this manner was like voluntarily agreeing to forgo any sense of time, and, after surrendering his meaningless resistance, he just moved on, often with his eyes closed, following the slow tolling of the bell.

He had almost become accustomed to being lost forever in the hateful waves when a ray of sunlight, too bright and glaring to be ignored, pierced the blue gloom, stinging his eyes into opening once more.

The water had gone from endless blue-black to a light shade of green. Achmed looked down to see that he was hovering over a shallow bottom, one that was stirred more or less constantly by the churning of harsher, stronger waves than those he had been passing through. He recognized them after a moment as surf that approached a shoreline.

I've come to land, he thought.

He wasn't certain if he should be pleased or not.

He allowed the surf to drag him onto the shore and vomit him up on a sandy beach strewn with shells and pebbles, rolling his body in the long drapes of his veils and robes to keep his sensitive skin from being shredded by the shards of rock and the husks of sea creatures. After he had lain for several moments on the slippery but undeniably solid ground, he unrolled himself slowly and brought his head up, opening his eyes fully for the first time in so long that the salty crust of the lids made it difficult.

He gave himself a moment to focus, then looked at what lay before him.

Then he swore in the ugliest manner he ever remembered undertaking.

Rising ahead of him in the distance was a city of gleaming buildings, polished in the colors of mother-of-pearl, and far away, a tall, slender tower made of what looked even more like shell, twisting like an enormous conch, rising into the low-hanging clouds.

Achmed put his head down on his soaking wet sleeves and contemplated what he had done to offend the Universe.

Gaematria, he thought in disgust. *I'm on the Isle of the Sea Mages.*

A moment later his fears were confirmed by the arrival of a guard unit dressed in the colors of the academics who had made this place their home since the sundering of the Second Fleet at the Prime Meridian.

He rose slowly to a stand and stretched out a hand in a gesture of warning as the regiment slowed to a halt before him. A strange heaviness, like a coating of seaweed, was hanging on him, light but tangibly there.

Achmed looked down at his body.

He had come into the water in simple clothing, a shirt and trousers, his cloak, robes, and veils.

Now, in addition to those garments, he was attired in a hauberk, a mail shirt of a sort, a coif, also seemingly of mail but a hood, and a mantle, a protective collar on his neck and shoulders. They were all comprised of the same strange carapace-like material that the scabbard of Kirsdarke was made of.

Before he could examine this new armor, the regiment came to a halt.

"I am the king of Ylorc," he said in a voice cracking from exposure to salt. "Tell Edwyn Griffyth I am here."

Then, overwhelmed with exhaustion and the beating he had taken in the sea, he collapsed on the sand again.

GAEMATRIA

When Achmed awoke he was, to his fury, lying outstretched not on the beach but in a comfortable bed, most likely in a hospice ward from the looks of the equipment around him.

Hovering near him was a hook-nosed man with a solid build, soft around the middle but still upright despite what the Bolg king knew to be advanced age.

"You carried me?" he demanded.

Edwyn Griffyth, the High Sea Mage, looked down at him with severe displeasure.

"The wind carried you, Majesty," he retorted dryly. "I make it a rule never to touch anything I suspect might be poisonous. I merely provided the elevation of your body and the direction of your journey into the bed you currently inhabit through the arts. To what do we owe the extreme pleasure of your company, unannounced?"

Achmed sat up shakily.

"I need to meet in council with some of your odious academicians."

"Ah, you came under the auspices of *diplomacy*." Edwyn Griffyth shook his head and sighed. "I should have guessed, given your polite address and graciousness. A thousand years in Alliance, and it's still a fulsome pleasure to speak with you."

The Bolg king noted that none of his weapons had been touched or removed, nor had his clothing, which apparently had been dried of seawater by some sort of magical means. He also concluded that news of Ashe's death or the buildup for war had not reached the isolated Isle.

He decided to allow that state of ignorance of both issues to remain in place for the time being.

"Given that you *have* known me for a millennium, I assume you understand that I would never have come here, especially through the sea, had it not been a matter of extraordinary urgency," he said, struggling to keep his voice from cracking, either from anger or salt exposure. "Kindly summon your experts in the subjects of tidal or other oceanic impacts of the Cataclysm that ensued with the rise of the Sleeping Child, as well as anyone familiar with the area of the sea that lies above what was once the Island of Serendair and the northern islands of Balatron, Briala, and Querel. Additionally, I need to speak to any scholar who knows anything of the lore of what sleeps within the Earth."

Edwyn Griffyth's jaw dropped open so violently that Achmed could hear it click.

"Surely you are joking," he said after he recovered the use of his tongue.

"I don't believe I yet know or like you well enough to joke with you, Edwyn," said the Bolg king testily. "Once again, let me reiterate the severe necessity of my task and the extraordinary patience I have already demonstrated. Now, for the last time, kindly summon the experts I have requested."

The High Sea Mage's jaw clicked shut violently.

He turned without another word and left the room, whereupon the Bolg king dropped back onto the pillows of his bed and closed his eyes.

Within the turn of an hour, Achmed found himself seated at a table in the Hall of Scholars, the central building in the academic complex that had long served as the seat of knowledge for the Known World.

Around the table was a gathering of some of the most brilliant minds in that same world, including the High Sea Mage and a number of other scholars unknown to Achmed.

And, to his consummate disgust, also in attendance was Jal'asee, the Ancient Seren ambassador whom he had hated on both sides of Time for millennia.

The tall, golden-skinned man had maintained a pleasant expression in spite of what could only have been interpreted as seething hatred coming his way from the Firbolg king, Achmed thought darkly. In his own pack a vial existed, packed carefully as he was making his preparations to travel, containing an elixir that he had brewed using the Lightcatcher in Gurgus Peak with this very scholar in mind.

It was one of the only experiments he had ever undertaken in the study of the ancient instrumentality, built from brittle drawings and schematics rendered two thousand years before by Gwylliam the Visionary, Edwyn Griffyth's father, that, in addition to the ability to focus the elemental power of the light spectrum as he had in the protection of Ylorc, was able to render certain conceptual or abstract entities into a liquid form of unsurpassed purity.

The abstract entity that Achmed had sought to render into utterly pure and potent liquid form was that of silence. It was a black potion, thick and unadulterated, that he had yet to test, but even in the very bottling of it, with just the faintest essence of it escaping into the air, the entire upper part of the Cauldron had been bathed in a lack of sound so encompassing that it was feared for a while that the soldiers guarding the entrance to the throne room almost half a mile away from Gurgus Peak had been struck deaf.

The pleasure that Achmed had experienced in contemplating Jal'asee's potential inability to ever utter another sound had been profound.

And yet, in a wry twist for Fate's amusement, the Ancient Seren ambassador was seated at the table, obviously selected as one of the experts he had requested.

In addition to the hated ambassador and the High Sea Mage, the seats at the council table were occupied by three other scholars.

The first seat held a silver-haired woman of Liringlas blood, aged but bright-eyed, who had been introduced as Aurelia, the historian with an expertise in the annals and accounts of Serendair, the exodus from it, and the rare and minimal records of its last days.

Another chair was occupied by a nervous oceanographer named Kasthien, a dark-skinned bald man who Achmed had recognized as being of the race of the Gwenen, some of the rarest among the Cymrian population.

The final chair held a monk named Fralwell whom Edwyn Griffyth had said was an esteemed geologist.

Edwyn Griffyth cleared his throat.

"Though I am aware that either you do not realize or do not care about the devastating imposition your lack of notice and demands for a meeting have put upon the research of these scientists and experts, I would like to bring to your attention the severity of that impact, Majesty," he said, his tone bordering on unpleasant. "I would ask that you would, therefore, make your inquiries brief and direct so that they may return to their important work."

Achmed swallowed the throatful of bile that had collected since he had arrived in Gaematria. He was suddenly visited by an image of Rhapsody from centuries before attempting to maintain a civil discourse between him and Jal'asee and failing utterly.

For her sake, he took a deep breath and addressed Aurelia first as politely as he was able.

"I need to know whatever you can tell me about the last days of Serendair, and specifically about the area of the Northern Islands, Balatron, Briala, and Querel," he said, struggling to keep his tone civil. "I have not traveled back to the gravesite of the Island of Serendair, but the Lady Cymrian apparently did, in the company of her family, and said that there is something different about the sea over the place where the Island once was. She noted that sailing over it, especially in the northern areas where the three islands are, was treacherous, even though the sea is no longer boiling there as it was at the time we lived on the Island. I am, by the way, not interested in hearing any nonsensical folktales about Gwylliam and his visions, and his brilliant plan to ferry the residents of Serendair across the world to places of nonviolence or sacrosanctity. Please spare me the heroic *hrekin;* I want a true reckoning and an accurate description of what happened to the northern part of the Island."

"Gwylliam deserved credit for all the lives he saved, yes," said Aurelia with a hint of nervousness in her voice. "But there was innocent blood on his hands as well."

"Would you care to elaborate on that?" Achmed asked politely.

She glanced to the side at Edwyn Griffyth, who sighed and signaled for her to continue.

"One of the things that Gwylliam did not account for in deciding that the entire population of Serendair needed to be evacuated before the Sleeping Child rose was the possibility that there might be people, individuals, certainly, but moreover tribes, clans, or whole races, that were reluctant to leave on his say-so, or because they accepted the upcoming cataclysm as an act of God, the One, the All."

"Morons," said Edwin Griffyth flatly.

"Perhaps. But in a situation where only a vision informs such a massively important decision, people can be forgiven for balking at the word of an as-yet-uncrowned monarch," Aurelia said. "And, particularly once it became clear that the Sleeping Child was, in fact, rising, those whose insistence on denying the reality or living with it should have been granted their decisions as their own self-determination. The responsibility of the Crown to attend to them becomes null at that point."

"Indeed," said Edwyn. "You cannot save a fool from himself."

"Gained," said Aurelia. "But Gwylliam decreed that there needed to be a volunteer to do just that—someone to stand in his stead as king and hold the right of succession. It is my adjudged opinion, and that of history, that this choice was more about Gwylliam doubting his own vision than about needing to 'maintain order in the last days.' Any tribe or race of people who had decided that they wished to remain behind—such as the Lirin with the Oak of Deep Roots, Sagia—were well prepared to care for themselves. They understood the risks and the consequences and accepted them.

"But Gwylliam himself was not entirely certain that the vision his vizier had granted him, as the man had granted each new monarch upon his or her coronation, would come to pass. History records him as a, well, a mercurial personality, steady and stalwart one moment, insecure and filled with nagging doubt the next." She paused and glanced at Edwyn Griffyth, mindful that she was describing the High Sea Mage's father, but Edwyn merely nodded for her to continue.

"It was Gwylliam's greatest fear that he had decimated the forests of his land, had pulled up every root that had been established, to accomplish one of the greatest feats of population movement ever recorded—only to discover that it had all been a trick, or a mistake, that the Sleeping

Child would not, in fact, rise from the depths to destroy the Island. He feared he would have surrendered his throne, and his birthright, for nothing."

"Which is why he condemned a man to a needless death to watch over that birthright," Achmed said coldly. "Hector Monodiere." He had heard the tale from MacQuieth, from the iconic soldier's very tongue as the major part of the explanation of why he hated Gwylliam.

"Yes," said Aurelia, "but Hector did not stay alone. Four others volunteered to remain behind with him, three of whom ultimately are believed to have perished with the Island."

Achmed sat up straighter, having never heard this part of the story.

"Continue," he said, undoubtedly violating academic protocol and not giving a damn that he was.

"Much of what is known about the final days of the Island comes from the writings of the only one of those who stayed that survived," Aurelia went on. "That man was the youngest of the five, including Hector, a recently dubbed knight named Sevirym. He was apparently the idealist in the group who felt that there was something they could do to avert or minimize the upcoming Cataclysm, such as the endless sand-bagging duty Hector continuously ordered, apparently to the dismay and good-natured grousing of the others.

"At the very last possible window, a rescue ship from Marincaer showed up unexpectedly, and Hector ordered Sevirym, against his will, or so he says frequently in his journals, to go with the ship, because its arrival had enabled them to secure passage for several dozen residents of the Gated City, a population Gwylliam had not accounted for when planning the exodus."

"I'm not surprised," said Achmed humorously. "That was a rough crowd."

"By the time the exodus had passed, and the final rescue ships had stopped coming over the now-boiling sea, all that apparently remained in the Gated City were some starving men, women, and children who became Sevirym's responsibility on the *Stormrider,* the ship that had come at the request of the king of Marincaer. The king had heard the tales of MacQuieth Monodiere standing in the surf, holding vigil for his son, and sent a last-minute rescue attempt to save Hector. All the ship returned with was the contents of the Gated City and a very traumatized, disappointed soldier whom Hector had chosen to send with them because of the youth's oft-expressed hopes that there would be a good ending to the situation—and, for him at least, there was. But anyone who knew MacQuieth, and apparently his son was a great deal like him, knew that he would never let something as petty as certain death take him from his post."

"I see," said the Bolg king. "Pray go on."

"Another one of Gwylliam's most valued knights and, apparently, one of MacQuieth's dearest friends, a Kith woman named Cantha, volunteered to stay, as did an army captain named Jarmon, about whom very little is known. Finally, Hector's best friend, a Liringlas soldier and knight named Anaias, remained behind as well. Their families—wives and children—traveled together to Manosse with MacQuieth. All three of these people are believed to have died with Hector when the Island was taken down in volcanic fire."

Achmed looked impatiently at Kasthien, the scholar noted as the expert on the oceanic impacts of the Cataclysm.

"What I want to know is this—there used to be a failed land bridge of a sort to the north of Serendair, east of the islands of Balatron, Briala, and Querel," he said, glancing in annoyance at Jal'asee. "Is it still there? Or did it disappear when the Sleeping Child rose?"

"I've heard nothing of a failed land bridge, Majesty," said Kasthien. "The entire underwater topography was reset as a result of the Cataclysm; as for the islands to the north of Serendair, Balatron and Briala lost leagues of coastline, and Querel for a long time was totally submerged."

Jal'asee cleared his throat quietly.

"The failed land bridge was, at least in part, a result of the attempt we made in the Third Age to cool the underwater grave of the Sleeping Child," he said quietly, not meeting Achmed's furious gaze. "The most recent reports of sailors is that it is occasionally seen, shallow below the surface, in the southern hemisphere's spring to summer, which is approaching. Storms or undersea activity of moderate to heavy strength can occasionally even partially reveal it."

Achmed nodded to Kasthien and Aurelia. "Thank you," he said as pleasantly as he could. "I believe I am done with questions for you."

The two scholars rose immediately and hurried out of the room. Achmed then turned to Fralwell.

"I seek your expertise and your opinion regarding the consequences of entombment of living matter within the Earth's mantle," he said, watching the monk's eyes gleam nervously. "If something that lives in geologic strata, taking up considerable space, were to die and decay, would it shrink, as it would in the air of the upworld? Or would it maintain its heft and mass, due to a lack of exposure to that air?"

Edwyn Griffyth and Jal'asee exchanged a glance of alarm.

The monk, however, did not seem to notice.

"That is hard to say, Majesty," he said, his voice low and musical. "Can you be more specific about the type of animal and geologic strata?"

"No." Achmed's voice stripped the air from the room.

The monk exhaled. "It would depend on the type of strata or substrate surrounding it, primarily. We have seen entire animals and trees maintain their mass if they perished in tar, for instance. So, without specifics, I would guess that an animal or plant, like a large root, that had great heft in life, but perished away from the decaying reach of the air, it would likely maintain a great deal of its mass.

"But the opposite is possible as well, depending on its chemical composition. Some structures and bodies decay quickly because of the acidity of their sap or blood, and can wither quickly, even in the absence of air. I could not say definitively even if I knew what you are referring to."

The Bolg king nodded and indicated the door. The monk rose quickly from the table and, with a puzzled look at the two remaining Sea Mages, made his way out of the room.

"Anything else you might possibly want to know?" Edwyn Griffyth asked archly. "We are clearly at your disposal, Majesty—or at least you seem to think we are."

"Yes, as a matter of fact," Achmed said. He pointed to the armor that had clung to him upon his exit from the sea. "Do you have any knowledge of this?"

Jal'asee coughed.

"I sailed with the Second Fleet, on MacQuieth's ship," he said quietly. "That appears to be his armor—or something like it."

The Bolg king merely nodded. "Do you know what material it is made from?"

The Ancient Seren shook his head. "I only know that it was always full of moisture, even when he was abovedecks on his ship, standing in a brisk wind that would strip the water from anything else. He wore just those few pieces, preferring freedom of motion to heavier armament.

I believe it was made from the discarded carapace of a rare sea creature, but what that was, I do not know."

Achmed rose from the table.

"Interesting," he said. "Now, with one more indulgence, I will be on my way and out of yours."

"And how do you wish to be further indulged, Majesty?" Edwyn Griffyth asked through gritted teeth.

Achmed smiled. "I would like to be taken to the tower."

Both Sea Mages looked at one another in astonishment.

"You know that is not possible," Edwyn Griffyth said tersely. "Only trained mages are allowed in that artifact, and only the most senior—"

"Is the conversation in this room secure? Spells and such having been cast to make certain it is not overheard, as I believe Rhapsody once told me?"

"Yes," said the High Sea Mage. "Everywhere in this building, as long as the door is shut, but as for the tower—"

"I am planning to enter the Vault of the Underworld," the Bolg king said quietly. "If I survive, highly unlikely as that is, I plan to see if there is anything I can do to address that which sleeps within the depths of the world, whose mass is a sixth or so of that world. Unless there is something else you know about that entity, or any special tool you wish to give me, I believe it will most likely continue sleeping after my visit. But if I survive, I will report back on its status."

The complete lack of sound from the two academics, whom he had long asserted were in love with the noise of their own voices, was devouring. Achmed smiled in amusement, then leaned forward and spoke in his sandiest tone.

"Now, take me to the fucking tower."

36

After the Sea Mages had recovered and assented to his request, Achmed made his way back to the beach again.

The telescope at the top of the White Ivory Tower had been useful in finding the coordinates of where Serendair had once been, and had shown him the shallow reefs that had once been where he believed the land bridge stood, but there was little else that it could do to reveal to him anything he else he sought.

This was largely because everything else he sought was hidden from the sight of the world, either beneath its crust, or beneath the sea.

He had left without as much as a word, leaving the Sea Mages stunned. They followed him down to the beach, hurrying behind him across the glimmering sand and nattering at him. What they said did not penetrate the sound of the wind in his ears or the words in his mind, spoken long ago by Rath.

You could walk the Vault alone, and when you were done the silence would ring with nothing but the whisper of your name.

You have often been given to wild assumptions that have not always proven true, Rath, the Bolg king thought, ignoring the two men desperately trying to keep up with him as he approached the water.

The voice in his memory turned sweeter.

You said that at some point this beast will be summoned, Rhapsody had said in the cold tunnel deep within the Earth, the wall of which was a scale in the skin of that very beast.

Yes.

What if it didn't hear the call? In order to summon something, you need to know its true name. Of course, I don't know this thing's name. But if we could obscure the call, keep the beast from hearing it properly, or feeling it, perhaps it would just stay asleep and not answer. At least for a little while.

The harp she had set in place had laced the air of the massive tunnel with threads of light, the vibrations of music she had played on the instrument to interfere with the hearing of the beast.

But the "little while" had passed long ago.

He walked into the arms of the sea, paying no heed to the shouts of the academics who chased him all the way to the water's edge.

SOUTHERN OCEAN, NEAR THE
GRAVE OF SERENDAIR

If Achmed had believed his journey to Gaematria to be a long one, he had not known the meaning of *long*.

His travels to reach the grave of Serendair introduced him to the definition.

He had come to realize early in his ocean trek that because he was carrying Kirsdarke across his back, he was benefiting from the power it granted for its bearer to become formless, no longer solid in the drift, much as the Firstborn race of Mythlin were said to be. That lack of solidity was an uncomfortable state for him, but at least it allowed him to pass, unnoticed, beneath the surface.

Days and nights blended, one into the next, as he made his way through some of the deepest parts of the ocean, across wide expanses of the undersea world. The creatures that passed him were so nightmarish in some parts of the wide expanses of water that he took to walking with his eyes closed.

He was able to do that because the bell that sounded every now and then grew stronger the deeper the sea got, calling to him insistently, louder as he got closer to the place where he had once been able to feel the heartbeat of every living person on the Island.

The place where the sound was the loudest turned out to be a small peninsula in Sithgraid, where MacQuieth had long ago stood vigil for his son, Hector, with no one but his daughter-in-law and grandson allowed by his side. Achmed had walked the sea respectfully there; the agony that the ancient hero had suffered at the loss of Hector was still present, nascent in the very water of the place.

Finally, he began to hear a different call, the sound of horrifying devastation and destruction in the distance.

Even as far away from it as he was, the Bolg king had no misconceptions about what he was hearing.

MacQuieth had described it to him once, staring out into the rolling surf that battered the rocks of Traeg.

I knew that I would find devastation there, but could not have begun to imagine how hellish, how truly terrible the sight of it would be. The towers of Tartechor, the great city of the Mythlin, once the jewel of the sea, gone, along with the rest, swept away by the roiling current. The hundreds of thousands of souls that lived there gone as well, atomized, turned into vapor, foam on the waves. In breathing the water around the place where the city had been, I knew I was breathing the dead. It was a kindness that Tartechor went the way it did, however. For all that it was horrific to view the place where there had once been such opulence beneath the waves, and now was nothing but ever-shifting sand, it could not begin to compare to the horror of the sight that was once Serendair.

Achmed, who, unlike MacQuieth and Rhapsody, had left nothing of sentiment behind when he ran from the Island, still could feel the unrelenting terror and sorrow in the turbulent waves of the sea, almost three millennia later.

He followed the sound of the bell slightly away and north of the dismal symphony of death that still rang in the depths of the ocean on his way to the small islands north of where the Island had been taken to its grave.

NORTH OF SERENDAIR, THE GRAVE OF THE SLEEPING CHILD

The night before Achmed made landfall on the Northern Islands, a ferocious storm had come through, a storm whose intensity was so fierce that he could not hide from it, even as deep as he allowed himself to sink into the sea.

He had passed the night hovering in the drift, trying to keep from being carried too far out to sea, keeping his eyes closed against the whirlwind of sand and sea bottom that was filling the water amid the roaring storm. He had struggled to maintain consciousness, but even that seemed impossible during much of the storm's duration.

Until, with morning's light, he found himself hip-deep in crashing surf at the edge of what looked like a sandbar, exposed by the storm from the shallow sea around it.

The Bolg king dragged himself out of the churning water onto the semi-dry land that led to what once had been a peninsula where the water met on three sides, to a failed land bridge.

And, shaking the water from his garments, he straightened the lightweight armor that matched the Mythlin scabbard he carried and made his way across the tidal wasteland, where the sea had once swelled to the land, now nothing but a desert of ocean sand.

The sea's retreat had laid bare the bones of ships, broken reefs, shells of every imaginable kind, cracked and jagged in the wet grit where the water once broke against the shore. Achmed ran around or jumped over them, hurrying to find the doors to the Vault before the sea roared back into place.

He ran for three or more miles, past waves of sand and flapping fish, sea creatures caught unaware by the storm and the drawback of the sea, expecting each time he crested a long sand hill that the crevasse the Sea Mages had described would be on the other side of it, but each hilltop yielded only another view of the endless expanse of sand.

Until finally, after struggling up a tall sand dune, he had to pull himself to a hurried stop.

He was standing on what appeared to be a great ridge in the seabed, a towering wall that led down into a crevasse a thousand or more feet deep, at the bottom of which the remnants of seawater pooled. Achmed followed the perimeter with his eyes, and could not see its beginning, nor its end. The depression seemed to stretch to the horizon; the cliff wall beneath him made the seabed seem as if he were standing in a vast meadow atop a mountain. Whatever the actual dimensions, it was clear that a man could not see all of it at once; it stretched out beneath the sand, hidden for millennia by the sea, into the place to which the water had retreated from the storm.

Achmed gazed down into the crevasse, deeper than the one in the Bolglands that separated the Cauldron and the guardian mountains from the Blasted Heath and the Hidden Realm beyond it.

There appeared to be an ancient path in the face of the cliff wall where it slanted inward, which seemed as good a possibility as any.

Achmed closed his eyes and loosed the pathfinding lore he had absorbed during his trek along the Root with Grunthor and Rhapsody. She had sung them through the fire at the heart of the Earth with namesongs that had approximated what she thought their true names were. As a result, by changing his name from the Brother to his silly current title she had cost him the ability to discern the heartbeats of any person in the world.

She had, however, given him the ability to unerringly track a path.

Grateful, finally, he thought as the second sight kicked in, looking around for the trail. *Heartbeats would be of no use at this point anyway.*

He closed his eyes and stood as still as he could as the inner sight took off, leaping over the rim in front of him, spinning madly toward the path that led down the face of the slanted cliff, until it came to a stop at the bottom of the crevasse.

Then it disappeared.

All right, then, the Bolg king thought. *Here's for it.*

He climbed over the rim and began sliding down the wall that his path lore had indicated.

He hurried down into the crevasse, slipping and falling occasionally, sliding on his knees or even on his back, rising and cursing. The seabed was thick here, like rock beneath the sand, but absent of the debris that he had seen in the open seabed near the shoreline.

Finally, when he had fallen on his arse far enough down to have descended a small mountain, he found himself at the base of a sheer cliff, staring up at a solid wall of rock.

The wind howled and shrieked above him, but stayed at the level of the sea, only venturing down into the canyon long enough to whip sand into his eyes.

Achmed sought the path again. A closer image of a trail filled his mind.

He slowly made his way over the scattered rock of the seafloor, following the secondary path lore until it came to an abrupt halt.

Above him towered what appeared to be two massive slabs of solid earth, smooth as granite and white as the rest of the sea sand. There was a slash of thin darkness between them; otherwise they appeared no different than the rest of the rocky undersea hills. Achmed's blood ran cold in the memory of the last time he had been here.

Along with the water that was shedding down the sides of the canyon, sand was falling in rivers off of the enormous slabs of earth.

Towering doors of titanic size bound in brass were revealed, with massive handles jutting from plates of the same metal, a strange keyhole in the rightmost one. The gigantic doors were inscribed with ancient glyphs and wards, countersigns and runes.

Attached to the door, interlaced through the brass handles, was what looked like a pair of bony human arms, wrapped through one another, calcified, barely recognizable for all the petrified ash that had hardened around them.

In the seabed behind them, a stick of driftwood, or something like it, jutted at a strange angle.

Achmed went up to the door.

For a notoriously unsentimental man, he felt a powerful twinge as he stared at the skeletal arms. Even as detached as they were, it would have been impossible to miss the stalwart strength that had put them there in the first place, a desperate grip and desire to prevent the doors from opening at obvious mortal expense.

What in the world is this? Achmed wondered, studying the arms. *They were not here when last I was led to this place.*

He looked at them from different angles, confused.

I wonder if this was once Hector, he mused. *I am almost certain this must have been him, given how MacQuieth had described him.*

They had built seawalls, levies, in the last days, in the vain attempt to hold back the inevitable, the great hero had said sadly. *That must have been Hector. My son would have been filling bags of sand to the last.*

The thought that, in addition to having to hold the abandoned Island together in the last days before the eruption of the Sleeping Child, Hector might have had to hold the Vault of the Underworld closed with his arms was more than Achmed could bring himself to think about.

He carefully removed the arms, which broke apart easily in his hands, and placed them in a hole within the rocks beside the enormous doors, then found another, larger stone to seal the hole as if it were a grave or a columbarium.

He turned away from the doors, remembering the time he had been escorted here, with an invisible chain around his neck, or, more precisely, his name, the true name that was being held prisoner inside the stone altar from which he had recently retrieved Kirsdarke.

He had been shown these very doors, and allowed to look inside through the keyhole long enough to meet the creature that was waiting to exit through them.

Get the key, the beast had whispered in a voice that scratched his brain. *Get it. Bring it here. You alone, Child of Blood. The key will be alive when it is pulled from the rib cage of the Child of Earth, but will die before it reaches this place unless it is in your hand. You must be the one to bring it to me.*

And then you will be the one to free us all. Our liberator.

Achmed turned to his right and looked behind him.

Then he bent down and plucked the sand-and-ash-covered piece of driftwood from the barely dry ocean floor. He brushed it off, scratching the ash from it.

He was not particularly surprised to discover that it was an ancient key, dark of shaft, resembling a rib bone of a Child of Earth.

Because it was.

He had never fully explained to Rhapsody the reason for his stalwart vigil of the Earthchild, because he tried whenever possible not to recall the time he had been brought here previously. The thought of a conjured child of Living Earth being harvested for a single bone made his gorge rise at the sheer depravity and cruelty of it, like the planned eating of Meridion's heart had seemed to him when Talquist, the long-dead Merchant Emperor of Sorbold, had planned to do so.

Carefully he held it next to the keyhole, trying to ascertain the angle at which it would fit.

Achmed cast a glance at the sky, so seemingly far above him. He thought of Grunthor, and Rhapsody, and wondered where they were, if they could see him or at least know what he was about to do.

He decided they couldn't.

He hoped they couldn't.

He remembered how sick and nervous Rhapsody had been within the depths of the Earth, particularly when they were crawling along the Root of Sagia that wrapped around the Axis Mundi, the centerline of power that bisected the Earth. He recalled how relieved she had always been to be out beneath the sheltering sky once more whenever she left the Bolglands, or any other underground place that he and Grunthor had found comforting, the dark, warm tunnels of the Earth.

He held the key in his hand, contemplating where it would take him, knowing that he would very likely never see the sky again.

Then, taking a breath, he fit the key into the hole in the massive door.

37

$\mathcal{T}$he glyphs on the doors glowed with life.

The calcified ash began to fall from the bone key, sliding off in white chunks.

Achmed drew Tysterisk, then pushed the key into the lock and slowly turned it counterclockwise.

Beneath his hand he more felt than heard an echoing *thunk*.

Ever-so-slightly, the crack between the stone doors widened.

He pushed carefully on the rightmost of the two, but could see very little.

The darkness was devouring in its depth, the immensity of the place even more than Achmed could fathom. There seemed to be no border to it, no walls below limiting it to edges, but rather it was more like opening a door into the night sky, or the depths of the universe.

Achmed patted his Mythlin armor, finding it reassuringly wet, then opened the vault and stepped inside.

It was silent and utterly dark.

Quickly and carefully he pulled the key from the latch and shut the door.

The noise of closing it, or the breath of sea air that slid in, caused a disturbance he could feel.

The dead air of the massive enclosure thudded loudly and echoed throughout the enormous vault.

At first he saw nothing move. Then, at the most distant edge of his vision, he thought he could make out tiny flames which began to flicker, then surge forward. Achmed felt suddenly weak, dizzy, as his head was assaulted from within by the cacophony of a thousand rushing voices, cackling and screeching with delight.

Like fire on pine, the living flames began to sweep down distant ledges within the mammoth pit, some nearer, some farther, all dashing toward the door, churning the air with the destructive chaos of mayhem.

Achmed, whose head was throbbing now with the gleeful screaming that was drawing rapidly closer, put Tysterisk behind his back, waiting as a legion of individual flames scrambled down the dark walls toward the doors.

From the floor of the place a figure rose, almost human of shape, and began stiffly charging toward him.

As it came, seven or so of the faster screeching flames leapt upon it, whirling about it wildly in cackling fire, followed by a galaxy of stars all roaring toward him.

The enormous chamber rocked with the sound, the hissing, screaming, laughing, sobbing, bellowing, whispering, and hooting of a thousand or more individual voices.

Steady, Achmed told himself. *Steady, now.*

The figure was almost upon him, being egged on, it seemed, by the half dozen or so flames whipping around it. Achmed saw its dark eyes sight on him, its skeletal bones clad in rotten cloth reaching for him.

Just as it was upon him, he drew forth the ancient sword of elemental air and, rather than slashing, impaled the charging beast where he believed its heart would have been, holding it as steady as he could.

For a moment he was engulfed in white flashes of searing heat as the pure air of Tysterisk swept the flames into even hotter fire, exploding them into bright white blinding light, singeing the backs of Achmed's forearms while blasting the human-like creature's arm and shoulder off.

The seven fastest flames, hooting and catcalling in glee a moment before, let loose agonizing wails of anger and pain, and expanded violently until they winked out, as more behind them disappeared into the darkness, the rest fleeing until their noise could be heard no more.

Both he and the humanoid creature were tossed back in the directions from which they came, both of them impacting walls of stone.

Silence, encompassing and menacing, filled the enormous prison once more.

Slowly Achmed rose to a stand, using the wall against which he had fallen for cover of his back, and sheathed the sword. It appeared as if the skeletal creature had been blown apart, its shoulder and arm lying separate from the rest of its body.

The Bolg king pulled his pack from his back, keeping one hand free to draw the sword again. When nothing approached, he opened the pack and did a quick check of the supplies closest to the top and the gear in his bandolier.

The swords and the cwellan were all intact, as were the herbs and potions that Rhapsody had made, tonics of health and healing, as well as many capsules of lightning-bug fluid which, when shaken, cast a gentle light. He cursed quietly when he discovered that several of the fungi similar to the ones they had used long ago when traveling the Root, which also emitted a glow when crushed, had already been activated by the impact of his pack against the titanic doors. He moved those to the top of the pack, and the black liquid tincture of silence he had originally planned to poison the Sea Mages with to the bottom.

He also had a supply of Tanist Root, which would keep him hydrated without the need for water, and Vigil Root, which would allow him to remain awake without the need for sleep, a small still to turn seawater drinkable, food rations, several skins of water, and the poles of potable drink he had purchased from Barney.

Finally, tucked away at the very bottom of the bag was the key of bone.

Mostly satisfied with the condition of his supplies, Achmed turned to the gigantic doors one last time and secured them again, assuring himself of their solid closure. He had laid his hand on the door in the course of his check and so knew that the sea had returned; the pressure was palpable, and the thudding of the Deep echoed off the entranceway and the ceiling above, so high up that he could not even see it for the darkness.

As he was finishing the check of his equipment, he noticed a terrible hissing sound coming from the pile of rags and bones that had been the creature the flames had ridden to attack him.

He spun, sword in hand, and pointed it at the pile of human refuse.

He heard the hissing sound again, louder this time, dry and brittle, and realized suddenly what he was hearing.

The creature was chuckling.

"Thank you," it said, its voice waterless on the verge of cracking. "Good to have 'em off me."

The Bolg king came closer. The creature appeared scorched and damaged, but purged of its flame passengers, at least temporarily.

"Don't move too quickly, if you value your life," he said to the rags and skin-wrapped bones.

A hissing sound erupted again, stinging the sensitive nerves on any exposed area of Achmed's skin.

"No worries about that," it rasped. "Been dead a *very* long time. Wish they'd let me stay that way permanently, but they use me; they need me. If I'd valued my life, I never would have stayed behind to guard the Island for my king. So, clearly you can see that I didn't value it much."

The Bolg king squinted in the dark. "Hector?" he asked.

A wheezing sound answered him, echoing in the oddly angled cave. He had the momentary impression that the sound was a full-blown laugh, but the concept of laughter existing in this place disappeared the instant it occurred.

"I was never Hector," the creature hissed. It had still not risen, but lay where it had fallen after the blast.

"Who, then, are you?"

"Not who I was."

Achmed scanned the cave, looking for movement or light, but saw nothing, heard nothing, except the faint rustling where the creature moved slightly against the earth.

The creature seemed to at one time have been human, being in possession of one remaining arm, two shriveled legs, and a human head covered only partially with what resembled hair. There was something about it that reminded Achmed strongly of a mummy, all except for the dark eyes, which were still set in the hollow face, eyes that burned angrily, even when it had been recovering from the shock of the air sword. It pulled itself up, slowly and deliberately, struggling to make use of only one arm, until it was sitting, leaning back against the heat-baked wall of the cavern.

"What do you have for me?" it demanded.

Achmed still did not answer. He noticed that the floor seemed natural, formed from some mineral other than basalt or clay or anthracite, but that there was not a single rock or stone or broken piece to be seen, nothing to kick, scatter, or throw.

"What do you want from me?" he asked in reply.

"I hope," the creature coughed, "you brought beer."

"Beer?" Achmed gave a short chuckle. "No beer. Sorry. Would have obliged if I had known I'd be making your acquaintance."

The creature spun slowly, like a snake, raising itself up a little higher. "Show some respect in the presence of a mighty desolation," it said, puffing raggedly in the dry, airless place. "Twenty-five or more centuries of thirst gaze upon you at this moment."

"I do have this." Achmed reached into his pack and withdrew one of the poles of Canderian brandy he had purchased from Old Barney what felt already like a lifetime ago.

Guardedly he approached the creature, which seemed to have trouble righting itself between its stiffness and the loss of its arm. "Brandy— of a quality vintage. Will this do?"

The remaining arm shot out, quivering. "Give. Give. *Give-give-give.*"

Achmed hesitated, then removed the seal and cork and handed it down to the seated creature, which he then had a chance to examine.

It might once have been a man. Few clothes remained, of indeterminate color or shape.

It snatched the flask from his hand, waved it in front of its face, as if it could smell, then poured the dark liquid into its mouth. Achmed could almost trace the path of the drink down the gullet into its leathern belly.

It paused, took another long drink, holding the brandy in its mouth for some moments before tilting its head back.

"Ahhhh," it said, its voice greatly warmed and wetter than it had been. "Bless you."

The Bolg king bowed his head slightly, making note of the word *bless.*

The desiccated man, if it had been a man, took another swig, then opened its mouth in a long *aaaahhhhhhh* again. The sound seemed to come from the depths of its body, down to its twisted feet.

"It is dry here," it said wistfully. "Dry as the heart of a sandstorm. Dry as—well, dry."

"Indeed. Who are you, and what can you tell me about the remaining F'dor?"

For the first time, the creature smiled, revealing sunken teeth and gums.

"Everything," it said.

38

THE VAULT OF THE UNDERWORLD

The all-but-mummified creature held up the pole of brandy and gazed at it intently.

"This is not beer—but it was not bad, either."

"Who were you?" Achmed asked, thinking of past times when he had commerce with strange creatures in strange places, though none could even begin to compare to where he was and what he was beholding.

What he thought might be the living remains of a man turned and looked at him intently, his dark eyes gleaming.

"I am honored that you thought I was Hector," he said quietly. "Hector was a great man. It was an honor to serve with him."

Achmed thought back to what Aurelia had told him in Gaematria, trying to remember names.

"Were you one of the men who stayed behind with him? Anaias, perhaps?"

The skeletal man chuckled again, another hissing sound that scratched Achmed's ears. "Yes. And no. Anaias stayed behind on the Island. I imagine he died in the arms of the Tree—he was Liringlas. Hector sent him home before he and I rode north." He struggled to sit up again, to little avail, exhausted from his words. He took another drink.

"No," he said when his throat was a little less dry. "I was Jarmon, an ordinary soldier in His Majesty's army. Came up through the ranks."

His eyes broke with Achmed's and he sighed, a rattling sound. "Hector died in the water; I died in the dust."

From behind his veils, Achmed inhaled, but just nodded.

"Now go up there," the skeletal form whispered, and tipped its head toward a gently sloping passage. "When you return, tell me what you see. I shall stay here and finish my libation, and dispose of my arm."

The Bolg king absorbed the words, then turned and made his way up the slope that the dried man called Jarmon had indicated.

First he walked as far as he could go and still be certain there was nothing hovering or hiding around him. A hum was brewing from the space beyond which he could see, so he lay on his belly as he climbed.

The watery armor left a thin, dark trail in the dust.

The farther he ascended, the more certain he was that he had come into the Vault almost at the very top, at what would have been similar to the highest floor of the tower of Gurgus Peak that held the Lightcatcher, and that the rest of it existed lower, deeper, wedged in the depths of the Earth. He was more convinced of it when he reached the top of the passage, which opened up before him, like the highest balcony in a concert hall.

He peered down over the edge.

A bottomless darkness lay below him, like an enormous stomach cavity. Spun around it were buttresses that appeared to be longbones or ribs, reaching down into the devouring darkness, with glowing, crackling flames crouched along the edges.

The pit seemed to go on forever, twisting into blackness.

The noise he had remembered from the last time he had been here echoed against his eardrums distantly, the sounds of pain and twisted laughter, the pounding of the drums of war and the wailing of children whose parents had been taken in front of their eyes. Armored as he felt by the Mythlin hauberk, coif, and mantle, it did not seem to spare him from the overwhelming wheedling, the taunting and the weeping, sounds of a sick world that thrummed against his skin and eardrums.

It was almost impossible to hear the noise of the Vault and not succumb to utter despair, a physical compulsion as well as a mental one.

Achmed shook his head and thought of the song in the darkness of his bedchamber that had wrapped around him while he slept some time before. It did little to ease the pain now, but it did coat his senses a bit, senses that were growing heightened with each beat of his heart.

He stared at the closest of the flames, high atop the descending stone longbones, gripping the hilt of the air sword as he lay there.

The creatures seemed to be hanging like bats at the top of the passage he had just ascended, asleep perhaps, or biding their time, buzzing with ugly noise.

It was almost as if they were snoring.

As his sight sharpened, he began to see each creature not as an indistinct flame, but rather like a moving shape within a screen of pure vibration, buzzing inconstantly, incorporeal. The fire it seemed to profess was actually very unlike real fires he had encountered over his very long life; it was more as if in seeing what looked like flames he was actually seeing vibrations of hate, of lust, or avarice, the dark, evil thoughts of dark and evil beings, rather than the natural element from which they came.

Suddenly, from around him was a swirling of flames that swelled like a flock of subterranean bats, screeching and snarling as their high-pitched voices, each a different tone of hatred, struck him, dashing against him and sliding off against the water armor.

Rolling fully onto his back, Achmed did a quick reconnaissance.

There appeared to be three or four; it was difficult to be sure, as they dashed, flashing like fire-colored lightning, strafing him, snapping like feral dogs but without form.

He drew the hilt of the air sword again and held it close to his leg.

Hooting, sneering, and howling, the fireless flames charged him from all sides as one.

Just as they attacked, Achmed struck with the air sword.

His speed was such that he was able to slash the first one on him before he swung back and slapped another as it flew past, shrieking in rage. He caught the second one on the now-visible blade of the sword and, using all his strength, held it still, above him, for a moment.

The flame-like creature screamed, flapping and fluttering on the blade of the air sword, seeming to spread apart the longer it was in contact with the weapon.

Then it blew into pieces with a horrifying shuddering sound, exploding as a small candle would be melted by a torch or as the sound of a bell might be erased by the wind.

Achmed waited, still on his back, but nothing else attacked him.

He remained a good while, listening to the noise over the edge of the opening, but the seething and jeering, the hooting, spitting, and whispering, had gone silent.

He rolled onto his front again and, like a spider, crawled back down the slope, noting that it went higher beyond where he'd been attacked.

*W*hen Achmed returned, Jarmon was standing erect, his skeletal back to him, engaged in what appeared to be a slow, ominous dance.

He was spinning painfully, stiffly raising one leg, planting his heel, deliberately and heavily pivoting, and then doing the same with the other foot. Achmed could not determine the meaning of the dance, nor whether Jarmon was conscious of him or his surroundings. The remaining arm limply held the empty flask that had contained the brandy. *Gesturing with the arms is apparently not part of this ritual,* he thought, still wondering what was going on.

Finally, Jarmon turned his head slowly toward Achmed and hissed in either greeting or amusement, it was impossible to tell. Then he fell to his knees, and began to use the round flask as a pestle to complete his purpose, pounding the floor repeatedly with it.

Achmed came closer to observe what was going on.

He was crushing the amputated bones of his arm into dust.

"What are you doing?"

Jarmon looked up at him and gave him a grisly smile. He did not stop in his task.

"When they return, I have no intention of digging again, especially—" He gave the Bolg king a knowing look and turned back to the tiny fragments of his arm bone as they yielded with whispers to his insistence, dissolving into dust as he rocked the flask over them as if he were rolling out dough. "I'm surprised they didn't think of using my bones before. I'll be damned if they'll force me to dig with what's left of my arm as a tool." The hissing laugh returned. "Well, I suppose I'll be damned in any case."

As he watched the mummified man grinding his bones into dust, every loneliness or stubborn determination Achmed could ever recall making seemed crushed with those bones. The academic and theoretical opposition he held for the race of F'dor stole away, and he discovered in its place, at last, comprehension of Rath's passion and urgency to see the race extinguished.

"My apologies," he said to the ragged being.

Jarmon shook his head. "Seven. Seven dead when you arrived," he said, almost happily. "If I had seven hundred arms, I'd give them each again. This is a good day. How many did you find? Tell me what you learned."

"Tell me why they made you dig."

"'Tis better if you see for yourself," Jarmon said, blowing the dust off the rock and starting on the shoulder joint. "What did you find up the slope?"

"Three attacked me. They burn well when mixed with wind. Then I came back."

"Go back and climb all the way up the neck to the head, to the eyes. Pay attention to how many are there, then come back and tell me what you've seen."

"What does that mean, neck, head, eyes? Whose neck, head, and eyes?"

Jarmon looked up from his task, seemingly annoyed.

"Did you study nothing about this place before you came here, King Ysk?"

Achmed's mouth dropped open in shock.

"What did you call me?"

The skeletal man grinned broadly. "I called you by your name, did I not?"

"No," said Achmed. "That has not been my name for a very long time, nor is it the most recent name before the one I now bear."

"Ah, a shame," said Jarmon. "You might want to rethink that. But we can talk more about this when it's safer—when I am done with my task, and you have seen more of the slope. This is a very big vault, and it is full of very evil things. I imagine you would like to know what you're up against, would you not?"

"Of course," said Achmed sullenly. "Whose head, neck, and eyes?"

Jarmon finally stopped working to crush the shoulder and came over to Achmed, holding the bone like a club or a gavel.

"When this place was built, there were many more of the folks that live here inside," he said, waving his shoulder bone for emphasis. "And their sheer number strained the facility, shall we say? The Wyrmril, the race normal people call dragons, gave their cache of Living Stone to make the place, and as you can see, they've only had one escape since the beginning of Time. But when that threat of rupture seemed possible of coming to pass, the Progenitor Wyrm, the originator of the race, saw the place bursting at the seams and wrapped him or herself around it, consuming it and, I believe, Ending."

"I know this tale."

The animated pile of rags threw its one remaining hand up into the air.

"Well, why didn't you say so?" Jarmon inquired. "If you know the tale, then you should be able to figure out whose head, neck, and eyes I'm talking about."

Achmed blinked. "Oh."

"Go."

The Bolg king watched as the dried-out man went back to work grinding his own shoulder into dust.

He returned to the place where the three F'dor spirits had swept down on him, silent now except for the endless drone of maniacal noise in the distance. He traveled up the slope, through a number of peaks and corners that he realized after climbing along them were the shoulders and neck of the enormous beast, a creature for which there was nothing he had ever seen to match for scale.

At one joint of the neck, another ambush occurred.

As he was turning through what appeared to be a series of hiding places, a circle of flames sprang up around him, chanting, cursing, insulting him, trying to overwhelm him with flashes of black fire pitched at his eyes.

The Bolg king responded by taking out Kirsdarke and drenching both himself and the corridor, raining water down upon the beasts and snuffing many of them. As each of them winked out, a puff of smoke was left behind, leaving the slope hazy with it.

The rest of the screaming fires fled to distant corners, sending up wails of agony that made his skin throb.

Finally he came to the end of the tunnel, an enormous cavern that was filled with wheedling sounds being emitted by disembodied voices, all trying to encourage him into foolish tasks or suicidal undertakings in the dark, spoken sensually or maliciously combative, voices calling mournfully or begging plaintively, a cavern full of lies and manipulations.

At the bottom of which, set into the enormous oval floor, were two reflective pools of silver mirrors that flashed with the movement of anything coming down from the slope above.

Achmed paused here.

He was uncertain at this point what to make of this place, because, unlike the endless pain and frustration, terror and threat of the rest of the Vault he had seen so far, he had come into what passed for a hopeful place.

A place of promise, where he could feel the palpable potential of escape. Demonic flames were chasing each other around the circular floor, entreating each other, and him, to help them out.

Many of the bristling fires were repeatedly slamming themselves into the mirrored pools, flashing and flaring and occasionally winking out.

See? the tempting voices were saying. *There is a world beyond here—the legends are true. Look out through the eyes; they are the windows of the soul.*

You have no souls, you monsters, Achmed thought disdainfully. But the entreaties were so powerful, so compelling, that he had the irresistible urge to do as they said, to look out through the ancient dragon's eyes, to see what lay beyond the Vault, as they did.

He did so, only to discover an image reflected back at him, an image of himself, twisted and rotten, thick where he knew himself to be thin, weak where he knew he was strong, the internal mirrors causing him, for the slightest of moments, to cease to believe in his own resolve as another squadron of flame grew nearer, whispering promises of power, of escape.

Then, as one, they all came roaring at him at once, only to be snuffed out by a sweep of the air sword that expanded their flame to the point of not being able to be sustained.

A series of explosions that looked for all the world like fireworks lit the interior of what had been part of the Progenitor Wyrm's skull, leading to a swelling chorus of screaming and acidic hatred once again.

As he was returning, he saw that the low ceiling of the place, well within his reach, was deeply scratched, and noticed light suffusing through, most likely dead rock that had once been Living Stone, as if it was a very thin layer of rock that he knew was part of the exterior of the Vault.

He reached out his hand in confusion and touched it with his glove.

This is clearly a place where the rock is directly submerged in the depths of the sea, he thought hazily. *Why would they be scratching their way out here? And how? Surely they must know their efforts will destroy the one thing that keeps the sea from pouring in—*

He looked more closely, only to discover that there was condensation and seepage all along the top, as if there were a million tiny grooves and cracks, behind which the seawater threatened to burst through at any moment.

It perhaps explained the lack of demonic presence in this part of the prison.

On the stone floor at his feet was a puddle of dampness that had been whitened by salt.

Achmed looked around to assure himself of a lack of ambush, then opened his pack. He set up his still to catch and purify the water for later use, not so much for himself but for Jarmon, whose thirst he could still feel in his skin, even this far away.

"What in the world are they trying to do up where the skin of the Vault is thinner?" he asked incredulously as he returned to see the skeletal soldier finished with his task. "If they want to drown, I am more than willing to help them."

"They don't want to drown, King Ysk," Jarmon said, settling his emaciated body under a column of Living Stone. "There are no cracks, for, unlike most of the Vault, that part's not stone. It is the skin of the great beast that gave its life. Some water passes through it, but they will not escape that way.

"They are not sentient creatures—they are sheer will, chaos, and destructive mania. They want out, so they compelled me, not long after I came to this place, to attempt to make an opening in what they thought was the roof, until the seepage was noticed. They feared being overwhelmed and drowning, so they made me stop. They originally were the ones who had made me dig in the first place. That's why the weapons that were on me when I came to this place are gone; they were worn away by my attempts at digging."

Achmed sat down in the dust of dead Living Stone and Jarmon's bones.

"I have more libation," he said, opening his pack and taking out two more poles. "Tell me your story, and at least one of them will be yours."

39

The animated pile of bones and skin sat down and extended an eager hand.

Achmed put a pole of whiskey in it.

"My story ended the day I entered here," Jarmon said, opening the pole with his teeth. "Nothing but dust since then, sunless, starless ages of dust. It never occurred to me that the bane of my existence would be a dry world, but it is."

"You said you could tell me everything of the F'dor," Achmed said, removing the cap of his own brandy and resolving to make certain that the next time he offered one to Jarmon, he handed it over open. "And how you know what was once my name."

"The latter is a quicker tale," the ancient soldier said. "I know of you, Ysk. I know every secret that has been put on the wind. When I stand at the top of the shoulder, at the thin place where they are mostly afraid to go, every secret that rides the wind comes by, or at least it does on the rare occasions when the sea pulls back, as it must have for you to come through the door you did. Whenever the top of the Vault is in the open air, the secrets pound at the roof, wail outside the Vault, demand to be heard, carried here on the sea wind.

"And the demons, they are impressive listeners. I learned from them how to hear the secrets brush along the scales of the peak, learned to guess their size and shape as they circled round the world. There is not much left of me. Bones carried by secrets, and anger and their creeping dread that they'll miss witnessing my self-destruction—and yours."

Achmed took a deep draught of his pole of brandy.

"I despise riddles," he said. "Can you speak clearer to me?"

"While there are stories on the wind about the great Dhracian assassin, there have also been tales of you within this place for as long as you've been alive—perhaps longer," said Jarmon, leaning back against the wall. "Your conception was an epic event in here, apparently, though I was not here when that happened. I am younger than you—easy to believe, me being the picture of youth!"

The skeletal soldier laughed. Achmed smiled in spite of himself.

"There is only one thing more terrifying to a F'dor spirit than a Dhracian, the race that has been patrolling outside the Vault since the Before-Time, waiting to sing their death chant and explode their host, or banish them to oblivion. And that, King Ysk, is the prospect of a Dhracian that has ties to the Earth itself. There has only been one such entity since the beginning of Time, at least in the lore of this place.

"And all their prophecies warn them of such a hunter, who can walk the Vault with impunity, free from their powers. They have feared your coming as much as the upworld fears their escape."

"That's hard to imagine," said Achmed, drinking again.

"As for the F'dor, the reason I could claim to tell you everything about them is that I have housed all of them in my time. I know their secrets, as I know yours."

"Housed them?"

"Whenever they can beat me into submission—and I'm proud to say that isn't very often—they attempt to catch me in thrall, or otherwise make me a temporary host. None of them would want me permanently, of course—to take on such a shambling midden of trash would be a terrible curse, since they would have trouble shaking me afterwards—but if they merely ride along, they are able to use me to feel solid for a while, like their fellows who escaped long ago, when the falling star hit the Vault and ruptured it. They are very jealous of those who made it out."

"I imagine."

"They are also very jealous that I move and act and see in the world, even such a world as this. Yet they know they should not destroy us, for we are all the chances they have."

Achmed sat up straighter. "Us?"

"There is an old man—or there was."

"Where did he come from?"

Jarmon finished his whiskey, then sadly held the pole upside down.

"Hmmm? Oh. There is a powerful F'dor, one who escaped during the rupture, named Brann. He came home to see if he could aid the Master in getting them all out of the Vault the second time the Sleeping Child arose. He took as a host an old fisherman who had rowed out from the fishing village of Dry Cove on the northern seacoast at Kyrlan de la Mar to see what was occurring during the days before the Rising, then lured Hector and me to this place, convincing us to take the king's scepter, which as regent he had access to, and open the Vault."

Achmed choked on his brandy. *"Hector opened the Vault?"*

The skeleton's black eyes turned darker.

"Do not gainsay my commander," he warned, his voice thick with threat. "You must remember that F'dor are superior liars and manipulators. It was a confusing time, to say the least. And the old fisherman led us here, to this wasteland, assuring us that he had found an ancient mine that might be able to offset the rising of the sea, like a levy or a sluiceway.

"Once we had opened the door a crack, he strengthened in power, no longer the old fisherman, but now the demon who had taken the poor man as a host. We battled over the door, and when it appeared the spirits might actually escape, I told Hector to open the door, and threw myself into Brann, wrapping my arms around his knees. We both went flying over the threshold, and Hector had the chance to slam the door closed and lock it again."

In a way, I suppose, Achmed thought, swallowing more brandy and remembering the arms through the door handles.

"At any rate, the fisherman that Brann took on was dragged into the Vault with me. And he's somewhere around here, if they haven't driven him to take his own life by now."

"So tell me what I should know about these fire demons."

Jarmon's eyes narrowed.

"The *first* thing you should know is that they are not made of fire. When you are looking at them, what you see is fire, feral, consuming, self-important, because that element is in their makeup, but they are not fire. Natural fire wishes unity, one flame seeks another until it becomes a colony, a column of flame that spreads but does not wish escape. Each of these is a spirit, selfish for its own chaos. It hates its brethren as much as it hates you and the limits of the world.

"The lore is that they are a race of creatures created this way, that a generous, loving god I no longer believe in made them of flame, but I know what they *really* are. You have been lucky, King Ysk, to have wrapped them in your sword, to keep them out of your heart and ears. Because what they really are is words."

"Words?"

"They are the words of a lonely, angry god who couldn't control his offspring, who wrestled the ether into this imperfect world.

"Each one is the utterance of that god—a curse, a sigh, a wail, a sneer. The dragons fled from them. My poor philosophy dares not attempt to translate the thoughts of a god, and I do not think you will be able to kill them, to silence them all. They will beat at you, slide between your certainties, unravel your logic, turn you against yourself. All that I loved, they drained of meaning, and then drained from me."

Achmed raised the pole to his lips, narrowed his eyes, and thought of the terrible potion he had made to silence the Sea Mages.

And plotted how it might silence the demons.

"You mentioned a Master," he asked finally. "Tell me of him."

"He is no king, though he fashions himself such. He lives in the very bottom of the Vault, where it is eternally cold, and where the souls of those whose bodies were taken as hosts, then their spirits eaten by the demons, wander, lost, for eternity in a great lake that is wracked with ice, but never freezes. It is the way that he attends to his most important duty, which requires there to be frost within the depths of a world with a core of raging, elemental fire.

"The Master has but one function, and he is the only F'dor patient and forethoughtful enough to be responsible for it. He is the guardian of the Wyrm."

Achmed leaned forward.

"I cannot imagine that it is wise to speak of such an entity in this place," he said quietly.

Jarmon shrugged. "Why not? It is common conversation here. The demons are incessantly proud of that Sleeping Child, that entity that dwells even deeper than the Vault, in the bowels of the Earth, that child, stolen from the Progenitor Wyrm, whose body encircles this prison, not far below its parent, asleep for all of Time. There is no risk in speaking of it, because it is given to conversation more than any other subject other than the escape that would allow the residents of this place to awaken it."

Achmed exhaled. "Go on," he said.

"And 'guardian' is a generous title, given that first, only the very fewest of minds in the world, known or unknown, have ever even heard of this Sleeping Child, and even fewer have seen it. I may be in the presence of one right now, but I am not one.

"Second, there is little responsibility to stand guard, given that he, like us, is trapped in here, and should something come that threatens the Child—imagine the irony of that for a moment—he would be able to do nothing to stop it. And, finally, there is nothing that *anyone* is able to do to stop it, King Ysk. It is the death of the world, known from the Before-Time to be so. Not a question of how, as they say, but when. All he does is guard the door. Their name for him, in their tongue is *He That Watches the Door*."

The Bolg king pointed up to the enormous entranceway through which he had come into the Vault. "Isn't that the door?"

"As I've told you, that's just one door. There is another, much bigger door. And it leads to a greater prize, from their point of view. He has no key to it—again, not much of a guardian."

"What else?"

Jarmon shook his remaining arm, and shrugged his remaining shoulder. "You don't have weapons to kill them all."

"You don't believe so?"

"Well, if you are thinking of the Thrall ritual, many of them have survived it before. And it is highly likely that you will be assaulted from all sides if you undertake it. Most likely not physically—but their weapons are not physical."

Achmed nodded. "Keep going."

"They have keys to your heart, your brain, your soul, even if you are of a race that is especially resistant to them, you are still vulnerable, because you have a beating heart. If you ever have loved a woman, or a child, or a parent, you are already in their grasp.

"They are expert liars, and they will tell you anything you need to know, anything, to convince you that you have lost the battle for life, or that you never really deserved to be in it in the first place. Imagine your wisdom, your coolness, your plans, your vision shredded to a ragged pile of thread that proves two things: that you never had an unselfish thought or impulse in your life, and that their victory is not only inevitable, but a blessing."

The mummified man leaned closer, a fetid smile on his sunken teeth.

"They will not all succumb to your weapons. Look, I'll show you how they work. I have learned enough of their lore, and enough of what they already know about you, to speak to you as they would. Hear me."

Achmed felt a sudden chill, but he said nothing.

" 'This man has come to our world, born to destroy us, and yet, look at his choices.' " He pointed to the cwellan. " 'Why did you bring *that,* Ysk? You knew it would do us no harm, and yet you lugged it along. You only brought it so that, should anyone ever find your remains in here, they would know who they belonged to—who you were. You are as vain as the rest of us.

" 'And how many years has it been since you've used it? The wind off the sea says that your land is more or less always at peace. Perhaps age has had its way with you, like a rapist or a harlot. If you don't keep up with the Hunt, you lose your skills, your reflexes—your edge.

" 'And you didn't make that weapon with our kind in mind, did you, Bolg king? You claimed to have made those disks for Anwyn, but we, who look within, we know your inner secrets. You made them to destroy Ashe. To what end? You jealous, grasping worm, Ysk—all you ever had was your loss.' "

Achmed's eyes widened in shock, then narrowed coolly. "How do you know these names?"

Jarmon chuckled dryly. "I've been around the F'dor long enough to have learned their skills of lying—and one of them is to listen to hear the names that *you* have heard most recently, spoken in love, or hate, or contempt. Those names, those vibrations, cling to you—and the F'dor are nothing but vibration. It's a skill unparalleled. I know what *none* of that means—those names mean nothing to me—but they lie, and manipulate, and twist your reality until it is no longer yours, but theirs."

"I see. Pray continue. It's fascinating."

Jarmon closed his thin-lidded eyes and listened again, his mouth ajar, like a door left open for the wind. Then he opened his eyes and looked at Achmed again.

"All right, one last attempt. 'Had she chosen you, what would that have made of you? Why be a king if not to gain her? If you had her, you would never have left the Root. Perhaps she would have grown tired of it—what then? Brigands, mercenaries, then curiosities—eventually when the end came, you would be nothing but a source of resentment to her.

" 'No unrequited love, no lost girl, dooms you to no kingdom, no Earthchild, no future. Savor your pain, Ysk—it made you who you are.' "

The dry man exhaled, exhausted.

"I have utterly no idea what any of that means," he said. "But I imagine enough of it is fresh to you, possibly painful enough to make you think twice, especially when you hear it from the mouth of an expert liar, whose race exists for nothing more than chaos and pain. Now, avail me of another drink."

Achmed watched him in silence for a long moment.

"That you can make use of their skills is a sign that when they have embodied you, they have left whatever vibration constitutes their spunk behind in you."

"No doubt," agreed Jarmon. "Welcome to what your world will be, if you are unable to get out of here. Now where's my drink?"

Once Jarmon had finished his libation, Achmed rose and opened his pack.

"Come," he said. "I am ready now."

The withered soldier looked at him in amusement. "Ready for what, pray?"

"I tire of this place," Achmed said, checking his supplies one more time. He pulled out a branch of Vigil Root and put it into his mouth at the corner. "No offense to the company."

"Oh, none taken, truly, Majesty."

"Take me to him, to them," the Bolg king said. "The longer I am here, the more they will know of me. Each moment we tarry from here out weakens me. Let's be on our way to the depths of this place."

Jarmon grinned and stood stiffly as well.

"Very well," he said. Then he struck a comic pose, like a street poet. "Let us descend into the blind world now," he intoned. "I shall go first and you will follow me. Let us go on, the way that waits is long."

Achmed's forehead wrinkled. "What's that about?"

The soldier shrugged. "I've no idea. It has been floating around on the dead wind in here forever."

The Bolg king rolled his eyes and followed Jarmon down into the belly of the Vault, his broken guide spouting random poetry all the way.

"Through me, the way into the Suffering City," he chanted. "Through me, the way to Eternal Pain; through me, the way that runs among the Lost."

"Perhaps you might consider 'Silence Is Golden' next," Achmed said, gritting his teeth.

"Before me, nothing but eternal things were made," Jarmon extolled to the unseen ceiling of the Vault. "And I endure eternally."

40

$\mathcal{T}$he descent into the deepest part of the Vault was accomplished, to Achmed's surprise, in total silence.

Having seen enough of the upper reaches, he had expected a nagging chorus of flames to accompany him, screeching and hissing, taunting and begging, strafing him from the corners and nooks and caves that freckled every wall of what had once been a very straight and plumb dungeon, and he had prepared for it. He was chewing on the Vigil Root as long as it lasted, both swords in hand as he traveled, his armor sealed fore and aft of him, but instead of the assault he had girded for, he was met instead with the devouring sound of hollow noiselessness, the occasional *plink* of something dripping in the dry prison—and nothing more.

The overwhelming emptiness was beginning to take a toll, he discovered, as he followed Jarmon farther and farther down into the blackness. While there had been noise and threat, it was easy to forget what he had left behind in the upworld, and what had left him behind in the same place. Even the comfort of the things that had once served as a happy touchstone to him had decayed and warped into painful memory and loneliness, accentuated by the thudding silence.

And, even more, he was haunted by the thought that below him lay nightmares he could not yet fathom.

The longer they descended, the more regular the architecture of the place became. It seemed to Achmed that they were traveling inward, away from the exterior that had been, in the Before-Time, encircled by the

Progenitor Wyrm and down into the narrow, regular Vault that the dragons had built in that Age to contain the Firstborn creatures which had sought nothing but glorious destruction and chaos.

And then there was the frozen stone.

Jarmon had warned him that the bottom of the Vault was eternally cold, but that had not been sufficient to describe the sensation that numbed his skin-web as they traveled farther into the silent prison. All light was gone now, except for the glowing spores and lightning-bug fluid that he had brought, and even the radiance of those things, made by nature to illuminate the darkness, only served to make the trek even more unbearable. The walls of the Vault were covered in frost, something that he never seen in the hallways and tunnels of Ylorc.

But when they finally reached the lowest level of the place, it was impossible not to know it.

The dry air of the Vault had long since lost its edge, the ability to desiccate the throat and nasal passages in what was obviously the presence of some sort of source or sources of water. But now water was everywhere, leaking in great streams of what in the dark looked like clear blood, puddling on the flat surfaces and pathways, until the water sword itself quivered in his hand, shaking like a dog to clear itself of the clammy condensation.

Jarmon's frailty slowed them greatly as they went deeper, but Achmed was loath to hurry him. The soldier had kept up a more or less constant patter when traveling what had been inhabited areas of the upper Vault, but once they had gone past the point of any light or sound, he turned inward, walking so quietly that Achmed could barely hear him.

The thought had occurred to him that he might be able to track the man by his heartbeat; Jarmon had been born on the Island, and therefore should have been among those to whom he still had a connection. But after trying and failing to find the soldier's internal rhythm, he remembered, annoyed at himself, that he was accompanying an entity that had been dead more than two thousand years, whose heartbeat had ceased when the doors of the Vault had slammed shut behind him.

For a long time they had been walking and skidding over pools of ice on a flat surface. Most of the Vault was built of inclines, but now it seemed as if they were following a prescribed route, an enormous and endlessly high hallway leading to only one destination.

Ahead of them, a gigantic opening loomed, a high archway that, like every other elevated place in the bottom of the Vault, had dripped water for Time Uncounted. The frigid cold had frozen the streams from which the water had cascaded, lending the appearance of fanglike teeth jutting from the top of the archway, a devouring mouth open to the only terminus, which seemed to be the throat and stomach of some beast of gargantuan proportions.

There is nothing to be lost here, Achmed reminded himself as he followed the shaking Jarmon, the cold light of the soldier's glowing spore flashing nervously about the tunnel walls from his shaking. *Any soul I ever had is beyond the reach of this place now.*

Graal's sweet face, reflecting his own eyes, appeared in his mind, reproaching him for the error of his thoughts.

Now the sound of water returned to the airless tunnel, the rush and whoosh accentuating the rising noise of cackling-crackling again.

The closer they came to the arched entranceway, the louder the voices became, all of the cacophony that Achmed had endured in the upper reaches of the Vault, magnified and elongated by their impact on whatever ceiling lay beyond the doorway.

Chanting could be heard, a deep and resonant sound that had the feel of charnel houses to it, words that he could not understand but knew to be obscene, profane, against the pounding of deep drums, the percussion of hate and rage echoing through the frozen walls. Above that deep sound, high, sliding notes of panic and pain, wild and insane laughter, weeping and bellowing, shouting of execution commands and the catcalls of blood-sport arenas all greeted them as they approached.

Achmed slowed to a stop. "Wait," he whispered to Jarmon.

The soldier shrugged nervously as he continued his shaking dance. "I'm in no hurry, King Ysk," he said. "Take your time, by all means."

The Bolg king's eyes scanned the immense threshold over which he was about to step, in sight, sound, and tactile sensation truly the most vile place he had ever beheld in a long lifetime of vile, onerous places traveled. *My life was a succession of dark paths,* he thought, *leading to this place of ultimate despair. If this is to be the end, I deserve the benefit of one last remembrance of those few things that I did right, the memories of those that I loved, to be my penultimate thoughts, not this poisonous darkness.*

He closed his eyes and, searching for the freshest memory he could find, summoned the image of the face that had taught him the meaning of friendship, the great grinning tusked smile beneath amber eyes that were always filled with humor and respect. In this particular recollection, Grunthor was sitting at a table, a handful of cards spread in front of him, comically whimpering or laughing aloud in the course of a game of Crusher.

Achmed's throat constricted as next he recalled the image of the person across the table from the Sergeant-Major, her face set in a comically serious expression of concentration, as if the outcome of the Firbolg card game were critical to the survival of the world itself.

Then, as she had done not so very long ago, the image of Rhapsody put down her cards and looked at him, rising and coming to him. Her smile had brought warmth and light to the longhouse, as well as to his heart, a heart that for most of its existence was almost as dark as the threshold he was about to cross. Achmed's strength of memory was such that he could almost feel her embrace, could banish the hideous odors of the Vault from his nostrils long enough to inhale and recall the scent of soap and spice, vanilla, and meadow flowers.

I love you, you petulant thing.

He gritted his teeth as the sight of her face in his memory turned to another night, as she listened to his words, tears in her beautiful eyes. His own voice filled his ears.

Whether you believe it or not, I do love you. In that way. And have for as long as I can remember. In fact, even though I know there was one, I can't recall a time when I didn't.

I'm glad I finally got the chance to tell her, at least once, he thought, keeping the image of her behind tightly closed eyes. *Grunthor nagged me for a thousand years to do it—he would be glad as well.*

When the image of Rhapsody looked up and her eyes met his, it was a recollection from the last time that they had, smiling over a glowing child that they had made together.

A last moment of joy, just before the world had fallen down around them.

Achmed exhaled slowly as the image began to fade, thankful that he could still summon a memory of times that had been happy in the black underbelly of the world.

This place has less power than I feared, he thought. *Even if this is the end, I take what I choose to remember with me.*

He swallowed, then cleared his throat.

"All right, Jarmon—here we go."

$\mathcal{F}$inally, they passed through the opening.

There they saw that they were on the elevated dam walls of a monstrous lake or, more correctly, a pool, filled with turgid black water, the crests of its churning waves capped in ice. The water was far below them, and in that water floated countless souls, beings of every race, their faces uniformly gray, struggling helplessly in the filthy drift. Achmed's throat tightened again at the sight of misery beyond anything he had ever seen, tiny children tossed and pulled under, to emerge, gasping, moments later, men and women in armor, struggling to get to the surface before they were dragged down again, old people battered by the current, bobbing helplessly.

None of whom seemed to have the blessed option of death.

All around, perched and floating high above the tribulation, winking flames of hatred leered, laughing, squealing, and chortling in malicious glee. Thousands of them, far more than Achmed had ever imagined could still be alive, given the numbers in the lore and the expeditious work of the Gaol, the Dhracian hunters over the millennia, tracking and destroying their kind.

In the center of the lake was a rocky pedestal, a phallic object that might have passed for a throne, around and above which an enormous mass of flame was hovering.

It was laughing in what seemed like a thousand separate voices, all of one mind.

Jarmon came to a halt before him, frozen in his tracks.

The vibrations of the place that were wreaking havoc on Achmed's sensitive nerve endings and skin were all of one thought about the roaring flame.

Master, they whispered, cried, and howled. *Master.*

Achmed slipped his hand into his pack, then pulled it out again. He held up a spore and crushed it gently, then raised it aloft, a tiny pinprick of light in the absolute darkness.

Laughter, harsh and vigorous, soft and amused, threateningly violent, filled the enormous cavern and splashed against the waves of the lake.

A squadron of flames swooped down, screaming as they came.

The Bolg king slapped them away with the water sword, blasting forth a immense spray of surprising heft and volume, drowning them in their own fury, winking them out.

The entity known as the Master rose higher above the obelisk throne. A shadow, vaguely human-shaped, changing moment by moment to the blurry likenesses of various beasts of prey, was wrapped in its fire-colored flame.

"Welcome," it screeched in a thousand different voices, each of them hateful. "Join the dance!"

A roar of fire rose from the multitude of flames hovering in the air, shrieking with laughter.

Achmed smiled sardonically. "Thank you, no—never have been one for it."

"Oh, but Ysk, it's all for *you*," the Master said in an obsequious tone. "We have been awaiting your arrival for a thousand millennia! Surely you can celebrate with us."

A wracking explosion of bellowing laughter roared through the Vault again. The icecaps in the lake bobbed and lurched violently in the turgid water.

Achmed sighed.

"Very well," he said. "I suppose a toast is in order."

He opened his hand. In it was a cylindrical metal flask, which he removed the cork from, then held high in salute.

"What shall we drink to?" he inquired, a nasty edge to his voice. "How about this? A toast to—truth."

The Vault exploded in arcane merriment, howls and sighs, burbling guffaws and hiccoughing glee.

The waves of the black lake roared as well, spinning and tossing the helpless souls within it.

"Oh, right—how foolish of me," Achmed said, lowering the flask in a thoughtful stance. "I had forgotten—none condemned to this place understand that concept. Allow me a second chance. How about this? Let us all toast to—silence. Shall we?"

The profane jollity dimmed a little, but continued to titter throughout the enormous cavern.

Achmed saluted the Master with the flask.

Then he poured it over the edge of the lake. The black tincture hit the frosty water with a loud hiss.

The cackling around the massive chamber and high above the turgid lake diminished.

Achmed's face darkened, the way it did when he was sighting his cwellan.

He raised both blades simultaneously.

And, with all the dexterity he had been gifted with since birth, he slapped the turgid waves of the lake with Kirsdarke.

The water surged and leapt like a tidal wave, reaching to the very top of the domed ceiling, immersing the hovering flame demons.

As, with a countersweep, Achmed summoned the wind of Tysterisk, spiraling it in vast, ragged rings swelling through the massive canyon.

The Vault was silent of demonic sounds for a moment; nothing could be heard save the roar of the water and the screech of the dusty wind blasting over the lake.

The howls of terror began, then were summarily choked off, as the flame demons expanded and blew apart, slammed into the cavern ceiling and walls, drowned, gagging and choking as their fiery, formless bodies sagged under the weight of the airborne water, or fell, spiraling, like a flock of thousands of birds plummeting into the cold lake.

They did not make so much as a *plink* as they winked out, wrapped in an all-consuming storm of complete and utter silence.

The Master, hovering at the center of the conundrum, let loose a roar of rage in the multitude of voices, all of which were smothered in the heavy blanket of water-filled air.

Rendering him speechless.

Achmed saluted again, then tossed the flagon into the lake.

The waves settled, ice floes spinning helplessly amid the still-floating souls, as silence resolved in the cavern, this time naturally.

Achmed reached out and put his hand on Jarmon's trembling shoulder.

"Look well upon this, the extinction of the bastard race, or the race of bastards, from the Before-Time," he said quietly. "I'm glad we lived to see this day."

"Speak for yourself," Jarmon mumbled.

The Master alone remained, hovering in the damp air. Its flame visage, roaring orange and yellow in panic the moment before, settled into a red burn.

"You've come a very long way for nothing, I fear, Ysk," it said in a solitary voice of surpassing anger, cold and deadly.

Achmed snorted. It was a laugh of pain and victory at the same time. He swallowed the blood in his mouth that had come from clenching his jaws, his lips contorting into a sneer.

"How do you see nothing in this moment?"

The monstrous shadow's vibration darkened to the color of blood.

"You will never leave here," it said menacingly. "You cannot get out again any more than we ever could. It will be a living death for you. You will be trapped, as we were trapped, in this place of endless darkness, away from all that you once knew, once ruled. You will never get out."

"I never expected to," said the Bolg king smugly. "I have lived most of my life redecorating underground palaces that have been crudely inhabited in the past. This may be a challenge compared to Canrif, but I have all the time in the world now."

The beast's vibration cooled slightly.

Achmed could taste its fear.

"You are the last one," he said, each word slow and deliberate. "The—last—one. All the others are gone, dead, dissipated, silenced— every target you had for hate, because you could not spread it to the world at large, is no longer here. You think that because your kind have craved freedom and wanton destruction in the wide world, every other living thing does as well. *Wrong.*

"All my life, the wind that is in my blood has been both bane and blessing. While I can ride it and find the heartbeats of my enemies on it, I have also found it to be an irritant. There is no wind to speak of down here, especially now that your playmates have been spun into oblivion. All of that cacophony is stilled. It will be a fine place to sleep. I am quite content, actually. If you could see how I decorated my royal bedchambers in Ylorc, you would know what a joy this will be for me.

"So," he finished, "I offer you an honor you and your kind definitely don't merit, but it is my pleasure to give it to you nonetheless. While I may not dance much, I have been known to *sing*. It is not for you that I do so, however; it is a dirge, not for your kind, but in honor of one who suffered at your lies, who vanquished your brethren in the upworld, and, like the rest of the world, has no need to fear you ever again."

In a harsh voice, filled with the grief and pain and loss he had carried all his life and in the recent past, he raised the sword of air and pointed it at the Master, then began to chant.

Mo hale maar, my hero gone—

The beast wrenched as currents of wind encircled it, wrapping it tightly in elemental bonds of power.

World of star become world of bone
Grief and pain and loss I know

The monster let out a roar of rage that echoed off the walls of the cavern, only to be swallowed a moment later by the whine of the wind as it rose in reply.

My heart is sore, my blood-tears flow, Achmed intoned, his throat ragged now.

He continued to sweep Tysterisk about, choking and dragging the flame that was the Master around the obelisk throne in the air.

His brow darkened as he held up Kirsdarke again. As the dirge neared its end, the lake beneath the monster rose up once more, this time in an immense column of black water centered around the stone.

Then, with a surging roar, the water swallowed it, blowing the beast and the stone into a thousand sparks that shot to the corners of the cavern, then winked out in the blackness.

To end my sorrow I must roam, Achmed whispered, his voice bloody and dry.

My terrors old, they lead me home.

41

The Bolg king looked around.

All throughout the cavern there was a heavy silence, but it was not as caustic as it had been moments before. The shadows of the tens of thousands of gray-faced innocents that had been tempest-tossed for ages, and especially in the throes of the ending of the race of F'dor, stared at him gauntly from the now-stilled lake.

He let out his breath slowly. "Where is the door?" he asked Jarmon.

The living corpse pointed to the lake.

"At the bottom," he said.

Achmed closed his eyes and muttered a muted curse.

"Of *course* it is," he said. "How good a swimmer are you, Jarmon?"

The remains of what had once been an intrepid soldier turned and looked at the Bolg king in what appeared to be terror. Achmed sighed humorously.

"That's what I assumed you would, er, not say," he said.

He slid Tysterisk into its sheath in the twin bandolier, then shook Kirsdarke free of the condensation that was soiling its blade.

"I beg your pardon," he said to the ancient weapon of water. "As truly as you deserve to be cleansed and placed back on the altar stone of Abbat Mythlinis, I fear I am going to have to make what I hope will be one last request of you."

Achmed took off his knapsack and felt around in the bottom. He pulled forth the last of the glowing spores, the large flask of Canderian brandy, which he tucked in a pocket, and the key of bone.

"Can you carry my gear, Jarmon?" he asked. The old soldier nodded quickly. "All right. Get everyone you can out of the lake, every shadow, every shade, every child, whomever you can. I'm going to the bottom to see if I can find the door. If I don't return, get these people out of here through the other door if you can."

"Majesty," Jarmon stuttered, "we—we are all—dead, sir."

Achmed shrugged. "I think I've done all that I can do in that regard, Jarmon," he said, checking the viability of his boots. "The woman who—the mother of my child told me often that she believed that paradise was not a common meeting ground in the Afterlife, but that each person made his or her own place in it. You will all just have to find your own paradise now."

"Aye, sir," said the withered soldier. His sunken teeth and parched skin seemed to spread into the approximation of a smile.

"If I am able, I will be back presently," Achmed said. He held the hilt of Kirsdarke tightly, squeezed the glowing spore in his other hand, and, making certain there was no one below him in the icy black lake, stepped off the rocky edge and fell, feet-first, into the water.

The sting of his eyes almost made him drop the sword.

Achmed waited for a moment for the ability to breathe underwater to kick in. When it did, the air in his lungs was dry and heavy, like that in the Vault.

He held the glowing sword, and the spore, outstretched in front of him, then kicked down to the bottom of the lake.

He started at the base of where he and Jarmon had entered this last part of the Vault, the ghostly light of the sword and the spore bringing a bluish illumination to the horrors of the black lake's depths. He swam past skulls and skeletal limbs, rusty swords and manacles and a host of other terrifying objects, brushing them aside and searching each rock, each silty patch, for something resembling a keyhole.

He found nothing.

How long he remained in the water, the element he loathed, carefully examining the bottom, he had no guess. The ringing bell that had led him on all his previous expeditions was sickeningly silent; the great Kirsdarkenvar had traveled the length and breadth of the sea, its trenches and abyssal plains, but Achmed imagined even MacQuieth had not ventured into this cold black lake of haunted water and ice.

After what seemed to be an endless search, he saw the obelisk above which the Master had been hovering and swam over to it, holding up the sword to aid in its examination.

Almost immediately he saw the runes glowing brighter with his approach.

A key-shaped hole outlined in what appeared to be gold was proudly displayed in the center of the runes.

Is this even possible? he thought sourly as he swam closer. *Can that possibly be the keyhole?—of course not. That never happens. Probably I will put the key in and it will snap off, condemning me to this place of everlasting darkness with ten thousand shadows, an old fisherman I have not met yet, and a living mummy who shows potential as a poet for all eternity, because Life has a terrible sense of humor.*

The keyhole gleamed.

Just as one like it had gleamed when he had approached Sagia, the Oak of Deep Roots, with just such a key, two thousand years before, on the other side of Time, with his Sergeant-Major friend and a struggling female hostage.

Achmed held his breath, and inserted the key into the hole in the obelisk.

He had to kick violently a few seconds later as the giant rock column began to turn and grind, disappearing before his eyes into a oxcart-sized hole in the bottom of the lake.

Well, he thought as he snatched the key from the spinning lock and swam back, still facing the obelisk sinking quickly from view, *I do suppose after walking the Vault of the Underworld, anything has to be luckier by comparison.*

The water around him began to race toward the hole. Achmed swam to the surface and signaled to Jarmon.

"Try to be calm," he shouted over the flailing of the panicking shadows. "It will all be over soon, one way or another."

After an indeterminate amount of time, the frigid water of the dark lake had drained, and the Bolg king sat at the edge of the hole in the floor of the Vault of the Underworld.

He was listening to the silence.

Jarmon had managed to help him round up the Lost, as they had been called, empty, lifeless souls without memories of who they had been or where they had even come from, men, women, and children who nonetheless complied with the dead soldier's commands and had formed an enormous line, waiting to enter the corridor through which the waters of the icy lake had drained.

"Take them into the corridor beyond the door, and wait for me there," the Bolg king had instructed.

Jarmon nodded.

Once the Lost had left the cavern, Achmed stood alone in the center of what had been the lake, listening to the silence.

He thought of the Dhracians he had known, Father Halphasion, the Grandmother, and Rath, and those he had met in the course of the Hunt, when he had deigned to join it. Stalwart protectors, with no thought of any life beyond the endless vigilance demanded of their race; he wished they could have been there, just for a moment, to see the Vault, now empty.

He thought of the night when he and Rath had sat out atop one of the peaks of Canrif, the ancient Dhracian telling him of his heritage, of his mother, of the race that sought him endlessly, wanting to bring him into the Common Mind so that he could be one of them.

Rath had looked at him with his strange, scleraless eyes, imparting all of the seriousness of his belief.

You could walk the Vault alone, and when you were done the silence would ring with nothing but the whisper of your name.

He closed his eyes, feeling the echo of the silence.

Ysk, the Bolg had called him. A grievous insult, the word for spittle or vomit. And yet from that race, that name, he had gained the lore to walk this place, to have standing here.

To vanquish it.

"Ysk," he whispered.

The circular vault caught the sounds and spun them around, ascending and descending what had once been the thoracic cavity of the first dragon in the world.

Ysk—Ysk—Ysk—Ysk—Ysk—Ysk—

Even as it layered onto itself, there was a fricative percussion to it, almost like the hand drums that the monks had played in the monastery where he had sought sanctuary as a youth, where he had been brought, close to death, by the first person who had ever shown him mercy and kindness.

In his mind he could hear the voice of Father Halphasion, the gentle Dhracian monk, as the priest bound up the wounds he had sustained in his escape from the Bolg. He could almost smell the candle wax of the monastery.

Child of Blood—brother to all men, akin to none.

He whispered those words next, listening with his eyes closed to them rise and fall in the dusty air, repeated endlessly, as if dancing with the fricative name the Bolg had called him.

Brother—the Brother—the Brother—the—

And then, a sweet voice, recently having achieved Namer status, even though she hadn't known it yet, spoke in the now-comforting darkness of his thoughts.

This is my Brother—Achmed—the Snake.

His voice trembled as he whispered the name she had given him, hearing the Vault ring with it.

Achmed—the—Snake—Achmed—the—Snake—Achmed—the— Achmed—Achmed—Ach—

Achmed clenched his jaw in memory, then spoke the names by which the Firbolg had called him.

Firbolg king, the Night Man, the Earth Swallower, the Glowering Eye.

The song of his name was beginning to become cacophonous, ugly almost, as all the appellations by which he had been called over the course of his lengthy life were clashing with each other, thick in the air.

He waited until each of them had winked out, like a disembodied F'dor spirit in the air of the upworld.

And then thought hard, trying as much as possible to recall the exact tone of voice, difficult given that it was the only one of all the names he had ever been given that had only ever been spoken once.

Welcome, little one. Meet your father.

The name rang like a small silver bell in the dark torture chamber.

Then it swelled to a symphonic sound, bright and warm, harmonic.

Until it descended again, into a quiet echo.

Father.

Achmed smiled at the overwhelming irony.

This would have been an even better name to have chosen if I wanted to hide it, he thought. *No one ever would have guessed it.*

He contemplated the only time he had used that word to address someone, Father Halphasion, his mentor and rescuer. The humble monk, brutally killed for a few coins given to a group of poor men, who had truly been the only parental figure he had ever known, not a father of blood, just as he was not to Graal, but of love, and sacrifice.

He stood in the silence of the Vault echoing with the word, only a whisper now.

Father—father—father—father—father—fa—fa—fa—

The Bolg king listened to the repetitive song until the word finally dissipated, leaving no sound whatsoever.

Well, listen to that, Rath, he thought in wry amusement. *Turns out you were right after all.*

He thought again for a moment about the ancient Dhracian, serving as guardian to the Sleeping Child, and hoped that his oldest child knew that she no longer had anything to fear from the Earth but the other Sleeping Child that slumbered within it.

With any luck, not for much longer, he thought.

He turned and went into the corridor, looking at the line of gray-faced souls, numb and terrified, with Jarmon at the lead, a glowing tube of firefly liquid in his remaining hand.

"I assume I don't have to remind you all of the need for silence," he said tonelessly.

The shades nodded or just stared in the requested state.

"Very well," Achmed said. "Follow me—let's go find paradise."

42

OUTSIDE THE VAULT WITHIN THE DEEP EARTH

$\mathscr{B}$eyond the door that had not been opened but once in all of history, the Earth was wet, dripping moisture from the radix, the hair-like roots that had filled its vast caverns and shallow tunnels all through the journey that the Three had once made through it. The scent filled Achmed's nostrils immediately, making him shiver with memory.

The rough tunnel branched off in numerous directions, some into even larger openings, some that withered down to dead ends.

The Lost, however, lost no longer, seemed to know exactly where to go.

Before Achmed could lead them anywhere, the gray-faced souls turned rapidly in multiple directions and quickly made their way, as if summoned, to different passages in the tunnel. It almost seemed as if they were in no need of following the openings, but rather rose slightly off the ground as they passed into the Earth, like dandelion seeds on a warm summer wind, disappearing into the black, cold darkness.

Achmed turned to see the desiccated corpse that had once been the soldier named Jarmon waiting beside him, still holding the glowing vial aloft, even as its light was beginning to dim.

There was an expression that he recognized on the dead soldier's face, one that he had seen many times on that of his best friend. Occasionally over the years he had known Grunthor he had caught a glimpse of longing, for what Achmed had never been certain, but clearly something other than what they were undertaking. It would disappear as fast as it came, as the stoic expression that came from military training returned.

Just as it was doing now on a face that was largely not even there.

Jarmon looked steadily forward, but it seemed to Achmed that his head was inclined slightly, as if listening to something on the underground wind.

"You hear a call?" he asked the skeletal man quietly.

Jarmon nodded slightly. "Aye."

"Go, then," Achmed said.

The soldier shook his head.

"Go," Achmed said, a little more strongly. "Your service is over, to Hector, and to me. You said you would lead me through the Vault, and you have. That Vault is now empty, and we are beyond the door. If you hear a call, follow it. Thank you for your aid."

Jarmon turned slowly and looked at the Bolg king.

"You are trapped here, you know," he said sadly. "You passed through the Vault, but not over the threshold of death. I can't leave you alone here; it wouldn't be right."

"Nonetheless, your service is ended," Achmed said, smiling slightly. "Go. I hope you find peace."

Jarmon's sunken, broken eyes fixed on him sadly. Then he lowered his head, resigned.

"Dismissed, soldier," Achmed said. He gave him an uncomfortable salute.

The animated corpse that was Jarmon chuckled in spite of himself. He put the vial of glowing fluid between his broken teeth, returned the salute with his remaining arm, then turned and walked away into the darkness, where he disappeared, dissolving almost before the Bolg king's eyes.

Leaving him alone in the emptiness of the bowels of the Earth.

For a very long time, Achmed stood in the tunnel, lost in memory. He was ruminating about the time he, Grunthor, and Rhapsody had spent, somewhere in the depths of the world, crawling along the Root of Sagia, known in Serendair as the Oak of Deep Roots, which had grown to gargantuan lengths, wound around the Axis Mundi, the line of power that was the centerline within the Earth.

One night, or rather, the sleeping time they observed in a place of endless night, he had awakened Rhapsody, after assuring himself that Grunthor was deep in slumber, with the same words Meridion had greeted him with the last time they had been in each other's company.

I have a story for you, he had said to the Lirin Singer, who was struggling to awaken from her nightmarish repose. *Its ending isn't written yet. Do you wish to hear it?*

He had taken her hand and led her to a place where the ceiling of the tunnel was toweringly high, and pointed into the darkness.

Over there is a tunnel unlike the others we have followed. There have been many like it, but I doubt you've noticed them. The tunnels were not carved by the Tree's roots, but have been here long before its acorn was ever planted.

His eyes stung, remembering the look on her face in the shadows. He knew from her heartbeat that she was terrified and confused, but she had adopted a solemn, thoughtful expression, and merely nodded, listening.

Deep within that tunnel is a beating heart. You have asked repeatedly how I know where I am going. The answer is that I can sense almost any pulse in my skin. I know that what I am saying frightens you, because even though your outward expression has not changed, your heartbeat has quickened. If you become lost within this place, if you fall down a root shaft or are buried alive by a cave-in, I can find you, because I know the sound of your heart.

Her eyes had glistened in the glowing light of the Root, the only illumination below the ground, but he could see she understood what he was saying.

Achmed winced and closed his own eyes, remembering the panic and desolation of her death, of how in the end he had been able to do nothing to save her, his promises notwithstanding.

Listen to me, he had continued. *I've been following a pulse. First it was that of the Tree itself, but once we found the Axis Mundi it changed; now I have been following that other heartbeat to this place. Something terrible rests in there, something more powerful and more horrifying than you can imagine, something I dare not even name. What sleeps within that tunnel, deep in the belly of the Earth, must not awake. Not ever. Do you understand me? You once said that you could prolong slumber—*

Sometimes, she had cautioned.

Yes, he had continued softly. *I understand. This must be one of those times.*

He had quietly continued to tell her the tale of the first of the race of dragons, the Progenitor Wyrm whose neck and head he had so recently seen in the Vault, of the theft of one of its original eggs, a wyrmchild that the demons had stolen away and kept, deep in the frozen wastes of the Earth's interior, growing until its coils had wound around the very heart of the world. It was now, he had explained, an innate part of the Earth itself, its body a large part of its mass.

It sleeps now, he had told her, *but soon that demon wishes to summon it, and will visit it upon the land. Rhapsody, I can't explain its size to you, except to say that Sagia's trunkroot was a mere piece of twine in comparison to the taproot, yes?*

Yes, he could still hear her whisper.

And the taproot was a thread compared to the Axis Mundi. The Axis Mundi is like one of your hairs in comparison to this creature. It has the power to consume the Earth; that was the intent of the thieves who put it here. It awaits the demon's call, which I know for certain is intended to come soon. I know this, because he planned to use me to help bring this about.

He had to admit a grudging admiration when she had nodded rather than panicking.

You named me Achmed the Snake because it sounded frightening to you, didn't you? he had asked her.

Yes, she acknowledged. *I told you that a long time ago. And I've been embarrassed about it ever since.*

Perhaps you shouldn't be. It may have been the only thing that allowed me to find the tunnel. When I was the Brother, I was tied only to the blood of men and women. It may have been the serpent name you gave me that helped me hear this beating heart.

He had led her into the dark, frozen tunnel, where the demons, he had explained to her, had taken the element of Fire with them when they went upworld, to keep the wyrm in hibernation. *They wanted it to grow to its greatest possible size before setting it free,* he had said.

He had been unable to relay much more information to her, because by this point he was freezing to death from the inside, except for the last fact he shared—that the tunnel wall which towered above them and off into the endless dark was but a scale in the skin of the wyrm.

A sense of warmth rushed through him now, his eyes still closed in memory. He could still see her, sitting down on the ground and taking up her harp, clearing her mind and attuning herself to the diffuse music in the frigid air around them.

She had begun to sing a slumber song, a simple roundelay, while he watched her from within the frozen prison of his body. She was staring at his eyes, having arranged for him to blink once for a normal maintenance of the rhythm he was hearing, or twice should that rhythm change, adding harmonic elements, raising the pitch of the song slightly in the attempt to mask the demon's call when it eventually came.

After what had seemed like hours, while he stood rigid in frozen pain, she had risen, still playing the harp, and walked back to the entrance of the tunnel.

Samoht, she had said to the instrument. Play on endlessly.

The harp had obeyed, continuing the lullaby, even as her fingers left the strings. Over and over the roundelay played, repeating the same complex melody. Rhapsody had set the instrument carefully on the floor of the tunnel near the entrance, then stepped back. On it played, endlessly.

Samoht.

His memory of what had happened after that was cloudy; he recalled her whispering his name anxiously, pulling at him, unable to bring him to motion or response, after which she had disappeared into the darkness, leaving him alone in the tunnel. After some time and considerably more pain Grunthor had arrived with her and carried him, unable to bend, away, until Rhapsody had taken his hand and given his arm a solid pull, as if to test the strength in his muscles. He recalled bending forward slightly and whispering in her ear.

Look.

When she turned around, she saw, as he and Grunthor had, that the tunnel was slowly filling with slender threads of light, like the gossamer of a spider's web. Each new repetition of the melody had formed a new strand, attaching itself in a circular pattern to the cavernous walls of the tunnel.

The song is freezing in place, she had murmured.

With each new round the threads grew thicker, the sound of the song louder. Its key was now up three notes from where it had been when she started, different enough, with any luck, she had said later, to jangle the namesong when the demon eventually spoke it. The roundelay, something Singers learned early in their training in order to be able to sing harmony with themselves, continued on, creating more strands of glowing spider-silk.

After a while it's going to be cacophony, Rhapsody had said as they left the tunnel.

Achmed opened his eyes.

He was wondering whether that cacophony had ever come to pass.

Then he decided, given a lack of other pressing social obligations, he should go and find out what the status of that larger Sleeping Child was now.

"Achmed the Snake," he said quietly in the depths of the world, renaming himself. He loosed his *kirai,* his seeking vibration.

Then he concentrated on his own heartbeat, and that of the wyrm he had once sought here.

For a long time he heard nothing but silence.

Then, for a moment, a distant flicker tickled his skin.

The Bolg king locked his heartbeat on it, catching the trail like a bloodhound, and followed it through the maze of twisting tunnels, like a beacon.

Until, at a juncture of a tunnel, he stopped suddenly, astonished to hear a familiar sound—a sound of the wind in the world above.

Ancient and deadly.

43

$\mathcal{A}$chmed froze.

The sound beyond the juncture was a discordant whistling in multiple voices, shrill and whining, an ancient song known at the very core of his being, inherited from his mother's race.

The Thrall ritual.

It was a rite he had known for millennia, taught to him by his mentor, Father Halphasion, in the early days of his life, when he was leaving behind the nightmare of his father's race, the Firbolg of Serendair, and being shown that of his Dhracian mother. Later, the Grandmother, the Earthchild's *amelystik,* her guardian and caregiver, had polished his technique in the depths of the ancient Colony where they had first found the sleeping entity.

Within your mind, call to each of the four winds, the Grandmother had instructed.

Chant each name, then anchor it to one of your fingers.

Bien, Achmed thought now, holding the waning light of the tube higher, trying to expand its scope of radiance. The north wind, the strongest. *Jahne,* the south wind, the most enduring. *Leuk,* the west wind, the wind of justice. *Thas*—the wind of morning; the wind of death.

"In the name of the four winds, I call to you—come forward!" he shouted in the language of his ancient race.

The whistling noise stopped, leaving nothing but its diminishing echo.

The light wavered.

"Come forward!" Achmed called harshly again.

Slowly, from around the tunnel opening's sides, shadows appeared, familiar forms swathed in robes of heavy cloth.

Achmed caught his breath.

Dhracians; more than a dozen of them. They hung back, their hands upraised in front of them, in the pose of the Thrall ritual.

"Peace," he whispered in their ancient tongue. "The Vault is empty."

The band of Dhracians glanced at one another but said nothing. Finally, one among them spoke in the hissing, fricative voice that Achmed himself shared.

"Ysk?"

Achmed swallowed, trying to contain his contempt.

"A misnomer," he said, his hand with the glowing tube returning to his side. "How do you know this name?"

The Dhracian who had spoken came forward, his scleraless eyes black and liquid in the dim light.

"If you are Ysk, your coming was foretold long ago, when the Vault was broken open by the falling of the Sleeping Child," he said in his sandy voice. "We have been waiting since that time—are the Unspoken all dead?"

"So it seems. You are the guardians, then? Those of our race who have been here since the Before-Time, standing watch over the door of the Vault, to keep the F'dor locked away?"

The shadows nodded slightly.

"Why are you not of the Common Mind, Ysk?" the lead Dhracian asked suspiciously.

"I am Uncounted," Achmed said irritably. "And I am called by another name now. How have you lived down here all this time?"

"We consume the Root—it is our nourishment." The Dhracian looked at his fellow guardians, lapsing into an awkward silence.

"Your guardianship has come to an end," Achmed said, signaling behind him. "The door into the Vault is open, as you know, or you would not have beset upon me with the Thrall ritual, assuming the F'dor had broached it. I suggest you make your way back to the upworld through it. You can search the Vault and make certain it is empty, though I would not have come through the door if I believed that any remained alive."

He reached into the pocket of his robes and pulled forth the rib key.

The Dhracian guardians reared back in shock.

"Take this with you," he said, holding it out to the one who had spoken. "When you get all the way to the top, there are two doors that open, once unlocked, into the depths of the sea." He smiled slightly. "You will have to swim if you wish to get back to the world of air."

He could only see the smallest glimpse of their faces, but by their stance and the way the dozen Dhracians glanced at each other, he could unmistakably feel their disgust.

It was a disgust he wholeheartedly shared.

Achmed shook the key impatiently at the leader once more, and the robed man quickly took it from his hand.

"Leave the doors open wide, and let the sea drown that place," he said, reaching back to his dual bandolier. He drew Kirsdarke from its sheath, then Tysterisk. As the air sword came forth, a breath of wind rose up from the loam of the dirt floor, filling the tunnel with a spinning breeze. He held both of the swords out horizontally, parallel to the ground.

"Take these with you—Kirsdarke, the sword of elemental water, and Tysterisk, that of elemental air. Both will allow you to breathe beneath the waves of the sea until you are able to rise into the wind. I suggest whomever is most displeased at being in the water hold on to that sword; it will help you become accustomed to the sea until you can catch an updraft.

"I have but one last request of you," he continued, annoyed that the guardians still seemed shocked by his arrival. "Go, upon getting your bearings, to the land of Ylorc on the Middle Continent, known in your time as the Wyrmlands, where the Great White Tree stands at the place where the element of Earth was first known to have appeared in the world. Travel east into the rising sun until you come to fanglike mountains, jagged and beautiful—this is the land of Ylorc, my kingdom.

"Within the depths of Ylorc, the homeland of the Firbolg, whom you are not to harm, as they are my subjects, is the last of the known Earthchildren, a Sleeping Child whom the F'dor have long sought. Standing guard over her is one of the Brethren named Rath. He, unlike me, is of the Common Mind, and a well-respected hunter of the escapees.

"Tell Rath that his guardianship is also now at an end, that the Earthchild may be allowed to sleep, alone and in peace, in the safe place she occupies, where an *amelystik* named Laurelyn the Invoker can tend to her from time to time. Ask him to return the swords to the altars at the elemental basilicae where they belong. And then, when you have completed this quest, I suggest you all go back into the wide world and allow the winds to take you wherever they will, at their whim. You deserve the pleasure of the element of our race washing you clean of the dust and the memories of this place."

The leader stared at him. "You are not coming with us, Ysk—?"

"No," the Bolg king said, gathering his gear. "I have another Sleeping Child to check on."

When the Dhracian guardians were long gone, and Achmed could no longer hear even the slightest whisper of sound coming from the passageway above him, he sat down and listened again for the serpentine pulse in the distance.

Again, he heard no rhythm, but after a seemingly endless wait caught a familiar flicker, followed by silence.

He struggled to make the connection to the faint noise, a single tap echoing very far away, and finally caught the memory of it. When he had last heard it, it was a deafening sound, and regular; he could sense the beast move as it stretched in its slumber, or settle back down into deeper sleep. But then he had been standing at the entrance to a tunnel where the wall was a scale in its skin, all but on top of it. Its heart must be very far away now to be so difficult to hear.

A long journey through the Earth. Again. The Bolg king exhaled, suddenly exhausted.

He looked down at his hands and was dully surprised at how thin and bony they had become. They had always been somewhat so, but now they were almost skeletal, the sensitive nerve endings and veins protruding like mountain ranges with deep canyons between them where his flesh and skin had sunken against the bone.

Idly he ran his fingertips over his face and discovered, to no real surprise, that it had sunken drastically as well. He had eaten the rations he had brought along with him when he remembered to do so, but the drive of his will had been so intense that he rarely did over the course of his journey. The elemental sword of water had kept him hydrated, but it, like the one of wind, was now gone, making their way, in the hands of the Dhracian guardians, back to the upworld and the altars of their elemental temples.

As is the last key out of the depths of the world, he thought.

Achmed let his head drop back against the earthen wall and closed his eyes.

Behind his eyelids an image of Grunthor appeared, pale and silent, sitting in the same position as he himself was now, his head back, eyes closed, in the light of a blood-red moon. It was a memory from long ago, before Rhapsody had even come into their lives, from a terrible night, a night of loss, of defeat, when the Sergeant's beloved troops were slaughtered to a one, leaving him the only survivor. He had continued to talk about them for years, as if they were still alive, most likely because the loss had been so profound that he could not really bring himself to actually believe it had happened. Achmed had always accommodated his friend's gentle self-deceit, but had been secretly grateful when the Firbolg of Ylorc had taken the place of the lost men whom the giant had mourned on both sides of Time and all throughout the trek of the Three through the belly of the world.

Achmed rubbed his eyes, trying to dispel the despair that had crept behind them.

The sad countenance of his best friend was replaced by an image of his newborn son's face, the infant's eyes sighting on his, almost in amusement. Achmed's heart cramped at the knowing look he thought he had seen there.

While he rested, his innate survival sense calculated the movement base of the ancient Dhracians, who were undoubtedly beginning a long and arduous search of every corner of the empty Vault, knowing that if he changed course and relented, following them up to the top levels of the ancient prison, he could eventually catch up with them, return to the land of the living, his kingdom, his life, as much of it was still intact, his people.

His son.

He exhaled again.

I wish I believed I had anything worthwhile to offer you in your up-bringing, Graal, he thought, a headache pounding behind his eyes, throbbing at his temples. *If your mother had lived, perhaps I would not have been afraid to ruin you. But now the only thing I have to give you is as safe a world as I can help make.*

He contemplated what lay before him, and wondered if he even had that.

Achmed mentally reviewed what gear he had left as he rose and shook the loam and dead radix from his robes. The cwellan was still there with a reasonable store of disks, and while he believed it might be useful against the endless armies of vermin, worms with sharp jaws that had slithered down sections of the Root when he had traversed it before, it certainly would have no bearing against what he was seeking. He also bore a thin longsword and a dagger, which were of even less use.

His food was all but exhausted, his water supply as well.

A diet of the glowing Root that ran along the Axis Mundi, as the Three and, apparently, the Dhracians had consumed, had worked before, though his lip curled at the memory of the taste and consistency.

No sane man would have even contemplated going forward.

Thankfully, sanity has never been a character flaw I've ever been accused of, he thought.

Then, looking around at the arse-end of the Vault of the Underworld, broken open, drained of the evil that had been contained there from the Before-Time, he turned away and started off in the direction of the whispered sound that he remembered from the last time he had passed through the bowels of the Earth.

44

HIGHMEADOW, NAVARNE

Once Graal had been successfully transported across Time and the sea, and into the temporary custody of Analise in Manosse, Meridion returned to Highmeadow.

As he came out of the tunnel he found himself nauseated and light-headed, something that had never occurred in traveling through the bonds of Time before, so he leaned up against a tree and took several deep breaths.

I should stay in the course of regular Time for the time being, he thought, rubbing his temples to try to ease the pounding in his skull and neck. *I think I need to remain where I am for a while.*

He inhaled and discovered what he thought to be part of the reason for his misery.

The air of the forest, the place that had been home to him for most of his life, was thin of magic, as if all of the nascent lore and power of the deeply magical place had been stripped from it. It was like a broken eggshell, an empty flask, though to the eye, nothing was different.

Nothing except for the air of the place, which was spinning strangely in a circular pattern.

The stars that had emerged in the darkening sky of the east winked brightly. The spinning of air in circular patterns, a trembling within the

Earth itself, carried with it an odor of primordial magic, an unmistakable sign of elemental power.

Meridion whirled around.

Hovering in the air before him, taller than the trees of the forest around their family homestead, was a filmy image of a wyrm, its red-gold scales glittering in the last light of day. Its enormous neck and head, dark of skin beneath the metallic scales and eyes of gleaming cerulean blue, drew power from the four natural elements that had been summoned by its appearance from the ether.

Though in form it was similar to Elynsynos, the matriarchal wyrm of the family, there was something younger, more energetic in its demeanor, a surging and ebbing of its movements that reminded Meridion strongly of the sea, as if the element of water was pounding through its blood like ocean waves.

The draconic image reared up and looked down at him.

Then its eyes took on an expression of fondness and excitement and unmistakable love.

Meridion—I have made my transition.

Meridion swallowed. "So I see. Congratulations, Papa. You—you make an impressive wyrm."

The diaphanous dragon smiled uncertainly, an expression of almost human reticence on its massive, serpentine face.

Thank you. It was a—an indescribable process. The dragon looked around. *It seems the apology, or my supposed execution, worked; the world is intact, at least. I see no signs of wide-scale war. That's a relief.*

Meridion nodded, his throat tightening, knowing what his father's next question would be, and dreading to hear it.

The beast looked around again.

Where is your mother? I must go to her, beg her forgiveness before anything else. Where is she?

Meridion opened his mouth, but no sound came out.

The dragon inclined its head as darkness began to settle in the forest glen.

Meridion? Where is your mother?

At last, even though he had been given them to speak by Rhapsody just before she passed through the Gate of Life, the Namer had no words.

———

*J*ust before sunrise, Edwyn Griffyth made his way to the beach at the southern shore of the Island, wrapped in the glow of a lingering dream of good hope.

In the distance he made out a long, thin shadow, and followed it until he was standing beside Jal'asee, who was standing at the water's edge, staring south as well.

"Good morning," the usually taciturn High Mage said, watching a gull dive over the waves, looking for fish in the froth.

"Good morning," Jal'asee answered, smiling. His elderly eyes, golden in the hues of his race, seemed brighter that day. "What brings you down to the waves so early?"

Edwyn Griffyth exhaled.

"I'm not certain," he said finally as the gull banked away out over the sea and was lost in the glare of the rising sun. "But something blew in on the night wind, I think, something—something promising; a bad word for it, really. Did you sense it?"

The Ancient Seren nodded, his face solemn as he watched the endless rolling of the waves.

"How would you describe it?"

Jal'asee was silent, lost in thought for a long moment.

"A relief of almost incomprehensible proportions," he said at last. "The air is lighter, the wind cleaner. I feel a lifting of a weight I did not even realize I was carrying. It seems a portent of goodwill."

The two men continued to watch the rolling surf.

"Care to hazard a guess as to why?" Edwyn Griffyth said at last.

"It is almost too much to hope," said Jal'asee reverently. "But last night, I dreamt of an empty Vault."

Edwyn Griffyth let all the air out of his lungs.

"So did I," he said.

The sun cracked the horizon, bathing the world in a golden light.

Epilogue

At dawn, the Sea Mages were standing at the dock, waiting.

The glistening ship had been in the harbor for more than an hour, its passengers and contents off-loading in an agonizingly slow process, causing Edwyn Griffyth to pace the boards of the quay restlessly, muttering under his breath.

Finally, when the ship was empty of all but the crew and a few remaining berths of cargo, two final passengers came forth from the hold and made their way to the gangplank.

In the lead was a seemingly young man, golden of hair and blue of eye, his dragonesque pupils expanding vertically in the light of the rising sun. As he walked, he kept a careful watch on the passenger behind him, an elderly man with golden skin. Edwyn Griffyth, watching attentively, turned for a moment and glanced at Jal'asee, comparing the Ancient Seren's coloring with that of the second passenger, then shaking his head and returning his gaze to them both.

"Great-nephew!" he called to the first man. "Here!"

Meridion looked up. He shaded his eyes from the morning light, then smiled and raised a hand in acknowledgment. He took the elderly man's forearm and led him carefully down the steps onto the dock, where they both came to a halt.

Edwyn Griffyth broke from the ranks of the other Sea Mages and hurried, puffing slightly, to the end of the dock.

"Well met, Meridion," he said, extending a hand to his great-nephew, who shook it firmly. "It's been close to three years with no news, except, of course, that of the tragedies on the Middle Continent. I'm terribly sorry for your loss, Meridion. Your dear mother, and—"

Meridion cleared his throat. "Thank you, Uncle."

Edwyn's expression of sympathy faltered, and he fell silent for a moment. "You were absent even from the sight of the Tower. We were beginning to fear the worst."

"I am sorry to have worried you, Uncle," Meridion said reassuringly. "With your permission, I would like to introduce you to a prospective student." He turned to the elderly man and took a step back. "This is Graal. Graal, this is the High Sea Mage, and my great-uncle, Edwyn Griffyth."

The Sea Mage blinked in astonishment.

The elderly man had two different-colored eyes, one green, one black as night, and skin the color of a golden beach. Around his neck a polished golden amulet gleamed, abstract in design but seemingly the image of fire solidly contained within a circle. His skin was lightly traced with what appeared to be veins or nerve endings, but in beautiful patterns which adorned his bald head, and his face was set in a smile of surpassing warmth that was filled with unmistakable wisdom.

The Sea Mage also sensed an undercurrent of humor.

"Well met, sir," the golden man said. In his voice was the music of the Ages.

"Graal is someone I feel you will want to make the effort to train in every lore, science, and art you have, Uncle," Meridion said. "He and I have a great deal in common, not the least of which is a rather tenuous relationship with Time." *He is, in actuality, less than three years old and appears to be existing backwards in Time, but we will discuss that with you at a later date,* he thought.

"Welcome, Graal," Edwyn Griffyth said. "Where—where are you from? Your family—"

"He has none to speak of," Meridion said hurriedly. "But he is as a brother to me. It would please me greatly if you would make him welcome, Uncle; studying with you is something his family always hoped for him."

"Well, by all means, let us return to the Hall and make you comfortable among us," Edwyn Griffyth said to Graal, who just smiled.

He glanced at Meridion, who was trembling slightly with anticipation.

Good, the Child of Time thought as the Sea Mages led Graal carefully up the dock. He smiled bemusedly, watching his great-uncle chat with the man who, in the Past, had given Edwyn's father his warning of the rising of the Sleeping Child.

And every other king of Serendair his prophecy on his coronation day, and had acted as vizier to each of them, giving them advice of the Future of which he had particular knowledge.

Having lived it.

Meridion hurried to catch up with them.

As he did, he passed a young woman, a passenger who had disembarked with the earlier ones, who was claiming baggage at the end of the dock. In his haste, he trod upon her toe, then stopped in mortification.

"I'm so very sorry," he said hurriedly, turning in apology but still looking over his shoulder to keep the Sea Mages and Graal in his sight.

The young woman looked up and smiled.

"Not to worry," she said.

Meridion's mouth dropped open in recognition of the dark hair and eyes, the studious nature, that he had seen so many times in his dreams.

He glanced at Graal again, who had turned to watch him amid the chattering of the Sea Mage delegation, and smiled knowingly before turning his attention back to the Mages once more.

Above all else, may you know joy, their mother had said.

Finally it seemed to Meridion as if he might.

THE SIXTH AGE, AT ITS END,
YEAR UNKNOWN

How long he had traveled the endless path of the Root along the Axis Mundi, Achmed had no idea.

His path had not been a straight one; he had encountered countless dead ends and cave-ins throughout his journey, rerouting repeatedly and taking new paths every time an old one closed. The *tap* in the distance was ever in his head, but not often in his ears. He had taken to filling them with wads of rotting cloth to keep all other sound out but that tap.

Until finally one day it had echoed loudly near him.

A chill ran through Achmed's body, wasted to little more than bone and sinew in the endless trek through the world.

After a moment, when his fingertips had been coated with frost, the Bolg king looked around him, and recognized for the first time since he had come back onto the Root where he was.

The cold breath of the absence of fire, taken by the long-dead denizens of the Vault of the Underworld, blew around him.

I'm here, Achmed thought, struggling to keep conscious. *This is the place where Rhapsody and I came, where she played her harp to change the name of the Wyrm—or, rather, to obscure it from the call of the demons.*

It was the place, he knew, where she had put out her hand to touch a tunnel wall and had rested it on a massive scale in the hide of that Wyrm.

As if in confirmation, in the near distance he could hear a buzzing sound, many repetitive notes that clashed in dissonance, almost unrecognizable as music.

Achmed exhaled his breath slowly, expelling the last of the air from his lungs, and taking in another, colder breath.

Slowly he made his way forward to a place where an opening yawned.

He came to the threshold and looked inside.

The tunnel he had once stood at the entry to was filled with countless crystalline threads of sound, frozen in place for centuries, spanning every possible opening or space.

The noise was cacophonous, each new thread of song produced by the harp layering even more soft, musical noise on top of what was already deafening. The Bolg king covered his ears with his hands, adding another barrier over the wads of cloth, but it did little to deflect the vibrations of the music.

Beyond the opening he could see that what Rhapsody had once mistaken for an enormous wall, the scale in the gargantuan Wyrm's skin, had both solidified and become at the same time vaporous, scored a billion times over with thin lines of light.

It looked for all the world like the silken sac of a spider, wound around the long-dead carcass of its prey.

The Wyrm that he had lived in terror of awakening was a gargantuan corpse, filling the tunnel with its ever-thickening body of wasted flesh and the tangible vibration of harp song.

Achmed, his body and spirit far beyond exhausted, felt a surge of warmth in the frozen belly of the world.

He thought back to the earliest of days with Rhapsody, still his hostage, when he first had come to learn she was a student of Liringlas music.

So I'll ask you again, Singer; what can you do?

He could hear her voice in his memory as clearly as if she were standing beside him.

Not very much, outside from singing a rather extensive collection of historical ballads and epics. I can find herbs to throw into the fire to mesmerize people. Obviously that isn't going to impress you much since you can, too. I can bring sleep to the restless, or prolong the slumber of someone who is already asleep, an especially useful talent for new parents of fussy babies. I can ease pain of the body and the heart, heal minor wounds and comfort the dying, making their passage easier. Sometimes I can see their souls as they leave for the light. I can tell a story from a few bits of fact and a good dollop of audience reaction. I can tell the absolute truth as I know it. And when I do that I can change things.

Achmed's throat had tightened to the point of choking.

Yes, yes you could, Rhapsody, he thought, his eyes stinging dryly. *And you did. You changed the predestined fate of the world.*

He swallowed and, in his fading mind, whispered what passed for a prayer, thinking of Graal, as he all but always did.

Finally you are safe as I can make you, my son, he thought. *Thanks to your mother.*

Then, with one last glance at the dead Wyrm, he continued on his way, back to where he had come from, back in Time.

Back, he hoped, to the remains of Serendair.

After a trek more endless than the one that brought him from the Vault to the Wyrm, Achmed finally began to recognize parts of the Root he remembered.

The vermin he had fought at the beginning of his journey had vanished, leaving nothing but the evidence of salt water all around him. *If this is Serendair, if I have made it back from whence I came, it's probably submerged,* he thought.

He remembered MacQuieth's description of what he had found when he had walked the sea to the site of the Island's destruction, hoping and failing to find and bury his son.

Where there had been highlands, there was nothing beneath the waves but rubble and ruin, melted statues and stone gates jutting from great mountains of broken earth, the towers of Elysian castle now pebbles in the swirling current. They had built seawalls, levies, in the last days, in the vain attempt to hold back the inevitable. That must have been Hector. My son would have been filling bags of sand to the last.

As he climbed the taproot, what had been the first of the pathways in their endless journey, he saw above him some of what MacQuieth had spoken of—broken walls and the detritus of cataclysm, clogging the tunnel above it.

Nothing recognizable except for what looked like a gate, crushed at the bottom of all the wreckage.

With the last of his strength, Achmed seized the handle of the gate

and pulled with all his might, knowing against all hope that he was trying to open a door at the very bottom of the sea, on which an entire
Island kingdom lay in pieces.

To his surprise, it opened.

Beyond the gate stood a woman he remembered, smiling brightly.

The elemental fire that had once burned at her core, turning her hair
the color of warm honey, was gone; it now hung loose to her waist, a
waterfall the same shade as pale flax.

Gone was the seraphic beauty she had gained in her walk through
the fire; she was now just the pretty young girl he had run into in the
back alleys of Easton. All of the flawless perfection of her beauty had
faded into a simple, dewy complexion and bright green eyes that sparkled when she smiled.

As she was doing now, beckoning excitedly to him.

"Come!"

Behind her a giant shadow loomed, broad as a two-yoked oxcart,
tall as an elder-oak, his skin the color of old bruises, his shaggy horsehair and beard red-orange once more.

He was grinning broadly, displaying neatly polished tusks.

Whole again.

"Come!" she called once more. Her voice was musical, but held none
of the power of the ring of the Namer. Her eyes met his, and her smile
broadened.

"Come with us, if you want to live!"

As the gate crumbled before his eyes, and the sea began to rush in,
Achmed's heart leapt, and he could not help himself.

He threw his head back, as he had never before done in his life, and
began to laugh uproariously.

Then he ran for the doorway and climbed through it.

Into arms that were waiting to embrace him.

Welcoming him.

After all his journeys through darkness, above and below the surface of the Earth, into the Light.